*Flood*Waters

by

Maggie Lett and Geoff Rowe

Published by ACM Retro Ltd

The Grange
Church Street,
Dronfield,
Sheffield S18 1QB.

Visit ACM Retro at:

www.acmretro.com

Published by ACM Retro 2011.

Maggie Lett and Geoff Rowe assert the moral right to be identified as the authors of this work.

A catalogue record for this book is available from the British Library.

Front cover: Victorian depiction of the 1864 Sheffield Flood

Contents

Just after midnight March 9/10 1864

Where in hell had all the water had gone? It's strange how sunlight can make the grimmest place look like the perfect spot: this place wasn't grim at all but perhaps a trick of the sunlight had blinded him to the trickling stream he knew to be here. Water was a rum thing: here one minute and gone the next. He knew all about water, it was his job after all and he knew this valley, he worked at its head, where the river held sway against all the banking and puddling and piping his men toiled at to stem its course. But he wasn't at work now; right now he could let his fingers trail through the long grass spotted with spring flowers and bathe in the chorus of birdsong and the susurration of the gentle breeze through the foliage. It was the idyll: he had found paradise, Eden nestled above the chaotic smoke of the town below. He walked on down the valley and again wondered about the river, what had happened to it? When he was a boy the river beside his house had burst its banks and tried to force its way into the house; he had stepped into the insistent flow, only maybe half a foot deep, and been immediately swept off his feet. Then the water had suddenly vanished, with only the jetsam of its visit left strewn about the garden. Maybe that was the moment he had decided to become an engineer, so he could learn about water and how to control it. Then strangely his feet felt soggy and he looked down and saw that the river had come back, totally unannounced and so much so that he was now wading through its current. There was a grumble of thunder but when he looked up at the sky there wasn't a cloud to be seen, it was a perfect cobalt blue, framing his paradise in a horizon of sunny calm that warmed his face and invited him to nestle in its warmth. And then he heard that the birdsong had stopped. Perhaps they too were nesting in the lazy heat of the sunshine. And at the same time he realised that somehow, quite unexpectedly, he was struggling to keep upright, just like when he was a boy. There was stillness, a quietness all around but he was panicked in his idyll, even the leaves seemed to have stopped their rustling but the water was running deeper and deeper and he was struggling more and more to keep himself steady and yet all around him was the stillness, the calm. Everything was all mixed up, nothing was as it should be, as it had been. He didn't understand. And then the sound came, he heard it, the sound. He thought it must be thunder again but this thunder didn't rumble and stop it just rumbled and rumbled growing ever louder and louder until it was roaring and roaring and he was going under in its sound, gasping for breath and straining for a hold on a tree, a branch, a clump of grass, anything, but even the ground seemed to be giving way and he couldn't get a grip, kept losing his grip. He

5

twisted to look behind him, up the curve of the valley, and his eyes widened to the horror of the future, a white tipped tumbling black wall of water almost as high as the valley itself surging towards him and powering on with its awful sound in the gentle stillness. He tried to swim, he tried to breathe, he reached out for air, he reached out for life but the water was relentless in its command and he was pulled back into the water and so he reached out again for air and he reached out again for life but the water was relentless in its demands and pulled him back, back into the water, back into the water...

John Gunson woke up thrashing and kicking, drenched in perspiration from his worst possible nightmare.

***

Part One
One week earlier

"Let me do that for you, Elizabeth. All these buttons and laces, I don't know why you didn't choose something simpler," said Anna Shaw, helping her daughter fasten her wedding dress. They had travelled into town together to have it made by Maria Hillier, a milliner and dressmaker who had a popular workshop in the Philadelphia area. Maria also created beautiful shawls so they had been able to order their entire outfits all under one roof. They'd even managed to buy Mr Shaw a new shirt for the occasion.

"What's it really like being married, Mam?"

"What's it really like? If I told you that you might call it off and I'd have wasted all this time on these fiddly buttons."

The two women laughed. There had always been a warmth between them: when Elizabeth had confided that she wanted to marry one of her father's tenant grinders, with her mother on her side, her father was an easy target.

"I wonder what Daniel's doing," said Elizabeth. "Do you think we'll be happy?"

Anna deliberately assumed a serious tone.

"He's a good hard worker and he always seems to take a pride in his work, not easy with all that muck about, and he's always paid his rent on time to your father. I expect he'll be able to buy his own wheel soon enough."

"Yes but do you think we'll be happy?"

Anna held the sensible note.

"Well happiness is a hard thing to define, I'd say. Sometimes you have to work at it, Elizabeth; sometimes the memory of the exciting wedding day will get overtaken by the hardships you might both have to face." Anna was struggling with the last button. "Breathe in, girl," she said. "That's it, all done."

"Do I look like a bride?"

"Let me just fix your wreath," said Anna, pinning a simple twist of tiny coloured blossoms on to Elizabeth's head and arranging the plaited tresses into place. "There now, let me look at you."

She turned her daughter around slowly and looked at the young woman: the girl's eyes, brown and open for all to read; her hair auburn and flowing - how Elizabeth had hated those red curls as a child and how one softly-spoken word from Daniel had turned the rough copper into gold.

"You look perfect," said Anna. "And do you know what?" She let go the sober pretence. "I believe you and Daniel will be very happy. You both have lights shining in your eyes which I don't think will ever fade."

The two of them stood grinning at each other and relaxed into the moment.

"Now, boots on," said Anna.

"I can't believe he chose me," said Elizabeth. "I remember when I first saw him at the wheel concentrating on his work, covered in that awful metal dust and his beard all greyed with the filings but still looking grand and handsome and somehow out of place. Most of the grinders who rent from father are thin and worn out. What horrible work they have to do in such terrible places. Their families must worry every day until their men get home. Daniel didn't look up when I walked in, I know it's too dangerous to take your eyes off the stone and anyway it gave me the chance to just enjoy looking at him. Mmmh! Then he got up to rack the blades he'd finished and he glanced over at me. One flash of those eyes, Mam, and I came out in goose-bumps."

Elizabeth turned scarlet, sucked in her lips with embarrassment. "I shouldn't say that should I?"

Anna pursed her lips and pretended to arch her brows. "And why not?" she confided. "Let's hope it was just the first crop of many."

Out along the lane wedding-goers and well-meaning nosey-parkers were now thronging along past the house. Footsteps hurried over the dirt road, some picking their way softly, some clacking against the uneven stones in their path. There was an excited urgency in the air. Voices chattered against the breeze as it rustled through the leaves and lifted wisps of dust around hemlines and newly polished shoes. Faces gentle and rough smiled in the weak sunlight. Outbursts of giggling ran along with the young girls in their best dresses, in their hands posies of spring flowers and field grasses. Groups of men swaggered authoritatively alongside, their thinning suits freshly aired and brushed ready for the day. Elizabeth Shaw and Daniel Fletcher were getting married.

The wedding was to be held in the chapel above the river in Loxley Bottom and the guests from Malin Bridge treaded their way along the water's edge. England at its most beautiful: here the dramatic gorges of the bleak Yorkshire peaks levelled out into a wide open valley where the rivers Loxley and Rivelin met before dancing down to swell the River Don and move on into the town of Sheffield. Upstream hamlets and farmsteads snuggled under the shelter of the hills and woodlands, small cottage gardens spoke of the pride cultivated by the inhabitants. All very pretty. Not so the encroachment of the grinding wheels, the mills, forges and workshops stamping their claims along the powerful streams. Malin Bridge itself had already grown from a small settlement into a village of several hundred people, attracted out of the clogging dirt of Sheffield by the opportunity to work and breathe. Today's marriage seemed to symbolise the union. Elizabeth, daughter of a modest landlord, was to be joined in holy matrimony to Daniel, a saw grinder who rented a trough on one of her father's wheels just along the river from Malin Bridge.

At the gate of Shaw Lodge stood the gig waiting to take the bride and her family to the chapel. Arthur the horse had had an extra special grooming for the occasion and bright blue and yellow ribbons were knotted into his mane and tail. Gabriel the driver had donned his one-and-only frockcoat (it had seen better days but still managed to give Gabriel an air of official coachman and the buttons did gleam) and he stood by the contraption at all but attention.

THE starch was enough to make Daniel call the whole thing off. He peeled his finger around inside the unfamiliar high-necked collar, already feeling a dampness of sweat and he hadn't even got his jacket on yet.

"By Christ, no wonder those town lot look so stuck up; you can't see past the end of your nose in this get-up." He wasn't talking to anyone, no-one was there, but the sound of his voice seemed to settle his jitters a bit.

He picked up the smudged mirror provided in the room and inspected the results of his shaving attempt. Daniel hadn't touched his beard since it had first sprouted when he was a lad. From wispy tendrils to a thick dark curly matting it had always been a feature of his face, not through choice but shaving meant razors and razors meant money. He might have made a living in the trade but what money he made he saved: another four or five years and he'd have enough for his own wheel.

He had fashioned this razor especially for today out of a spare piece of metal, honed an edge on it and then glued the blade to bone. But he hadn't expected his facial hair to be so coarse and tough. For a good twenty-five minutes he had soaked and lathered and scraped, nicking and irritating the sun-shy skin of his neck and chin. Now he peered again, suspicious of the results. He looked like half a face, the pinkly pale skin where once had been a decent beard looked abused and affronted. With his chin exposed now, even in the close and dingy surroundings of the room at the Stag Inn, he felt in some way unclothed despite the suffocating collar. God knows what Elizabeth would say; although he had always made the effort – cleaned, brushed and combed when they went out – she had never seen the lower half of his face before. He suddenly regretted his decision to shave, Elizabeth had liked him well enough without all this pampery and primping. Above his station, that's what people would think. Three troughs don't make you a gentleman just another grimy grinder. He looked in the mirror again. Maybe he shouldn't have shaved, maybe Elizabeth liked the beard. She'd surely prefer it to this mottled face.

But then he was marrying his landlord's daughter; he had to make an effort. Although he loved Elizabeth he was still in awe of her a little, couldn't understand why such a young lady had entertained his attention at all. Her father seemed decent enough, jolly in a way, always polite. But Thomas Shaw was first and foremost a businessman and Daniel had seen the evidence: grinders evicted for falling behind with their rent, while claims for better ventilation and safety precautions were dismissed as too costly. Daniel thought that being a son-in-law would always be secondary to being a rent payer as far as Thomas Shaw was concerned.

He rubbed his newly tender jaw and put the mirror down. The beard was off and he couldn't start sticking it back on again.

He knew what John would think. John Hukin, his best-man (right now downstairs, trying to con the publican out of a few cases of ale for the wedding) would call him a preening, poncing peacock. Daniel could hear him now: "Just wait til you're back at the Yew Tree, you won't last a minute with a face like that." Then again how often would he be out drinking with John once married and living in the family home. He had mixed feelings about that: Daniel had known John for well over half his life, twelve years give or take, and would miss the wild nights and scrapes they had fallen into but recently, since meeting Elizabeth, the desire to go out drinking all hours, fighting and whoring, all seemed a bit childish and a waste of time. He didn't think John quite appreciated the changes that were going to happen to their friendship and would probably be less enthusiastic about the forthcoming celebrations if he did. Still, that was something to deal with in the future.

Daniel pulled on his woollen jacket and fiddled with the collar again. He inspected his boots: polished for an hour with spit, the soft leather shone dully, too old and worn and supple to be worked up to a real gleam but presentable.

He looked around at the shabby room where he had spent his last night as a single man, thinking that the Stag was better to enjoy a pint in than to spend a night in. He shoved his hat on, picked up his bag and headed downstairs.

"Here he is, the man of the hour!" John roared, tankard in hand, as Daniel entered the bar. The best man appeared as broad as he was short, red faced with wiry ginger hair tufting from under his hat, suit dishevelled and shirttails hanging out. After seven years working for Neepsend Brewery down in Sheffield as a drayman, John's chest and arm muscles had swelled to rival the proportions of the very barrels he hauled, while the weight of his deliveries seemed to have consolidated his body and legs. He rested them unsteadily against the bar, the only person there other than the landlord, who was looking bored and hung over.

"Dammit John, how many have you had already?" Daniel walked up to the bar, pulled the tankard out of John's meaty hand.

"Just enough my friend, just enough." The best-man squinted up. "Dammit, Daniel, what have you done to your face?"

"What do you think?" Daniel pulled John upright, "Come on, we've got to get going. And tuck your bloody shirt in won't you, we're trying to make a good impression."

He had paid for his and John's rooms the previous night and now just wanted to get moving. John was providing the transport up to Loxley Bottom and had spent three hours yesterday afternoon scrubbing and polishing and garlanding the dray so it looked fit for a groom.

John drained his drink and hurried after Daniel, chuckling: "You know what you look like without that beard? You look like…"

"Yeah I know."

ELIZABETH shooed her mother out of the bedroom on the pretext of collecting her thoughts and calming her nerves. She looked at herself in the long mirror, this time taking in the picture through her own critical eyes and not as someone's beloved daughter. The figure who stared back seemed almost a stranger, someone who somehow seemed older, more grown, more - what was it? - positioned. Instead of the flibbertigibbet child of the house, here confronting her was the intended Mrs Daniel Fletcher. Even her cheek muscles flexed in an unfamiliarly confident way. Her hands had assumed a knowing confidence, her whole body had gained a significance that was both frightening and reassuring. This was Elizabeth Margaret Shaw, past, present and future all melded into one image in the glass, on her wedding day.

Turning away from the mirror she wanted to absorb the room she had had since she was born. A dishevelled bundle of embroidery lay cast aside on the chair - she never could see the point of women spending long hours just to sew one sampler, what for, for heaven's sake, what use was there for a small square of fancy cloth covered in the alphabet no matter how neat the needlework? Her teacher in the village school, Mrs Etchell, wouldn't agree with that. She even used to warn the girls to be sparing in the way that they peeled potatoes and not waste too much of the flesh: a man would frequently judge a potential spouse's virtue by the thrift shown in preparing a humble potato, she used to say. The girls used to joke about The Great Potato Test but now Elizabeth did wonder if Daniel would ever fret about how much potato would still be attached to the peel when his future wife got his dinner ready. She also wondered if Mrs Etchell had become carefree with the peeler when poor Mr Etchell passed away and was no longer around to keep an eye on her.

On the dressing table with her brushes, combs and clips sat the rosewood workbox her brother David had sent to her from India when he was a lieutenant in the army many years ago. It was inlaid with tiny seed-pearls and decorated with a painting of a strange elephant head, bright pink with coloured squiggles on it, which David's letter had explained was an Indian god. Right in the middle of the head was a small emerald. She was only a child at the time but loved the beauty and silliness of the box. Elizabeth tried not to think too much about her older brother; just wishing he could be here for her wedding day brought back too many memories of that awful day when they got word he had been lost during the mutiny, all that way away. Sometimes she cried to herself because she couldn't truthfully really remember him any more. He hadn't been so much her big brother as a kind of kindly uncle and now that she was seventeen she felt the guilt of her feelings.

On the mantelshelf were shells and pebbles picked up on the beach in Scarborough; a few ornaments, gifts and mementoes collected over the years; there was the small crucifix presented to mark her Confirmation Day, when she became a Soldier of Christ; there were a few books, gothic novels and, standing not-quite-upright was her rag-doll, Jenny, who had cuddled her company on scary nights when howling wind and thrashing rain had threatened to burst their way into the house.

There also, in a place of honour next to Jenny, was a small bunch of flowers, wilted and dried now, which Daniel had given to her as a token to mark their engagement. Elizabeth snatched them up quickly and tucked them into her bodice for good luck and because she wanted something of Daniel with her right now.

"WELL it's a fine morning for it, not too cold." John urged the big carthorse on a bit quicker with a tongue-click and switch of the reins as they approached a steeper incline. He glanced over at Daniel. "Mind you," he said, "your face might feel a bit chilly what with that new dandy look of yours."

"Leave it alone will you?" Daniel instinctively rubbed his chin again. The thing about John was that once he got something in his head that he thought was amusing he would harp on about it, trying to crack a joke with every comment. The thing was, the jokes were never funny.

The chapel wasn't far now and Daniel looked over at the river on his left. Not much of a river really, he thought, more like an energetic stream, still it powered enough wheels and mills in the eight or so miles between Low Bradfield and Sheffield.

"You alright? Seem a bit quiet." Occasionally John would know when to stop acting the fool. "Just a few last minute nerves, the big day and all that."

Around a bend in the track and through the trees Daniel could see the top of the chapel. He hoped he was doing the right thing: although he loved Elizabeth and wanted nothing more than to be her husband, he did wonder if he was ruining her life through his own selfishness. Elizabeth was marrying down, he knew that: Daniel wasn't the kind of man her family had expected her to marry. He didn't have the background, education or money to provide her with the same privileges she had grown up with. Daniel could see that her father thought the same way too but, to the man's credit, he had given his consent no matter. Still, disappointment is hard to hide and every now and again Thomas Shaw unwittingly displayed both that and concern for his daughter. With Elizabeth's brother missing in India, she had become like the Shaws' precious only child.

The dray rounded a corner and the chapel was there, quite a few people still waiting outside. Someone saw the approaching cart and shouted a cheery welcome. Daniel gave the assembled crowd a vague wave and said to John: "Well this is it, wish me luck."

"HURRY up, my girl, the groom's just arriving." Mr Thomas Shaw had been posted on discreet watch at the porch window to ensure that the bride herself didn't set off for the chapel too soon. It wouldn't do for a landlord's daughter to be kept waiting by a common tenant, a grinder of all things: his daughter had elected to marry a dirt-encrusted saw-grinder. Of all the worthy young men in the district, men of status and prospects, men of good family, educated, this Fletcher character was the one who had turned his Betsy's head. She had been dazing around the place for days, preoccupied, in some silly romantic world of her own, lost to her father and already another man's responsibility.

"I only hope the lass is happy," said Thomas to himself.

He had been lucky with Anna, a man couldn't have wished for a better wife: she had seen past his own coarseness and in time rounded his rough edges and tempered the worst of those traits he needed to be a successful businessman, albeit a minor one. Perhaps Fletcher had been just as lucky. Certainly his behaviour where Betsy was concerned had revealed nothing but respect and, yes, Thomas had to admit it, love.

The women of the house bustled down the stairs, the uncustomary stillness of the last quarter of an hour broken unceremoniously by a new energy.

"Ee lass you look like a royal princess," said Thomas, holding his daughter at arms' length. He gently rubbed her fingers as he cupped her hands on his then raised them to his lips. "Now hurry, your prince is waiting."

THE bells rang out and the congregation spilled out of the chapel, youngsters played around the leaning graves, bulbous women and haggard men gathered in huddles grateful for a bit of buzz and, as if from nowhere, an archway of bent canes strung with flowers and ivies held aloft by proud villagers tunnelled a path down from the church door to the lych-gate.

First out of the main party was the happy couple sweeping all before and aft in a haze of glorious joy. Next came the bridesmaids, friends with whom Elizabeth had spent her childhood playing in the fields and paddling in the waters of the Loxley. They were led out by Sally Bisby, chief bridesmaid and best friend of Elizabeth. Sally lived at the Cleakum public house in Malin Bridge with her father and mother and sisters and brothers. Following them were the bride's family, Anna and Thomas, but there were no parents to support the groom: Daniel's father, Robert, had died of silicosis after a working life spent huddled over a grinding wheel and his mother, Mary, had died in childbirth when the younger of their two sons, Nathan, was born. (God knows where he had ended up and who could blame him for getting away. He and Daniel had grown up in Bungay Street in a Sheffield area called The Ponds, a filthy, stinking, debauched place where hovel leant against hovel and sewage puddled and slopped in the confined alleys.)

After the bride's family came the Tricketts, family friends of the Shaws: James Trickett, a local dairy farmer, had offered his garden for the wedding party. (The garden was something of a talking point in Malin Bridge, not just for the size and well-tended lawns, the ornate shrubs and decorative borders but because it was kept by a gardener. To have a fine garden was grand enough but to pay someone to look after it, that was something else again.) Leading the rest of the crowd was John; relieved to have performed his best-man's duties without obvious hiccup – literally - he strode through the chapel door with gaggling children hanging off him, one dangling from his broad neck and two more clinging to his legs and balancing on his heavy boots. He was beaming and roaring like a giant for the benefit of his passengers but his eyes were already searching out the direction of the festivities.

All-in-all there were about thirty guests invited to the party. The Tricketts had set out cloth-covered tables adorned with wild flowers picked by their daughter Jemima who was now helping to pour out mugs of cider and lemonade and jars of porter. Daniel and Elizabeth stood arm in arm looking slightly self-conscious as well-wishers came up to congratulate them. Thomas and Anna, more at ease, stood a few feet away chatting with the guests, benevolently glancing over now and then at the newly-weds.

"Well here's to you two then." John, finally discarded of children, came up and gave the couple a drink each. "Mr and Mrs Fletcher."

"Cheers," Daniel said, relieved at the presence of John, a familiar face at last. Elizabeth studied John with a mixture of curiosity and friendly amusement having met him for the first time today. "A pleasure to meet you at last, Daniel has told me a lot about you."

"Not too much I hope." A coarse chuckle started from John's mouth before he remembered where he was and stifled it. Elizabeth laughed and Daniel, still linked to her, felt some of her tension ebb away as she finally started to relax and in response felt his own nerves settling. He had worried about what impact John would have in this company, needlessly it would seem.

"You two grew up together, I believe," said Elizabeth.

"We did indeed, it was me who struggled all that time to keep Daniel here on the straight and narrow and I must say, looking at you now, Mrs Fletcher, all my hard work seems to have paid off. You see, Mrs Fletcher…"

"Please, my name's Elizabeth…"

"You see, Elizabeth, he was a bit of a lad, our Daniel, a bit of an urchin as you might say, always trying to lead me astray and into mischief and that wasn't difficult round Bungay Street, I can tell you. We were born within a few houses of each other but he was the one who got to know all the dodges and all the dodgy places round about and he'd drag me along on his escapades, putting horses to fright when the grand town folk were climbing aboard their carriages or he'd be hopping on and off the buses without paying any fares. I'd better not go into too much specifics on the rest of his carryings-on, especially when the good Mrs Fletcher passed away and Mr Fletcher had taken to his bed with the coughing. Suffice to say that in the end I decided he had to be taken in hand, probably for my own sake as well as his."

"Pay no heed to him," said Daniel. "If either of us was up to no good it was John himself. It was no surprise to anyone when he landed a job working for the brewery; by the age of ten he already knew every tavern and pub in Sheffield and how to work the customers going in and out."

"Sounds as if you were both as bad as each other," said Elizabeth. "I don't know your part of Sheffield but from all I've heard I think it must have been quite hard for two young boys growing up there, though I admit some of it does sound like fun too."

"Not too much fun, I'm afraid," said John, downing another jug, "but we had our good times. Remember that time outside the whorehouse behind Blonk Street, Daniel?"

"I think Elizabeth gets the picture," said his friend, "no need to pencil in too many details."

As the drinks were passed out the party began to polarise: the children ran riot, tumbling and chasing each other, the women grouped around the tables, with Elizabeth and her dress the centre of attention. They chatted and speculated on her future while the older ones dropped hints about the joys and-the-rest-of-it of childbirth. The men moved further away, down towards where the garden met the banks of the Loxley. Pipes were lit and ale supped, accompanied by satisfied grunts of approval. Later they would re-group to eat and toast the couple but for now they could chat among themselves and enjoy the mildness of the weather.

"It'll be good to see the last of those damned navvies."

"Aye, we've had enough vegetables stolen from the patch to feed us for months."

"My runs have been raided I don't know how many times. We've had so few eggs to collect over the last few months you'd never think we had any layers and then some of the chickens seem to have managed to fly away despite the latch being on."

"It's their cussing and swearing back up the road from the pub that gets me."

"Aye they're a rough lot. And have you seen the way they live? Beats me how they get any work done sleeping so rough. That's the price of progress I suppose. The town needs the water and so do we for the engines or we might as well pack up and leave now."

The navvies had been working on the new dam farther up the valley at Dale Dyke; work had started on New Year's Day back in 1859 and hundreds

16

of itinerant labourers had been taken on. It was gruelling work perhaps deserving of a few mugs of ale at the end of a long arduous shift. The men got on with the work whatever the weather, digging with picks and shovels, humping mountains of earth and rubble up into barrows to be tipped in turn into waiting carts ready to be moved off and stored for future use. In some circles the navvies were regarded as the elite of the working classes for their unquestioning determination to just get on with the job and take the well-earned money but, for the residents of Loxley valley, their leaving would be not a day too soon. The swearing and womanising of the dam crews were legendary; over the last four years or so the sight of them fetching women up from Sheffield's whorehouses had become so routine it hardly warranted a self-righteous comment any more. Now that the dam was practically finished, only a few navvies remained and their presence had once again become the subject of local disapproval.

"Some of them are actually quite helpful," said Samuel Hammerton who lived up near the navvies' camp. His farmlands straddled the stream near the dam and he frequently had to cross from one side to the other to check on his animals. In fact he had gotten into the habit of making the crossing via the dam embankment rather than stumble down the river banks and over the boulders on the river bed. For him it was a welcome short-cut and he felt some peculiar sense of the navvies' deserving of some defence. "They are polite enough in their own way. And they've always been more than ready to lend a hand or two when I needed to lift the cart out of the mud. You know how bad it gets up there after heavy rain when the ground is water-logged. "

"Well maybe the dam will solve that problem," said James Trickett who had just joined the menfolk. "Come on, fill up your jars. It's not often we get together for a grand do. In fact we should do it more often. What do you say we organise a May Fair. We could have it here at Malin Bridge. We could get in some rides for the children and hire a few entertainers from Youdan's music-hall in Sheffield, I hear he has clowns and tight-rope walkers and such like. We could arrange it so the fair ran through the length of the village and I bet people would come from miles around so it would be good for business too."

"I'll drink to that," said Richard Ibbotson, not averse to the odd sup of ale to mark an occasion despite his respectable position as the treasurer of Bradfield Sunday School. "And here's to Sam's navvies," he said raising his jar again, perhaps more eagerly than people might have expected. "Not a job I'd want to do myself."

"Hear hear."

"Hear hear."

"All the same," said James, tipping his head generally in the direction of Dale Dyke, "whatever we might think about the navvies they certainly seem to know their job."

"Aye, they do that."

"It's to be hoped so anyway."

Jars were suddenly halted within lip-reach of open mouths. "Come on you men, come and join the ladies and don't be keeping yourselves to yourselves." Lizzie Trickett interrupted what looked to her like some very enthusiastic toasting going on: it was a little too early in the proceedings for anyone to be getting tight. "Look now, all the food is set out ready. There are potatoes and vegetables and a roast pig to be enjoyed. We've hunks of bread and cheese and pickles for you all to get stuck into so come on and get stuck in."

"Sounds more than tempting, my dear," said James.

"Aye it does."

"Sounds a grand spread," said Richard. "We were just talking about perhaps organising a May Fair in the village. What would your thoughts be on that, Mrs Trickett?"

"I say let's enjoy ourselves today before we start worrying about tomorrow," she replied. "We've a young couple here who deserve our undying attention and don't need their own big day to be diluted with talk of another."

"You're quite right my dear," said James. "Come, lead the way."

The hosts moved back up the garden to where the festivities were overtaken by the feasting at hand. They certainly knew how to lay on a good spread, this time extra special because it was the Tricketts' wedding present to Elizabeth and Daniel. They had known the girl since she was just a slip of a lass: she had often helped look after their own youngsters and certainly wasn't afraid to get her hands dirty when the cows needed milking or the pails emptied into the churns. The Tricketts and the Shaws had become good friends over the years and James had been quite proud to see his friend Thomas gradually build up his own business. Together they had watched their village grow, with rows of new brick cottages going up from and along the river, attracting more families into the place and in their wake more shops, making Malin Bridge not a bad place in which to live. It was certainly a thriving community but still managed to retain a village feel to it.

The Tricketts' own house stood in one of the prettiest positions. Quite a substantial residence, it was built right on the triangular spit of land where the river Loxley joined the Rivelin and it enjoyed views up both valleys. A lawn in front of the house sloped down to the Loxley, ending in a cluster of fruit trees which now provided a beautiful overhanging bower for the guests.

"There you both are," said Elizabeth, anxious for a chance to thank her neighbours yet again for their kindness. She wasn't sure really which way to turn her attention, everything was so perfect and her friends were all here having a good time and here was she, arm in arm with Daniel. "I was just telling Daniel that this place has always been like a second home to me and I couldn't have wished for a better place for our wedding meal."

"You just make sure you don't go slopping around in the cow sheds like you normally do," said James. "You've got a goodun there," he said to Daniel. "She's not one to turn her nose up at a bit of hard work, you just need to make sure she remembers she's a young lady; she's always been a bit too fond of getting right stuck in with the cows. Mind you, I'll no doubt have to take on some extra hands now that we'll be losing Betty's."

"Stop it, Mr Trickett,"said the young bride. "Daniel will be wondering what sort of a woman he's gotten married to."

"Too late," said Daniel. "I'm regretting the whole thing already. I'm off now to have a word with the minister to see if it's not too late to cancel."

Everyone laughed as he made to walk off up the hill and pretended to shrug off Elizabeth's pretence of despair. He was working hard at making easy conversation with the Shaws' friends. It wasn't that he felt particularly uncomfortable or in any way unwelcome, just out of place. After all, people like the Shaws and the Tricketts bought and sold people like Daniel Fletcher, they took you on when they needed to and got rid of you just as quickly when they didn't. Your money was actually their money. They were nice enough people once you got to know them but you could only ever get to know them on an unequal basis. He could see that his Elizabeth was warm in their company and that the Tricketts in turn looked on her like another daughter but he wished the whole thing was over so he and Elizabeth could get away and be on their own: he never felt out of place in her company.

"Don't you think he looks wonderfully handsome without his beard," she asked Mrs Trickett. "I hardly recognised him when I got down the aisle, I thought the wrong man had shown up. Do you know this is the first time I've seen his whole face?"

Daniel was aware of a deep blush colouring his unweathered cheeks.

"He certainly does look handsome," said Mrs Trickett. "But even handsome bridegrooms need to eat, you know, and so do their brides, so go and get your man some food, Mrs Fletcher."

After the excitement of the morning, the pace slowed as people busied themselves with plates piled high with roasted pork and buttered mashed vegetables: greasy dribbles ran down chins and threatened upright white collars, drops of drink spilled on to Sunday-best, fingers dunked hunks of bread into pools of rich gravy which then filtered down hairy arms. Then, as the dishes and leftovers were finally being cleared away by women hired in for the occasion, Thomas Shaw rapped the table, he'd an announcement to make.

"Well, everybody, thank you all for coming. I'll try and keep this short, I'm not really one for speeches." There was some laughter at that: Thomas Shaw was not known to use one word where five could be employed. Anyone who had dined with the Shaws knew that once the brandy was poured and the pipes lit Thomas could quite happily talk continuously for hours. "Anyway I should start by thanking James and Lizzie for providing their garden and wonderful spread on this wonderful occasion." More toasting, more cheers. "And I'd like to thank all you esteemed guests for turning out to share this wonderful day with us." More toasting, more cheers.

"Of course I'm not supposed to be losing a daughter," he said. Thomas looked at his Betsy. "No, I'm not supposed to be losing a daughter but gaining a son. Well I don't go along with that," he said. "I watched that baby girl being born, I've seen her learn how to toddle around and find her feet, seen her helping her Mam in the kitchen doing a bit of baking or whatever and making more mess than a whole pen of pigs. I've watched her doing her alphabet and begin to make sense of reading and words – not something I was ever that good at myself. Then suddenly she grew up, became a proper person in her own right and returning the love of her mother and me. She has been a central, warm glow in our lives so don't anyone tell me I'm not losing a daughter because I am, she's leaving home."

Thomas paused and (not a moment too soon for already people were getting sentimental and rheumy on his behalf) then signalled that his reverie was over with a dance in his eyes and a change of tone.

"Fortunately what is true and what I wholly agree with is that I am gaining a son, another son. Most of you will know that Anna and I lost our first boy, David, when he was fighting for Queen and Country out in India. Well," he said, turning to Elizabeth, "thanks to you we now have another man in the family and a fine man at that. And, while I might no longer have my little girl all to myself anymore, I do now have the two of you."

Time for a general outburst of more cheers and more thirst quenchings.

Thomas carried on, in full flow as ever, digressing from family memories to the price of coal to the navvies at the dam to the plans for a May Day fair and back to the odd memory until Anna finally brought him right back on track

20

with a very deliberate nudge and a knowing flick of her head.

"Right you are," said Thomas and he raised his glass and surveyed the gathering. "Right, I would like to propose a toast to the happy couple. To Daniel and Elizabeth."

The toast was repeated around the group, this time with a bit more solemnity. Some, like John, took noisy big swigs, others demure sips.

"Just one more thing…" Thomas checked the murmur of conversation. "Elizabeth, Daniel," he said, "you may have noticed that Anna and I have yet to give you our wedding gift."

Daniel started to protest but his father-in-law waved him quiet and who was Daniel to argue.

"You see it's not something we could bring to the party." Thomas paused and sipped his porter. "You may well know that I've a small number of properties up and down this valley. Well one of these has been empty for some time now, a cottage, just sitting there gathering dust, quite a lot of dust I would imagine, although I haven't been up there for some months now. So Anna and myself thought this cottage would be an ideal present for your wedding day, a new start in a place all of your own."

Daniel was stunned. Elizabeth's hands flew to her mouth with a gasp. Daniel sat there, mouth still hanging open, unable to fully comprehend what Thomas had just said but somehow recognising that he had in the course of one day gone from being a bachelor tenant-grinder to a husband and man of property. Elizabeth clutched on to him, perhaps already imaging the luxury of privacy and having her man all to herself.

"I really don't know what to say," said Daniel, at last managing to speak. "Your allowing Elizabeth to marry me was blessing enough. This, this is just more than I could ever hope to deserve."

Rewarded by their reaction, Thomas said: "I warn you it does need a fair bit of work doing to it and it's a few miles up the valley in Damflask but, as I said, it should set you nicely on the road to your new life together."

He signalled his arm across the garden and the band struck up. The music jigged everyone on to their feet and even Daniel found himself only too happy to take a swirl around the lawn.

IT was late afternoon and the sun was low in the sky casting long shadows behind Daniel and Elizabeth as they made their way along the road skirting the Loxley. She had insisted that they spend their first night together in the new cottage and had over-ruled Daniel's objections about the state of the place with an airy: "Oh we'll manage." In fact Daniel had been feeling the effects of too many ales too early in the day and the thoughts of a three-mile hike to Damflask hadn't initially struck him as very appealing, especially after the Shaws had insisted on them staying the night at the Lodge. But Elizabeth had been adamant, so they had packed up some basics in Daniel's bag and, after a round of boozy fond farewells, had set off up the valley. John had to get the cart and horse back to Sheffield before nightfall the following day but had offered to come up with the dray beforehand with more of their belongings.

Now that the air was much cooler, Daniel's head had cleared and he was glad Elizabeth had been so determined. Walking hand in hand with her at a leisurely pace, the overhanging oaks and elms dappling the path and the sound of the river persistently but pleasantly rushing along in the background, Daniel felt at last that he was married and together with his bride. The service and the party had been fine, if a little formal at first, but now he had Elizabeth to himself and they were on the way to their new home.

He had never expected to be given a cottage and at first what he had perceived as charity had rankled but common-sense had prevailed and negative thoughts had quickly been replaced with realism: there was injured pride and there was stupidity. After all, Thomas Shaw would never have allowed his daughter to slum it in some rented rooms, which was all Daniel could have offered, and it would have been another four or five grindingly hard years before he could have even contemplated getting their own place. He still had ambitions and would have to work hard to achieve them but life seemed that bit easier now. Giddy no longer from the beer but with sudden elation, Daniel whooped aloud, grabbed Elizabeth up in his arms and broke into a run. Twenty feet on and breathless he put her down: the effects of the drink hadn't completely subsided.

Elizabeth smoothed down her dress, laughing. "What was that for?"

"I don't know, life just seems too good. I've got you, we've got our own home. For the first time in my life everything's just, I don't know, just perfect." He couldn't really put his feelings into words but he knew that Elizabeth would understand what he meant.

"I know," she said as they started walking again. "I wonder what it's like, the cottage."

"Haven't you been there before?"

"No, I've only seen a few of Father's places."

"Well it's our place now and even if it is in a mess I'm glad we're on our way there now. I'll have it fixed up in no time. It'll be the finest cottage in the valley."

"I wonder if it has a garden."

"I'll make a garden with all the flowers you want in it."

"And vegetables, I'd like to grow vegetables."

"Sure, we'll have vegetables and anything else you want."

"And perhaps a cow," said Elizabeth. "I would like my own cow. We could have fresh milk and I could make butter and cheese. I do come with good references, as you know. I'm not sure I'd like to keep pigs, though. You get attached to animals and I'm not sure I could cope when it came to slaughter time. Oh and we forgot about chickens, we've got to get some chickens."

"Hold on, young woman, I'm still only a grinder."

"Yes but think of the money we could save. And I'm sure father would help out."

"Your father has been help enough already." Daniel heard the edge in his voice and regretted his curtness. "Come on, girl, nearly home."

The path took them down to the bank of the Loxley. Across the river there was a small wood and they paused for a moment to enjoy the sounds and smells of the evening. "I can see us living here for the rest of our lives, Elizabeth. It really is perfect."

"It'll be perfect for a family too." Elizabeth looked up shyly. They had never discussed having babies and she felt embarrassed at what was actually a reference to them living as man and wife. Her mother had told her what was what in that department and sometimes with her friends the conversation had included silly and sometimes quite rude girly comments about what follows when the kissing stops and everything else starts but she was nervous about the whole thing. Sometimes after they had been out together and Daniel was kissing her goodnight, she had experienced a wonderful physical excitement but it scared her just the same. Picking up on her silent blushes, Daniel smiled, putting his arm around her. "Yes, from now on it'll all be perfect."

They carried on, the light was getting poor and they still had about a mile to go.

THEY first saw the cottage as they rounded the bend in the lane by the Damflask paper mill, across the mill pond exactly where but not quite as Mr Shaw had described.. The village itself, more of a hamlet really, was snuggled into the bottom where several minor valleys met. There were a few cottages and a pub, the Barrel Inn, and a pretty stone bridge across the Loxley. But they picked out their wedding gift straightaway, realising that Thomas had spun them a bit of a tale. For there just up from the water's edge was a fine small cottage, with candles glowing warmly through the windows and smoke dancing merrily out of the chimney and there at the open door a one-woman welcoming committee, bearing a grin from ear to ear and holding her arms out to draw the newly weds in from the gloom.

"You must be Elizabeth and Daniel," she said. "I've been expecting you. My name's Mary Ibbotson, from the Barrel across the bridge there. Mr Shaw asked me to knock the place into a bit of a better shape for the two of you so come on in and see your new home."

What a day this had been. Instead of the ramshackle cottage they had been led to expect, there was not a mound of rubble nor a door hanging off its hinge nor even a speck of dust to be seen.

"There's a fire in the grate and I've fetched some water up. There's some ham and bread and basic stuff in the larder, eggs, cheese, tea and milk and bit of sugar. And I thought you might like a bit of honey to sweeten things up a bit. No doubt you'll be anxious to do the place up to your own taste so all I've done is clean and make the place presentable. I would have had the kettle on the hob but I wasn't sure whether you'd be coming tonight or not. Mr Shaw said something about you maybe deciding to stay at Malin Bridge for the night. I'll just do that now in case you fancy some tea."

Mrs Ibbotson bustled around, sorting the kettle and the crockery and at the same time showing them where everything was.

"I'll leave you two alone now, you've had a long day and no doubt a long night ahead of you. My husband Jon, he's the landlord up at the inn, sent this bottle of sherry over by way of saying hello and to toast you in as our new neighbours. So goodnight now."

Daniel and Elizabeth had been speechless with gratitude during the whole of this whirlwind of a welcome, only managing to mumble some inadequate thanks when the good Mrs Ibbotson was already half-way down the garden path.

Yes indeed, there was a garden, with its own willow tree dripping and brushing across the grass. And how lushly delicate it looked in the moonlight, even now when only in bud.

JOHN woke up in a barn, the sounds of cocks crowing and cows lowing not the usual ones that greeted his regular morning rises down by The Wicker. The dawn chorus he was familiar with was traffic, what with the early morning trains smoking and chunting off to Rotherham or Manchester over the big arched bridge across the road and the horse-drawn buses and sundry other carts and gigs clockling along on the cobbled street. And instead of animals wishing each other good morning it was people he normally heard, nor was there ever much good about the morning for them to be wishing each other a good one: not for them working under the skies surrounded by trees and fields, more likely dingy pokey cutlers' workshops, cramped forges, sparking-hot furnaces and hellish glowing steel mills and all other such horrors of man's invention. He himself was quite lucky really, he thought, working with the horses and being out and about on his dray. All the same it was thirsty work. John tried in his reverie to moisten his lips but his tongue stuck to the roof of his mouth when he tried and he realised abruptly that he wasn't on his cart but lying in some hay: he knew right enough why his mouth was so dry, he'd slept all night with his jaws hanging open like a drunken idiot, not for the first time and undoubtedly not for the last. He snorted his nose clear and tried to take in his surroundings through still-bleary eyes, not yet remembering where he was or why.

The scene certainly wasn't all that familiar but then John had had some experience in waking up in strange places. A platter-sized shoed hoof clopped down next to his head causing John to jolt aside, quicker than his body was prepared for, and he groaned loudly as all his muscles began to ache in their awakening. Stanley the horse had determined that John was now in the land of the living and was demanding attention. John sat up, brushing hay from his beard and clothes, and looked around. No, definitely not slept in this barn before. He was in a stall with Stanley and it was obvious that the big horse was getting restless. He was amazed that in his drunken state he'd had the wherewithal to unharness the animal and house him in the stall the previous night. He wasn't that amazed to find that he had ended up in the same stall to sleep it off.

"Well we've kipped in stranger places, hey boy?" John muttered as he stood up, smacking the horse on its rump. Judging from what he could see around him he reckoned he must have pulled the cart into the barn, leaving the door wide open, sorted Stanley out and then passed out. "I think it might be time to beat a hasty exit before we get some angry farmer wondering why we're using his place as a doss house." Stanley snorted in response and John led him out of the stall, re-harnessed him and clambered on to the cart. They managed to get the contraption turned within the confines of the barn and back outside into a grey and chilly dawn. "Wait here," John ordered and got off to close the door of the barn. Back on the dray he confided to Stanley: "With any luck no-one will know we were here."

On the road up to Damflask, John tried to piece together what had happened the previous night. He'd left the party after carousing and dancing all afternoon with the sole intention of returning with the cart and horse to the Stag and getting a good night's sleep before helping Daniel and Elizabeth with some of their belongings. Somewhat the worse for wear and giddy from his exertions with the village lasses, he'd left the party with a few bottles and in high spirits, that much he remembered, but somewhere between leaving the Tricketts' farm and Loxley Bottom, all of a few hundred yards, he'd had a change of heart and decided it would be good sport to head straight on up to Damflask with his cargo and surprise the newly weds. It had seemed like quite an amusing idea at the time. Fortunately he hadn't had the staying power. He'd obviously finished the bottles and decided that there was no way he'd be able to get all the way. Whichever barn he'd ended up in had seemed a much more inviting idea than trying to keep aloft on the cart for a few bumpy miles. Well, he had a sore head but the party had been worth it and now the fresh air and spring morning was clearing his head. "Thank God you didn't let me go and spoil their night, Stanley."

"THERE, what do you think?"

Daniel stood back to admire his work and Elizabeth linked her arm through his. It was the first full day of their life together and she was positively bursting with pride. The closeness between them was palpable. John had been and gone after trundling up from Malin Bridge on his cart with the pieces of furniture and other essential items the Shaws had donated and it had been a simple but delightful novelty to welcome him into their home together, sparse though it was before his arrival. A few hours' arranging and changing and re-arranging had followed until Elizabeth was satisfied with the position of everything, right down to that sewing box she had never before regarded as having any significance whatsoever. Daniel, of course, wasn't the least bit bothered, he just did the shifting to order.

"Isn't it a bit up on the right?" she said.

"What? I thought you said it was straight. Are you now telling me I have to take it down and start again?" Daniel tried not to grimace but he felt grimacey.

Elizabeth sensed his impatience and pulled a silly face at him. "Only joking," she said. "I think it looks grand."

They had decided to give their new home a name, or at least Elizabeth had: Willow Tree Cottage. Inwardly Daniel had thought it a bit twee but he appreciated the gesture of making the place truly their own and had so warmed to Elizabeth's romantic enthusiasm that the idea had become headily irresistible. For all his roughness of manner, he loved the reality of this being their home and he couldn't remember a happier time ever in his life. He had grown up in a desperate area of Sheffield where dead cats and dogs regularly floated past in the River Sheaf and street gullies carried piss and god-knows-what down into the river past hovels and privies and motley factories. How could he resist christening his own Willow Tree Cottage? He had fashioned a cross section of wood into a plaque and burned the words into the surface with a hot poker from the fire. Then Elizabeth had painted some dangling willow branches around the name and the initials, D&EF, across the bottom. Now the whole confection hung next to the door, at once intimate and welcoming.

"Well, Mrs Fletcher, not a bad suggestion of yours, I have to agree." He hugged Elizabeth to him and in a moment's quietude they simply enjoyed looking at each other, the breeze drifting down the valley gently shifting the willow tips. They had awoken early and dallied in bed, revisiting the pleasures of the night before and whispering and loving until the Sunday sounds of Damflask out-and-about had become too persistent to ignore.

Just as well, for John arrived soon after they'd risen and breakfasted: married they may be but, for Elizabeth at least, John appearing while they were still undressed on their first morning would have been more than she could bear. He would have known exactly what had been going on and she would have been desperately embarrassed.

"What other jobs have you for me now?" said Daniel. "Isn't that what a husband is supposed to do on a Sunday, little jobs about the house?"

"The only job I have for you, Daniel Fletcher, is to take care of me," said Elizabeth. She took him by the hand and led him back into the house, back into the bedroom.

"What, aren't you going to start cooking my dinner?" he said.

"First of all I have to build up your appetite."

RETURNING to Sheffield in the early afternoon after helping Daniel and Elizabeth with their belongings, John stabled Stanley at the brewery and walked home through the back streets to his room in The Ponds. The street was already full of people hanging around in small gaggles in the middle of the road, leaning on window sills or sat on doorsteps. The banter was raucous and bawdy, nearly everyone was swigging gin or beer from misshapen bottles, smoking roughly-fashioned cigarettes or clay-pipes, gambling with cards or on the toss of a few coins. Every now and then a girl raced by screaming or laughing, long skirts hitched up in one hand, drink in the other, being chased by one or more leering, jeering men. There was the occasional flurry of fists as young bucks showed-off in front of the women and established their status within the pack. And it was a pack, a wild unruly pack in which every extreme of behaviour surfaced at some time or another: the good and the bad, where loyalty was something hard won and never lost and violence was easily dispensed and knew no boundaries, work was hard and brutal and fun was something you had until you passed out. It was the pack of the people of The Ponds and John was one of its top dogs.

On the way to his room he was constantly met with acknowledging shouts, men would greet him with a respect forged from previous encounters with his fists – there weren't many in the area who hadn't at one point or another been laid out cold by John – and more than a few women approached him with the inevitable propositions. John weaved his way through exchanging a few words here and there but keeping it brief. All he really wanted was peace and quiet and a couple of hours of kip. It had been an early rise for him for a Sunday and more exertion than he had anticipated: Elizabeth Shaw had an incredible amount of stuff for one so young.

He bought a bottle of ale from one of the beer shops nearby and once home took it with him to bed. Before lying down he looked around at the dingy room, surveying his meagre possessions: a few worn-out clothes and boots housed in a cheap chest; a table bearing a dog-eared Bible (passed down on his mother's side) along with a dented bowl and a chipped mug; two chairs; a box with some of his Dad's souvenirs in it; a flash of fading colour from the rag-rug knotted by his Mum and a knuckleduster and assorted sheathed knives. Compared to how much Elizabeth seemed to have, this was less than paltry. John didn't know whether to be concerned about his lack of worldly goods or glad he hadn't too much to worry about, after all he didn't need much. He lived out of the one room, rarely using it for anything other than sleeping. He ate downstairs in the public diner, cleaned up in the jakes down the corridor and paid a woman further down the street to wash his clothes when they began to smell too high. Now weariness caught up with him and he closed his eyes to the scene; nursing the bottle, he lay down on the bed, fully clothed, and within minutes fell asleep.

The sounds of baying and snarling woke him up. He checked the time: nearly five-o'-clock. Looking out of the window he saw that someone had set up a dogfight almost directly under his room. Two Staffordshire terriers were tearing the hell out of each other surrounded by a ring of onlookers. At the edge of the crowd John could see the familiar sharp-pointed nose of William Pickens protruding from under the brim of a tatty bowler hat. He was clutching a fistful of paper money and was obviously acting as bookie for the fight. John's temper rose at the sight of the man in his gaudy jacket and trousers, prancing on the spot with the excitement of the fight and the profit to come. John grabbed his bottle of beer and lurched out of the room. Once out on the street, he stormed up to Pickens, grabbed him from behind, spinning the man around by his shoulder, and pushed him into the road. At first nobody else was aware of John's intervention, the sounds of one dog yelping in pain suggested the fight was nearly over and everyone wanted to witness the kill. Their attention was soon diverted. "I thought I told you I didn't want to see your ugly bastard face around here anymore," John roared. He shoved Pickens in the chest and then again shove, shove, shove, propelling the man backwards down the road. The crowd turned, relishing the prospect of a more interesting duel. John Hukin was always good value when it came to a brawl.

William Pickens was one of the men John had always suspected of having something to do with his father's murder. Five years ago the man had suddenly appeared in the neighbourhood and set up a money-lending and gambling racket. John's Dad had been an inveterate gambler and was often in debt to a number of bookies. It ended up being the death of him. If it wasn't for the fact that John had got solid evidence that Pickens was not in the area that night, the cheap bookie would already have been another body dragged out of the nearby open sewers.

Pickens stumbled away from his attacker, stuffing the money into a pocket and pulling out a wicked looking knife from another. He crouched over with the blade weaving in front of him, the stance of an experienced knife fighter. "You don't tell me where I can or can't go John Hukin. This isn't your town."

"You're right," John said, switching the grip on his bottle so it hung loosely in his fist. "But this is my part of town and, like I said, I don't want to see your damned mug in these streets." He started forward, feinting to one side, and then, as Pickens rushed in, fooled by the dummied move, cracked the bookie over the head with the bottle. The man collapsed instantly, folding on to the street without a sound.

A few of the braver elements from the dogfight rushed forward and inspected the prone man.

"Fucking hell John, I think you killed the cunt," one of them said as he bent down and started rifling through Pickens' pockets, pulling out a wodge of notes.

"He'll come round and he'll have a hell of a sore head when he does." John plucked the money from the man's hand and said: "I'd better look after that for now."

The rest of the crowd started to gather, leaving behind them the corpse of a dog and its owner, who was trying to bundle the limp body up ready to toss into the river. At the same time the door to a house near the commotion opened and a statuesque woman stepped out, wrapped in a frilly robe. She looked at John and smiled a nod of greeting. Then she noticed the unfortunate Pickens and the smile disappeared. "Well bugger me backwards with a barge pole, that's one fight you shouldn't have picked, John." She had a strange lilting accent having come down from Newcastle years ago.

"Don't worry about that piece of scum, Melanie," John said, "his type just needs to be taught the hard way, that's all."

"No, you don't get it, you great lunk." She walked up to him and almost whispered: "Will Pickens has fallen in with Jack Quinn and his lot. They'll fucking kill you if they find out about this."

Jack Quinn ran the biggest gang in Sheffield: protection, robbery, intimidation and murder were just a few of the activities he excelled at. He was not a man to upset, even John knew that.

"You'd best finish him off and dump the body, let the police find him. No-one here will talk." She put her arm around the back of John's neck and pulled his face down close to hers. "Seriously John, it's the only way. Quinn won't let anyone get away with having a go at one of his lot. He'll gut you like a rabbit. But if it's just a body then he'll never know what happened. Will Pickens was such an arse he was bound to get what was coming sooner or later."

John felt tired all of a sudden. He didn't need this hassle; all he wanted was to enjoy the remainder of his Sunday but things were never simple with John, his temper had always led him into trouble. This time the trouble seemed to be a whole lot more than the usual altercations and petty feuds he normally found himself embroiled in. No-one messed with Jack Quinn and survived to tell the tale. John knew that what Melanie had said made sense. If he got rid of Pickens now and spread the word that no-one was to talk, he'd be off the hook with Quinn. He had always disliked Pickens anyway, the man was a piece of shit and deserved anything that befell him. Maybe now was the time to put an end to Pickens and that whole chapter about his father.

The crowd began to lose interest and drift away; Pickens obviously wasn't going anywhere and John was in close conversation with Melanie and not likely to provide any further entertainment.

"You have to do it John, there'll be no end of trouble if you let Pickens go. First thing he'll do is run to Quinn and then your life won't be worth shit. Even you can't fight him." Melanie tugged her robe around tighter and then smirked. "And I can't afford to lose the trade."

John grinned sheepishly but shook his head. "I can't do it Mel, not in cold blood. If he'd died in the fight I could accept that and I wouldn't lose a wink of sleep but not now. Not now he's out cold. I'll have to take my chances with Quinn. I've enough reasons to hate Will Pickens but I'm not going to have his murder on my conscience."

"Well it's your funeral John Hukin and when Quinn comes looking for you don't forget you could have solved the problem right here and now." The busty madam turned on her heel and went back to her door. Just before she went inside she turned: "If you ever need to get away let me know, I've some money put aside and a lot of friends up in Newcastle who'll look after you."

John's mind was a maelstrom of thoughts and emotions but he was touched by her offer and even felt his eyes tearing with gratitude. "Thanks love but I think I'll take my chances here in Sheffield." He took one last look at Pickens lying in the street and then walked away. He had planned to visit Melanie's place later but now his heart, let alone anything else, didn't seem to be in it. Everything had changed in a brief moment. As he crossed the plank bridge over the Sheaf he was hardly aware of the smell of the raw sewage that oozed into it but he couldn't not be aware of the carcasses and the swarms of flies hovering. There was enough death around without adding to the tally. John wondered what Daniel would do in his place, probably he'd have killed Pickens and lived with the guilt, it was the logical thing to do. But what John did in the heat of the moment was left in the heat of the moment, he didn't give much thought to the consequences. Until now; now the consequences could turn out to be the end of him. John's response was to go find a drink, then find another and to keep going until he no longer cared. He knew Daniel wouldn't approve but he wasn't Daniel and Daniel wasn't there.

NEITHER could resist a quick nuzzle. It was Tuesday, Daniel's first day back at work since the wedding, but the two of them were still in honeymoon mood and what must become the routine of daily life was struggling to get established amid the wedded-bliss. "Get away from me woman. I'd best be off to work before I get tempted to dally here," said Daniel. "Three days' holiday away from the wheel is the most we can afford right now but you'll see; thanks to the start your father's given us already I'll be able to concentrate now on earning some extra money and perhaps in a year or two we'll have more time for ourselves. I want to get another wheel and take on an apprentice and then we'll be on our way, girl. I want you to have the best of everything.

Well, the best a good grinder can give you," he said.

"I've everything I need, Mr Fletcher, right here."

Elizabeth decided to walk down to Malin Bridge with Daniel and spend some time with her folks and Sally. She hadn't seen Sally since the wedding and there were lots of things to tell her best friend, now that she could speak with the experience of a married woman.

Daniel collected together his tools and put on his warm coat: it could be quite cold walking home late in the evening and (he hadn't told Elizabeth this) he would have to do some late shifts over the coming weeks to make up for the last few days: he had quite a big order on and he couldn't afford to lose a customer through being behind with a delivery just because he'd got himself wedded. This was his real world, far removed from his wife's seemingly idyllic life spent playing with the Tricketts' cows and all, but it had to become hers too, although he'd prefer it to creep up on her gradually and not spoil things right away. He was about to start busying around the kitchen to get himself some snap for his midday break but decided against it, not wanting to make Elizabeth feel she had fallen down on one of her wifely duties.

Then Elizabeth presented him with a parcel of ham and bread wrapped in muslin and a flask of cold tea to be warmed at the wheel house. She'd also snuck in a shiny red apple and some pickle in some greased paper. "There, your first lunch prepared by your very own wife," she said and he glowed. (Actually she hadn't been sure how thick to cut the bread and fretted ridiculously over whether it would seem too stupid to slice it as thinly as they did at home when the recipient was a big working man who'd be bent over a grinding wheel all day long. She was only too aware of the differences in their backgrounds and somehow the thickness of a slice of bread seemed to encapsulate it: Daniel's life in The Ponds was in stark contrast to her own and she loved him for it and for the way it had honed him into a strong, proud man who refused to apologise for his origins even while working to escape them into a better future, but she wasn't about to draw attention to it all with a dainty cut of loaf. Where was Mrs Etchell when you needed her?) Then she snatched up her basket ready for the off.

"You're spoiling me already," said Daniel.

They left Willow Tree Cottage behind them and headed off down the lane to Loxley. It wasn't a bad day but the gentle breeze of the morning soon started whipping fitfully through the overhanging branches and skitting up the loose soil off the roadway. "What's that saying?" said Elizabeth. "'The March wind doth blow and we shall have snow.' I hope not, don't you?"

"Whisht, girl, it's just a bit of a breeze."

DANIEL left Elizabeth at Malin Bridge and carried on down the lane to his wheel. She passed the Trickett farm and decided to call in to say a quick hello.

"Ah, just the girl," said James Trickett. He was bustling about the yard having already driven the cows out of the barn and on to the pasture land and was just about to pour some swill for the pigs. "We've been talking about organising a May Fair and, as an established married woman of the community, perhaps you'd like to consult with Mrs Trickett on what jobs you and the other ladies could do."

"A May Fair, that's a wonderful idea," said Elizabeth. "The whole village would love it I'm sure, and all the hamlets up and down the valleys. People always love a bit of music and fun and we could decorate the streets with ribbons and flowers. You can certainly count on my help and I'm sure Daniel would like to join in. Is Mrs Trickett in the house and we can start the ball rolling now?"

"She is, she is. Go on in and see her."

Elizabeth went on over into the kitchen. This was always her favourite room in the Tricketts', always busy and full of life: there were so many children around and that's what made the difference from her own home, or at least from her parents' house (she'd have to get used to the idea of having her own home now) much as she loved it, where there were only the three of them since her little sister Elspeth had died of tuberculosis and David had been lost in India. Mrs Trickett had a large dresser along one wall, full of pretty cups and plates and saucers on display and jars of this and that and small bundles of the children's sewing and drawing things; there was a big case-clock in the corner which chimed every quarter and pompously counted the hours; there was a plump mahogany-framed sofa which had seen better days and a scrubbed dining table surrounded by an assortment of mismatching wooden chairs; pots, pans and a couple of large kettles were stacked in working order in the inglenook and a well-worn wash-tub dominated the space between the sink and the back door; piled next to it were discarded boots and shoes of sizes tiny to huge and sundry bits of rough matting to clean up muddy soles and keep the farmyard out in the yard. Anna Trickett was busy peeling vegetables into the sink and her father, Tom Kay, was eyes-shut on the sofa when the visitor popped her head round the door.

"There you are, Mrs Trickett," said Elizabeth. "Oh, I'd better be quiet, I didn't realise Mr Kay was asleep. Is that why the children aren't here?"

"He's just dozing," said Anna collecting up the skins and throwing them into a bucket for the pigs. "He's still getting over the journey yesterday, short but hard for him, and I suppose he's having to get used to leaving his own place to come and live with us. I feel a bit guilty at having to ask Joe to leave after he's been with us these last few months and I'll miss having such a personable lodger around but we really don't have any room for an extra body now Da has moved in. Joe's going back to live with his parents in Arbourthorne on Saturday so it's all a bit of a squeeze til then, just a few more days to go of chaos."

"I'm sure Joe knows it can't be helped," said Elizabeth. "Anyway no doubt he'll be able to get his own place soon. Didn't you say he's got a good job?"

"More than just a good job, he's a partner with Mr Johnson at the Limerick Wheel, you know, that big place on the way to Hillsborough. He must be worth a bob or two. He's certainly a gentleman of means but I'll be sorry to see him go. No airs and graces there, just a well-mannered, nice young man. In fact if you hadn't hitched up with your Daniel I might have considered a bit of matchmaking there. Speaking of which, how is married life?" she asked, turning a wicked glint on her guest.

Elizabeth found herself blushing at the directness: she'd only been married a few days and was still overly conscious of the physical connotations of her being a new bride, even with Mrs Trickett, who'd had three children already and could have more yet, after all the youngest, George, was only five.

"Life is really very nice, thank you," was all she could manage.

"Come on now, tell me, does that handsome man of yours live up to his promise?"

An unstoppable grin creased across Elizabeth's face and she instinctively bit back her lips and at the same time hunched up her shoulders in embarrassment. She knew she'd shown too much and immediately shuttered her eyes.

"You don't have to say a thing, girl, your face is like a book." Anna Trickett pretended to switch her attention to the vegetables allowing the girl to compose herself.

"What's this Mr Trickett was saying about helping you with a May Fair?" said Elizabeth, anxious to be off the more personal subject. "Has a date been set yet?"

"Not yet. The men are meeting in the Stag on Friday night to discuss the when and what. Any excuse, of course. And you know what men are like, they think only they can do the organising and then they'll tell us women what to do."

"Well I'm happy to get involved, just let me know what you'd like me to do. I'll have to go now, I want to go and see Mam and Father quickly then I'm off to Sally's."

"Isn't she off visiting her relatives this week?"

"Yes, she's off to Oughtibridge on Thursday for a few days to visit her aunt and uncle."

"Bit of a welcome break for her, I should think. It must be quite noisy at the Cleakum, what with all the customers and the tribe of children, not much privacy for anyone. How many of them are there?"

"Five," said Elizabeth, "not counting Sally herself. She has three sisters and two brothers."

"That's right. Hugh, the baby one, sometimes comes to play with George. It gives George a chance to be bossy because he's a full year older and that's quite important when you're just a boy. Say hello to Mrs Bisby for me and perhaps I'll see you later in the week. Tell Sally I hope she has a good little holiday. Bye now. And keep that grin to yourself, remember, or you'll have the whole village talking."

Elizabeth waved to Mr Trickett as she walked up the path and out of the farm gate. It was a dry enough day with a high clear sky but the breeze hadn't abated, orchestrating a low hum through the tall elms against the counter ripples of the Loxley. The river seemed to be playing on its bed, quickly investigating fallen branches and stubborn boulders in its way, nosing mischievously in and out of every small inlet like a cheeky child with a stick in an ant-hole and dislodging whole flotillas of broken twigs to sail along with the flow. Elizabeth stopped to look over the bridge: she did love the sound of the moving water and its selfish energy and she imagined the excitement as it reached the sea and streamed out to join in and travel the world. She thought of her brother and of what it must be like to sail across the oceans as he had. Standing in the wind then conjured more unpleasant images of storms and angry waves and she hurried over and along the lane to Shaw Lodge.

"Hello, anyone at home?" she called hurrying through into the shelter of the porch and putting down her basket on the hall table. "Are you in, Mam?"

"Is that you, Elizabeth? I'll be down in a minute. There's tea on the hob if you fancy a cup. You must be tired and cold after walking all the way from Damflask. I'm just putting some laundry away, nearly finished. I'm dying to hear all about your new home. Are you hungry?"

Minutes later the two women were sitting in front of the parlour fire cupping their tea and feasting on some of Mrs Shaw's home-made fruit cake while the details of the Willow Tree Cottage christening were recounted.

"It sounds a picture," said Anna. "And did Daniel's things arrive alright?"

"John brought them all up on Sunday in the dray. We've still got work to do but the cottage already seems like home," said Elizabeth, quickly excusing any suggestion that she had forgotten all about Shaw Lodge in a matter of days.

"You don't have to apologise," said Anna, "it's only natural to feel like that. You've your own place now and that has to be your home. It's where your husband is, after all."

Anna slowly studied her piece of cake. "I hope you don't mind me asking," she said, "but you are my daughter and I've a right to worry about you – is Daniel alright with you, I mean, he's not rough is he, you know, in bed?"

"Mam, he couldn't be gentler or more understanding," said Elizabeth. She'd expected some such questioning – she would probably feel the same if she had a daughter – and had decided that the best way to get this particular bit of the conversation over and done with was to be open and not to be so silly as she had been with Mrs Trickett. "He's a good man, Mam, and he's been very considerate towards me. And if I can speak plainly to you," she smiled, "I can't say it's been any hardship on my own part whatsoever. Quite the opposite, in fact. Now, can we talk about something else?"

"We can now," said Anna. "My mind's at rest. Did Mrs Ibbotson have the place fixed up alright when you got there?"

"She did. She's been so nice to us, not intrusive, you understand, more like taking us into her bosom…"

"…and an ample one at that."

"Really I feel as if I've a friend up Damflask already. She's been telling me all about the neighbours and some of the regulars at the Barrel. Her husband's a bit worried about how business has gone down since most of the navvies left. Most people up there seem to think the dam workers were bit of a mixed blessing but now that they've gone the traders are beginning to feel the difference."

"It's always awkward when you get a lot of itinerant workers moving in and people don't like the way they live. Then they stay for a while and the shops and the pubs get used to their custom," said Anna. "No doubt some of the traders down here will also mourn their leaving. Have you been up to see the dam yet? I hear it's an incredible sight."

"Mrs Ibbotson says it's so grand that she can't remember now what the valley looked like before but couldn't believe it to be so wide. Daniel suggested we might go up on Sunday to take a look," said Elizabeth. "We're hoping you and Father will come to visit and then perhaps we could all stroll up in the afternoon. What do you think?"

"I should like that very much but, more importantly, I'm anxious to see Willow Tree Cottage for myself. I want to be able to picture you at home, that way I'll feel closer to you."

"I can't wait for you to come, Mam, but I want everything to be just right. It's Tuesday today so come of Friday, that gives me a few more days to get it all perfect for you. Now I must go, I want to see Sally and help her get things ready for her trip."

THERE had been metal grinders at work utilising the energy of the tumbling rivers in the Sheffield area since the latter half of the fifteenth century. The idea to harness water to drive the wheels used in putting hard-honed edges on tools had apparently originated in Germany. It wasn't the start of water power – up at Damflask itself a great millwheel was well established in the business of grinding corn – but it proved such an affordable technical improvement in the working of metals that soon the natural advantages of the local landscape had given rise to the development of grinding mills up and down all the area's rivers.

The setting couldn't have been more conducive. All the necessary resources were abundant and accessible around and about: massive quarries gave up their innards to be fashioned into grindstones; iron ore was already sourced in the region while the forests and woodlands and mines provided all the fuel needed. By the year seventeen hundred, some fifty per cent of the men in Sheffield were employed in some metal trade; years later still, skills were so well defined that different crafts were distinguished in the whole cutlery process, forgers were distinct from smiths while specialist grinders worked on a variety of edges from razors to saws, files and sickles to the finest table ware; the production methods were improving all the time, leading to greater output and quality. With the advances in steel making going hand-in-hand with this huge pool of skilled men, Sheffield was no longer a leading world player but the leading world player.

But it was dangerous work, filthy work, even in the rural-based wheels along the rivers' edges, like that in which Daniel Fletcher ground out a living. Surrounded by lush green countryside and swards of cut grass, the stone workshops let out a constant shrill of metal on rotating stone.

Daniel's was no better or worse than any. He sat inside his trough astride a narrow wooden bench, the horse, as he bent towards and over the heavy grindstone wheel turning noisily towards him, all fixed and operating in unison; his elbows rested on his knees as he hand-held blade to stone; his booted feet were cramped firmly in the bottom of the trough in the mess of metal shavings and stone dust mounting around him after flying off the stone to churn and fog and float through the air before descending to the floor. Even in the summer there was never enough ventilation for the thickened atmosphere to be sucked out of the place; in winter, with doors closed against the elements despite the heat of the toil, the grinder worked as hard at trying not to gulp in too much of the dark concoction into his lungs as he did trying to make sure the wheel stayed tethered in its mount. For that was the main immediate hazard of the occupation: if the strap holding the wheel broke, the grinder had little chance of survival in the face of a huge whirling grindstone suddenly hurtling towards him from only inches away. Like others in the same trade, Daniel would be lucky to still be alive at forty, if a life spent wheezing and coughing and choking with silicosis could be considered in any way a lucky way to be alive.

But lucky he was already: it was generally agreed that the wheels along the Loxley valley were marginally healthier than those further into Sheffield and, with a landlord like Thomas Shaw, at least the workshop was slightly better aired than most – Shaw had at least spent some of their rent money on that.

Daniel broke from his work to eat his snap. He smiled to himself when he pulled out the apple Elizabeth had included as a treat. He looked around the workshop as he greedily feasted on his humble meal and sat thinking about his new life as a married man, with its additional responsibilities, responsibilities which demanded more focused determination than he'd had before. He loved his Elizabeth, with her red-golden hair falling untidily over her shoulders, her wide-open brown eyes and that pretty face of hers with its small but distinct mole to the left of her mouth that bobbed about her cheek whenever she chattered; she was fairly tall for a woman – he was just above six feet and he didn't have to lift her too high or arch himself down too far whenever they kissed - but her slight frame gave her a delicacy which was wonderfully alien to this man from The Ponds.

It made him think of his mother: she too was slight of frame but through poverty not figure. That's what did for her when his brother Nathan was born, her body was too frail to provide both herself and the baby with the strength to survive. Then Daniel thought about his Da, about those awful last months he spent lying on the cot coughing up blood as he tried to wheeze in some breath and in the end being beaten by both. He couldn't see his Elizabeth put through all that; he'd work at the wheel for a few more years and put something by each week to build up an escape fund. He finished off the apple core and straddled the horse again: several hours of hard grind had to be got through before he could go home to his wife.

AT last John could begin to shake off the clogging, smoggy, soot-laden atmosphere of Sheffield as he rolled into open countryside on the way to Hillsborough. He spat out a gob of black and grimy phlegm and took a swig from his water flask. He had two deliveries at Hillsborough: the Blue Ball and the Hillsborough Inn and then on to Malin Bridge for the Stag and finally the Cleakum before he returned to the brewery for his last few rounds in the town centre. He felt tired having slept little since the affair with Will Pickens: every noise in the night had brought him jumping out of bed, knife in hand. So far, however, he had seen neither the bookie nor any of Quinn's men. It was possible that Pickens had revived, crawled somewhere and died anyway. John had seen that happen to men before when they'd been hit on the head: they got up, declared they were fine, only to collapse later on and never get up again. In the end John was John and he couldn't change that. If something came of the whole affair then so be it, he would deal with it there and then, but there was no point in worrying and losing sleep over something that might never happen.

He let Stanley choose his own pace, which was inevitably a plodding walk. The dray was still nearly full with barrels, John having made only one drop so far, and the big carthorse wasn't getting any younger. Anyway John was in no rush; with his inherent strength and willingness to work long hours, his job with Neepsend Brewery was secure. Good draymen were hard to find, many youngsters started out but found the work back-breakingly hard and soon quit. John was one of the few who worked without an off-sider, a workman who helped the driver with the off and on loading. The secret was in the rhythm and posture of carrying the barrels: a smooth fluid motion transferred the barrel from cart to shoulder, allowing the body to absorb the weight and the arm merely keeping the balance. If pushed John could carry a barrel on each of his broad shoulders but he rarely felt inclined to push himself that far.

It was hard to convince the novice draymen that a few weeks' work would give them the experience to make the job easier, aided by toughened skin and better-developed muscles. Most quit within the first fortnight. John blamed schooling for this: kids were soft these days; some had their noses stuck in bloody books until they were thirteen. They had no chance to get out and know what it was like to work for a living, proper hard work. John on the other hand had started going out with his Dad when he was nine.

Thinking about his father, John felt a familiar lump rise in his throat. It had only been three years since the old man had been killed, throat slit at the age of thirty-five. John had rampaged through the neighbourhood that night, destroying whatever got in his way as he tried to find who'd done it. To this day he had yet to identify the killer and the impotence he felt when thinking about someone walking away scot-free from murdering his Dad would boil up until his fingernails were embedded in bloodied imprints in his palms and his jaws were working overtime as his teeth ground away. The police had been unsurprisingly useless; a crime had been committed, that much they would acknowledge, but another body floating in the scum and rotting flotsam of the Sheaf was just that, another body. John found his mood darkening but, as always, found no way of lightening up. Then a stone rattled against the barrels behind him. The noise shook him out of his brooding and with a smile on his face he roared out: "I'll have none of that you bloody vandals." He heard a voice off to his left, its source hidden by the undergrowth.

"Eh up John, you're running a bit late aren't you?" Out of the bushes a small dishevelled figure came bounding up to the dray and leapt on to the seat next to John. The boy's head was almost totally engulfed by a floppy cloth cap and his clothes appeared to be held together by just a few well positioned threads.

"Now then Jimmy, what makes you say that?" John asked the lad. Jimmy was the son of one of John's cousins who lived out on the road to Hillsborough. The youngster would often run alongside the dray or jump aboard for a short ride and pester him with questions or bombard him with juvenile chatter.

"Dunno, just summat to say I suppose. What's the time anyway?"

John squinted up at the pale sun and pulled on his beard. "You see where the sun is now, just peeping out behind that cloud there?"

"Yeah I see it, so what does that mean? What time does that tell me?" Jimmy bounced impatiently on the seat, staring up.

"Well keep your eye on that and count to twenty," John said and while the boy's attention was skywards he sneaked a quick look at his old battered pocket-watch from the depths of his old waistcoat.

"…twenty. There I've done that so what time does it make it?" Jimmy pushed back the peak of his cap and thrust his face up demandingly.

"Why, that means it's eleven minutes past ten of course." John stared solemnly down at the boy, poker-faced. He watched as a gamut of expressions ran across Jimmy's face: at first a grimace of concentration followed by a nod of acceptance changing to puzzlement and finishing with a frustrated doubtful glare suspecting that he'd just been hoodwinked. In the end Jimmy just tutted in disgust and gave John a sharp elbow in the ribs.

Instantly forgotten and just as instantly on to another subject Jimmy suddenly announced: "It's my birthday on Saturday."

John already knew that and had been into town the other day to buy a spinning-top for the boy. Although he had never really got on well with Jimmy's father, he had a deep-rooted affection for the young lad and always enjoyed his fleeting hi-jacks on his route out west. He feigned ignorance however and said: "You can't have a birthday on Saturday, you've already had one, last year, I remember, because you fell into that pond and ruined your new clothes."

"I can too!" Jimmy protested in a slight panic. "You get one every year, me Ma says so."

John let out a theatrical sigh and nodded. "You might be right. I'm just getting forgetful in my old age. So how old will you be on Saturday?"

"Ten years old," Jimmy said proudly. "And then after that I'll be eleven."

"Oh, so you can count too." The dray was approaching Hillsborough. "Look now, you'd best get back home, lad, I've got work to do and your Ma will be wondering where you've got to. Maybe I might just pop over on Saturday. How would you like that?"

"Would you? That'd be great. And you could get me a present for my birthday. That's what folks do you know?" Jimmy jumped off the wagon and trotted alongside.

"A present eh?" John mused. "Like what?"

"Well like a pocket-watch, same as what you've got." Jimmy laughed triumphantly and set off at a dead sprint back in the direction they had come.

"He's a sharp one that kid. What do you reckon Stanley?" The horse's ears pricked up at the mention of his name and he snickered gently. "Yeah, I thought you'd think so." John flicked the reins and they picked up a little speed. He could see the Blue Ball's yard across the river and the landlord waiting at the gates. "C'mon Stanley, we'd best get this miserable bastard his ale."

Sometimes John had help shifting the barrels and sometimes he was left to manage on his own, it depended on who ran the inn. At both of the Hillsborough pubs he would be working alone with barely an acknowledgment from either publican whereas up at Malin Bridge John knew he'd get help from both the Bisbys and the Armitages who ran the Cleakum and Stag respectively. John didn't mind working on his own: although he always got on well with the various kids, he was seldom comfortable talking to the landlords themselves. He'd find himself saying something inappropriate or a little too colourful for the company.

As he started bringing the empties out from the cellar, John was thinking that he might call in on Daniel at his wheel and see how married life was treating him. He finished off at the Blue Ball and left without even seeing the landlord again. The Hillsborough Inn was a quick drop, only three empties and three to deliver. John knew that the bulk of his load was destined for Malin Bridge.

Daniel worked just this side of the village and John decided to drop in before the heavy work had to be done. He pulled Stanley up at the side of the road and tied him to a sturdy oak tree. Daniel worked at one of the workshops down near the Limerick Wheel on the banks of the Loxley and John could hear the god-awful sound of the grinders at work as he sauntered down the gentle slope to the building. He pushed the door open into a scene from hell. The four grinders who occupied the wheel were all hard at it, the noise was horrendous and fine black dust billowed around the room. Daniel heard the door swing open and John's bellowing voice. He gave a quick nod and slowed his wheel, letting it trundle to a stop on its axle. He got up from his narrow seat slowly, allowing his cramped muscles and spine to re-adjust to an upright position, stretched his arms out wide and rolled his shoulders. Wiping most of the dust and grime from his face with his neckerchief, he gestured to John that they should go outside.

"Gods you look like shit Daniel. I don't know why you do this work, I really don't," John said as they walked down to the river. "I could get you working on the wagons tomorrow if you just said the word."

"Aye but they don't pay the money do they? I've got responsibilities now and, short of crime, this is the best money I can make." Daniel pulled out his pipe and stuffed it with tobacco, John sparked up a match and lit him. "Sometime soon John you'll meet a girl and stop all the whoring and drinking and settle down. Then you'll realise that a drayman's wage just doesn't cover all your needs."

John didn't feel like being lectured by Daniel. "Give it a rest and lighten up won't you. For all you know we might all be struck down by the plague tomorrow and then my wage or your wage won't matter a damn." He picked up a stone and sent it skimming into the river. "For now I'm happy enough with my lot and I've got no plans to settle down with any girl. I don't reckon I'm the marrying type."

Daniel too spun a pebble out across the water. "Six bounces, not bad." He sighed: "I don't mean to get at you, John, it's just that since the wedding I feel like old man Shaw's breathing down my neck, making sure I don't ruin his precious daughter."

"What are you complaining about? God you can be a stubborn git sometimes, Daniel Fletcher. He's given you a house hasn't he?" John sat down, leaning against an old tree stump, and lit his own pipe. "All he's doing is giving you a helping hand. Any father would do the same. We're just unfortunate that ours aren't around anymore. You can't do everything yourself."

Daniel settled down next to his friend. "I know, it just seems that I should be able to provide for Elizabeth, I'm her husband after all."

"Well bloody provide for her then but don't turn down any extra help when it comes knocking. Look, if your Dad wasn't dead he'd have helped you out. And if my old man was still here he'd help me out. That's what parents do, accept it and quit thinking that it makes you less of a man."

Daniel inspected his pipe then bashed it on the ground to empty it. "You're right, it's just that I'm so used to looking after people, first Nathan, then me Da when he got sick. It seems funny accepting stuff from someone else."

"Well if I was you I'd think myself damned lucky. So stop moaning and start to enjoy life a bit more." John wondered whether to mention the business about Will Pickens and Jack Quinn, Daniel was always a good man to have in a fight, but he decided against it. The man was married now and John didn't want to get him mixed up in that kind of trouble. He stood up and brushed himself down. "Look I've got to get on, I think I must have drank the Stag dry when we stayed there, apparently he's desperate for barrels. I'll be back later in the week and call by again."

Daniel got up as well and the two men roughly embraced. "Cheers John, I know I can be a miserable bastard sometimes. Look, why don't you come up to the cottage sometime, maybe on Sunday again? The place is looking good now and our lass can fix you up with some nice grub."

"That'd be grand." John left with a wave and headed back to his cart. Daniel watched him go, feeling a great swell of affection for his old mate. Then he turned towards the wheel and braced himself for the work ahead of him.

As he untethered Stanley, John rubbed the old horse's mane. "We'll see if we can't get us something to drink at the Stag, hey boy?"

"MY goodness look at you. Married life is obviously working for Mrs Elizabeth Fletcher." Sally held her friend by the hands and then twirled her around under an approving gaze. "Whatever that man's doing to you, it certainly seems to agree with you," she said. "You look like a right grown woman, look at you, look at your chest, you're almost heaving before my eyes."

"Stop that Sally Bisby or I'll go straight home," said Elizabeth, feigning disquiet while adopting what she imagined was a right grown woman's demeanour. Then the two of them burst into laughter and fell into hugging each other with the novel thrill of it all..

"Come on in Lizzie and tell me what's what," said Sally. "I'm dying to know all the things it wouldn't be proper for a mother to tell a daughter and I know I can count on you."

The two girls headed for the back parlour behind the public bar of the Cleakum. "Everyone's busy outside so we can talk in here," said Sally. "If I shut the door then we'll hear anyone coming in and we can change the subject quickly if needs be."

Sally bundled Elizabeth into the deepest armchair in the room. "I want to make sure you're really settled and comfortable so you can talk freely. Would you like some lemonade?"

"Yes, fetch me some lemonade," said Elizabeth, waving her arm as if instructing a servant and pulling a know-all face.

Sally disappeared into the pub leaving Elizabeth to snuggle down into the chair with a simple proud grin on her face. She was the first of her group of friends to get married and delighted in the silly status it gave her. It was a wonder Sally hadn't lined them all up in the parlour to be told "what's what". Elizabeth couldn't help but run her hands down over her chest just to feel if it was actually heaving. A frisson trembled through her as the simple physical gesture made her think of Daniel and it was a blushing new bride not an experienced matron who greeted Sally as she swept back into the room bearing a tray laden with supplies of lemonade.

"My goodness, can't leave you alone for a minute without your mind wandering heaven knows where," said Sally as she set the tray down on a side table. She poured out the drinks and manoeuvred a smaller armchair into place so she could face her visitor full on. She settled down ready with her legs tucked up under and arranged her full skirt accordingly. Sally was a fresh-faced country-looking girl, with bosoms and hips nurtured by a childhood spent in a country pub and by the jolly mother that went hand-in-hand, but the knowingness suggested by her looks was belied by the innocence that same jolly mother had worked hard to protect: with so many men hanging around all the time in the bar, typically often the worse for drink, Mrs Bisby had made sure her blossoming daughter had remained as cocooned as possible. "Alright," said Sally, "I'm all ears. Tell me, what was it like?"

Loud, embarrassed, amused splutterings escaped from the two of them before, looking each at the other over the rims of their mugs, they sipped supposedly demurely on their lemonade.

"Come on," said Sally hurrying matters along. "You must start at the beginning but leave out the boring stuff. Tell me, did you wear that beautiful cotton-lawn nightdress you'd been drooling over for weeks?"

"Not all night," said Elizabeth and they both started hooting again.

"What do mean 'not all night'? Did he rip it off you?"

"He didn't have to, I didn't even put it on."

"You didn't even put your nightdress on?" More hysterics. "My but doesn't it sound wonderful, the two of you lying next to each other on a big plump bed, both of you naked, the skin up and down your whole bodies touching. Mmmh! Is it as good as it sounds?"

"Sally it makes you just tingle all over, the slightest touch is so incredibly exciting, but it is scary at first."

"Lizzie start with the 'at first', at the beginning. How did you actually get round to... you know, how did it start off?"

"Well it was late, of course, and we were both tired because we'd had the wedding and the party and then we'd walked up to Damflask."

"Was that romantic, the walk in the moonlight with your new husband, looking up at the stars knowing you were with a big strong man who was all yours?" Sally rolled her eyes and pouted her lips and rocked her shoulders backwards and forwards, all busybody and dreaming.

"It was so nice, really. Mam and Father had asked us to stay at home but I insisted that Daniel and I went up to Damflask instead. I said it was because we were anxious to see their present to us – wasn't that wonderful of Father, to give us a cottage? Anyway, to be honest, Sal, that wasn't the reason at all. I wanted to go because I couldn't bear the idea of going up to bed while Mam and Father, you know, were in the house while we were, you know, and them knowing what we would be, you know, doing. Can you imagine it, how embarrassing it would be?"

"I'd be exactly the same," said Sally. "Sometimes I can hear Mam and Da in their room and I'd hate it to be me they could hear."

"When we got to the cottage – I've not told you yet: we've decided to call it Willow Tree Cottage because there's this beautiful willow in the front garden sweeping over the grass and you can hear it swishing across the ground when the door is open."

"What a beautiful name! Oh you are so lucky, Lizzie: a handsome husband and all so romantic too."

"When we got there a woman from the village had already lit the fire for us and left in a few things; you might know her, Mrs Ibbotson from the Barrel?"

"I've met her a couple of times, that's all, but Mam and Da sometimes go up to the Barrel no doubt to discuss pub stuff. It doesn't interest me. I want to marry someone who's got nothing to do with pubs or bars or beer, someone who'll take me away from the smell of empty barrels and swilled floors and will lavish me in luxury and listen to everything I say because he's not worn out with talking to customers and drunken oafs. Anyway, I don't want to hear about all your domestic details, get to the real business. How long before you kissed?"

"It was a bit awkward to start off with; when Mrs Ibbotson had gone and the door closed behind her I felt really self-conscious and couldn't think of a word to utter so I just pottered around like some fidgety fool. Then Daniel came up behind me and just held me in his arms and I started to shiver with goose-bumps. He turned me around and, after all my worrying and nerves, it seemed the most natural thing in the world when he bent down and took my face in his hands and kissed me. Sally, I nearly collapsed, so heady was the effect that it rushed right through my head and I could hardly breathe properly, my legs went all trembly and I got a peculiar kind of an ache, you know, down there, that's so scary. But it's a delicious, overwhelming kind of scary and what surprised me so much was that far from dreading going to bed I wanted to, so much; I wanted to see Daniel and touch him and have him touch me. Sally, it's just so difficult to describe."

"And the first time he actually put his thing inside you did it hurt? I've heard that it really hurts."

"It did a bit the first time but not so much after that, after that it didn't matter."

"The first time? You mean he did it to you more than once?"

"I wanted him to."

Sally gulped down a cooling mouthful of lemonade. "Well," she said, "if it's as good as you say no wonder we get told the opposite, it's just to put us off. I can't wait until it's my turn."

"I think it's all to do with loving someone very much."

The two girls sat in silence staring at nothing but thinking of everything when the sound of the angelus rang out from one of the local churches and broke the spell.

"Midday already," said Sally. "John Hukin will be here any minute with the week's delivery from Neepsend. He comes here every Tuesday but I didn't realise he was Daniel's friend until the wedding. He's a real flirt when he comes here. He's always making funny comments to my Mam and winking at me at the same time. Shall we go out and see him, Lizzie?"

"Perhaps a change of scenery would calm us down," said Elizabeth, pulling herself up out of the chair and not a little conscious of how personal she had gotten in her conversation with Sally. "I do like John though I've only met him a couple of times. You probably know him much better than me."

"He's nice enough, certainly friendly with his banter and talk," said Sally, "but what's there to know for an ambitious young woman like me, he's just a brewery man."

It was a giggling pair of haughty lasses who went out to greet the dray.

THE two Masters Bisby, Thomas, a strapping lad of nine with the knees out of his trousers, and his younger brother Hugh, all cuts and grazes and runny nose, always took on an air of grand importance when Mr Hukin arrived at the Cleakum with the supplies, aping their father, as they thought, in guiding the operations to get the heavy barrels off the back of the cart and the light ones up on to it. Their main job concerned the two wooden doors over the hatch into the cellar: they were set the task of unlocking the bolts and lifting the doors with strict instructions to be careful not to fall in, which they did anyway with regularity, it being great fun to go sliding down the chute and into the cave below. It did nothing to complement their assumed importance but they could never resist it. Once they'd scrambled back up the chute they tried to look busy and in-charge all over again.

"Now Master Thomas, Master Hugh, is the cellar open and ready," said John. "Stanley here is getting a bit tired hauling all this beer about the countryside all the way up from Sheffield and he's anxious to off-load some of it now, only if that's convenient to you young Sirs, of course. Perhaps you'd like to give him an apple or two while your Da and I see to the heavy work. We don't want you young gentlemen getting any dirtier than necessary now, do we?" he said, giving them both the once-over with his eyes and silently commenting on the state they were in. "It's a fine couple of sons you have there, George," he said to the landlord, "and a fine looking daughter too," he added as Sally emerged from the building. "Hello there, Miss Bisby, you're looking very well today, always a pleasure to be seeing you. Oh and you've a visitor I see. Elizabeth, you're looking well too, quite a rosy new bloom to those cheeks now."

"You should mind your implications, John Hukin" said Sally. "That's no way to address your friend's wife."

"Now now, Sally," said her father. "Let the man get on with his work. Come on, John, let's get those bloody barrels down before it rains." George Bisby could be a somewhat pompous man for a landlord, often curt in manner, saving his amiable face for the working side of the bar.

47

John slightly bowed his head and tipped his cap lightly at the girls. "I don't think it'll rain today, George," he said, looking up at the sky while he took the pins out of the u-hooks and uncoupled the endgate of the dray. "The wind's dropped and we could be in for a pleasant afternoon. I hope so, anyway, I've at least one more round to make when I've finished here. How many do you want today?"

"Twelve if you have 'em," said George surveying what barrels were left on the cart. "We got through some last weekend, what with the wedding and so on. There's nothing like nuptials to bring out the thirst in people."

"That's true enough. I got through a few myself, to be honest, not whole barrels, you understand," said John, quickly glancing at the ladies present. "Are you alright there lads?" he called to Thomas and Hugh. "Keep Stanley steady now while I climb up, I'm relying on you, keep him busy with those apples." He clambered aboard the dray and did a quick calculation. "Let's see, George, I can let you have nine today and then if you need more I can perhaps bring up a few more when I'm back this way to see Dan, that's with Mrs Fletcher's permission, of course." He nodded towards Elizabeth and arched his eyebrows with a smile. It was returned with what John recognised as an unmistakable warmth.

"That'd be handy," said Bisby. "Come on now, let's get to it." He went off to station himself in the cellar.

John took off his outer coat and worked in his rolled-up shirtsleeves. His waistcoat was threadbare and couldn't have given him much warmth but at least it was protected down the front by his long leather apron, polished to a shine through use. He rocked the barrels to the back edge of the cart then jumped down and hauled one high up on to his shoulder, almost as if the thing was weightless. Sally nudged Elizabeth to make sure she was catching the eyeful.

"Aren't we the muscle man," said Sally. "At least you're fit for something, John Hukin. I doubt if schooling was ever your strength."

"Schooling was never my anything, Miss Bisby," he answered as he strode across the yard. "We never had much call for it in town."

"And there's certainly no call for it in a man humping barrels of beer all day long," said Sally.

"And you're certainly not your mother's daughter, not with that sharp tongue," said John. He lowered the barrel carefully to the cellar hatch, taking the weight on his shoulder for as long as possible before dropping it on to the cushion to send it rolling down the chute to George below, then did the whole thing again eight more times, all the while feeling more inadequate than he cared to admit. Aware that he was shining with the sweat dripping off his beard and running down his arms and his breath heavy with the exertion, he looked around expecting some more caustic comments from Sally but the two women had disappeared. John wiped his brow, disappointed but more relieved.

"Come in and have a drink before you set off," said George.

"I'll have a quick one out here, if you don't mind," said John. "I must get off." In less than a minute his reddened face was hidden behind the rim of his mug of ale and very welcome it was. "I'll be back in a few days then, George. Okay boys, is Stanley set for the off?" he asked the youngsters who had taken it on themselves to brush down the old horse. "You've done a good job there," he told them and gave them a small coin each. He put his coat back on, sprang back up to the driving seat and set off back to the depot, thinking on the way that he might get Daniel to teach him how to read and write properly. "Sod it," he decided. "She's right, what does a drayman need with fancy reading and writing. Certainly nothing that would have come in handy last night," he chortled and gave Stanley an extra flick of the reins.

THE sound of voices and activity at the gate of Willow Tree Cottage brought Elizabeth to the door. It was a calm night but quite late, nearly nine-o'-clock, and she had been anxious about Daniel being so late: he had warned her he'd probably have to do some overtime at the trough but, still in the first flush of marriage, Elizabeth didn't realise quite how late he had meant and she missed him. Mixed with the voices – with some relief she recognised Daniel's and was surprised to hear Gabriel as well – were shuffling, scuffling noises and the unmistakeable whimpering of a dog. When she opened the door, there in the lantern light was Daniel holding aloft for inspection four squawking chickens in each hand while Gabriel was struggling to control a small, agitated terrier and trying to prevent its escape.

"Let me get rid of this thing," said the driver. "Here, dog, this is your new home, get down now and leave me in peace." Gabriel tied the dog's leash to the porch post. The terrier sniffed around a bit and wagged its tail before deciding to play the sympathy card and hide in the shadows at the side. "Well that's a relief," said Gabriel, straightening himself up and brushing dog hairs off his topcoat. "That poor puppy has been yelping and whining all the way from Shaw Lodge. I told Mrs Shaw it was a silly idea to fetch it out here so late at night in the gig but she was adamant that it would be a lovely surprise for you."

"It's so cute," said Elizabeth, bending to make friends with the new arrival.

"And your father sent these layers up," said Daniel, standing tall and looking out of context for a scuffed up grinder just finished work. He wasn't quite sure what to do with the damned things, a jabbing mass of wing-flutter and pecking beaks getting aggressive with each other in their fight for flight; of course there was no coop as yet to put them in and they couldn't go in the house but he couldn't hold on to them much longer, he'd already been wrestling to hold on to them all the way from Malin Bridge. "I wondered why he sent me a message to call in to the Lodge on the way past. This is why." He held the frantic chickens aloft and Elizabeth and Gabriel burst out laughing at the sight, poor Daniel surrounded in a haze of flying feathers, his dirt-encrusted face relieved only by the lantern reflection in two wide-open eyes and a set of teeth lined top-and-bottom in a hang-down mouth. Then even Daniel, who could err on the side of being overly serious, felt his grimace crease into a smile.

"Right," said Elizabeth taking charge. "There is an old bit of fencing round the side of the cottage: we could lean it up against the wall and block off the ends with some wood to keep them in and the cold out, just for tonight. Could you give me a hand Gabriel?"

"I don't want to complain but could you be quick about it," said Daniel. "These might look like innocent chickens to you but they're actually mad creatures on the run from a witch's brew and they've been stirring me up long enough."

The makeshift shelter was completed and the birds penned. The dog instinctively betrayed his curiosity and ran madly round everyone's feet, now and then barking at the chickens to let them know who was boss: a cosy corner inside Willow Tree Cottage was to be his bed.

"Come inside, Gabriel, have some supper with us."

"Thank you, Miss Elizabeth, but I think the menu at the Barrel might be more to my taste at the moment, if it's all the same to you" he said. "They serve a good drop of porter and Jonathan the landlord is always abreast of the latest news and gossip of the district and that always helps the drink hit the spot more directly."

After the farewells, the Fletchers went inside the house, the latest addition yapping at their heels, and only the faint moonlight remained to guide Gabriel on his way. He didn't need it: he mounted the gig and clattered over the stone bridge and into the courtyard at the rear of the pub. "I expect you wouldn't mind a drop of something yourself," he addressed the horse: Arthur knew well where he was and let out a thirsty whinny. Gabriel tied up in his usual spot, away from any potential nosy parkers; quite who would be bothered where the man went for a drink was anyone's guess but for some reason he thought it better to be discreet.

"I didn't realise Gabriel was such a regular up at Damflask," said Elizabeth, trying to do the impossible in brushing down Daniel's work clothes. She had hung large pots of water over the fire while waiting for him to come home and now he was soaking in the tin bath in front of the hearth. Elizabeth kept sneaking glances at his broad back, watching him soap his arms and chest, scrubbing it in with his fingers to help get the black out of his nails at the same time and then rinsing off with a flannel, all in the flickering firelight.

"Come and scrub my back, Mrs Fletcher," he commanded, as if he had picked up on her gaze. "Get you hands over here, your husband needs you."

This was an intimacy of married life that had come as a unforeseen pleasure to Elizabeth and she duly started rubbing Daniel's back as he leaned forward, exploring the contours of his body, the blemishes on his skin, noting the roughness on his elbows and the cuts and grazes on his hands, the redness at the back of his neck where it met the pitch-dark of his hair.

"I saw that scoundrel John Hukin today," said Daniel, rotating his shoulders and easing his muscles in the warm tub as the water and gentle fingers ran down his back. "He was up this direction doing his deliveries."

"I saw him, at the Cleakum. Sally insisted we went out to see him and then she was really nasty to him. I've never seen such a spiteful side of her before. She was so unpleasant to him I couldn't understand why she'd insisted we went out to see him in the first place. It was definitely peculiar. I tried to let him see that I wanted no part in it. Has anything ever happened between them? I didn't notice anything odd at the wedding."

"Not as far as I'm aware but then there's no understanding women, as I'm beginning to realise more and more. But then John can be a bit odd himself."

"Perhaps but I like him, not just because he's your friend but because it's easy to see why he is. He strikes me as someone who'd be very loyal and kind. He was really good with the Bisbys' young boys and he can be very funny."

"He can also be the exact opposite," said Daniel. "You've only met him a couple of times and you've seen the good side but there are things that have happened in his life that have left him quite explosive, especially after a few drinks. He can get very free with his fists can John. There's a few been on the receiving end of his temper and had the black eyes to prove it, myself included."

"You? I thought you and him were as close as brothers." Elizabeth poured a pan of water over Daniel's head and started massaging the day's dust off his scalp.

"We always have been," said Daniel spluttering as the soapy water poured down his face inducing a breathless sensation of drowning. "We grew up together and always looked out for each other. I suppose we had a lot in common; our parents died when we were young and I for one would have felt very alone without John there for me. My Ma was a very kind woman, what I can remember of her anyway, which to be honest isn't much, I'm ashamed to say, but then I was only two when she passed away. But it seems she made my Da promise her he'd make sure Nathan and I learned how to read and write, whatever it took, and he was as good as his word. It broke his heart when Nathan walked out without even a goodbye and it broke my heart to see my Da close up inside. He loved me, I know, but he couldn't hide his hurt. Ma had died giving birth to his second son and then that same son just cleared off. Broken hearted, I suppose, that's what they call it isn't it?"

"It must have been hard and lonely for both of you," said Elizabeth, "I can't really imagine it, I've had such an easy time of it by comparison. Even when we got the news about David going missing in the war in India our life seemed to carry on as normal. I missed him but I suppose I never actually stopped to think about how Mam and Father might be feeling deep down inside. You make me feel very selfish."

"Well you shouldn't. We don't all lead the same lives, thank goodness, it wouldn't do for us all to go round crying and wailing all the time."

"Did you cry and wail?"

"Every day until I met you, young lady. Anyway, lass, I think I'm as clean as I'm going to get so pass me that towel will you and let me dry myself before I turn into a fish." Daniel stood up, dirty water dribbling down his body back into the tub. Elizabeth teased him with the towel, holding it out of reach until he managed to grab it and pull her towards him. "I'll deal with you later," he said but she couldn't resist tickling him and touching him as he tried to dry himself. She loved that he had no embarrassment standing naked in front of her. She couldn't help but press up against him, soaking though he was, and get lost in his eyes and they started to kiss and discover each other's faces for the umpteenth time. Unfortunately the puppy decided to join in too; it jumped up on to Daniel, who yelled as claws dragged down and tore scratch lines into his bare legs, and then started tugging for all its might on the hem of Elizabeth's skirt. Water splashed everywhere as Daniel thrust the dog away, straight into the tub. The shock of the wet sent the thing into paroxysms of panic as it fought to get back on to dry land where it began frantic shaking sessions to shed the water off its coat. Daniel snatched up the tub and emptied it out the door while Elizabeth rushed around trying to mop up the mess. The terrier, having made his presence felt and got a dunking for his trouble, slunk off into the corner in self-imposed disgrace.

All mayhem subsided, it made a cosy picture, the three of them in front of the fire, Daniel now dressed in some fresh clothes, Elizabeth curled up at his feet, him curling his fingers through her loose hair, and the terrier supposedly asleep but with one ear cocked and one eye on the proceedings, just in case.

"So tell me, what was it that happened to John? You said he'd even hit you."

"His father was knifed in the street in Sheffield and killed about three years ago and John's still tormenting himself over not finding the person who did it. It was a long time ago now but the sore still festers in his mind and makes him go crazy sometimes. Anyone who gets in his way then has to look out, even me." The gravity of the history led them into a momentary silence.

"Tell me about the first time you saw me," said Elizabeth; she wanted to change the conversation into something warmer to match the situation and this had become one of her favourite topics.

"Well I was very surprised that Mr Shaw had sent his daughter down to the wheel to mix with all us rough types. I remember looking up from the stone and seeing you standing in the doorway, pencil and notepaper in hand, all nervous and shy like the young miss you were. I thought I noticed you blush when you looked at me but I decided that must have been wishful thinking."

"Wishful thinking, eh, on just one glimpse of me. One glimpse of you and I did blush, you were right and I knew you had noticed. I remember feeling my face burning and having to turn away from you quickly, I thought I was going to die with shame."

"We all wondered what you were there for." (Daniel adopted a high-pitched squeaky voice.) "'Hello, I'm Elizabeth Shaw. My father has sent me to do a maintenance report. I hope I won't disturb you.'" (Elizabeth slapped him on the legs at the imitation.) "You seemed like a little lost girl fighting the urge to run off yet you had a certain determination about you to do what your father had asked."

"I was scared, I felt really out of place. I thought you'd all be staring at me and whispering things I'd not be meant to hear." (It was Elizabeth's turn to put on a voice, deep and supposedly sonorous.) "'What's the Shaw girl doing here, spying on us or what? Not much to look at is she, spoilt cow.'"

"Is that the best you can do?" Daniel mocked her attempts at mimicry. "You'll never make a man," he said.

"That's a relief."

"I'm forced to agree," said Daniel. "Now move over while I put some more wood on the fire."

The new logs crackled and spat in the grate, exploding little sparks amid the odd hiss of sap bubbling out through the bark. Their faces glowed in the flicker of the flames, fanned by thoughts of how that first visit at the wheel had led to their courtship. None of it had been straightforward because of the difference in their social status but they met constantly thanks, initially and ironically, to Elizabeth's father. Thomas Shaw had devised a strategy of gradually educating Elizabeth in the running of the property business: as the only remaining child of the family, she would be the one to inherit the portfolio of workshops and cottages from which the Shaws derived their income and Thomas wanted to ensure that she understood it all; he didn't want her, as a simple woman, to end up the ignorant dupe of some fancy lawyer or, worse even, of some unscrupulous husband. For a while Elizabeth and Daniel had both deliberately engineered encounters - Elizabeth showed unexpected enthusiasm in wanting to learn the business and do the property rounds with or without her father, while Daniel took to calling at Shaw Lodge, to pay his rent instead of waiting for the collection or to report some minor repairs needed to the troughs – then they had to go through that awful formal meeting with her father when Daniel asked for permission to walk out with his daughter. Mr Shaw was not impressed. He recognised Fletcher as a good tenant, not as husband material for his precious Betsy. Gradually, though, he was talked around by Anna: he saw his daughter's eyes light up whenever the man was around and saw that same light reflected in return. Shaw began to take note of the grinder, certainly a hard worker and with ambitions of his own to get on in his trade; he looked into his background and couldn't resist a growing respect for this man who had taken sole care of his father through some terrible months of disease, all the time never failing to meet an order date. Why the young man could even read books, as Anna was at pains to point out: the couple undoubtedly had his wife's blessing and her instinct was seldom wrong. Thomas saw them as a happy match after all.

The fire was dying down and the night chill had begun invading the room. "Time for bed, I think, lass; I've an early start in the morning," said Daniel at last. "Are you coming?"

"I suppose so, I've nothing better to do," said Elizabeth with a knowing look. They might be married but she still enjoyed flirting with her man. They stood up, Elizabeth blew out the lamp and Daniel picked up the candle to lead the way upstairs. The dog was all action again.

"Any ideas for a name for the puppy?"

"I think we should call it Waterbaby," said Daniel.

"That's no sort of name for a dog."

"Okay, how about Pebble?"

"Pebble?"

"Well it certainly seems to swim as well as one."

"Alright, Pebble it is. Come on, Pebble," said Elizabeth calling the terrier. It didn't yet know its name but the dog knew an invitation when it heard one and bounded through the door with them, a flurry of tail-wagging and excitement.

***

Part Two
Friday March 10

Charlotte Gunson put her husband's breakfast in front of him and poured out a cup of tea. "There's still a strong breeze out there, I've just seen someone's laundry blow past the kitchen window."

"Mmm? What's that dear?" John Gunson peered over the top of his newspaper. It was his habit to read most of the morning paper with his breakfast and he seldom changed from his habits.

"I was just saying that a large pair of bloomers has just flown past the window." She smiled at his absent-mindedness. They had been married for thirty-three years but she still found his mannerisms and slightly quixotic traits endearing. "The wind is still up," she said.

Gunson turned to the weather section and scanned the information. His attention was suddenly held and he brought the paper closer to his face. "By the looks of things it's going to get worse before it gets any better. Fitzroy forecasts a gale coming in from the west."

Charlotte knew that her husband always read the weather avidly, it was part of his job as a chief engineer, she supposed. She also knew that he put great store in Fitzroy, who had instituted a system of storm warnings that were published in the press when applicable. Gunson put the paper down and removed his spectacles, his forehead creased by a slight frown. "I might have to change my plans today. I was going to take the gig out to Redmires but I think I'd better go and check on Dale Dyke this afternoon." He finished his toast and washed it down with some tea. "We're not quite finished up there and I'd like to make sure everything's as it should be before this gale blows in. I might be back a little later than usual tonight love."

"No problem, we're only having cold cuts. I'll have it waiting for when you come in." Since the last of their children had left, the Gunsons had become more relaxed about meal times. Even so John still liked to eat in the formal dining room with the best cutlery. Some rituals had to be observed.

Gunson stood up, slipped his spectacles into his breast pocket and folded the

57

paper under his arm. "I'd best be off love, it might just be a busy day."

Charlotte held out his jacket and said: "Don't forget your coat, that wind has a definite chill to it."

Outside, Gunson, still shrugging on his heavy overcoat, walked the few yards to the offices next door: the premises of Sheffield Waterworks Company. He nodded to a couple of colleagues in the foyer and made his way up to his office.

"Morning Mr Gunson, looks like the weather's turning for the worse." A young man in his mid-twenties bounded up the stairs until he had caught up with his boss.

"Morning Pearson." Gunson waved his paper: "Fitzroy's issued a storm warning in from the west. I'll be taking the gig over to Dale Dyke later just to check up on how things are proceeding."

Mathew Pearson, a junior surveyor with the company, looked at him with slight alarm. "You don't think there'll be any problems do you?"

"None at all I'm sure but if the storm breaks a bit hard we might have to open a couple of the outlet pipes to ease the pressure on the embankment. A safety precaution that's all, nothing to worry about. I'll have a better idea when I get there."

Gunson's office was on the second floor. He watched as Pearson continued up to the third floor, two steps at a time, and wondered when last he'd had that same energy.

At his desk, Gunson immediately pulled out the latest reports on the progress of the dam at Dale Dyke. He had been the company's resident engineer for fifteen years now, rising slowly and methodically through the ranks since he had joined at the age of twenty-two. If he was honest with himself, he didn't expect to rise any further but that didn't bother him. He led an uncomplicated life, enjoyed his work and was comfortably set up so that he needn't have to worry about his and Charlotte's future.

AT Damflask, Daniel's mood matched the heavy, overcast day. "That bloody goat," he growled, crashing into the kitchen clutching the eggs he'd been out to collect in the yard. He only had three and he held them up in Elizabeth's face and shook them.

"Whatever's the matter?" Elizabeth was still waking up and in the last couple of days had begun to realise that her husband wasn't at his best first thing in the morning. It wasn't that he was bad tempered with her personally, quite the opposite, he was quiet, sullen almost, as he looked forward to yet another full day's grind. He tried hard to be kind in the middle of it all, she appreciated that, but she accepted his nature and had taken to being just as quiet to help ease him into the day. Usually he'd come round fairly quickly but today he seemed particularly cross: it was Friday, they had been married for almost one whole week, the happiest week of her life so far, the happiest week she could ever have possibly imagined and it was ending with him in the blackest mood she had experienced.

"That bloody goat," he said again. "I was bending down picking the eggs from the straw and it butted me, that's why there are only three eggs today because the rest got smashed when I fell headlong into the coop. Now I'm covered in egg yolk and chicken shit and I've got to go to work stinking like this."

Elizabeth tried to swallow hard and covered her mouth with her hand but it was no use, she couldn't help it, she started to laugh, exactly the wrong thing to do.

"Yes it's all very funny isn't it," snapped Daniel. "It was funny enough when your father gave us the chickens and that blasted dog but what do we want with a bloody goat? I didn't realise when I married you I'd be taking on a whole menagerie. I'm a grinder not a smallholder. Does Shaw think I can't provide for my wife? What shall I expect Gabriel to bring up next, that ridiculous cow you were dreaming about?"

The look on his face, the tone of his voice, the anger in his manner were new and brought Elizabeth up short.

"Daniel why are you being so nasty?"

"Do you think I like not being able to provide you with all the things your father can?" he replied. "Cottage, animals, what next – a cart? a wardrobe of new clothes so his poverty-stricken son-in-law can look more presentable? perhaps a few fancy bonnets for his Betsy so she doesn't look like a grinder's wife?"

"I'm going outside, I'll not listen to any of this." Elizabeth was angry at the resentment pouring out of the man whom she had thought of only as loving and caring. "My father has been more than good to us and I for one am glad he has. Here we have our own home thanks to him."

"Yes, exactly right, thanks to him. But it's my responsibility to look after you now and I don't need your father rubbing my nose in the fact that I've less money than perhaps you and he would like."

"That is so unfair. My father has accepted you totally and he's only doing what he can to help both of us, not just me. I've never heard anything so stupid and all because you got butted in the backside by a goat. Come on,

Pebble, let's go outside." She slammed the door behind her.

Daniel did indeed feel stupid and mean but, rightly or wrongly, he had had enough of Thomas Shaw interfering in his life. He knew the man had been more than generous but so much generosity was difficult to take and even harder to repay. After all, it was his wheel rent and the rent from others like him that allowed people like Thomas Shaw to make his grand gestures. Daniel pulled on his cap and muffler and, muttering curses he tried never to say in front of Elizabeth, left the house.

Outside she was pretending to play with Pebble and had even tied a bright red ribbon around the dog's neck. "Aren't you waiting for me to walk to work with you?" she asked plaintively as Daniel stormed up the garden path. "What about your breakfast? I haven't made your snap yet."

"No time," he snarled back. "I'll see you this evening but I'll be late home, I've a big order to finish by tomorrow. By the way, I don't think a ribbon's going to last very long on a stupid dog do you?" Daniel strode off down the road, already regretting his outburst. She was right: he was being stupid, a right stupid bastard.

Elizabeth stood tearfully watching him cross the bridge and head off down the lane. "I'll keep your supper warm," she shouted after him. He stopped, turned to look at her, smiled and waved and went on his way. She didn't see the smile, he was too far away, so she was left wondering if the wave meant that everything was now alright again or that he was brushing aside her promise. She couldn't wait to see him later when, she knew, everything would be better.

"FOOL. Fool. Fool." Daniel breathed the words out in time with his long paces. He could be such a dunderhead sometimes. The sight of Elizabeth crying as he left the cottage had hit him far harder than he would've ever expected. Suddenly he felt like such a fucking idiot. In a brief moment of temper he had reduced the person he cared about more than anyone else to tears. Even as he had stormed away, the vision of his distraught wife had almost stopped him in his tracks, almost turned him around to rush back and gather her in his arms and make things better again, but he had been too ashamed. He knew that if he had returned Elizabeth would have excused his behaviour and accepted his anger, just so everything would be alright once more, but that wasn't good enough. That was the scene Daniel had witnessed time and time before in The Ponds: the wife an image of domestic placidness, dutiful and heeding, merely because she was more in fear than in love

60

with her husband. "Bloody, stupid, stubborn, pride." Again the words were punctuated by his strides. John was right, he needed to lighten up, relax, enjoy life more and not get so pent up with trivial irritations. Thomas Shaw was only doing right by his daughter, looking after the one child he had left.

Daniel knew that the top and bottom of the problem was their difference in upbringing. The Ponds wasn't that far from Malin Bridge but it could have been on the other side of the world. Elizabeth wasn't used to the way people talked and treated each other down in the cesspits of Sheffield and Daniel sometimes forgot to curb his language and modify his behaviour. He was only too aware of his own shortcomings and, as John never failed to point out, he often missed the funny side of things even when they slapped him in the face with a custard pie. The problem was that there had never been much to laugh about in Daniel's life. There had been plenty to worry about, plenty to rail against and plenty of reasons to put up your fists rather than talk. But... there he was again, getting bitter and humourless, thinking about a life which was no longer his. He had a better one now, a beautiful wife and an idyllic home, soon there would be children and even the young puppy had its charms. So long as he hadn't blown it with his crassness this morning. He'd have to do something to make it up to Elizabeth. Maybe he could craft her something at the wheel, a token. His mood lightened as the thought took hold. There were enough scraps in the workshop to fashion something. He could make a pendant or a locket or something like that, shape it into a love-heart. If he returned to Willow Tree with a gesture like that he might be able to make things alright again, along with a shovelful of grovelling as well.

Feeling more cheerful now, Daniel quickened his step. Even the deteriorating weather, spitting rain and strong gusts of wind from the west, failed to sink his buoyancy. A pendant and a posy of flowers would hopefully make amends. Like John had said, you need to enjoy life every now and again, blast the order for the next day, that could bloody well wait. Today he'd take as much time as was needed to make the prettiest thing he could for his girl.

Thinking about John, Daniel wondered if his friend was alright. Last time they had met, the big man hadn't seemed as cheery as usual. Now that was a laugh, because John always accused Daniel of being too stiff and serious; an accusation which always rankled, not because he denied it, far from it, but because he was scarcely allowed to forget it in John's company. John had been lucky in a way: when his father was alive the man had been the life and soul of the party, always cracking jokes and fooling around. Okay, he had lost everything on the toss of a coin but he had been fun to be around. Daniel smiled as he remembered the times when, as young boys, he and Nathan would turn up at the Hukins' house, when they still had a house, and Matt, John's father, would entertain them with wild stories. He would regale them with adventures in deepest darkest Africa or in the Araby world of Turkey and even though the boys knew the man had never gone further than Doncaster they'd believe his tales wholeheartedly. The sight of him dancing around as he demonstrated how he fought the Fuzzie-Wuzzies in east Africa or how he managed to capture a battery of Russian guns despite the charge of the Light Brigade never failed to leave them rolling on the floor howling with laughter.

Daniel actually laughed out loud thinking about old man Hukin, startling one of the numerous squirrels just out of hibernation and loitering on the ground. Daniel laughed again as he saw the little animal, fluffy tail bobbing, scuttle and clamber for the shelter of the tree tops. He was in a good mood and, for the first time since he got married, he no longer felt that Thomas Shaw's involvement was a slur upon his pride. He would have to remember to thank the man properly later tonight for all he had done and try to get to know him, treat him as a man rather than as his landlord or father of his wife. Yes things would be fine, he mused, and he'd make sure that Elizabeth knew that he had changed so she didn't need to, he'd make sure of that, he'd do anything that was required to make sure of that. Then on Sunday he would find out what was troubling John and sort his problems out too. The thing about John was that he was always getting into scrapes and more often than not Daniel managed to solve the issue with a few well-chosen words.

They had been good times though, Daniel thought as he entered Malin Bridge, when John and he had been young kids charging around causing mayhem and always Nathan, no more than a snot- filled teetering little toddler, determinedly following them everywhere on his stubby, sturdy legs, gurgling some kind of nonsense or another. The havoc they would create around The Ponds: pilfering pies and apples from the local stores, hurling freshly laundered sheets into the quagmires of shit that pooled around the area and picking fights or arranging full-scale wars with the kids in neighbouring streets. Daniel knew there had been plenty of terrible times as well – you couldn't avoid those growing up in The Ponds – but by and large they had been good times, carefree and running wildly amok throughout their childhood. The best of those times had been when Daniel and John had been about eleven, Nathan about nine and his Dad had still been healthy and John's Dad hadn't run up so many debts that he had become a crotchety old bugger. Then they had been a proper gang: the Fletchers and the Hukins swaggering in high spirits and regarded with high respect around the neighbourhood.

Times would be different from now on but good once more, better than they had been: there'd be children, loads of children, and Elizabeth would blossom into the woman he could already see but she was still trying to discover; John would find some girl, despite his protestations, and move up into the valley. They'd be a gang once more, the Fletchers and the Hukins striding out and conquering all. But this time they might not bother chucking the laundry into the shit.

As Daniel approached the wheel, for the first time in ages he actually picked up his pace and hurried to get there. There was a pendant with Elizabeth's name on it waiting to be made. And that night he'd make sure he showed his face at the May Fair meeting at the Stag, have a chat with Thomas Shaw and hopefully start to get to know the man. He'd have a couple of drinks while he was there too. Although he was confident he could make it up to Elizabeth, a bit of dutch courage wouldn't go amiss.

THE Dale Dyke dam had been Gunson's headache for the last five years. The company had started work on New Year's Day back in 1859 and it should have taken only two years to complete but underwater springs, not discovered in the original surveys, had permeated the area, keeping the ground sodden and making it nigh on impossible to build a watertight core to the embankment. In the end the company had had to transport two pumping engines up the valley and keep them running non-stop for months on end just to keep the ground water from welling up and flooding the place. Even with the pumps there had been some minor subsidence during the building of the outer wall and talk that some of the materials used had not been given sufficient time to set properly. Work on the dam was finally nearing completion. The number of workers, navvies mainly, had been cut to the minimum required for the finishing touches.

Gunson's main concern was that until recently the dam hadn't had to hold back much water; last summer, however, they had closed the outlet pipes in order to begin storing it. Rain and snow-melt from the winter had added to the accumulation and now the reservoir was near to full capacity for the first time. He knew the effects that strong winds could have on a large mass of liquid, churning it up and increasing the pressure on the embankment. There was no doubt that the dam would hold but Gunson would feel happier if he knew the sluice-gates were open just to provide a release in the forthcoming storm. He just didn't know if the remaining workers knew about the gale about to hit the area and felt it prudent to go up there this afternoon just to make sure. He would finish off some paperwork he had pending on another project and then take the company's horse and gig up just for his own peace of mind.

"COME on in quickly out of the wind and get yourselves warmed by the fire. I'll pull the chairs close. Watch out for the dog, he's great fun but he's a real scallywag especially when there's any activity going on." Elizabeth had to work hard to put on a good front for the two women, her mother and Mrs Trickett, who had just arrived to view Willow Tree Cottage now that Elizabeth had had time to start turning it into a home: it was a few hours since Daniel had stormed off and her eyes were no longer red from crying but she had spent the morning going back over the scene and back over it again trying to figure out how things had gone so wrong. She still didn't know. The idea of taking some snap down for Daniel's midday break had occurred to her but that wouldn't be possible now she had visitors.

"My you've got this place looking like a little palace and you only here a matter of days," said Mrs Trickett. "To think just last week it was a dirty old place no-one would even glance at twice and now you've got it looking lovely."

"Thank you but it's not all thanks to me. Mrs Ibbotson had given it a good clean before we got here and then John was a big help when he brought up all our stuff on Sunday. What do you think of the cottage Mam, you haven't said anything yet?"

"That's because I've been too busy looking around at all your nice touches. It's beautiful and it's lovely and cosy. This is just the sort of place I would imagine as perfect for a young couple in love setting out on their life together," said Anna. "The two of you have worked wonders. And how is that husband of yours, back into the routine of work I suppose?"

"He's fine, Mam," said Elizabeth, not elaborating but looking away, unintentionally hinting to her guests that perhaps "fine" wasn't the full story. They weren't blind and had both been married long enough to men to know that everything isn't wonderful all the time. Anna didn't press the matter.

"And how is the puppy?" she said. "I hope you didn't mind me sending it up. I thought it would provide good company for when Daniel's down at the wheel all day."

"Ay there's nothing like a few animals around to add warmth and life to a place," said Mrs Trickett.

"We call him Pebble," said Elizabeth, visibly softening, quickly recounting the incident with the bath water. "He's great fun but he does like to get involved in everything. Sometimes Daniel has to rescue his slippers when he comes home and Pebble thinks it's a signal for playtime but that's what puppies are all about, I suppose. I love him, the dog, I mean, we both do." She started to get flustered and decided the best solution was tea. The guests glanced silently at each other. She put the cups and saucers out – they weren't precious but they had been in Anna's family for years and reminded Elizabeth of childhood and playing at ladies' tea-parties with Sally – and the biscuit barrel. "Did you get a ride up or did you walk?" she said to divert attention from herself.

"We walked," said Mrs Trickett. "It's not that far as you well know yourself but the weather seems to be on the turn, the wind is certainly whipping up. I thought my skirts were going to carry me away like a balloon when we hit the brow of the hill, especially when my bloomers filled with air, whoosh. Fortunately your mother kept me earthbound but it was touch and go for a few moments. I thought I was going to get a bird's eye view of your cottage instead of just walking in through the door and goodness knows what view you would have had of me, the whole valley would have had of me."

Her silly conversation seemed to turn on the light in Willow Tree Cottage in the gloominess of the day and her two companions were both inwardly grateful for it. Mrs Trickett could always be relied upon to chatter everyone into good humour.

"Will you be coming back to Malin Bridge with us, Elizabeth?" asked Anna. "Gabriel is coming to fetch us later. I thought you might enjoy coming to the meeting this evening. All the men are going to the Stag to discuss plans for the May Fair and us women are gathering at the Lodge to sort out our roles and you might enjoy the conversation and seeing all your old neighbours. Would Daniel be able to meet you for walking home? We could always get a message to him."

"He expects to work very late this evening, Mam," Elizabeth replied noticeably quickly. "He had to go off to work early this morning as well because he has a big order to finish for tomorrow. But I'd love to come to the meeting and see what I can do to help."

"In that case I'll get Gabriel to drive you home when it's all finished."

"Well I might just take a look outside so I can get the picture of Willow Tree Cottage firmly into my head," said Mrs Trickett, giving Anna a hintful look. "If you hear me yell come rushing, I really don't want to get blown away."

A waiting quietude settled over mother and daughter. "It really is looking nice here, Elizabeth. Perhaps when they start piping water down from the dam you'll be able to get your own running water, save all that messing about at the well."

"Mmmh." The young woman was nervous of displaying any upset but felt her mother's knowing gaze.

"Alright, what's happened, tell me? Have you and Daniel had words?"

"No."

"Come on now, do you think I don't know your face well enough," said Anna. "You don't have to be shy with me."

Elizabeth blurted out the story of the goat and the broken eggs and her laughing and the row that followed, in particular about Daniel storming off still in a temper and without any breakfast or midday snap. "I don't understand why he got so angry with me, Mam, everything had been so good up to then. I was going to walk into Malin Bridge with him like I usually do but he wouldn't even wait for me."

"Oh Elizabeth, believe me you've nothing to worry about; I'm afraid that's men for you, that's what they're like, all loving and considerate one minute and then boar-headed as that goat of yours the next. Daniel's no different and neither is your father but it doesn't mean anything, it doesn't mean he doesn't love you just as much as he did yesterday."

"But we've only been married for a week."

"That's about right," said Anna. "I remember what it was like with your father and me after we'd been married for a week. I was just the same as you, still silly with the happiness of it all, still convinced we were so in love that nothing could touch us, certainly nothing as awful as a big row, but it did. Your father always had a bit of a grudge against my family too, just like Daniel, I think that's what made him into the good businessman he is, he was so determined that no-one but Thomas Shaw was going to look after his wife and I'm sure your Daniel's got that same stubborn streak. Your father and I see that in Daniel too, that's why we were only too pleased to give you both our blessing."

"Tell me about your row, how did it happen?"

"It was all over something stupid, just like yours. Your father had inherited some money on his marriage, a small amount but enough to invest, and he decided that the safest idea was to buy some property associated with the cutlery business. I can hear him now, working out the whys and the wherefores. 'People will always need knives and forks for their tables,' he said. He had arranged to look at a wheel near Hillsborough and was getting ready to meet the agent; he had his best suit on, the one he had worn for our wedding, and he'd polished his shoes to a shine; he had his watch chain linked across and he'd spent time curling his moustache to just the right position. He was desperate to look the part and not like he was actually, a complete fish out of water. Anyway there he was, all spick and span, and me floating around fixing his collar for the umpteenth time and generally getting in his way. I put a flower in his buttonhole and stood back to admire him. 'Where's my hat?' he asked, already in a lather, probably because of me fussing so much. 'Here,' I said, 'my father bought you this one specially for today, he wanted you to make the right impression.' And that was it. He exploded. He flung the hat across the room and marched out, leaving me there completely stunned. Then he stormed back in, demanded to know where his old hat was, found it, said it had always been good enough for him and still was, he put it on and disappeared off out again, slamming the door as he went."

"Oh Mam. Did you cry?"

"Of course. Like you I was very upset but you see I hadn't made allowances for him, it was only his nerves and his need to show me he was the man of the house, that he didn't need my family interfering. I believe your Daniel's the same; he's feeling a bit smothered by your father's generosity, perhaps, and he may take it as some sort of criticism of him so that when you laughed, well, the floodgates opened and all that pent up stubbornness poured out."

"Was Father alright when he came home?"

"When he came home he was as contrite as they come. We both laughed about it as I'm sure you will tonight. And your father and I are still together, aren't we? We've been very happy and there's no reason why you won't be. And don't forget, Daniel's been living on his own for a long time and it takes time to get used to living with someone else. Now cheer yourself up and fetch Mrs Trickett in, she'll be flattened against the wall trying to keep her balance in this wind."

"Thank you, Mam. I feel a lot better. I suppose Father and Daniel do have a lot in common."

"And that's no bad thing."

Mrs Trickett was still oohing and ahhing over the delights of Willow Tree Cottage when Gabriel pulled up in the gig to take them all down to Shaw Lodge. The women were glad they didn't have to go back on foot: the weather had turned a lot duller and windier since their arrival. The tops of the trees were reaching up trying to a get a fingerhold in the sky only to get blown down about themselves for their efforts.

THE morning passed quickly and at noon Gunson picked up his coat and hat ready to leave. He popped his head into the office next door to let its occupant, Edward Stanwick, a clerk in accounting, know that he'd be out for the remainder of the day and then made his way to the company stables.

Steering the small trap on to Division Street, Gunson immediately felt the strength of the wind tugging at his hat and plucking his collar. It was certainly blowing harder than it had been this morning and he pulled his hat on tighter and fastened the top button of his coat. The midday traffic was quite heavy and he found himself sandwiched between two horse-buses and progress was slow. Once he turned off on to the road to Hillsborough he was able to let the horse pick up a bit of speed. He wasn't in any particular hurry, however, and kept the animal jogging at a comfortable trot.

Gunson was only vaguely aware of his surroundings as he approached Hillsborough. He was thinking about that bloody man John Towlerton Leather, a foolish name for a foolish man. Leather had been the company's engineer-in-chief until twenty years ago; Gunson had held only a junior role when the man had left but Leather had been retained as the consulting engineer and had prepared the plans and specifications for the reservoir. He now lived in some fancy house over in Leeds and spent more time occupied with his contractual work, which was far more lucrative, than on his consultation obligations with the waterworks company. Leather's specifications for Dale Dyke had been based on theory and previous projects; when writing them up he'd had no idea of the core materials which were to be worked in order to build up the embankment. Gunson was aware of maybe only six site visits Leather had made since the dam project had commenced and at some of the most vital structural moments in the construction, most notably the building of the puddle wall, Leather had been absent.

The puddle wall was the core of the dam embankment, a mixture of clay and sand wetted and kneaded into an amalgam impervious to water. It didn't need much structural strength, that was provided by the inner and outer embankment walls made out of heavier material. The sole purpose of the puddle was to prevent water seeping through the denser but porous inner wall and across and out through the outer wall but they'd had problems: the specifications stated that the core needed to be built up simultaneously with outer and inner embankments but this had been impossible to achieve and the inner puddle wall had always played catch-up. Sometimes rocks and stones would fall into the clay as it was setting and these had to be picked out to maintain the integrity of the puddle. Gunson was confident that the dam was structurally sound but he would have liked to have had a more frequent professional liaison with Leather. After all it was meant to be Leather's experience and knowledge that had had him retained as a consultant. That was what he was being paid for. Although the project was now nearly completed, Gunson felt that Leather had let him down; the entire responsibility for the construction had weighed down on Gunson's shoulders alone.

Crossing Hillsborough Bridge, Gunson turned left on to Holme Lane and was soon on his way up through Malin Bridge. Gunson was old enough to remember when Malin Bridge had been a mere smattering of buildings tucked away in the countryside. Now the village had hundreds of inhabitants as the community grew and thrived on the boom of industry.

Gunson reined in his horse, easing the pace to a slow walk as the long climb up the valley to the reservoir began. He put thoughts of Leather out of his mind, determined to enjoy the open country and the tranquility he rarely experienced on Division Street despite the bad weather. There was also a constant background screech emanating from the small workshops down by the river's edge but the noise seemed to be absorbed as one with the beauty of the scenery and contained within the almost-picturesque mills responsible for the sound.

As Gunson passed through Damflask, he noticed that one of the empty cottages he had always admired on his passage through now appeared to be occupied. He had always thought the place had looked shamefully neglected for such a well-situated property and was heartened to see that at last there were signs of life. By the looks of things the new occupiers seemed determined to spruce the cottage up to its potential. Gunson gave out a rueful chuckle and clicked on the horse. There had been a time early on in the dam's construction that he had entertained thoughts of enquiring into who owned the cottage with the intention of making an offer to purchase it; a romantic dream of an idyllic rural life for him and Charlotte now the children had left home.

A light rain began to smatter as he approached Low Bradfield, about a mile down from the reservoir. It was a wispy rain, more a gentle flutter against the skin than a dousing. Gunson wondered if this was the herald for the forthcoming storm or just a sporadic spring shower. As he drew closer to the dam, still climbing a steep gradient, the embankment rose so massively ahead of him that his senses were spun in a dizzying vertigo, warping his perspectives and dwarfing his stature. It seemed to engulf half the sky and it was only as he brought the gig to the top of the dam, with the valley falling away behind him and the rippling expanse of water ahead of him, that he felt in control of himself once again. For the last ten months, since completion had been in sight and despite visiting the site more than twice a week, the dam had never failed to have that effect on him. He checked his fob-watch, nearly three-o'-clock. He'd spend a couple of hours looking around and then head back home.

The rain had either grown heavier up here or the wind was whipping spray off the surface of the reservoir lake. Either way Gunson found his face dripping wet and his clothes drenching darkly. The water level was within a few feet of the top and furling in choppy white crests but Gunson had seen far rougher water at Redmires reservoir to the south. He knew the dams were designed for such conditions, especially in this type of terrain, and anyway the level had yet to reach the waste weir which would spill the water, channelling the excess down to the river below. Much more exposed at this height and no longer enclosed by the sides of the valley, Gunson caught his hat just before it was torn away by the wind. He thought it prudent to take it off and let his thinning hair take the brunt of the gusts rather than lose what had been a Christmas present from Charlotte. He set the brake on the carriage and clambered down.

Not far off, standing in the shelter of the work hut, he could see George Swinden, one of the company's overseers, chatting with a group of navvies. That didn't surprise Gunson: Swinden, a Londoner who had gradually migrated north working on the canals and railways, liked to talk. He liked a drink as well. The reason why he was the overseer on site was that despite the talking and the drinking he got more done in a day than most got done in a week. Also it was impossible not to like the man. Clutching his hat in one hand and clasping the lapels of his coat together in the other, Gunson leaned into the wind and moved towards the men.

"Afternoon guv'nor, didn't expect to see you up here today." Swinden broke off talking to the navvies and stuck his gnarled hand out. He was a small, wiry man, with a wind-burnished face and traces of bluish veins worming his cheeks and nose. Deep lines were etched around his eyes which were always sparkling and friendly and furrowed creases travelled down his cheeks to the corners of his mouth. His coarse and frizzy grey hair was being tousled haphazardly in the wind. Gunson, nearly six foot and with a figure the proud result of decades of Mrs Gunson's good cooking, loomed over and around Swinden, he fumbled with his Homburg, nearly losing it in the wind again, and shook Swinden's hand.

"Afternoon George, just thought I'd pop up and see how things were going." Gunson nodded at the navvies who all muttered a cheerful greeting. Gunson was rare amongst the senior staff at the company in that he had seldom failed to get on well with navvies despite their coarseness and wild ways. Although there were only a handful of them left working on the Dale Dyke project, Gunson always felt reassured by their presence; they were rough, foul-mouthed drunks but they were also tough, hard-working and rarely fazed by the most arduous of work and they got the job done.

"Well best get on with it lads while I have a word with the gaffer here." Swinden waved them away and then turned back to Gunson. "Like I said Mr Gunson, I didn't expect you up here today, I hope there ain't no problem."

"No problem, I came up just to check that you knew there's a storm brewing, coming in from the west. You might want to think about opening the outlet valves later on if it gets rough up here." The two men moved into the hut to get out of the wind and to hear themselves more easily.

"Funny you should say that but you know them navvies have just been saying the same thing about a storm coming. Don't know how they know, ain't no newspapers up here, as if they could read anyway; they're like gypsies I reckon, they know stuff like that. Anyway talkin' of brewing, I got some tea on the boil, fancy a mug?"

"That'd be more than welcome, something to warm us up on a day like this."

"Well if it's warming up you want, I got something a bit stronger than tea." George winked and pulled out a small bottle of rum. He took a swig and passed it to Gunson who hesitated and then said: "Why not, it's a foul day and it's only going to get worse." Gunson swallowed some and nearly choked on the liquid. It wasn't the oak-aged liquor he was accustomed to. Coughing he managed: "I might have that cup of tea as well George."

George cackled and poured out a steaming mug of sweet black tea. "Get your laughing gear round that guv'nor, it'll sort you out."

The tea was densely sugared and should have tasted sickly foul but Gunson found it warming and strangely satisfying. He suspected it had been laced with George's tipple. He finished the tea and pulled his hat on. Remembering the weather outside he took it back off and said: "I'm going to do the rounds while I'm here, have a look and make sure everything is shipshape."

"Right you are Mr Gunson, I'll keep an eye on the water level: if it gets up I know what to do."

Gunson opened the door and stepped out. It already seemed like the wind had grown stronger. He decided to cross over the dam and take a look from the other side.

On the south side the navvies were struggling in the wind to finish off the last portion of the embankment. Gunson looked over at them but he could scarcely see them through all the spray now being blown over the top of the dam. He had a look at the outer wall. There was no sign of any seepage so he inspected the inner wall where the water lapped against the containing structure. Again there was no cause for concern, the wall appeared solid and immovable and there were no depressions or evidence of slippage.

Gunson decided to observe the movement of the windswept water for a while. He was confident that there were no problems; the dam was sufficiently complete to contain the reservoir and, if the level did rise, Gunson knew that the combination of the weir and George opening the outlet valves would ensure there would be no overloading of the embankment. He waited around for an hour or so just looking at the different elements but as the weather degenerated and the workmen started finding shelter rather than work he decided to push off home. It was gone four and Gunson couldn't see any point in hanging around any longer.

THE scene at Shaw Lodge was one of chatter and chinwag and the delicate clinking of spoons in cups and cups on saucers as the ladies of Malin Bridge – all the women who were anyone in the village had made it to the May Fair women's committee - caught up on gossip, heard all about the transformation of Willow Tree Cottage, Sally Bisby's visit to relatives in Oughtibridge, the imminent departure of Joe Barker from the Tricketts' back home to Arbourthorne and the latest bulletin on the state of Grandpa Tom Kay: evidently he was feeling much better and was looking forward to staying in with the grandchildren while their mother was at the Lodge and Mr Trickett went early to the men's committee over in the Stag.

"He got there very early," said Ann Armitage, the publican's wife, "so early I was able to leave him to help Bill set up so I could get away on time."

Mrs Bisby was there, she had left fourteen-year-old Teresa in charge of the children at the Cleakum in Sally's absence.

Mary Ibbotson had come down representing the Barrel, keen to make the May Fair a valley event and get Damflask involved.

Also there was Lizzie Price, who ran the general store across the Loxley with her husband; he saw the fair as a great opportunity to shift some of the stock he'd had lying about for too long – nothing like an influx of strangers to boost trade and if he could get the order for the ribbons and street bunting so much the better. Mrs Price had brought along her niece, Hannah Hill, who had recently arrived from Mortomley to help look after the Prices' recently confined daughter Sarah and their new two-day-old grandson: Lizzie thought the girl deserved a bit of time out.

Ann Mount was there too - she ran a small shop and also hoped to get a bit of trade out of it all - and Emma Barrett, the shoemaker's wife, also glad of a few hours out and relieved to have left her two-year-old, William, in the charge of a babysitter for a change.

The Lodge was certainly full. Even Mrs Etchell the old schoolmarm had made it to the meeting, giving rise to more subdued chattering over the sandwiches and cake as it was generally agreed it was time she got herself out and about again now that Mr Etchell had been dead these last few years.

"I still remember what you told us at school about peeling potatoes and how it could influence any potential husband," said Elizabeth, deftly steering the conversation away from any maudlin topic. "'Don't pare too much off or he'll think you're wasteful,' you used to say."

The lesson had stuck in the memory of quite a few ex-pupils, judging by the nudging and gentle laughter that ran round the room.

"It's to be hoped you remember it well now you do have a husband," said Mrs Etchell, warmed by the unexpected, kind attention. "Really it was quite a silly thing of me to say: I'm sure the eligible young men of today have other things on their minds than how much skin comes of a spud when their betrothed wields a knife but I'm glad to hear it has remained one of your more important memories of life in the classroom."

Polite applause greeted her attempt at humour: Mrs Etchell had never been known for lightheartedness but on several occasions she had revealed an unexpected lightness of spirit since the old man had passed away. Perhaps he was the sour one all along. Perhaps her more frequent presence about the village in future would prove a not unpleasant bonus for the neighbourhood.

The main business of the session had been sorted out quickly and early on, with responsibilities delegated and jobs handed out with minimum discussion or argument. No-one could resist devoting most of the meeting to being sociable and enjoying themselves and before they knew where they were they heard the clock chime seven. No-one could believe the time had gone so fast, that it could be so late already, that they'd spent so long talking, that they'd managed to sort out everything so amicably, who was to be in charge of this, who was to be in charge of that.

Shawls, hats and gloves were sorted and distributed to their relative owners - judging by the sound of the wind outside they'd all be needed – and the meeting broke up with satisfied smiles. The local women all left, huddled together against the gale for moral support as they started off home in the darkness. It was agreed that Mrs Ibbotson would have a lift home with Elizabeth in the gig: "Don't forget we'll see you Sunday, Mam, you and Father, up at the cottage, and I'll cook you a nice dinner and we'll have a walk up to see the dam. Goodnight, give my love to Father."

73

"Goodnight now." "Goodnight."

Gabriel flicked Arthur's reins to get the horse moving: it was no night to be out, he thought, his two passengers were tucked up under blankets in the back but he was sitting up top all exposed despite his big coat. "Still Arthur, at least it's early and we've the rest of the night off after this trip. Perhaps a quick visit to the Barrel might not be amiss as we've got to go there anyway."

JOHN Hukin wiped the dirt off his hands with a grubby cloth. The last of the empties had been off-loaded and the barrels stacked in the brewery yard. It had been a tiring day and he wouldn't be sorry to see the back of it: on Fridays all his deliveries were to town-centre pubs so he didn't have any long trips to do but it was always the hardest day of the week for the big man, always busy, all the pubs getting fully stocked for the weekend. He gave Stanley a good rub down after removing the yolk and tack and led the horse to its usual stall in the Neepsend stables. "See you tomorrow, old son," he said quietly, fastening the stall door. "How about a trip to the country in the morning, take Bisby his extra barrels out at Malin Bridge, eh? I bet he's already panicking in case he doesn't get them." John locked up and left the yard, looking forward to partaking of some of the supplies he himself had delivered. He was pulled to one side on his way out by one of the other draymen. "Seems you've been up to your usual carryings-on, Hukin, I hear Jack Quinn's looking for you, something to do with someone Pickens or other." "Pickens, Pickens? I don't know anyone of that name," said John and he bade the drayman goodnight. He decided to go straight home, the long way round.

AS ever when the gaffer was around the few workers left up at Dale Dyke were on their best, attentive behaviour when Gunson had turned up unexpectedly that afternoon. They thought it was a lot of fuss over nothing; fancy coming all that way out from Sheffield just because of a weather report in the bloody newspaper, as if they'd never had strong winds up there before: if they didn't know how to build a bloody dam by now after all their experience with the Water Company then nobody did. They weren't sorry to see the back of him, old woman. The men piled up their tools and started off home, braced against the storm and glad of the excuse to pack in a bit earlier than usual. Perhaps in the circumstances a quick stop-off at the Barrel would be in order.

"Might see you over there," said Bill Horsefield, "I'll just put these shovels

74

in out of the rain first." Bill had been quite pleased to get this job with the Water Company: he only lived just across the river from the site office, couldn't have been more convenient, and he often volunteered to stow stuff away at the end of the shift and let the others go on home. He did a general tidy-round of the site as was his habit, collected all the discarded picks and spades together and opened the door of the storage hut to stash everything away inside. The door whipped out of his hand with force and crashed back against the side of the hut. "Bloody hell," he muttered. "I wasn't expecting that." He managed to get all the tackle into the hut and made fast the lock, setting a heavy rock against the door as an extra precaution – "blow that away if you can" – and set off to short-cut home along the ridge of the embankment. Not a good idea: the strength of the gale now rushing down the valley was far too strong and it was all he could do to stay on his feet let alone walk. "Bloody hell," he muttered again, "I wasn't expecting that."

Bill scrambled some way down the embankment to escape the full force of the wind; it wasn't that easy to get a foothold on the slope but at least he was in the lea of the wall and he slowly started his way across the dam face, quite slippy now because of the rain that had started falling. "Bloody hell, I'll be glad to get in out of this, bugger the pub," he muttered. "It's too bloody windy and too bloody dark and I'm getting too bloody old for this lark. Mind you after this I might need a drink."

With the image of a mug of porter taking shape in his mind, Bill edged his way across the dam wall, bent into the slope to help keep his balance. That's how he happened to notice the crack.

He gave a bit of a start and near lost his footing. "Bloody hell, would you look at that." It looked to him like a frost crack, he'd seen many such like in the course of working on various dams but they'd all been in the winter, this was near two weeks into March already. He looked at the evidence with a professional eye and estimated the crack to be only just wide enough to get the blade of a penknife in but it followed in a long line about twelve feet from the top of the embankment and ran on for about fifty yards. "I wasn't expecting that," he muttered, confused and looking around, wondering what he should do. The engineer had already been out and said everything was shipshape but perhaps he hadn't seen this, thought Bill. "It's probably a frost crack," he tried to kid himself but really he was feeling anxious. "Trust me to find the bloody thing," he muttered.

Seeing one of his colleagues heading up the lane alongside the river to the pub, Bill shouted him to come over, desperate for a second opinion. "Hey Greaves, come on and look at this, I'm a bit worried, see what you think." The two men looked and looked again, scratched their heads, decided it was a frost crack, decided there was no frost, and agreed to seek a third opinion.

The person nearest by to consult was Sam Hammerton, the farmer often to be seen crossing from one side of the river to the other to get to his fields, not a bad bloke and quite sensible enough, one of the few locals who at least was always civil to the navvies. He wasn't too overjoyed at being summoned out earlier than he needed be in such appalling weather but then he had to go out to the fair committee in Malin Bridge sooner or later so it might as well be sooner. The men's approach also made him feel quite important.

The three of them hunched and struggled back against the weather along the dam wall. When he saw the crack in it, Sam was more alarmed than he'd expected. "We should get George Swinden out to take a look," he said. "I for one would feel a lot happier."

It was now nearly seven and, what with the lateness of the hour and the heaviness of the stormy skies, it was too dark to see such a narrow crack with the naked eye. Nevertheless all the toings and froings along the dam wall had also roused the curiosity of several of the residents of nearby Bradfield and it was quite a procession of men who clambered their way along the embankment with lanterns held buffeted in the wind to illuminate the safest route. Several had come up from the cottages grouped around Annett Bridge just down the road and a few had made their way up from Low Bradfield to investigate the commotion. Not one to miss out on a bit of excitement, the Sunday School teacher Richard Ibbotson also put in an appearance, perhaps it would provide a good excuse for a bit of a hot toddy to fight off the elements.

Swinden had just finished his first beer when Greaves came hurrying into the inn. "I wondered where you'd got to mate, what do you fancy?" asked Swinden getting his money out ready. Greaves came up to the bar where the Londoner was sat and bent his head forward conspiratorially. "I need a quick word with you George."

"Sure, whatever, but let me get a round in first."

"No, we need to talk, outside."

"Bleedin' hell what can be so important that a man can't have a quick drink on a Friday night?" All the same George followed the man outside. Greaves closed the door. "I didn't want to panic anyone unnecessarily but I think you should come and have a look at the dam wall." George looked at Greaves as if the man had lost his senses and grumbled: "Why, I've only just bloody well left the place haven't I?"

"Bill's found a crack and we think you should come and take a look, you know more about that dam than anyone."

George was instantly alert. "A crack? There shouldn't be no cracks, there hasn't been a frost for ages. We'd best go and have a gander." The two men trotted up the road towards the reservoir.

DOWN at Malin Bridge the good and the worthy men of the village were getting in their drinks at the Stag Inn: it promised to be thirsty work setting up the various working parties and sub-committees for the May Fair. The women of course could be relied upon to do their bit but the real responsibilities lay with the menfolk: success lay in the detail of the planning and that was a man's job.

"I don't know what's happened to Sam, he said he'd be here," said Thomas Shaw, eager to call the meeting to order. No-one had envisaged this sort of weather when the meeting was arranged in the balmy circumstances of Betsy's wedding.

"He's probably just running late. It'll take him a bit longer than usual to get down here in this weather," said James Trickett, relieved he had only to cross the Loxley and he'd be home and dry. "Don't forget Richard said he'd be here too. He's keen that the whole event should open with a proper blessing ceremony, though quite why it should be him do it and not the minister at our own Chapel I'm not sure."

"Let's not put off anyone who wants to get involved," said Thomas. "Sometimes people start out full of enthusiasm for these things but when it comes to it the real work is left to the few."

"Give them a few more minutes then. Meanwhile we can perhaps just sound out a few ideas," said James. "You all know Joe Barker, here, he's off home back to Arbourthorne tomorrow but he's got a few good suggestions for the fair and is keen to stay in touch and see them through. Take the floor, Joe."

BY now there were a couple of dozen men at Dale Dyke huddled in against the storm on the dam embankment. The wind was howling around them, blowing scarves and mufflers into all sorts of frenzied shapes and patterns in the gasping lantern-light and drowning out any voices that weren't at shouting pitch. Several feet above the adventurers, on the other side of the dam wall, the surface of the body of water somehow appeared unnaturally still, shiny as a rich black mirror, but out towards the edges along the valley sides and against the dam wall waves were erupting up from the calm like so many angry demons, spitting their spray this way and that, black and white, agitated, the crests of the swelling waters in turn lighting up and dying down in the reflected night sky. A lantern was blown out, then another. "Bloody hell," said Bill, "it's a rough sort of a night." Another thunderous gust and the last of the lanterns was extinguished, leaving the men stranded on the rough wall in total darkness, lost together in a hell of roaring noise and howling winds. Below them, the River Loxley streamed along innocent and unconcerned. By the time someone managed in the confusion to get another light to catch long enough to re-ignite a lantern, they saw the crack had grown: one of the men could easily put his arm into it while the lantern flame showed it was now perpendicular, heading right down the face the dam, almost top to bottom.

DANIEL wiped the sweat and dust from his face and stood up. His cramped muscles protested at the movement and his joints cracked and creaked as he tried to unwind the tension from his back which had built up in the hours of sitting at the wheel. He brought the newly-fashioned pendant up to the oil lantern to inspect it more closely. As the light reflected off the metal Daniel could see that all his labour had been worth it, the pendant was simple but elegant in design. He had made it from an offcut piece of steel, first creating the rough shape and then honing the metal so that it was a perfectly symmetrical miniature heart. Next he had ground away the splinters so the edges were rounded, this had been the tricky part, Daniel was so used to putting a sharp blade on to steel that his fingers and hands instinctively pressed the metal on the wheel too hard and at the wrong angle. After a few mistakes and the pendant a little smaller than intended he had grown used to this new technique. He had drilled a hole near the top of the metal and then spent his energy on burnishing the steel so that it shone with a soft lustre. Once polished to his satisfaction he had set about engraving the surfaces. On one side he had etched, in a floral script, the initials D&E and on the other he had replicated, as best he could, a sprig of willow similar to the one Elizabeth had painted on the cottage plaque. He had finished off with some gentle polishing and then threaded a leather thong through the hole: he thought he could replace the leather with some ribbon when he got home that night.

Daniel was pleased with his efforts and quite surprised that he had managed to occupy the entire day without once worrying about his other work which was due for delivery the next day. "Maybe I am learning to lighten up," he said to himself. Time was getting on, however; Daniel thought that it must already be after nine and by the sounds of buffeting outside the workshop the weather hadn't eased off at all. He put the pendant in his pocket, pulled on his coat and hat, killed the light – the other grinders who worked in the same building had left hours earlier – and locked up.

THE meeting was threatening to fall into boozy anarchy at the Stag where there was still no sign of the men due from Bradfield. Joe Barker had exhausted his suggestions for the May Fair and the committee had exhausted all discussion on them. They'd all agreed on which of them were good ideas and which weren't feasible and they needed to move on. "We'd better start without them, I can let them know what they've missed," said Thomas. "Alright now, order everyone. The first item on tonight's agenda is to nominate a chairman and treasurer and then we can get down to allocating tasks. Any nominations for the post of chairman?"

As always on these occasions there was silence: no-one wanted to put himself forward and no-one wanted to be left out.

"In that case I nominate James Trickett," said Thomas, "after all the fair was his idea."

"Hear hear." "Hear hear." "Quite right." "Good choice."

"That's settled then," said Thomas. "Over to you, James."

"Thank you, Thomas, thank you everyone. Next item, a treasurer, can I have your nominations please."

As always on these occasions there was silence: no-one wanted to put himself forward and no-one wanted to be left out.

"In that case I nominate Thomas Shaw," said James, "After all, he's got one of the best heads for business in the village and if he can't sort out the finances then no-one can."

"Hear hear." "Hear hear." "Quite right." "Good choice."

"That's settled then," said James. "Now we need someone to take charge of the sub-committee responsible for booking the fairground acts. Any nominations?"

LAST to arrive at the dam face was one of the contractors engaged by the Water Company to build the Dale Dyke reservoir. "Ah Mr Fountain," shouted Bill Horsefield against the growling wind when he recognised someone with a bit of authority. "Take a look at this bloody crack. What do you make of that?" Urgent exchanges of opinion passed between Swinden and Fountain, following the path of dancing light as a lantern weakly traced the sharp route of the crack for their close inspection.

"It looks as if it's coming out from inside of the embankment."

"Some water must have gotten in behind the puddle."

They looked at the fissure, they felt the wall, they studied the situation.

"Look at the way the top of the embankment is leaning over the lake, it's not by much but it wasn't like that earlier," said Swinden, "I know because we had a good look when Mr Gunson was here."

"It must have sunken a bit with the water getting through."

After much deliberation they agreed that there was no immediate danger, which came as a bit of a relief to the assembled company as the excitement had long since worn off and they were to a man anxious to get inside and out of the awful weather. The top-most branches of the trees were almost level with their roots, bending reluctantly to the ground under the force of the gale and adding a ghostly whining to the bellowing of the wind. The men's feet were starting to slip and slide, too many of them squeezed into the limited shelter of the embankment and losing their balance as each wrestled to keep collars up and mufflers tight.

"What I'll do is send young Stephenson here to fetch Mr Gunson back, he'll know what to do," yelled the contractor. "Son, take your horse and ride to Sheffield to get Mr Gunson, tell him a crack has appeared in the embankment and he'd better come straight away. Explain that we know it's late and a horrible night but there are people here who need reassuring."

Stephenson Fountain picked his way carefully over to the valley side where he'd left his horse tied to a tree. He mounted the animal – the saddle was soaking wet and not at all comfortable for a ride all the way to town - fixed his feet in the stirrups, took hold of the reins and kicked in his heels, spurring the horse on into the blackness. At least he had the wind at his back but it was a narrow tortuous road round the hillsides and down into the valley and it was difficult to make good progress.

Meanwhile his father organised the men to carry out some basic safety procedures. The lake water was just a few inches below the height of the embankment and Fountain wanted the pipes opened which would allow excess water to pour out through the waste weir if the level climbed any higher. A double set of pipes had been included in the design, right at the bottom of the dam wall, but opening the valves proved a trying and arduous job: it took four or five men almost half-an-hour struggling to turn each of the huge screws
to raise the sluices, all the time being beaten about the face and hands by the driving rain, trying to catch their breath against the wind and squinting their eyes to see as best they could in the darkness and squall. The pressure of

the water added to their difficulty and when the sluices were at last opened rushing water was discharged with such force that the men shuddered to feel the ground tremble beneath them and heard such sounds as they never in their life wanted to hear again.

But their efforts seemed to have done the trick. Swinden and Fountain took a look at the crack again and it hadn't gotten any worse. They were also able to reassure everybody that, thanks to their actions, the level of the water in the reservoir had fallen and was now below the level of the crack.

"Thank God for that," said Bill. "I can't deny I was getting a bit worried there."

"I think it's safe for you all to go home now," said Fountain. "Thank you for your help. Mr Gunson will take things from here when he arrives."

It was a few very wet men who made their way home, relieved but with a good tale to tell when they got there. They might also play it safe and keep an ear open, just in case.

STEPHENSON Fountain had only got as far as Damflask when he felt his saddle slip. "What a bloody nuisance." The young man was panicked. "Jesus, that's all I bloody well need right now. My Da'll go mad when he finds out, and me the one supposed to be looking after the tack. I've only managed two bloody miles." He reined in his horse abruptly and dismounted, patting the horse to stop it getting any more spooked by the sudden stop in such god-awful weather. The girth under the horse's belly had snapped. "Bloody hell, bloody fucking hell." Stephenson looked around him for inspiration: there wasn't a soul to be seen, only the rays of the rain sheeting and those bloody trees still moaning in the wind. The good news was that he was almost level with the Barrel Inn, a place his mother had warned him to steer clear of until he was older but he had no choice tonight but to disobey: he had to get the strap repaired as quickly as possible or he'd have hell from his father instead.

Jonathan Ibbotson was behind the bar when Stephenson walked in, soaked and sodden, his hair stuck to his face and his boots caked with mud. "Well well, I never expect to see Fountain Junior in here on a good night never mind one like this," the publican addressed the assembled company. "Will it be lemonade or a man's drink as you're here unsupervised?"

"I'm not really here," said Stephenson, "well I am, but not why you think. But I do need a drink, yes, I do need a drink, a glass of ale please. And I need some help, urgently." Stephenson called out to the men in the bar. "I've just ridden down from the dam. There's a big crack in it and I have to fetch the engineer from Sheffield as soon as possible. Is there anyone here who can repair my saddle-girth quickly?"

"There's a crack in the dam, you say, whereabouts?"

"At Dale Dyke."

"I know at Dale Dyke you ninny but whereabouts is the crack?"

"Oh, in the wall, a long crack too, it's probably almost from top to bottom by now. There's a load of people from the Water Company up there inspecting it. They reckoned it was quite safe but they want Mr Gunson to take a look tonight, just to be sure."

"Mr Gunson?"

"Ay, he's the engineer."

"So they're not that sure?"

"As sure as they can be," said Stephenson, enjoying the grown-upness of the occasion and the ale. "They were opening the overflow sluices as I left, I should think that'll do the trick." (He might be enjoying the attention but he didn't want to alarm people unnecessarily and then get blamed for it later.) "Once they're open the pipes will carry off any water that shouldn't be there." (He wanted to sound knowing without really knowing anything.) "It'll be fine once the sluices are open, that'll do the trick."

"We'd better get that strap fixed then," said Jonathan, inwardly not feeling totally reassured. "Don't let it be said we refused to help a young man on important company business."

GABRIEL perked up when he saw the lights of the Barrel ahead and even Arthur pricked his ears up against the onslaught of the wind, fully alert to the treat ahead: slop of the usual, eh, Arthur. The coach had been heading full-on into the wind for most of the journey along the Loxley, allowing for the twists and turns in the road; there was some temporary respite as the road dipped south west down into Low Matlock just below Broomhead Tilt and the gusts came side on but then the lane led directly west again with a climb up into the valley.

"Not far to go now, Arthur, then let's you and me get out of the storm," called Gabriel, before shouting over his shoulder to his two passengers that the end of the road was in sight. His voice was lost against the whooo-ing drone of the wind but something else did catch their attention, the persistent clocks of galloping hooves on the dirt cobbled road.

"I wonder where he's off to in such a hurry," Mrs Ibbotson shouted into Elizabeth's ear. "What is he doing?" she wondered as the horseman rode past at speed without stopping. "Something's put a thistle under his saddle," she said.

The gig carried on up to Damflask and Gabriel guided Arthur over the bridge to drop Elizabeth right at Willow Tree Cottage gate. "Make sure you have that door shut tight behind you," warned Mrs Ibbotson. "I'm sure Daniel won't be too late, not in this storm."

Elizabeth struggled to catch the latch back on the gate and ran up the garden path: then she struggled to hold the door from blowing out of her hand and letting all the flying debris find sanctuary in the house before she was finally able to close the door to behind her. It was very dark inside and even with the curtains closed and everything shut tight she could hear the ghouling noises outside. She was glad when she'd lit the lamps. She took off her wet shawl and hung it on a door hook then spread her coat out to dry on the back of a chair and knelt to attend to the fire; before going down to Malin Bridge earlier she had banked it up with damp paper and coal slack so there was still the faintest glow of embers to be rekindled. Some welcome relief at least but every now and then a sooty drought gusted its way down the chimney driven by the hysterical wind outside and Elizabeth shuddered, wishing Daniel was home.

Across at the Barrel, Gabriel helped Mrs Ibbotson out at the door and then went to tie up in his usual place but it was too exposed for Arthur and he led the horse around the corner. "Don't worry I won't leave you here too long," he said.

"ORDER, order."

"Thanks, make mine a stout."

"Oh very funny that man there," said James Trickett as general rumblings of laughter filtered round the room as the joke was repeated in hushed tones. "Right, can we just spare a few more minutes to review what's already been decided," he tried again. The gathering at the Stag was getting merrier and rowdier by the hour but the drinkers felt that congratulations were due: they had sorted out chairman, vice-chairman and membership of all the various committees and sub-committees and you can't get anywhere until that's done, they agreed. Fortunately Joe Barker's suggestions had put at least some practical ideas on the table, ideas which would be reported back to womenfolk as part of the successful outcome of the meeting.

"I vote we call the meeting to a close," shouted Charlie Price, the upstanding proprietor of the store, giving his moustache his customary tweek

– he was very proud of it, he always thought it looked rather distinguished above his full-length apron when he was in command behind the counter in the shop and now he practised the same gesture as he rose to take the floor. "Joe here's leaving tomorrow and I reckon we ought to take time to wish him good luck for the future. He's only been in the village a short time but he's played his part, not least tonight with all his excellent recommendations for the fair. I know he'll be back but I believe we should mark the occasion of his departure with a toast. I give you, Joe Barker," said Charlie, raising his glass before James Trickett had a chance to argue.

"Joe Barker." "Joe Barker."

"Thank you all," said Joe. "It's been a great pleasure getting to know you all and I look forward to the next meeting."

"Hear hear." "Hear hear."

The men raised their mugs once again and supped.

James was a bit put out and said as much to Thomas. "That's that then, Thomas, meeting over."

"Don't worry about it, James, we've accomplished as much as could be hoped in the first meeting."

"That reminds me," said James, springing to his feet for the last time and attempting to make himself heard. "Next meeting same time same place next week," he called. "Any apologies for absence will be noted."

Most of the men settled down for another couple of hours in the pub, a few decided it was time to get off home. What with the warmth of the inn and the business conducted, all in such a friendly spirit, they'd all forgotten about the storm now raging outside.

"I'm off," said Thomas.

"And me," said James. "I'll just get a couple of bottles for old Tom."

"I'll walk back with you," said Joe. "I came straight here from Sheffield and I've still got the men's wages in my pocket for tomorrow. We can't have the Limerick Wheel out because I got drunk on the men's pay."

The three men battled out into the night together, hunched up and barely tilting their hats at each other to say goodnight let alone remarking on the success of the evening. They were friends, the niceties would keep. James and Joe trudged off to the farmhouse, Thomas staggered a path to Shaw Lodge.

WHEN the road surface was good, Gunson pushed the horse to its limits despite the fury of the storm. He knew that the road from Holme Lane right through to Low Matlock was pretty good. The well-established wheel ruts carved into the surface after years of commercial use were broad and acted more like tracks, aiding their progress rather than being an obstacle. After that the road deteriorated and he'd have to be more cautious but by then the horse would be exhausted anyway. He glanced at Robert Craven next to him who was hanging on to the side strap for dear life. At some point his hat must have blown away because his bald pate was glistening wet but from the terrified look in his eyes the hat seemed the last thing on his mind. "Don't worry," Gunson shouted, "we'll get there."

When young Fountain had burst breathlessly into the Gunson household and explained the situation, Gunson had straightaway gathered his coat and got ready the horse and carriage. He had immediately thought of Robert Craven who had been one of the original contractors on the dam. Craven had worked on countless reservoir projects and lived in Hillsborough. It wouldn't take long to pick the man up and what Craven didn't know about dam construction could be written on the back of a penny-black, his advice could well be essential. Meanwhile Stephenson had stood shivering in his sodden clothes asking what he should do. "Do you think it's serious Mr Gunson, me Da's up there and all. Do you think I should get back up there?"

As he was pulling on his topcoat Gunson had called Charlotte. "Keep the lad here for now love, he's done in and his horse must be exhausted." His wife had bustled into action and had taken the boy by the arm: "You'd best stay here and get some warm broth inside you, my John will sort out any problems and if needs be you can stay the night. Goodness, it's not as if we haven't the room to spare since the children left. I tell you what, you can have Toby's room."

"What about me horse, I've left it tied to the gatepost."

"Well go and bring it round the back. There's stables where you can house him for the night, he'll be fine."

"It's a she Mrs Gunson."

"Well whatever, the sooner you get her in out of the rain, the sooner you can get warm and dry."

Gunson had cracked the whip all the way to Hillsborough. Craven had answered the door and didn't hesitate one moment. With a shout to his wife as he wrapped up he followed Gunson on to the gig and they were off back into the storm.

Approaching Malin Bridge Gunson couldn't see a thing: heavy clouds blotted out any moonlight and the driving rain was blinding him anyway. He knew he was relying purely on the horse's eyesight and instinct to get them up there in one piece. They sped through the little village, Gunson noticing that the Stag, illuminated by a cosy interior glow, seemed unusually full for such a small place, and then they were out the other side.

"Not far off now, maybe three miles," Gunson once again yelled out to Craven but still the man didn't seem to hear. He kept on gripping that strap and staring into the distance like he was on a one-way trip to hell.

OUTSIDE in the darkness the force of the wind coming down the valley almost blew Daniel off his feet. He steadied and braced himself and bent into the wind. With one hand clutching his coat together and the other keeping his hat on he re-joined the road. Almost immediately he was forced back off the lane as a small two-wheeled carriage came rocketing past, muddy water from the puddles in the wheel-ruts spraying up and drenching him as he stumbled backwards. "Bloody idiots, why don't you look where you're damn well going!" he roared but the gig was already racing off into the distance and Daniel doubted that the occupants had even noticed him. He thought about going straight home but then remembered he had decided to go and thank Thomas Shaw. The May Fair meeting would have been going full swing for some time now and the last thing Daniel wanted, after his long day, was to walk into a noisy, smoky pub full of half-drunk men arguing the toss over some sidestall or another. He decided to have a couple of quiet jars at the Cleakum first, then he'd pop into the Stag when hopefully the meeting would be finishing off and he would have a better chance to talk with Thomas privately.

He pushed open the door to the pub. At first he thought the place must be closed, there were no other customers and no-one behind the bar but the lamps were burning and a fire blazing in the hearth.

"Evening, what can I get you?" The figure of the landlord rose up from behind the bar where he had obviously been tinkering with something. Daniel moved over to the fire, finally relinquishing his hold on coat and hat. He let the heat start to warm him through and dry his wet clothes. "Evening, a pint of porter, cheers." He warmed his hands: "God but it's bloody filthy outside. Any idea how long it's meant to last?"

The barman finished off the pint with a frothy head and placed it on the bar. Daniel was sure the man had been at the wedding but couldn't for the life of him remember what his name was.

"I reckon it'll blow itself out pretty soon, these things normally do. It's Daniel Fletcher isn't it?"

Daniel walked up to the bar, fishing a few coins out of his pocket. "That's right, you were at the wedding weren't you." He put the money on the bar and said: "Get yourself one at the same time."

The landlord picked out the right change and dropped it in the till. "Thanks, I'll join you in a porter, it's a good brew. Aye, I was at your wedding, a good bash that was, but I know we weren't properly introduced then, the name's Bisby, George Bisby." He stuck his hand out across the bar and Daniel shook it. They both took a drink and Daniel nodded. "You're right it's a nice beer that." He looked around at the deserted pub and without thinking said: "It's pretty quiet in here for a Friday night, even with the weather."

Bisby pulled a face and said: "They've got that meeting down at the Stag, it's taken all my custom. I just hope the next meeting they have they'll hold it here. It'd only be fair."

Feeling a little awkward having inadvertently raised what was obviously a touchy subject, Daniel busied himself with his pipe.

"Your new wife was down here the other day," Bisby said after a while, "she's good friends with our lass Sally, they're thick as thieves when they get together."

"Aye, she said she'd dropped in earlier in the week. No doubt Sally will be up to Damflask visiting Elizabeth soon." Daniel drained his mug and said: "I'll have another one of those, it's been a bloody long day and that ale is just hitting the spot."

"How's that cottage of yours coming along?" Bisby asked as he worked the pump.

"It's looking grand, there wasn't much to do really and Mrs Ibbotson had done most of the cleaning before we got there. Do you know Mrs Ibbotson?"

"Mary? I've known them a long time, run a good little pub up there." The landlord passed Daniel his drink. "That one's on the house," he said. "Chances are you'll be the only customer I get all night."

"Cheers, I'll make sure I make this my local, bring some of the lads in from the wheel now and again." Daniel felt a little guilty that he would be leaving after this drink to join the others at the Stag and also because before tonight he had never set foot in the Cleakum before. Whenever he had been drinking in Malin Bridge he had always frequented the Stag.

"Oh aye, where do you work?

"Just down the road by the river, just before you get to the Limerick, I've been there for a few years now. One of Thomas Shaw's places." Even as he uttered the words Daniel realised he was digging himself a big hole.

"Oh, then I'm surprised I haven't seen you in here before."

"Well before I got married I used to live down in Sheffield, I didn't really spend much time here outside of work."

"Whereabouts in Sheffield? I know it quite well, I've got a cousin who lives in Sharrow."

Daniel felt a little like he was being put on trial and wondered if these were just casual questions or whether Bisby was digging for gossip. "I used to live on Bungay Street, near the middle of town."

Bisby looked quite surprised and said: "That's down in The Ponds isn't it? I've heard it's a bit rough round there."

Daniel became a little defensive but was not particularly surprised: The Ponds had quite a lurid reputation and more than a few of these villagers had raised an eyebrow when they found out where he came from. He knew that all kinds of stories were told about The Ponds, most of them blatantly untrue, some of them blatantly true. "Well I suppose we all have to be born somewhere. It's not as bad as people lead you to believe, not as nice as Damflask obviously but there really aren't riots and orgies going on all the time there." Actually, thinking about it, Daniel wondered if The Ponds might in fact seem like hell on earth to some of these backward bumpkins.

"Aye it's a nice spot you've got up there in Damflask. I sometimes take the kids up in the summertime and now we've got that reservoir I was thinking about making some toy boats for them to play with. I bet there'll be some decent fishing too."

"Well I'm just glad to be out in some fresh air at last. The worst thing about Sheffield is all the smoke and soot in the air. When me and Elizabeth raise kids I'm glad they'll be able to breathe clean air and have the run of some countryside." Daniel glanced at the clock behind the bar, surprised to see it was already after ten. He finished his drink: "I'd best be making tracks then, thanks for the beer."

"My pleasure, thanks for coming in, it's been nice to meet you." Bisby took Daniel's glass and put it behind the counter. As Daniel walked out he called: "And don't forget we serve good food here as well, the wife is well known around here for her cooking."

"Cheers, I'll remember that."

Once again outside and the weather, if anything, seemed to have got worse. Daniel hadn't realised how late it was. He thought about just setting off for home but he knew he couldn't, he had decided to have a word with Thomas and so he would. Now would be the best time; Daniel felt quite mellow after his two beers and he knew that Elizabeth's Dad would have had a few as well. He hurried over to the Stag.

"SEEMS you've been up to your usual carryings-on, Hukin, I hear Jack Quinn's looking for you, something to do with someone Pickens or other." "Pickens, Pickens? I don't know anyone of that name." John had been more than usually bothered by the drayman's comment, perhaps because he was too sober to shrug it off: he wasn't stupid enough not to know Quinn wasn't the kind of villain to mess with too much. "That fucking wretched sniveller Pickens, I should have finished him off when I had the chance." John was walking aimlessly round the wettened streets, passing taverns he might normally be tempted into and keeping his head low: the wind turned out to be a bit of a bonus, no-one had a mind to look up at passers-by, he'd probably be quite safe from snooping eyes. Maybe Daniel was right, he should take himself in hand. He wasn't sure about the idyllic image painted by his friend of new generations of Hukins and Fletchers frolicking together in the fields around Damflask but there again it did make for a pretty picture. Of course John would have to find himself a good woman first: that could be more difficult than him changing the bad habits of a lifetime.

AS the embankment loomed up, a huge dark black mass within the darkness, Gunson and Craven could just make out the moving pin-pricks of lanterns on the outer wall. The trap was moving slowly now, the climb up the valley having exhausted the horse. The two men could see the silhouette of a figure walking down the road: as they drew nearer Craven said: "I think that's Greaves."

Gunson pulled the gig to a halt as the approaching man came up to them. It was Greaves, looking cold, wet and miserable.

"What news of the dam?" Gunson yelled, the wind whipping away his words so they barely reached Greaves even though he was standing right beside them.

"Seems like it's a false alarm. There's a crack alright but the dam's holding up well and good." Greaves bawled back at him. "I'm getting off, I've had my fill of this place for today."

Craven looked over at Gunson with an unspoken question plainly on his face. Gunson simply nudged the horse forward and said: "We're going up there."

Outside the work hut they could see George Swinden, Steven Fountain and William Horsefield talking to another group of men; Gunson recognized the farmer Samuel Hammerton and assumed the others were locals who had come up out of concern. "George, Steve, William," Gunson greeted them as he got down from the carriage. "How's it looking?"

It was Swinden who answered. "I don't know guv'nor, it seems to be holding, the water ain't even up to the level of the weir yet. I just don't know, I'd say we're fine but you never know with things like that."

Gunson was relieved that the water level had still to reach the weir, it meant that the reservoir was yet to reach its capacity. "What about the outlets, you did open them?"

"Sure we did."

Gunson felt confident now; the pipes were open and the reservoir wasn't full. "Well let's go and have a look at this crack shall we?" Swinden went and got another couple of lanterns, lit them within the shelter of the work hut and passed one each to Gunson and Craven.

Gunson, Fountain, Craven and Swinden proceeded in single file across the embankment until they reached the point where the crack started. Gunson actually lay down on the top of the wall and swung his lamp down, trying to get a better look. The crack was about twelve feet beneath them but it was almost impossible to tell whether it was below or above the water level on the other side. Gunson got up and paced along, silently counting. He estimated the crack was fifty yards long, give or take, and a few inches wide. He turned to the man behind him and shouted: "Let's take a look at the weir." Out in the open with no shelter and the wind roaring straight down the valley and across the water, Fountain cupped his ear to indicate he couldn't hear. Gunson gestured that they should continue onwards and the men crossed to the bank on the other side.

Gunson inspected the weir and saw that the water was still some way down from entering it. He beckoned to the men that they should shelter in the lee of the valley side. "So what do you think?"

Fountain was the first to speak: "I reckon if we don't relieve the dam of water there'll be a blow up in about half an hour."

Gunson looked around at the others. Craven merely shrugged. Swinden said: "I've got a nasty feeling about this. Maybe the weir wall's too high to be much use right now. I think we should blow the fucker up and let more water out."

Gunson nodded. "I agree, it's better to be safe than sorry. Get some powder and we'll blow it."

A CHILL in the air roused Elizabeth from dozing, curled up in the chair in front of what was no longer a roaring fire. She jumped up suddenly to look at the clock, past eleven and still no sign of Daniel. All her worries about the morning row came flooding to the surface again and tears started flowing down her cheeks once more. Perhaps she was over-reacting: he did say he would be late but this was very late; he did wave from across the river but maybe it was a goodbye wave because he'd already decided he wasn't coming back. She looked out of the window but could make out nothing but wind and rain and the fronds of the willow whipping around like ribbons on a maypole: even the gate which she had particularly fastened was clapping and creaking backwards and forwards on its hinges. She opened the door but couldn't hold it open and went back inside. "Daniel, Daniel, please come home to me." Pebble flapped around her skirt, wagging his tail, glad she was awake at last and he had someone to play with. She tied his red ribbon back in place and picked him up for comfort.

GABRIEL was about to order his fourth pint: no need to hurry back to Malin Bridge, no-one would be needing his services any more tonight in this weather, he could just take his time and relax. "I'm afraid we're closing up now and clearing out up to Sam's place for the night," said Jonathan Ibbotson from behind the bar.

"You're closing?" asked the old man, puzzled, this wasn't usual for a Friday night, was he going to miss out on his relaxation after all?

"Haven't you heard?"

"Heard what, what is there to hear?" said Gabriel.

"They found a crack in the dam wall up the hill and the engineer is coming all the way out from Sheffield to take a look as we speak, as a matter of urgency."

"A hole in the dam wall?" Gabriel couldn't quite take it in. He had never had much call for working things out other than making sure he was where he should be and when with the carriage for Mr and Mrs Shaw.

"Yes, Gabriel, a hole in the dam wall. The young man they sent to fetch the engineer said it wasn't anything to worry about but holes in dam walls and urgent visits by engineers in the middle of the night doesn't sound to me like nothing to worry about. We're not taking any chances. We're going to Sam's place up on the hill and I suggest you find somewhere safe yourself to hole up. Most people in Damflask are heading to higher ground for the night, just in case."

"They sent a young man to Sheffield, at this hour?"

"Yes, on a horse, now get yourself off. I hope nothing does happen or that we haven't left it too late already."

"Right, right," said Gabriel reluctantly gathering his stuff off the counter.

"Safe, hole up for the night because of a hole in the dam wall, everyone going." Then the penny dropped through the fug. "Not safe here, everyone leaving... I'd better go over and warn Miss Elizabeth and that husband of hers."

Gabriel walked out of the Barrel only to be forced back against the wall. The rain was beating down as he trudged his way through the muddy yard to find the gig. "Come on Arthur, we have to get ourselves off out of here. I'll just lead you across the bridge to Miss Elizabeth's, I think that might be easier." In the looming dark of the storm he could make out groups of people clutching bundles and children and anxiously making their way out of Damflask and up the surrounding hills. "We'd better get a move on Arthur."

ONLY the diehards were left supping up in the Stag when Daniel walked in shaking the water off his cap. "Daniel, has that young wife of yours let you out on your own already? Will it be the usual?" asked William Armitage getting ready to pull the porter for his regular.

"I've just come from work," said Daniel, deciding to leave out the bit about having a drink in the Cleakum. He hadn't realised how sensitive landlords could be. "I was hoping to see her father; has he already left?"

"You've missed Mr Shaw by a good hour. He left when the meeting broke up. Are you stopping for one?"

"No I'd best not. I told Elizabeth I'd be late home but I hadn't reckoned on it being this late. The weather's awful, have you looked out? It won't make the way home any easier. I've never known it so bad. I might leave that porter til tomorrow, goodnight now."

It was a lonely walk as he headed off into the night; Daniel felt totally alone, overwhelmed by the howling noise and the power of the gusting wind. He fingered the pendant in his pocket and the thought of Elizabeth cheered him as much as anything could in the circumstances. "Please God she'll love it," he thought.

GUNSON was sure that this was the right thing to do. Only God knew how long the howling wind and rain would continue but if the weir was blown at least the pressure against the dam would be relieved. He knew there was a risk involved: the amount of water released through the weir channel would far surpass what the outlet pipes could carry off and that volume of water could cause some major damage further down the valley but, compared to what would happen if there was an actual break in the dam, this excess water would be a mere trickle.

Swinden, soaked and muddied to his knees, had dug a hole right on the edge of the river bank next to the weir. Fountain had crossed back over the dam to the hut and now returned with a keg of powder.

"Right, George, you've dealt with explosives more than the rest of us, set the powder and lay a train." Gunson felt happier now they were actively doing something and was sure this would alleviate the problem. Swinden took the keg and filled the prepared hole, then bent down, backing towards the others and spilling the powder, laying a train to be ignited from a safe distance.

"Fuck me but it's hard to see; I think I've got a complete line. You'd better light it before the rain completely ruins the bloody stuff."

Gunson got ready to light the powder: "You'd better put in some distance from here, get up the valley. I'll be right behind you." He applied the match to the powder and made ready to run. There was a spark then a fizzle then the powder went out. "Damn it." Gunson edged forward and located the end again. He fired up another match and this time the powder took hold sending a fizzing sparkling train towards the main explosives. "That's it lads," Gunson shouted as he hurried up the valley, "take cover it's going to blow."

The four men huddled behind a boulder watching the progress of the train, each braced against the imminent explosion. Then the powder went out again. Just a couple of feet from the hole, it just petered out.

"Fuck, fuck, fuck," George shouted, "it's got to be too damp, or the wind has blown the powder away. It's useless, we ain't going to blow that fucker unless we stick a torch right down the bloody hole and go up with it." He looked around at the others and said: "And I for one ain't prepared to do that."

Gunson stood up after they were sure there was going to be no explosion: "Well before we try again I suggest we take another look at that crack. If there isn't any leakage by now I think we'll be alright."

The men scurried past the hole full of explosives, still cautious of it, and made their way along the embankment. As they got to the start of the crack, Gunson once again began to sweep his lantern down over the wall to see if anything had changed. Everything looked the same. They reached the end of the embankment and stood shivering while Gunson thought what to do next.

THE knock at the porch had Elizabeth on her feet in seconds. "Daniel, you're back," she called, flinging open the door ready to pull him into her arms and hug him and hold him and say she was sorry for laughing out of turn this morning.

"It's me, Miss Elizabeth, is Daniel not home yet?"

"Gabriel, oh." She slumped back in disappointment. "I thought you were him. I don't know where he is."

"Well now, Miss Elizabeth, I expect he's down at Shaw Lodge sheltering from the storm. I believe he was expected at the Stag for the big meeting and no doubt Mr Shaw has insisted he stay with them until this terrible storm has passed. Don't you be alarmed," he said, then realised this wasn't perhaps the best thing to say as he was about to alarm her right and proper.

"Do come in, I'm forgetting my manners," said Elizabeth, wanting desperately to cling on to Gabriel's explanation but not totally convinced. "I'm afraid I fell asleep and let the fire go out. What are you doing up here so late anyway?"

"That's what I need to tell you," said Gabriel. He had known Miss Elizabeth since she was a wee lass and had come to regard her almost as his own grand-daughter; it pained him to see her so obviously distraught but he had to take care of her again this time. In a peculiar way he suddenly found himself temporarily the man of the house. He had to take charge. "We have to go out, get out, both of us, you and me, we have to get out of the house and go some ways up the hill, just for a short while. Do you know anyone who lives up the hill on this side?"

"Anyone who lives up the hill, whatever for?"

"Well I'm sure it's nothing but they were saying in the Barrel that a crack has been found in the wall of that new dam at Dale Dyke and that it would perhaps be safer to get up on to higher ground for a bit, just in case like. It seems there's an engineer on his way up from Sheffield now to sort it out but meanwhile I need to get you to safety, that's what everyone told me."

"Get me to safety? Wouldn't we be better off staying in the cottage? It's been standing here long enough, it must be quite sound."

"I'm sure it is," said Gabriel, "and no doubt it will be waiting for us when we return but Mr and Mrs Ibbotson were insistent that I get you up that hill for a while and I don't want them refusing to serve me for not doing what they said. So come on, Miss Elizabeth, put on your warmest hat and coat and we'll be off."

"Couldn't we just go over to the Barrel and stay with them?"

"They've already gone. The Barrel's deserted."

GUNSON stood there at a loss as to what to do. Finally: "Okay, I'll check the outlets, make sure there aren't any leaks down there."

The pipes appeared in good order, although it was hard to discern much in the dim light, and Gunson hauled himself back up to the reservoir. The others were waiting at the top: "I'm going to take one more look at that crack." This time only Swinden followed him. They walked rapidly along the embankment, studying the outer wall as best they could but again could see no change. They came back and paused at the near end of the crack. As the two men stood there the water unexpectedly foamed up in the reservoir behind them and plunged over the top in a white sheet, covering their feet. Gunson studied the liquid as it poured down the wall and spilled into the crack. That didn't look good, he thought, and hurried back to the others. Maybe there was something he could do back at the valve house, maybe he could open them up more, do something.

Swinden followed after Gunson and saw the man once again running down to the valve house, skidding and slipping on the wet grass. Swinden had a notion that something was terribly wrong. As Gunson entered the building he roared as loudly as he could: "Get the fuck out of there you fucking idiot, get back up here."

Gunson re-appeared from the valve house and as he cocked his head up towards George he saw a section of the dam wall suddenly collapse, a big section, maybe thirty feet wide. "Holy Mother of God," he screamed and sped up the incline. He reached the top, Swinden grabbing him by the scruff of his collar and dragging him up when they were knocked off their feet by an immense explosion. The dam had burst. The gunpowder had gone off. They reeled back on the ground and watched, helpless, as millions of gallons of water started to surge through the breach.

"MISS Elizabeth we really ought to get going. Arthur's just up the track with the carriage, I left him tied to that huge oak, you know the one, not far to go and then you'll be safely tucked up in the back out of the weather. You might want to take an extra blanket."

"I want to leave a lamp lit in the window, for Daniel, just in case he makes it back before we do. I don't want him to think I've run away or anything."

"Now why would he think that, Miss Elizabeth. Come on now, coat on."

Gabriel picked up Elizabeth's bundle – she had taken the precaution of quickly packing some bread and cake and a flagon of water, she wasn't sure how long her great protector would insist on this enterprise – and opened the door of Willow Tree Cottage. Elizabeth picked up Pebble, wrapped the small terrier in the spare blanket and followed Gabriel out into the storm.

The threesome started up the lane to the gig. The noise of the storm seemed suddenly to boom louder and louder.

GUNSON watched in horror, still lying where he had been knocked to the ground as the water poured through the huge break. The spectacle was horrifying: a white seething mass of water spewing forth. The sound was deafening: a thundering roar so loud that everything else was soundless. He watched as everything in the path of the onrush was ripped and torn away but all he could hear was the barrage of a thousand waterfalls in his head. Trees were plucked out of the ground by the roots as if they had been mere blades of grass and chunks of rocks and boulders were rolled and carried off as if they were no more than bouncing balls. There seemed to be no end to the water, it just kept pouring through. Gunson sat up and bowed his head in his hands as he thought of the fearful nightmare about to be unleashed on the people further down the valley.

THE flood dashed down the ravine. For the first three-quarters of a mile there was nothing for the water to destroy other than the vegetation and natural features of the geology. A piece of stone, having split slightly from the valley side after eons of weathering erosion, was rent from the bedrock, it was thirty-six feet long and weighed more than sixty tons but was carried along easily, acting like a battering ram. Annett Bridge was the first man-made structure the water hit. It was swept away in an instant. The first house the water encountered was Annett House farmstead. Fortunately it was empty; the owner, John Empsall, was one of those who had gone up to the dam earlier and he hadn't trusted the reassurances that the crack wasn't dangerous. He had gotten his family out and now watched from above on high ground as his home and entire livelihood was completely eradicated. The devastation rushed onwards exploding into Low Bradfield carrying away the bridges, mills, chapel, school and stores. Some inhabitants having heard of the crack in the dam had decided to play it safe and, like John Empsall, had sought safety up the valley side. The Ibbotsons were one such family and helplessly witnessed the destruction of their village; they could see some of their neighbours thrashing about in the mad waters below as others, now corpses, bumped and swirled rapidly past the struggling victims. The onslaught careered towards Damflask.

A VERY bedraggled Daniel was relieved to see the Barrel just ahead of him but couldn't fathom why the pub was in darkness, in fact the whole of Damflask seemed to be in darkness. "Surely everybody can't have gone to bed early, not on a Friday," he thought, "not with all this storm going on." He was soaked to the skin and had been buffeted and blown about all the way up from the Stag and couldn't wait to get home to his beautiful wife, especially when he spotted the lamp lit in the window and he knew he'd been forgiven.

THE roaring thunderous noise got bigger in their ears and Elizabeth and Gabriel turned to look in its direction, back towards the Loxley. Through the driving rain she could make out Daniel on the other side of the river and the tension of her long, lonely day melted away as she saw that he was coming back to her. "Daniel Daniel," she shouted joyously but her voice couldn't carry. Pebble leapt out of her arms as he saw his master, barking and wagging its tail with all the excitement. Daniel heard the faint sound of the dog and looked up. He saw Elizabeth and his heart started thumping in his chest.

THAT was the last they saw of each other. A wall of raging black water some fifty feet high suddenly fell crashing down the valley between them carrying in its tide whole trees, ancient boulders, huge stones, cows, sheep, pigs, sections of demolished walls and the debris of people, their homes and their very lives. Daniel saw Willow Tree Cottage completely engulfed by the torrent seconds before he was washed off his feet to become part of the flood. Elizabeth's scream as she saw him swept away pierced the storm and she passed out. In the water Daniel was pulled under by the weight of the flow, twisting and somersaulting, his lungs bursting as he fought to get to the surface. Every time his head burst through he thrashed and paddled his arms wildly desperately trying to keep afloat, gulping in as much air as he could, panicking and struggling for survival against the onrush before going under again. The torrent seemed to be gaining momentum all the time adding deadening strength to the awful flotsam travelling down-stream with him and his body was bashed and battered in a relentless assault. As the leading wall of the flood water speeded and rumbled on just yards ahead of him he grabbed hold of a kitchen door and at last managed to stay on the volatile surface, gasping for breath, bruised and bloodied. Then not two feet away from him he saw a small dog, drowned, being carried along in the water, a soaking red ribbon mangled around its neck.

THE flood smashed its way down the Loxley valley, twisting and turning
as it followed the river bed, funnelled and fuelled into renewed devastating
power by the steep contours of the hills; but the wider-bottomed valleys held
no respite, for the leading edge of the water was being pushed from behind by
the waiting latent power of hundreds of millions of gallons of water frantically
rushing to freedom from the breached Dale Dyke reservoir.

By now the flow had added machinery and metal supplies ripped from the
mills and wheels near Beacon Wood to its load, innocuous cargo such as the
twenty huge sacks of potatoes from a house in Little Matlock and, tragically,
the innocent bodies of men, women and children, snatched from their sleep.
At Damflask the residents had had some warning but for people living further
down the valley the only announcement was a deafening roar and by then,
for most, it was already too late. In Little Matlock, Thomas Chapman was
awoken by the hellish noise of the water rising in the bedroom, just in time
to see his young son, William, about to be washed out through the window:
Thomas grabbed the boy and held on with all his strength but the flood
brought down a ceiling beam on the man and he could only look on in anguish
as his son was whipped and eddied out of his grip.

In Malin Bridge, for the Shaws, the Tricketts, the Bisbys, the storekeepers,
the workers, the farmers and grinders and other residents, the deluge arrived
without any notice. The distance from Little Matlock was about one and a half
miles but it proved a lethal one and a half miles, for the valley at that point
was narrow and steep-sided and the ground dropped sharply, funnelling the
water and allowing the flood to build up its tremendous power once more.

Immediately in its boiling path, in that once enviable position on the spit of
land between the merger of the Loxley and the Rivelin rivers, was the home
of the Tricketts, with its beautiful gardens running down to the verdant river
banks. They'd all had a good evening: old Tom Kay with his grandchildren;
Mr and Mrs Trickett enjoying the company of friends and planning the May
Fair; young Joe Barker sleeping off his night in the Stag with the satisfaction
of his ideas being the only decent ones to be put forward, now all packed
and ready to go home to Arbourthorne the following day: they were all in
bed sound asleep. They were in the habit of going to bed round half-ten and
tonight they were all particularly tired after their socialising. But even the
Tricketts were roused by the noise and James struggled out of his warm bed
reluctantly and lit a lamp to find out what on earth was going on. He looked
out of the window to see a terrible scene: the farmhouse was surrounded by
violent currents of water rushing at and into the house. It rose unstoppable up
the stairs and even gushed up through the floorboards and floated the oilcloth.

Less than seconds later the whole house was literally picked up by the flood and carried along by the water; it twisted and spiralled and was dashed out of existence. Not one of the household survived.

Round the corner at Shaw Lodge, Anna and Thomas fared no better. A huge chunk of machinery clattered and shoved against the house like a battering ram and pounded through the gable wall ripping the place apart: as the bedroom floor collapsed into the insidious water Thomas frantically tried to get a hold of Anna, reaching for her arm for her hand for her head only to see her slip out of his grasp to disappear out of sight as their heavy oak furniture toppled over into the swell and pushed her under. The loss robbed him of any will to try to save himself.

Across what had been the bridge, whole rows of cottages were destroyed, bombarded by the maelstrom of debris dashed about by the flood water: all manner of domestic items had joined the melee in the water - iron bedsteads, wooden cots, upholstered furniture, carpets, pots and pans, crockery, mattresses, jars of jam and bottles of sauces, shoes, books, items of clothing, toys, all the simple, heartbreaking evidence of everyday life. Other homes were lifted up by the water, just as with the Tricketts' farmhouse, and turned around violently and rolled over to crumble into more fuel for the flood. The shoemaker George Barrett and his wife Emma and their lodger were washed away with their terraced cottage: their neighbours Lizzie and Charlie Price vanished along with their store – he wouldn't be providing ribbons or bunting for anyone any more – and their family, including that precious bundle of a two-day-old grandson; the old schoolmarm Mrs Etchell left this earth to join her husband, dead these last few years. No evidence of any of them remained. Opposite the terraced cottages was the Stag, where eleven people, including Bill Armitage, the publican, and his wife, Ann, were all crushed or swept to their deaths as the pub was demolished by the torrent. By the bridge itself was the Cleakum: all the Bisbys were drowned, George and Sarah and five of their children, the outer walls of their inn ripped off and all but its chimney stack left to mark the spot.

The flood relentlessly poured on respecting neither people nor property. Down the lane at the Limerick Wheel, part-owned by the unfortunate Joe Barker; here the water commandeered rolls of crinoline wire, iron castings, heavy tools and with them Bill Bethel, who had earlier left for home but been asked to return to the wheel to work on a late delivery of steel which had to be made ready for the following day. Bill had five furnaces fired up and on the go, all red hot and scorching the air and heating huge quantities of softening steel. He was alone when the water forced its way in: it flooded into the open furnaces, attacked their hellish innards and overwhelmed the workshop with hissing searingly hot steam, disfiguring Bill's body with agonising burns moments before the place was blown apart.

But the water didn't stop to investigate its aftermath, instead it ruthlessly carried on hurtling down the valley, still travelling with manic speed over fields, over roads, swallowing up anyone and anything in its path, the wall of water still thirty, forty feet high. It swept down to Hillsborough, where more houses, more people, were dashed apart or sucked under to their death. Some people managed to escape by climbing through upper-floor windows and scrambling to safety on to the hillside just inches above the high tide: a tailor, Joe Chapman was wearing just a scrap of old nightshirt and had climbed into a large crate to keep out of the draught of the sudden and unexpected cold blast and so bizarrely he saved his life; the crate floated. Others weren't so lucky. The toll collector, shopkeepers, householders – many were lost as the merciless water claimed their homes as its prize.

The inundation swept on through Owlerton - the boundary wall of the new barracks was dashed to pieces as if made of pebbles not heavy stone - and rushed down to the confluence of the Loxley and the Don. An entire haystack surviving its journey remarkably intact finally escaped and was surreally thrown on to solid ground after travelling down from a country field. An iron-shuttled weir was dismissed like some flimsy doll's house while seconds later yet more machinery, stone and bodies were added to the deluge as it made ready to hit Sheffield.

JOHN heard a voice shouting out in the street; it somehow rose from the middle of a loud and totally unrecognisable noise and John hid quickly in the shadows fearing he'd been rumbled by one of Jack Quinn's spies. He had given in to his thirst, too easily really, and had had a few jars in some pub or other round Bacon Island, not one of his usual haunts, before venturing back out into the storm. "I should have stuck to what I bloody well said," he staggered cowering in a doorway not in the mood for a fight… perhaps if it had been later than half past midnight… He was cold and very wet and listened out for the direction of the voice, very hard to make out over the wind howling and whatever else was going on: "What the hell is that noise?" He carefully poked his head out of the shelter of the doorway and saw a policeman running desperately from house to house knocking on doors and shrieking up at windows to those inside to wake themselves bloody quick and get the hell out. Then John saw that the policeman was paddling. "What the fuck?" Then he realised he was paddling too, his feet hidden suddenly in swirling water that was quickly deepening as he stood there. Too soon it was up to his waist. "Run now," he heard the copper shout, "run for your life." He tried to, wading against the flow and struggling to keep upright as the water caught his legs and the wind whipped around his body, the elements combining to try to drag him down. "Jesus Christ," he muttered, the first prayer he'd uttered since asking God to reveal who'd killed his father so he could take his mortal revenge. Just yards away the bridge to Bacon Island crashed into the molten stream as it fell victim to the force of the flood and John was pushed back into the doorway. The thunderous noise filled his ears, the sight of dead bodies bumping and turning and speeding past him in the broil filled his eyes. As the flood's impetus roared on its way, he saw before him one vast sheet of filthy, clogged water. By the time John fully understood the situation, he was up to his chest in the ferment and realised he'd have to move or die. He left the deadly sanctuary of the doorway and felt his way along the wall, gripping on to anything that gave any sort of a hold as the water and its lethal mix sucked and plucked at him. "Thank God," he said as the wall gave way to an opening where a flight of worn stone steps led up out of the pool. He clambered up dripping and sweating despite the cold, any threat of Quinn put into a distant perspective as he looked down on the devastation below. He'd lost only his boots, the people floating past him had lost everything. There was a crowd of silent onlookers gathered at the top of the steps. "Where the hell did this all come from?" John asked no-one in particular. "What the hell happened tonight?"

***

Part Three

"Poor child, I thought she'd never fall asleep but she's dropped off at last, though what sort of a night she'll have I don't know, God have mercy on her. I just kept looking at her poor head lying on the pillow. She's worn out. It'll take a long time before she gets over all this."

Kitty Scott had joined her brother Gabriel in front of the hearth, where he sat wrapped in a woollen blanket, his feet in a bowl of hot water and his hands cupping a mug of broth. He was still shaking a bit but the rigours of the long drive over the hills to Bamford were beginning to ease in the warmth of the fire. The wind was still blowing up a storm outside but at last they had arrived safely. It had taken a few hours to get there from Damflask and the cold, wet ordeal had taken its toll on Gabriel and the horse but they had made it. Elizabeth had thankfully remained unconscious for almost the whole of the journey, waking only when the cobbled streets of the village had registered a change of sound in her ears and by then Gabriel had reached his sister's house. They had helped the girl out of the gig – she didn't seem to know what was going on, let alone care where she was – and Kitty had put her straight to bed while Gabriel unhitched Arthur and stabled him, leaving a small supply of water and feed for the faithful old bay.

"Kitty, you've never seen anything like it, the whole place was flattened, flattened, even the big pub opposite, all by this huge tide of water, and then seeing poor Daniel swept away, well, that was just too heartbreaking to behold. Jesus I felt so helpless, Kitty. God knows what happened to folk further down the valley, I can't see as they would have had any chance at all. I didn't know where else to come."

"You did the right thing coming here," said Kitty.

"I keep thinking of what would have happened if I hadn't gone to fetch Miss Elizabeth or if we had left the house a couple of minutes later."

"What matters is that you did fetch her so don't go accusing yourself of being helpless because you saved that girl's life. If it hadn't been for you she'd be dead by now. As it is she's upstairs sleeping in a warm bed."

"Kitty you've never seen such a happy couple as those two youngsters. She might not be that grateful that I saved her after seeing her Daniel drown like that."

"Go on now, Gabriel, stop talking so soft. It will take time for her, that's to be sure, but we all have to get on with it and do our best, not many people are blessed with an easy life, sad though it is to say. God deals us all our own hands and we have to play them out. Now finish up that broth and be off to bed yourself, you've done more than can be expected of any man tonight. I'll sleep up in the girl's room, just in case she wakes."

JOHN came to with a nasty crick in his neck. He found himself slumped on a bench, his head lolling forward on to his chest with no support and the damp of his clothes having seeped through into his bones and his tired muscles until they were set into the most uncomfortable position. His boots were clogged with mud and he had a tidemark of dried dirt across his coat as high as his shoulders. There were other people around him in the room, wherever he was, talking in sombre tones and with sombre words. The talk was all about the flood, of the horrors seen, the mothers, fathers and children lost, the homes and possessions disappeared into the black. "Where am I?" he asked another lost soul in ragged clothes sat next to him. The young man looked at him with empty eyes, jaw set in a permanent gape. The man couldn't speak but his eyes were witness enough.

"You're at the police station," a woman called to John. "You'll get nothing out of poor Joel Midwood there. He's just seen his little brothers and sister swept away and his mother and father slip off the roof and drown right in front of him. You get yourself a hot drink and then grab a lantern, some of the men are out looking for bodies and they could do with all the help they can get."

"What time is it, has the water gone?"

"It's about half-six," she said. "The level of the water has dropped alright but there's still enough of it about where it shouldn't be and mountains of mud and garbage and God knows what piled up everywhere and bodies sticking out in it all over the place."

"Where has it all come from?" he asked.

"I'm told that new dam burst, the one up at Dale Dyke. Gallons and gallons of water escaped. I'm told that's where a lot of the bodies have come from, up the valley, but God knows there's a few from round about here too, bodies and bits of bodies."

Bodies. Bits of bodies. The Dale Dyke dam. Jesus Christ.

"I've got to go," said John, "got to look for some bodies."

He left the relative comfort of the police station and ventured outside into the street, still barely able to stand up properly. The stench nearly knocked him back off his feet and he had to smother his nose and mouth with his hands to try to keep out the smell of filthy water, machinery oil, rotting vegetation, grounded animals... The night was still dark and the weather not much improved but he could make out the moving bobs of lantern-light as searchers poked and prodded and called out among the ruins. He set off to make his way back up through the streets of Neepsend to the brewery.

"Have you lost a horse?" he was asked by one of the many passers-by wandering round, bewildered, utterly distraught, "have you lost a big grey horse?"

"No," said John, "why do you ask?"

"Because there's a big grey horse floating around in my parlour and it wasn't there last night. Are you sure you haven't lost a big grey horse? Do you know anyone who has lost a big grey horse?"

"I can't help you there," said John,.

"But I don't know what to do with it, I don't know what to do with a dead horse. How do I get it out of my house?"

John guiltily shoved his way past the stranger and climbed up the back alleys to the brewery stables, trying to ignore the complete devastation all around him and the harrowing cries for help. He found Stanley where he'd left him, and safe. "Come on now," he said to the shire, "we've an unscheduled call to make and I'm not sure what we'll find." He hitched up the dray and was pulling out of the yard when a man grabbed hold of the reins.

"Where are you headed for, friend?"

"Do I know you, you're certainly no friend of mine?" Instinctively John's mind turned to Jack Quinn.

"My name's Matthew Blagdon, I'm a reporter for the Sheffield Telegraph and I'm trying to get up to the valley to see where the dam burst."

John studied the man for a second or two while he made up his mind. Perhaps some company would be welcome in the circumstances and perhaps this Blagdon reporter bloke might know a bit more about what had happened. "Climb aboard," he said and they started out for Malin Bridge.

THE ground was drifting, swaying as if it was lapping against something more solid. The sensation was dreamlike until the freezing cold and wet seeped through to Daniel's consciousness waking him abruptly. He started upwards, jerked blearily into awareness, his sudden movement almost tipping him into the water. He found himself lying on a door. One corner of the door had lodged itself into the soft earth of a river bank, another had become caught in the tangle of branches from an overhanging bush. The current of the river was trying to shift the door downstream but it was anchored enough so it merely bobbed with the flow. Daniel forced himself on to all fours and crawled up the door until he could reach the bank and then, even though the pain in his body screamed in protest, pulled himself up on to dry land. He rolled over, confused and bewildered, not sure if the wetness he felt on his face was water or blood – it seemed heavier and more viscous than water – and passed out.

When he came to again the day was lighter, the pale dawn had matured into morning and the dull reminiscence of aches had grown into sharp spasms of agony that racked his body. His head felt like someone was pressing it down on a grindstone and not letting up, his vision was blurred and his tongue felt thick and swollen and dirty inside his mouth. Despite the torture wrenching his arm and shoulder, he wiped his hand across his eyes, trying to clear his vision; it came away sticky and red but at least he could see more clearly. What in hell had happened?

He sat up gingerly and felt and heard the sound of bones grinding against each other. The stabbing shafts of pain in his side suggested he had cracked a few ribs if nothing more. What in the hell had happened? Where was he? Why was he here?

Memory came back to him in an anguishing sob. Pictures formed in his head as he remembered. He saw Elizabeth waving across the valley. With someone? Then the image of a foaming, roaring mountain of water racing towards him and engulfing him. He remembered seeing her and then the water and then the struggle to keep afloat, gulping in water, spitting it out, trying to swim to shore, trying to survive. He remembered the limp body of Pebble floating past just as he managed to clutch hold and clawingly haul himself up on to that door. That was all.

Slowly he managed to stand, staggering from one side to the other and hugging himself against the pain. He had to get back to the cottage, Elizabeth would be worried because he was so late back and he still had to give her the pendant. In a panic it occurred to him that the pendant might have been washed away and he furiously patted down his sodden clothes until he felt

106

the reassuring shape of it in his waistcoat pocket. Another memory suddenly hit him and he reeled back from its force. He now saw the willow tree being uprooted and smashed by the wave. He struggled up the slope of the bank and started hobbling up-river. If their home had been hit by the water, what had happened to Elizabeth?

Daniel found the path running alongside the river and recognised where he was. The river was the Don and he was stood on the road between Sheffield and Rotherham, just on the outskirts of Rotherham. Daniel was astonished, how had he ended up here? He had been washed away at Damflask down the Loxley, which he knew joined up with the Don somewhere in Owlerton, just south-east of Hillsborough, and he knew that from there the Don flowed through Sheffield then meandered north-easterly to Rotherham. But the journey between Damflask and Rotherham must be a good fourteen miles by road and God knows how much longer by river. Somehow he had managed to remain on the door, out cold, for all that distance, floating and drifting. Why someone hadn't fished him out as he floated and drifted through Sheffield was a complete mystery to him. Again he wondered what the hell could have happened and again his thoughts returned to Elizabeth. She would be in a right panic by now and in the state he was in it could take him over six hours to walk all the way back to the cottage. Still, he had to get moving otherwise he'd never get home.

As Daniel walked he felt some of the aches and stiffness begin to loosen up. The bruises were still painfully apparent and various cuts and gashes continued to seep blood, his ribs continued to grind and seemed to send shards of splinters into his chest but the overall chill and drenched feeling began to wear away as the effort of walking brought out a sweat and the wind, still stiffly blowing, started to dry his clothes.

He had travelled this road several times when delivering finished goods to his customers and had hoped to flag down a passing tradesman on the way back to Sheffield but there was no traffic at all. In fact Daniel could see no-one, not even in the far distant surroundings. By this hour of the morning, even though dawn had only recently broken, the route should have been fairly busy as the farmers took their goods to town and the haulage companies started their rounds. Where was everyone? Where had all that water come from in the first place?

It was only then that Daniel remembered the dam they were building up at Dale Dyke. He'd heard the rumours about the doubts of the integrity of the construction but had dismissed them as the inevitable moans and grumbles that the mill-owners and village folk always had about something or other. He was also aware of how foul the weather had been the previous night, the wind and the rain blowing like there was no tomorrow. Surely the dam couldn't have burst? As the possibility dawned on him that so much water could have only come from the reservoir, Daniel forced himself to walk quicker. If the dam had burst it might have damaged the cottage. Maybe even now Elizabeth was surrounded by chaos and mess. Daniel knew his lass and knew that she wouldn't be able to cope with all that on her own, especially as he also knew that her little dog had probably been washed out to sea by now. He searched frantically around trying to spot someone else, a cart, a rider, someone who, even at a price, could speed up his progress. Elizabeth needed him now more than ever and here he was stuck somewhere outside bloody Rotherham and crippled to boot. There was no-one. It was like someone had cancelled the day and somehow only Daniel was still around to witness it. He stumbled on as fast as his battered body would allow.

By Christ, there were so many things to sort out and time was getting on. Daniel was still on the road to Sheffield, having left the course of the Don but heading more directly into town. He weaved from one side to the other as if drunk and his mind raced deliriously over the tasks he had before him. He still had to give Elizabeth the pendant and even before that replace the leather thong with a fancy ribbon, then he had to get back down to the wheel and finish the job he had put off yesterday. Then he had to pay a visit to Mr Shaw and get to know him better and then he should probably go and call on John and find out what was bothering him. Then there was that bleeding chicken coop he had promised to finish and after that he should fashion a proper collar for Pebble, no self-respecting dog would settle for a bit of ribbon round its neck.

As he stumbled to and fro Daniel began to sing in a hoarse and slurred voice: "There was a jolly grinder once, lived by the River Don, he'd work'd and sang from morn to night, and sometimes he'd work none." As he finished the first verse Daniel collapsed on the verge, sweat sheened his face and he could barely sit up. With tears in his eyes he realised that he couldn't make it back to Willow Tree.

A PIERCING scream jolted Kitty out of her slumbers and she rushed over to the bed where her unexpected guest was sleeping. Elizabeth had cried out in the middle of a nightmare too real and frightening for even the subconscious to absorb. "Daniel, no, no" she called and started sobbing uncontrollably. "Daniel."

"There, there, child," said Kitty, cooling Elizabeth's brow with a cold wet cloth. "It's alright, you're safe here. You're running a bit of a fever but you'll be fine after a good night's rest. Now you go back to sleep and please God we'll sort everything out in the morning."

Elizabeth's head was turning fitfully from side to side on the pillow, her eyes were still closed but behind them replayed the image over and over of the sight of Daniel disappearing under a falling mountain of angry water. Kitty kept mopping the girl's face and gently rubbing her head until finally the sobbing subsided and the poor lass fell back into the same restless sleep.

The sun had risen by now to show a clear day dawning. Out through the curtains Kitty could see the puddles and streaming gullies from the previous night's rain but at least the trees weren't bending over backwards like they had been and some calm was being restored. She glanced over at the girl again and decided it was safe enough to leave her and go on down to the kitchen. Gabriel was already up despite the previous night's experience and had put the water on to boil.

"How is she?" he asked. "Did I hear her scream just now?"

"You did but she's dropped off again, thank God. And you should still be in bed, my man, you need your rest too."

"How could I lay in bed just thinking thinking."

"By thinking of yourself for once, that's how."

"I suppose I'll have to go back, see what the place is like, see if Mr and Mrs Shaw are safe," said Gabriel. "That at least would be something to cheer Miss Elizabeth, then when she's recovered a bit I could take her home to Shaw Lodge."

"If there is a Shaw Lodge anymore," said Kitty. "Who's to say whether or not that great wall of water you described hasn't wiped the whole lot off the face of the earth and the Shaws with it."

"Ay but I'll have to go and take a look, make sure," said her brother. "Otherwise I can see Miss Elizabeth determined to set off there herself and I'd hate to think what she might find if you're right. For all we know Daniel's body is lying there right now on the river bank waiting to be found and then if she saw there was no Shaw Lodge either, well, I don't know how she'd cope just now."

"I know, I know, but not today. If you won't think of yourself think of that poor horse of yours. A trip like that straight away back over the hills could kill him. And then perhaps you don't want to alarm the girl unduly by rushing back so quickly. Let's give it a couple of days, Gabriel, and then perhaps her fever might have gone down too."

109

"No doubt you're right as usual, Kitty, it does sound sensible. Perhaps I'll get one of the lads from the village here to take a ride over tomorrow. Now I think I'll take some of that good advice of yours and go up to bed for another hour or so."

"HEY wake up, wake up."

The next thing Daniel knew was a nudging prod in his ribs, each probing dig sending waves of pain shooting through his body. Without thinking and with a snarl he grabbed at the thing that was the cause of his torment. It was a walking stick. He plucked it out of its owner's hand with the ease of plucking a blade of grass out of the ground. Although the stick was a good inch and a half thick in diameter, Daniel snapped it like a twig. Only then did he actually wake up. He was staring up into the face of an old man who had backed away fearfully. Behind him were a horse and cart with a woman sat on the passenger side.

Daniel pushed himself up so he was sat on the grass verge. "Who are you and what in the hell do you think you're doing?"

"Now look here we don't want any trouble," the man said, stepping back further and grabbing hold of the horse's halter.

"I'm not looking for trouble," Daniel said and slowly stood up. He tried to remember how he had passed out again. He reckoned he must have a touch of fever and vaguely recalled stumbling about all over the place, crying and singing like a fool. Aware of the old man's wariness, he opened his arms in a placating gesture. "Look, I've been injured and must have passed out. Unfortunately you were sticking me just where it hurt the most. I'm sorry I broke your stick but I wasn't really aware of what I was doing."

The old man still looked cautious, understandably: Daniel towered over him and his bruised, battered and brooding face was never going to instil confidence in anyone. Daniel stuck his hand out, wincing as fresh spasms lanced up his shoulder but he smiled and said: "I'm Daniel Fletcher, I seem to have been washed down river. I mean you no harm but I would ask you for some help. You seem to be headed towards Sheffield, if I could hitch a ride with you I would be very much grateful."

The old man seemed to relax slightly and shook. "You're from Sheffield? Well I'm Ralph Jackson and you're welcome to a ride into town, you'll have to sit in the back I'm afraid." He turned to the woman sat on the cart. "Do you hear that Eileen? The man's from Sheffield, been washed down river by the flood."

Daniel's head suddenly cleared. "You know about the flood? It was a flood? Was it the Dale Dyke that broke? Can you tell me what's been going on? I've been out of it most of the night. What's happened up the valley? What's happened to Damflask, do you know? Has anyone been killed?"

"Easy, easy son. I don't know much at all, I've never even heard of Damflask. All I know is that our lad came back home about six-o'clock this morning, he works on the railways, and he said there'd been an awful flood. All I know is there was water up to a man's chest down at the station, the Wicker Station, and me and the wife decided to come and take a look. That's all I know." Ralph hauled himself on to the cart and settled down next to his wife. He collected the reins and said: "Climb up in the wagon if you want a ride."

Daniel dragged himself painfully on to the rear of the cart, it was empty other than for damp clumps and strands of hay matted to the wood. He lay down, happy to be on his back again, and watched as a few clouds, no longer thick with rain, rolled past his vision.

"You alright there son?" Ralph called back from the front. "We'll be there within the hour."

"I'm alright thanks, I may just sleep for a while." Daniel closed his eyes and sank back into his oblivion, lost in an unconsciousness that came as a welcome relief.

"This is as far as we go." Ralph Jackson was leaning over the side of the wagon and shaking Daniel.

"Eh what?" Daniel woke up, disorientated once again.

"I said that we aren't going any further. We turning back, the wife can't take this anymore."

Daniel sat up and looked around. They were parked outside the Wicker Station and the devastation even here was appalling. There was mud and detritus everywhere; he could see upturned traps and gigs, household possessions scattered randomly and, incongruously, carcasses of animals and what could be dead bodies jammed up against shattered buildings and twisted street lamps, huge blocks of stone and building rubble strewn across the road. Daniel could see why Eileen Jackson wanted to go home. "Well thanks for the ride, I know where I am now." He watched as Ralph manoeuvred the cart around in the street and headed back to Rotherham and then Daniel turned towards the centre of town.

MATTHEW Blagdon's notes following path of flood back up from Sheffield:

Last victim of flood in Sheffield, Thomas Gill, on duty at Hornby's Brightside Lane chemical works: knocked into water by fence, screamed for help in water but no-one could get to him

Willey Street – resids escaped up on to roofs

Lady's Bridge arches piled high with trees, furniture etc, blocked up with debris forcing water up and over parapet of bridge; naked man seen clinging to gas-lamp died before could be reached

Blonk Street full of dead bodies and rubbish

Jonathan Turner floated up to ceiling in back room of house in Nursery Lane and drowned

Cast-iron footbridge washed away: furniture seller Mr Carr kept vigil all night to make sure no-one tried to cross bridge no longer there

Widow – Wallace? - trapped ground floor house in Cotton Mill Row; neighbour threw sheet out to pull old woman up through window but she was swept away inches from his grasp

Check story Cotton Mill Walk; two children found asleep top of cupboard on flooded ground floor of house – name Wells

Sheffield Workhouse Kelham Street under 4ft water, also came up thru sewers: one inmate, George, climbed to top of boiler to escape and sat whistling surrounded by rushing water; in hospital and lunatic wards beds floating around; male inmates rescue screaming sick women and children – smallpox, measles, venereal diseases etc – thru v deep water and saved many lives

John Eaton, Kelham Island, smashed against mill and killed trying to save his pig; Eaton's wife died trying to save him

Ball Street rescue; three men on way to work saved when lodger in Hallamshire Hotel tied cord to bedpost and dragged them thru window

Several people drowned in ground-floor rooms in Green Lane district: row of gas lamps picks out dead bodies floating in flood

Only one woman drowned as whole terrace wall ripped off Waterloo Houses, pet birds still singing in their cages

Horse washed over 8ft garden wall, found standing knee-deep in mud, alive, still in halter, Philadelphia

Must interview Policeman John Thorpe, hero, saved many Bacon Island residents

Family of James Sharman in Shuttle House 5 adults 3 child + 1 baby roused by Thorpe: fam trapped in house by iron security bar bolted across window, Sharman somehow found strength to pull out bar, baby thrown thru window to Thorpe + Walkers brothers (?); rest of fam pulled out thru window mid raging water

Baby found asleep in bedroom, candle still lit but five other people in house (Wright fam) drowned

Harvest Lane mother – Crump – found dead on bed, son dead on sofa

John Parkes, Orchard Lane, woke wife & children to rush out of house to escape what he thought was fire, he was washed round rooms in house then out thru window & survived, rest of fam drowned

Couple in Neepsend, she invalid, piled table and box on bed to get out of water, whole lot fell in but they were rescued

Boy climbed up inside chimney and survived, fam drowned, most of house destroyed, Parkwood Springs

Woman, Mrs Needham, holding child in her arms, already dead – Parkwood Spr

General:

Wicker Station under 4ft water so no trains in or out

Lots of mills, factories etc ruined, great loss of stock, plant, boilers, machinery, forges etc ripped from foundations

Lots of animals lost - pigs, horses, chickens, cows etc; lots of food stores lost

Sheffield Workhouse turned into temporary morgue for laying out bodies for identification

"What's that you've got?" asked John seeing his passenger leafing through a book and jotting down lots of words. Far from being welcome company the Telegraph bloke had been quiet the whole way.

"My notebook," said Blagdon. "I was making notes of all that happened starting from town and working my way back up the path of the flood but there's just too much, I've given up. I can't believe how many people have died tonight. In this day and age you just don't expect to witness people being killed on such a terrifying scale because of an engineering failure."

"Read it to me," said John. He remembered well enough trying to get out of the water to safety and he'd have had to be blind not to see the awful sights around him, mud piled high and ruination everywhere as he drove his dray out through Sheffield now that the flood had subsided, but he had fallen asleep innocently in the police station and wasn't sure what this man was talking about when he talked about 'people being killed on such a terrifying scale'. "Go on, read it to me."

Blagdon read out his jottings, very matter of fact but their contents were still too dreadful not to hit home. John sat there silently for a few minutes trying to take in the scale of what had happened through the shorthand of Blagdon's notes. Jesus Christ, he'd been luckier than he'd realised.

"Who told you all that stuff?"

"I've been out since the alarm was raised. People are always ready to talk practically non-stop when something like this happens, not that it happens very often, fortunately. I suppose it helps them, to talk, I mean. They need to, I suppose, it's a kind of release for them and for me, well, it gets me my story for the paper. I've never reported on such a major event before."

"You got all that from people in the street?"

"And from the police, where I found you. Only you were asleep when I got there or you'd have heard most of it yourself."

"So why did you ask me for a lift if you know so bloody much about it already?" asked John, not feeling that comfortable alongside someone admittedly there for some sort of professional curiosity value when he himself was on his way to see how his friends were coping.

"I want to see where the dam burst and see what's left in its wake up the valley. We'll be bringing out special editions today."

"Do you think it'll be as bad there as in Sheffield? Surely it can't be, there are fields and things up there for the water to spread out."

"Well obviously not enough," said Blagdon, "otherwise there wouldn't have been so much water rushing into Sheffield, would there. I would imagine it's not a pretty sight up there."

John flicked on the reins and clicked on the horse to get a move on. He had been worried when he heard that the dam had burst but surely it couldn't be as bad as this man threatened?

"Well if you doubt me just look around you," said Blagdon, sweeping his arm in an arc to take in the shattered landscape. John followed the man's arm with his eyes: he was beginning to feel very stupid and very anxious, he'd been so busy with his thoughts and following the road that he hadn't actually looked too much at the scene around him and, now that he did, he felt his pulse race and his face drain with fear and shame. They were just outside Hillsborough and had left the destruction of Sheffield behind them but the images meeting him here were every bit as horrific. It was a route he knew well: he had delivered to the pubs up this way for years and he knew the landmarks and the bends in the road like the palm of his own hand. Where were the whole rows of houses that had been there before? Where was the other half of Hawksley's rolling mill, the dry-stone walls, the lovely gardens? What had happened to the Old Blue Ball Inn, where John had never got on well with the landlord, Bill Cooper? And what about the Mason's Arms, where Will Pickering always kept a fine cellar? Where was the toll house and the toll collector, old Tom Winter, who used to sit outside the place morning, noon and night to make sure no-one got over Hillsborough Bridge without paying up. And where was the rest of the bridge?

THE streets of Sheffield were busier than normal even for a Saturday with thousands of people milling around trying to help, trying to find lost relatives and friends or just being there and trying to find out how on earth such a disaster could have befallen their town. The burst dam was the talk on everyone's lips but only gradually did the full horror of the situation dawn on them. They saw the devastated mud-raked ruins along the Don and they heard tales of death and survival and bodies recovered naked from the sludge; they wondered at the if-I-hadn'ts and the if-it-hadn't-been-fors; they peered into once-private homes now thrown open to public viewing through walls no longer there, tutting sympathically at the sight of the odd birdcage still dangling on its nail, at photographs miraculously still hanging up, at what colour people had painted their bedrooms. They had a nice clear day for their promenading although the smell could have been better. Between them wandered the homeless, the distraught, the utterly lost and the ghost-like bereaved.

Then people heard about the state of things further up river and they shook their heads and prayed at the news of whole villages no longer there and no-one left to bear witness to the events of the night. Some decided there and then to take a trip up river to see for themselves.

The rescue parties in the town had a heart-rendingly difficult job unearthing mangled people and what was left of them from the sludge and debris. One group of men cried as they came across the two halves of a young girl's body which had been severed right through its middle. Some faces were crushed beyond recognition, some were frozen into dreadful contortions, some still smiled that innocent smile of undisturbed sleep. Recovered remains were taken to the workhouse to be laid out for identification but there were so many collected that the rescuers had to start lying bodies and torsos and limbs in a small field not far from the river.

By noon, the number of dead was put at about two hundred and fifty.

"You want to check the workhouse pal. That's where they've got the dead 'uns, fucking bodies piled high, hundreds of the poor buggers."

Daniel had stopped the first man he had seen as he walked up Pond Street. "What, the workhouse at Kelham Island?"

"Yes, mate, that's where they are, what's left of 'em. You wanna brace yourself before you go in. It looks and smells terrible, not the sort of ending I'd want for my family, I can tell you. Best of luck to you if you're looking for someone. I don't envy you that."

"What do you know about the flood? What about up past Hillsborough?"

"There's nothing up past Hillsborough, pal, everything's been destroyed past there, there's no-one left, they're all killed."

"But their bodies wouldn't be in Sheffield Workhouse would they?"

"Washed down here by the water, they were, some of them without a stitch on 'em. No way to go, stripped of everything. Anyway, hope your lot have been spared, bye now, I'll keep my fingers crossed, you look as if you've already taken a bit of a battering yourself."

Daniel watched as the man walked away and disappeared into the crowd. There were a lot of people about but he felt utterly, totally alone, trying to take in what the stranger had just told him, trying not to believe the obvious. He wandered about aimlessly, refusing to face what might lay waiting for him in the workhouse, his lovely beautiful Elizabeth, the life taken from her. Out of his pocket he took the pendant, thinking of how simply happy he'd been just yesterday when he'd fashioned it at the wheel instead of doing his work: someone bumped into him – "Sorry pal" – and he had to scrabble on the ground to find the pendant as feet bustled and hurried past and threatened to kick it out of his grasp but he thrashed out at the mob of legs and managed to retrieve it. Everything suddenly seemed ridiculously irrelevant. He stood straight and determined that he had no alternative but to go to the workhouse to look for Elizabeth's body.

He headed up Nursery Street and on through the back alleys to Kelham Street. Even for a product of The Ponds it wasn't exactly a smart part of town. Sheffield Union Workhouse was an ugly, miserable-looking place at the best of times, an old cotton mill brought back into use to put a roof over the heads of some twelve hundred inmates, the poor, the bedraggled, the deranged and the sick of the town. It provided grim accommodation for the living and now it had taken in the dead.

The stinking bodies were laid out side by side on straw in rows, with narrow gaps between to allow both the bereaved and the gawkers to pass between. Daniel welled up with fear and disgust in equal measure as he entered the hall and grasped for the first time the extent of the carnage wrought by the broken dam. The victims were of all ages and of all degrees of wreckage: some bodies were complete, many had parts missing: some looked as if they were just asleep, others were hideously contorted; some already had name-tags tied around their necks. Visitors shuffled around respectfully, handkerchieves swaddled to their noses but this was no quiet scene; above the sound of shuffling feet were the sounds of sobs and moans and useless murmurings of comfort; occasionally screams of recognition perforated the general hum, signalling one of the volunteers on duty to rush over to attach yet one more identity tag.

Daniel forced himself to join the slow procession of viewers moving up and down the rows, heads bent, couples holding on to each other for support, trying not to wretch, eyes constantly peering from one unclaimed corpse to the next. Attempts had been made to clean the victims' faces but sometimes people had to bend closer for a proper look and a mist of flies would rise up disturbed in their probings. It was a disgusting, draining ordeal. The man in the street had been right, it was no way for any human being to end their days.

There was no sign of Elizabeth. Daniel thanked God and rushed out of the workhouse gasping for air and relief from the dreadful place. There was still a chance, he kept telling himself, still a chance. Perhaps he'd been seeing things when he thought he saw Willow Tree Cottage collapse, he might have got confused as he was so suddenly swallowed up by the flood. He set off for Damflask feeling better than he had since he'd come to on the river bank and not even the wails and destruction around him could destroy the one glimmer of hope he had been given.

THE sun was well up when Jimmy awoke but the grass was still damp with dew. He looked around in confusion until he remembered what had happened. Standing up he realised he still had three rabbits hanging from the inside of his jacket. He tore the carcasses out and dumped them into the bushes, suddenly they didn't seem to be important at all. He didn't understand what had happened. He was wet through, muddy and stinking; his body hurt all over and he'd lost his hat and somehow one of his shoes. He guessed that the hat was floating off somewhere and the flimsy material of his shoe had just fallen apart in the water. He limped on, feeling thorns and sharp stones cutting into the sole of his foot. He didn't know exactly where he was headed; he just needed to go there anyway.

Things had started out so well. A little after his Ma and Da had gone to bed, which was normally about ten-o'-clock, Jimmy had snuck out of the house to check on the traps he had set earlier in the day. After months of exploring, Jimmy had discovered that the best place to lay the snares was about a mile up the hill from the house. There was a smallholding there which grew vegetables for the markets in town. The rabbits loved the veggies and invariably a few were caught in the traps. The very first time he had come back triumphantly with a brace of rabbits he'd had one hell of a scolding from his mother and a beating from his father that he felt for a week. "Honest folk like us needn't resort to poaching, James, we can go to the stores and buy what we want there," his mother had said. Jimmy had felt more than a little aggrieved at that; he liked rabbit and reckoned the farmer would have appreciated his effort to reduce the number of pests on his land. Anyway poaching was what you did on rich people's land, that's why Robin Hood was made an outlaw. He didn't stop trapping though, it was too much fun. But the next time he went he had laid the rabbits out on the doorstep and, after denying all knowledge about where they came from, his mother had said: "It must have been cousin John who brought them up here for us, he knows we like a nice bit of rabbit." A delicious stew was the result and after that Jimmy simply left his catches outside the door. Since then his meals had improved enormously, mostly rabbit but also occasionally pigeon pie and even once roast pheasant. Jimmy suspected that his Ma knew that he was still catching the animals himself but, now that she had an alternative explanation, she was happy to enjoy the free meat.

Jimmy knew he'd never have another scolding from his Ma or another beating from his Da and there'd never be another delicious rabbit stew or any other kind of fancy meal. He stumbled on towards Hillsborough. Maybe it was God's way of punishing him for his poaching, maybe he had gone too far.

While Jimmy had been collecting the rabbits the previous night, he had heard an incredibly loud roaring sound, so noisy that he had taken shelter in the hollow of a tree fearing that the sound was something to do with him, possibly God sending a host of angels down to punish him, but the roar had eventually subsided and Jimmy found that he was unharmed. With the three rabbits secured inside his coat he had made his way home only to discover that the house wasn't a proper house any longer, it seemed to have collapsed in on itself; it was a rubble of stones surrounded by pooling water. He had waded into the water and then clambered into a gap where once had stood the front door. Inside it was so dark that Jimmy had to feel his way around with probing feet and flailing arms. He had found his parents that way; things kept bumping into him as they floated by in the lapping water and through touch he had encountered first his mother, cold and lifeless, and then his father, limp and dead. He had screamed then, from terror rather than grief, this seemed like a nightmare rather than any reality he could accept. Panicking he had torn himself away from the touch of the bodies and had splashed unseeing this way and that, bumping into things, knocking his shins, stubbing his toes and grazing his knees as he fumbled and stumbled and floundered his way out. Once outside again, he had found his way to the higher dry ground and then collapsed in a heap convinced that he had definitely angered God and this was definitely his punishment. He waited for the host of angels to return and carry him down to hell.

GABRIEL found there was no shortage of volunteers to ride over to Malin Bridge, quite the opposite. The storm of the previous night had given way to a clear, bright sky and, when news of the tragedy just the other side of the hills had spread around Bamford, whole families and groups of day-trippers were already packing their hampers to have a day out and take a look for themselves at the burst dam. Miss Elizabeth was mercifully still in a deep sleep, undisturbed by the general buzz of activity not yards from her bedroom window.

"I think it's disgusting," Kitty had said, peering out from behind her curtain. "Just look at them all, can't wait to enjoy other people's misfortune. May God have mercy on your souls," she shouted, unheard and ignored. "Thank God you're not joining the ghouls, Gabriel, you're best off out of it for the time being."

"Perhaps but I need to know what's happened to Mr and Mrs Shaw and the Lodge. I spent a good many happy years in their employ and I've a duty to find out for myself how things go with them."

He had eventually given in to her insistence that he rest for the day and had gone outside to find a rider. In the village square he found a young man, Billy Nightingale, who was just saddling up his horse to head across to Low Matlock for news of his brother who had started work at Broadhead's Wheel only three weeks earlier. "Our Mam told him not to go, she said it was dirty work and too dangerous and that he should stay here in his own village," said Billy, "but our Jim had an eye on Sheffield, he fancied moving to the town eventually and perhaps setting up in some business of his own, there's a laugh, our Jim with a business of his own."

"Have you been there before, to Low Matlock?" asked Gabriel.

"I been there a couple of times alright, with Jim."

"How about Malin Bridge, do you know Malin Bridge?"

"That's just up the river ain't it? Sure, I been there once, with Jim like," said Billy. "We went to a pub there, can't remember what it was called, a funny name, Cleggum or Creggum, sommat like that, not the usual sort of a name

119

for a pub I thought at the time. Boy we had a laugh that night, Jim and me. I'm thinking of going over there meself to join him, if Our Mam'll let me."

"Was it the Cleakum, by any chance?"

"Ay that's it, Cleakum, I told you it was a funny name. I bet that's where Jim is right now, having a few jars while the Master fixes up any damage to the wheel. Folks here are saying it was quite a flood they had last night."

"I think they might be right," said Gabriel, deciding not to spoil Billy's hopes with his own fears. "Would you do me a favour, Billy? I'm staying here with Kitty Scott, she's my sister, do you know her?"

"Ay I know Mrs Scott, a God-fearing woman, I'd say."

"She is that, Billy, she is that. Well I'm visiting with her for a few days but I work for a family in Malin Bridge and I wondered if you'd mind looking in on them for me, as you're going over there anyway, just to make sure everything's alright, you understand?"

"I'd be glad to if I can find them."

"Well their house is rather grand and it's just across from the Cleakum, you can't miss it, it's called Shaw Lodge."

"Shaw Lodge, eh, it does sound grand, a lodge, well. And who shall I say was asking after them? Mrs Scott's brother?"

"My name's Gabriel. I'll pay you for your trouble."

"Never mind about that," said Billy, "though something to buy a drink for Jim and meself wouldn't go unwelcome."

"Of course," said Gabriel, "here you are. Will you be back today?"

"That depends on our Jim, it could be tomorrow if he is off work. I'll call in at Mrs Scott's as soon as, let you know how everything is."

"Thank you, you're a good lad."

Billy swung up on to his horse and gathered up the reins. "It beats me why all these people are heading over there," he said, "they can't all have brothers working over there. Right, so I'm looking for Shaw Lodge, a grand house, Shaw Lodge. I'll remember that because I've an uncle named Shaw, lives over in Manchester. See you later, Mr Gabriel." He kicked on his horse and was gone.

Gabriel watched the young man thread his way between the bustling sightseers and then ride out of Bamford village, breaking into a gentle canter as he reached the hill road, the same one Gabriel had fled down not ten hours ago. The old man stood there watching awhile, not seeing, his mind full of images of the previous night, in particular the sight of Daniel washed suddenly away into… into what… into where… Gabriel felt some comfort in not knowing what had happened to the Shaws, not knowing meant there was still a chance they might have come through it all, whatever it all was. He had worked for Mrs Shaw's family before she got married to Mr Thomas and had easily been persuaded to accompany her to Malin Bridge and take up duties there with her new family and they had always treated him well. Then when Master David was born, a happy liveliness filled the house; he was a real boyish little lad, the sort of son any man would want, always playing at big adventure games and forever getting into scrapes as he sailed the seven seas along the Loxley or went mountaineering in the low-lying hills. Miss Elizabeth's arrival was the icing on the cake, a lovely little girl who was just as at home playing the lady as playing the tom-boy. And now, she might be the only one left. Gabriel silently made a promise to look after her for as long as was needed and then he made his way back to their refuge.

Kitty had already opened the door of the house. "Any luck?" she asked, wiping her hands in her wrap-around pinny.

"Yes, someone called Billy Nightingale. He's going over to find his brother, on his own, by horse."

"That'll be Jim Nightingale, the brother, he went there looking for work a few weeks ago but if you ask me it was the bright lights of Sheffield that beckoned. Still, they're neither of them bad lads, good family, the Nightingales, though the father gets drunk a bit too often, if you ask me. Come on in now and have some breakfast. When does he expect to get back?"

"He's not sure. He seems to think he'll be going out for a drink with Jim tonight. We'll have to wait and see." Gabriel looked directly at his sister through tearful eyes. She hugged him close for a moment before drawing away as if it was unseemly.

"I'm sure he'll call straight here with any news when he gets back," said Kitty. "Now, breakfast. While you eat I'll just check on that poor girl, see if she's still fast asleep." She put some bacon, eggs and sausages out for Gabriel and a good helping of bread and butter and then left the room, shut the door behind her and leaned on the doorpost: she had never known her brother to be so affected by anything before, she had always thought of him as a bit slow on the up-take, and she offered up a quick prayer for him and for his employers, who had obviously become like family to him.

IT was worse than anything John had imagined, even in his blackest thoughts. Malin Bridge had all but disappeared, at least the part he knew. John looked out on to an expanse of ruins, mud and loss, loss everywhere. Blagdon was busy off with his notebook again, foraging here and there, trying to discover the survivors among the many trippers so they could relate their personal tales of death and horror. John could only stand there and look. All the way up the valley he had tried to focus his mind on being positive, trying to convince himself that his friends would be alright on the simple principle that they were his friends. Some of those around him were in un-muddied clothes, obviously maudlin spectators up for the occasion from Sheffield and God knows where, others were dirty, desperate, slopping about in the mud trying desperately to find anyone who might even now be alive in the puddle. There were bodies, mostly half-naked, and limbs no longer attached to the owners who but a matter of hours ago had been full of life. There was the surreal mix of broken animals, furniture, nature and industry which had become only too familiar as he'd made his way up the valley. It was difficult to figure out exactly where he was, so much had disappeared; ironically it was only the river itself that gave any clues, that same river which had acted as a deathly flue down which the torrent had poured. Over there used to be the Stag Inn; up there used to be the Tricketts' farm, now all gone, where just a week ago happy, smiling people filled the beautiful garden celebrating and dancing and toasting to mark Daniel and Elizabeth's wedding; across there stood Shaw Lodge, now vanished without a trace but for a stubbled corner of stones marking what used to be the side of the house.

"Hey, come here," Blagdon shouted him. "You know your way round here, what's that place?"

John turned to see a defiant chimney stack still pointing skywards on the other side of the Loxley, the rest of the building robbed of most of its outer walls, the floors hanging down over the mud and filth and debris, no longer supported, the whole place defying any logic as to how the flood wrought so much damage and not more, not less. "I used to deliver there every Tuesday," said John, "that's the Cleakum pub."

"Come on, let's take a look."

Almost unconsciously John followed the reporter, picking his way through the sickening aftermath of the flood., glad of someone to take some sort of charge. They paddled across the Loxley – it would have been once again reduced to a gentle dancing stream but for the constant flow of cargo still bobbing down-river and the silt and soil and mud thickening its waters – and emerged in front of where Shaw Lodge used to be. John paused, still shocked by the complete waste of it all, and tried to work out in his head where the different rooms might have been. He had never been inside Shaw Lodge but there had been nothing unusual about the house and it was easy to imagine where the family might have sat in front of the fire reading, where Mrs Shaw might have made her husband a cup of tea or cooked his supper, where Daniel might have been received when he called on Elizabeth. All gone.

"Hey, looks as if there's an idiot girl survivor at the pub," whispered Blagdon. "Look at her, what's she doing? Let's find out who she is."

John couldn't move; there scrabbling through the rubble was Sally Bisby, surrounded by a group of onlookers. She was picking things up, throwing them away, giving them away, stowing them in her pocket, all the time shaking and concentrating on the task at hand in a frantic, distracted manner. The people gathered about at first seemed to be offering to help the poor girl, realising that she was sifting through what was left of her home and family, then John realised they were no more than gruesome souvenir hunters, stuffing their pockets with anything Sally discarded. Sure, they offered her money for their curios but she paid no attention. They gladly stowed away cups and saucers and anything else she didn't want.

"What the bloody hell are you lot doing?" screamed John as he weighed in towards the group ready to challenge anyone in his grief and confusion and concern about the Bisby girl. "Leave that stuff alone, get your bloody hands off that, you fucking bastards, fucking vermin."

"Hey gaffer we're only trying to help out," said one bloke reeling back from the unexpected onslaught. "You don't think this broken cup's actually worth the few shillings I've paid do you, or any of the other stuff? It's only a way of giving the lass a few bob."

"Just clear off anyway, bloody ghouls," said John.

The crowd dispersed amid much cussing of John and self-righteousness on the part of the trippers but Sally didn't notice, she was still on her knees in the mud trying to uncover any important relics that would link her to her family. "Only Hannah to go now," she mumbled, "only Hannah to go now."

"Do you know this girl?" asked Blagdon.

"Shut up," snarled John. "You're as bad as the rest of them." Then he bent down, put his hands under Sally's arms and gently coaxed her to stand. "Hello there Sally, it's John here, John Hukin, your Da's drayman, you remember me don't you? I used to deliver your Da's beer every Tuesday. Come on now, let's get you up and out of this mud."

"But I've still got to find a Hannah," said Sally, "I've found something for everyone else, though they all need a good wash, of course. I've found my Ma's sampler, my Da's pipe, one of our Tessie's gloves; I've managed to find Thomas's wooden horse and Hugh's spinning top but I haven't found a Hannah yet. I can't go until I find a Hannah, it wouldn't be right."

"Let me help you then," said John. "I'll fetch a stick so you don't have to kneel in the mud. I can poke it around and you tell me if you spot anything."

John tried methodically to shove the sludge around this way and that while Sally gazed intently at the saturated mess, her eyes fixed on every lump and clump and bit of thing that was unearthed and then submerged again. "Stop stop," she cried and sank on to her knees again to pull out a drowned doll. "That's it, now I've got my Hannah." She cradled the sodden doll in her arms before carefully opening her bag and cosseting it away inside with the rest of her treasures. "Hello John, will you take me home now?" she smiled and linked her arm into his. "I think I would like to go home now."

John fought to hold back his tears as he led the girl away. "I've got a good idea," he said, "how about a trip into Sheffield, you can come and see where I live."

Blagdon caught up with them as they waded back across the river. "What's the girl's name?" he asked.

"Never you bloody well mind," said John.

"Hello, I'm Sally Bisby and I live here at the Cleakum, though it's going to need a bit of a fix-up when Ma and Da come back," said Sally with a beaming grin on her face. "It's not usually so run-down looking is it John? John delivers my Da's beer you know, every Tuesday, from Neepsend Brewery, don't you John."

"Pleased to meet you Miss Sally Bisby," said Blagdon, scribbling it down in his little book. "Where are you off to John? Up the valley or back to Sheffield? I thought I'd go up to see Damflask, I'm told it's completely washed away. Coming?"

"Not right now, I've Sally to look after. Damflask is washed away did you say?"

"So I've been told. Houses, pubs, everything gone that was anywhere near the river. Honestly, some of these visitors have been out here for hours. I believe the sight up at the dam wall is quite something. Sure you don't want to come?"

"Thank you but I think I've seen enough."

BILLY Nightingale kept telling himself it was because he couldn't really remember the exact location of Jim's wheel that he couldn't find it now. He knew there was a big tree just where the short dirt-track led off from the riverside lane into the wheel yard but he couldn't find the damned tree. He put out of his mind the giant elms and oaks he'd already seen uprooted and left to rot in the mud, he refused to think about all the terrible sights he'd seen already today: he wasn't from around these parts but even he recognised that lots of bad things had happened and that places that were there before weren't there any longer. But Jim would be alright, nothing could have happened to his brother, not to Jim, Jim was a sharp tool, he wouldn't go and let himself get killed like these other poor buggers, he wouldn't get stuck inside some bloody workshop and wait to be drowned. Billy vaguely pictured a big tilt and forge near to where Jim worked. "There was something about that place, what was it?" he kept asking himself.

He let his horse walk at its own pace along the direction of the river, stepping carefully, as horses do instinctively, over the slimy cobbles and the rubble and the drifts of rubbish. The smell was sickening, sickly sweet, rotting and mouldering. A few yards down the lane Billy saw what he had been trying to recall, a huge water wheel, huge, that's why he'd noticed it before, it was huge. Now it looked even more huge, standing alone and looking disturbingly ridiculous, more like a huge mistake than a huge water wheel, propped up by an assortment of mismatched boulders and stones piled randomly against its flanks: the rest of the works had disappeared. So had the wheel nearby, so had the big old tree. "God, Jim, I don't think I like the look of this," Billy admitted to himself before shooing the very notion out of his head.

He nearly choked when he saw a hand protruding from the mud, its fingers clutched in a fist. In one awful rush of realisation he thought it could be his brother. He leapt off the horse and looked around frantically, too nervous to go and investigate by himself. He didn't want to find what he thought he might. "Help, help someone, there's a person buried here."

"Well get them out of there," shouted a voice, he didn't know whose, couldn't see anyone nearby. "We've got enough bodies down here to dig out." The voice seemed to be coming from down the riverbank, out of sight from where Billy was hovering helplessly.

"I don't know what to do," he yelled back.

"Just dig."

Billy turned back to the hand; he walked over to it, he hovered, he squatted down and he looked at the fingers, all clenched and wrinkled and puttied, dirt still encrusted down the nails forming a black-black arc across the top of lifeless wet-swelled flesh, a man's hand, a workman's hand, a dead hand.

"Jim, Jim," he cried out and set to pawing away at the mud and filth. His pants were warm and damp, he couldn't help it, he'd wet himself. Shame filled him, fear shook his body, his eyes wept. Gradually he clawed his way through the slime until the feel of sodden cloth met his touch, then the bulk of the body attached to the hand. It was impossible to tell anything from the clothes, they had been reduced to rags and strips of anonymous cloth. Billy paused, he would have to wipe the mud off the head, see the face underneath. He looked up, hoping someone might come to help after all; it shouldn't be left to him on his own to find his brother Jim. He pulled a handkerchief out of his pocket and almost reverently and with great tenderness he cleaned the dirt from the smothered face.

Billy let out a howl of disbelief and screamed his brother's name before crumpling to the ground, laughing through his hysteria and relief.

"What the bloody hell are you doing here?" A foot gently nudged him in the ribs. "Hey, Billy Nightingale, what are you doing here, I said? Why aren't you back at home with Our Mam? This is man's work here."

The two brothers stood for a long time hugging each other, almost dancing in a circle as they held on tightly, not wanting to let go. "Jim, I've shamed myself, I've wet my pants," said Billy, pulling away and hanging his head. "I saw this hand sticking up out of the mud and it's so close to where your wheel was and I was so scared because the wheel was gone and I thought the hand was you and I couldn't help it, it just happened."

"Never you mind about that, though I'm a bit disappointed in your lack of faith, Billy boy: you didn't really think your big brother was going to let some drop of water kill him off did you? Mind you, it was quite some drop. And now we've both of us got to help out here, there are a lot of bodies buried round about and it wouldn't be right to just leave them, that's what Our Mam would say, so come on. Don't worry about your pants, they'll soon be covered in a lot worse than your own piss."

"How come you escaped it all, Jim? I can't see anything left of Broadhead's."

"No, well, I wasn't in there at the time, silly. Don't tell Our Mam this but I was up the hill aways, with a young lass from the village."

"That's just like you, Jim, just like you." Billy couldn't help smiling, reassured that all was well in his world, with his brother up to his usual tricks with the girls. "Don't worry, I won't tell Our Mam."

"I tell you what though, Bill, we saw it all and I don't mind telling you it was some sight you never want to see. There was this, like, mountain of water, about a hundred feet high it was and moving faster than the fastest of horses can gallop and the noise it made was louder than the loudest thunder you can imagine. And the screams and shouts of all those poor people caught in it all, my God I never want to hear the like again. I stayed up the hill until it had passed and then came down to see what was left. We've been working all night searching for anyone who might have been trapped alive somewhere but

126

I'm afraid it's a hopeless job. What made you come over here? Did you hear what had happened?"

"Everyone in Bamford was talking about the dam bursting when I got up this morning so I came to make sure you were alright. I didn't expect to see so many people here."

"Yes, suddenly there are lots of visitors to the valley, all wanting to nose and have a look. People are even picking up bits of stuff out of the wreckage to take home as keepsakes. And do you know what, I may become famous: I was interviewed by a reporter from the Sheffield Telegraph. He was telling me that the flood carried on all the way down to Sheffield itself and on to Rotherham and a place called Doncaster. I believe Sheffield was pretty badly hit."

"You'd never expect it to get as far as Doncaster," said Billy. "Where is Doncaster?"

"Away to the east from here," said Jim, "now let's get to work."

"Okay, Jim. By the way, do you know anything about what's happened at Malin Bridge? There's a man staying with Mrs Scott, you know, her that lives in one of those cottages with the fancy gardens, Gabriel he said his name was, asked me to find out about a big house called Shaw Lodge, Shaw, like our uncle in Manchester, said it was opposite that pub you took me to, the Cleggum."

"The Cleakum, you mean, daft lad. I'm told most of Malin Bridge has gone but we'll go down later and take a look and if the pub's still there we'll have ourselves a drink."

"Sounds good to me," said Billy. "In fact this Gabriel bloke gave me the money to buy us both one if I checked up on Shaw Lodge for him."

"Then that's what we'll do. Why does he want to know about Shaw Lodge?"

"He said he worked there."

"Well let's hope he still has a job."

EVEN from a distance it was clear that the ruined landscape that had been Hillsborough had suffered a terrible fate. Jimmy could hardly believe his eyes. He began to suspect something serious had happened which had nothing to do with God punishing him for snaring a few rabbits. He came to Hillsborough Bridge or what was left of it – to Jimmy it looked like a strong puff of wind would blow down what was left of the thing – the walls and parapets which used to grace the bridge were missing and all sorts of things cluttered the road. There was tumbled masonry, animal carcasses, tree trunks, wardrobes and cupboards and other stuff which should have been in people's houses and not

127

lying scattered on a bridge. As he picked his way across he saw the body of an old man lying face down in the mud, his legs trapped under a large bookcase. The man was motionless and one arm was stretched out at an impossible angle, he was dead and Jimmy was thankful he couldn't see the corpse's face. Seeing the body discarded and alone reminded him of his Ma and Da and the way when he had first found them they had been so completely lifeless, so unlike the people his parents had been, more like bits of flotsam bobbing and boating where the water took them within the darkness of his destroyed home. It was as if their bodies had actually just been soft shells, like something to carry a person about in and when the person left all that remained was an empty container. Jimmy knew that the difference between a live and dead person was a soul. He remembered puzzling over that at Sunday School not knowing exactly what a soul was, now he finally understood: the soul of a person was the person. In a way Jimmy was kind of glad that at least he knew his Ma and Da were now in heaven and in a way it scared him so terrribly that he felt the tears start to come. He rubbed his face roughly, smearing the wetness away with a grubby sleeve, and carried on walking. The blood from his foot was flowing quite freely now, leaving a one-print smeared trail behind him but the pain helped to distract his thoughts and contain his panic. As he looked around he wondered if this was what the world had looked like after Noah's flood; he tried to recall the Bible stories but couldn't remember why God had sent the flood in the first place. He was sure it had been a punishment for something but was fairly sure it hadn't been for poaching.

Once on the other side of the river Jimmy didn't recognise the village. The road on his left, leading up the valley, was still there albeit gouged and torn up into a shoddy mess but so many of the buildings he expected to see were no longer standing. He had only headed for Hillsborough because it was nearby and his Dad had some friends who lived there but now it seemed like a pointless journey. There was nothing left of the place and Jimmy reckoned that whatever friends his Da had had were up in heaven too. Amid the ruins, struggling in the churned up ground, were people, some blank-eyed and aimlessly wandering, others sifting through piles of destruction, no-one paying any attention to anybody else.

Jimmy sat down on what looked like a part of a roof ridge and lifted his injured foot on to his knee. He couldn't tell how bad the cuts were because the sole was caked in mud and dirt. He knew he had to be strong, life had dealt him a shitty blow but it seemed like he'd have to look out for himself now. Anyway only sissies cried. Then the tears came in waves of wracking gulps; his Ma and Da were gone and he was alone, everyone dead and no-one there to be with him, no-one there to look after him. He knew he had to be strong but it was awfully hard when he was so scared. As he opened himself to all his grief and despair and hopelessness, some part of his mind was dimly aware that it was his birthday. He sobbed and sobbed.

"My God, lad, Jimmy? Jimmy?" John pulled up the horse and clambered down. "Jimmy you sight for sore eyes, come here lad."

The poor boy felt strong arms scoop him up and he gave in to the warm relief of being cradled by the care of another human being. Through the mist of his tears he recognised his Uncle John and no longer felt so alone. "They're dead, Uncle John, they're all dead, my Ma and Da have gone, their souls have gone to heaven. It wasn't because of me was it, Uncle John, it wasn't because God was punishing me for a stupid little bit of poaching that Ma told me was wrong?"

"Of course not, lad, the dam burst, that's what, nothing to do with your few rabbits. Now I want you to concentrate while I ask you a hard question: you are sure they're dead, aren't you, otherwise we'll all go back and take a look now, just to be certain?"

"I'm sure as sure, I found them myself, floating about in all the water. They were bumping into things and not moving."

"Alright then, Jimmy, you'd best come home with me til things get sorted, we can't have you stuck here on your own, can we, especially on your birthday. You see, Jimmy, despite all the terrible things that have happened I still remember it's your birthday and birthdays are birthdays, they're important. I can't say as you'll get that watch you were after, what with all that's gone on I haven't had time to do any shopping, but we'll see, later perhaps. First of all we'll get you back to my place and then tomorrow I'll see about sorting a proper burial for your Ma and Pa, they deserve for it to be done right."

"Will I be able to help, I want to help?" pleaded Jimmy. "I know their souls have gone, that's what it says in the Bible, that our bodies are just vessels, but I want to help bury their vessels, Uncle John."

"Well of course you can help, you don't think I could do such an important job on my own, do you? Up into the cart, then, and Stanley will take us all back to Bungay Street."

Sally had fallen asleep on the dray bed, exhausted but still clutching her bag of treasures. "Who's that?" Jimmy had never seen Sally before. "Is she your girlfriend?"

"No, she's the daughter of one of my old customers, rest their souls. You and she have got a lot in common, Jimmy, her folks were killed by the flood last night as well. Her name's Sally. She's got nowhere to go either, we're all a bit lost together, but at least we are together so don't you worry none. Why don't you have a sleep in the back and I'll wake you when we get there. Then we'll all sit down and talk about what's to be done. I expect you're quite hungry too, eh?"

"But I don't want no rabbit," said Jimmy. "I don't never want no rabbit ever again."

ELIZABETH was just coming round and, with eyes closed and a still-sleepy grin on her face, she stretched out her arm to find Daniel. He always slept on the left so, he said, that he could get out of bed early for work without disturbing her, knowing full well that she wouldn't dream of him going off to work without first sharing breakfast with him and perhaps walking with him almost as far as the wheel. She opened her eyes when she realised he wasn't there. She couldn't quite understand it: not only was there no Daniel beside her but she didn't even know where she was, certainly not in their bedroom at Willow Tree Cottage, nor in her old room at Shaw Lodge. She looked around but nothing seemed in any way familiar. "Daniel?" she called out, "are you there? Please stop fooling with me, where am I, where are we? Daniel?"

A hesitant knock on the door made her sit back relaxed into the pillows. Daniel must have kidnapped her away to some little hotel for a surprise late honeymoon after that silly row and that would be him at the door now bringing her some delicious breakfast in bed. "Come in," she sang, quickly arranging her hair. Even that was peculiar; her hair felt flat and matted to her scalp and she tried to tease it out with her fingers fearing to look too much of a mess first thing.

She needn't have worried, it wasn't Daniel at the door but a small, homely-looking woman whom she didn't recognise.

"Hello," said Elizabeth. "Is Daniel downstairs already?"

"Not right now," said Kitty.

"Perhaps he's getting washed then, is he? At least it will give me a bit of time to sort out my hair, I don't know what's happened to it."

"I'm afraid he's not getting washed either," said Kitty, seating herself down on the bed. "Do you not know where you are, do you not remember coming here?" asked Kitty.

"Not at all, I believe Daniel must have whisked me away on a late honeymoon and here I am, so ungrateful, lying late in bed."

"You're not on honeymoon, child, and Daniel's not here. There was a terrible terrible accident last night and your poor Daniel's gone, God rest his soul. And you yourself have had a bit of a fever: I thought it best to let you rest in bed, you were so worn out when Gabriel fetched you here in the early hours of the morning."

Elizabeth looked totally uncomprehending. "Gabriel? What's he got to do with… An accident, Daniel gone? I don't understand, what are you telling me? What accident? Daniel can't be gone, he loves me, we've only just got married."

Kitty took hold of Elizabeth's hand. "I'm sorry, you poor girl, but Daniel's dead, he was drowned last night in that terrible flood."

Elizabeth pulled her hand away. "What terrible flood? He was at work yesterday, that's all, I even saw him coming home on the other side of the river."

Her face set in distant concentration, motionless, drained, as she saw Daniel coming home on the other side of the river and then that sudden torrent of water that swept him away. A burning fear filled her eyes and all her features shrank against the memory. Elizabeth had woken back into the nightmare and met it with tears and heart-breaking, anguished crying.

Kitty cradled the girl in her arms, rocking to and fro to provide some comfort, no matter how seemingly useless. Gabriel crept in through the door but left quickly: he couldn't bear to see Miss Elizabeth so emptied and him not being able to do anything to help with her pain.

"I COULD do with a drink, Billy boy. I don't know what's worse about this situation we find ourselves in, the shocking sights we're seeing or the physical graft. But I've been at this rescue business for over twelve hours now and I need a break. How's about we head down to Malin Bridge, we can see to your bit of business and make sure all's well at the pub. What do you say?"

"I'd say that's not a bad idea at all, Jim. To be honest I'm finding all this very upsetting. I have to work really hard not to puke up over the bodies we're finding."

"I know, I know, I told you it was man's work. Now how are those trousers of yours? Fit for a quick one with mine host at the Cleakum?"

"Aw, I was trying to forget all about that," said Billy.

"Let me take a look at you. Turn around." Jim eyed the lad's breeches. "They'll do," he said, "no-one would ever know it wasn't all mud."

"You won't tell Our Mam, will you Jim?"

"I won't tell Our Mam about your little accident and you won't tell Our

Mam about me being up the hillside with a young lass. Agreed?"

"Agreed."

"Time to go, then."

The two brothers handed back their shovels to the rescue gang and explained that they had to go find someone at Malin Bridge. They were wished good luck and thanked for all their help. A churchman from Bradfield invited them to a remembrance service to be held the following day and they promised they'd try to be there.

"But not too hard," muttered Jim as they turned away. "Hey Billy, do you think that horse of yours can take the two of us? I'm actually feeling done in; these legs of mine have been carrying me around for long enough in one go."

"No problem, Jim, and I can always walk alongside if the horse gets fed up."

"Right you are. Malin Bridge, here we come."

It wasn't far and the scene was unchanging as they followed the path of the flood down to Loxley Bottom and on to Malin Bridge. Here even these two hard-bitten body-diggers were stopped in their tracks. They had seen workshops and wheels and forges and stuff destroyed, trees pulled up by the roots and boulders where they shouldn't naturally be but this was different, this was people's homes.

"My God, Billy," said Jim, "this isn't good, it's not good. I'd no idea it was going to be as bad as this. You just wouldn't think a bloody pile of water could rip through houses so much that there'd be no houses left. And just look at all these people. If the locals are dead who's this lot?"

"I bet they're like some of the people in Bamford, Jim. When I was leaving there were loads of them packing up to come over here to have a look. I tell you, I was glad to get away on my own on my horse."

"I suppose you can't blame them in a way," said Jim. "It's an awful thing to have happened alright, all those people dead and that, but it is a bit of excitement for the living I suppose, that's the way of things. What was the name of that house you have to look for?"

"Shaw Lodge, Shaw, same as our uncle in Manchester."

"Opposite the Cleakum, you said. Well I think that chimney stack over there is what's left of the Cleakum, if I've got my bearings right. We'd best ask someone where Shaw Lodge might have been."

Jim got down off the horse and tried to pick out who looked local and who didn't, not too difficult when you looked at the faces and the clothes. He found one likely character and called over. "Hey mate, any idea where I might find Shaw Lodge?"

"At the bottom of the river in Hillsborough, probably. You're standing where it used to be."

"Oh. Any idea if any of the folks inside survived?"

"I doubt it. I myself saw the house just before the flood hit. There was a light on and signs of someone moving about but then the whole place was just ripped up by the water and twirled around a few times before it just sort of fell apart and crashed into the water. I didn't see any sign of anything after that, nothing. No-one could have lived through it. Nothing has survived along this stretch of the river. I believe they're using the workhouse down in Sheffield as a sort of mortuary if you want to check."

"Thanks," said Jim. He turned to his brother: "Did you hear all that, Billy?"

"I did. I don't think Mr Gabriel's going to be too happy when I tell him. What shall we do now Jim?"

"I'm thinking that perhaps we should make our way home. I've nowhere left to work, we can't get a drink and I believe a good plate of Our Mam's stew would be just the ticket after the day we've had digging up corpses. I don't mind telling you, Billy, I think we've both seen more than our fair share of misery and death today."

"Right you are, Jim. We'll take turns on the horse, you can ride first."

THERE were things to be decided if the news was as bad as Gabriel suspected and Miss Elizabeth had become a widow and an orphan in the course of one tragic night. He felt sure that his sister would be only too willing to have the girl stay with her here in Bamford but it was his duty to work things out properly and try to figure what was best. It would take time for Miss Elizabeth herself to be able to think about the future let alone make plans so for now it was up to him. Of course he wouldn't know anything for sure until the Nightingale lad had come back but he wanted to at least have started to work things out in his head. That was something he was never very good at, working things out in his head, he knew that, and life had been so easy with the Shaw family all these years that he hadn't really had to sort even himself out in his head, he just got on with his job, driving the family around, going on errands and doing odd jobs here and there to keep himself busy meantimes, but things were different, suddenly unimaginably different.

The immediate problem might be how he could keep Miss Elizabeth away from Damflask and Malin Bridge. It would just be too heart-breaking for her yet he knew she could be quite a determined young lady and she might insist on going over there. He'd try to persuade her not to but probably end up agreeing to drive her. In a way he wanted to go himself, to pay his last respects.

In the longer term there was the matter of how Miss Elizabeth would manage financially. Even if she decided to stay in Bamford she would need some income and if she wanted to live elsewhere she would only more so. That raised the question of whether or not she would have to work but the very question made him shudder: what on earth job could such an innocent young lady do?

Gabriel sat there puffing on his pipe, staring into space and concentrating hard. Then he had it, of course, what an old fool he was in truth: there were all Mr Shaw's properties and investments, which must surely pass to Miss Elizabeth; even if some of the buildings had been lost there was the land he owned. That was it, the solution. When Miss Elizabeth felt up to it, he would drive her over to Sheffield to visit Mr Shaw's solicitor. Pleased with his success, the old man started tilting back and forth in his rocking chair feeling able to relax a little for the first time since he'd left the Barrel all those long hours ago.

"Hello Gabriel, are you asleep?"

"What, oh Miss Elizabeth, no I'm not, I was just sitting here going over things."

"I tiptoed in, I didn't want to disturb you."

"Don't be silly, child, come and sit down. Has Kitty been talking to you?"

Elizabeth clutched her hands in her lap, her fingers fidgeting and twisting constantly. "Yes," she said softly. Her reddened runny eyes flitted from one corner of the room to another, as if to look directly at the dear family friend would bring on yet more uncontrollable aching sobs. "Gabriel I don't know what to do, I don't know if I can cope."

"I know."

The two of them just sat there in silence, a bond of grief closing the distance between them.

"You're welcome to stay here as long as you like, for good if you like," said Gabriel.

"Thank you. Your sister's very kind, you're both very kind but I need to go home, I need to see where he died, I need to look out across the river as I did when I last saw him. I don't think I can do anything until I do that. Do you think you could take me, Gabriel?"

"Of course, Miss Elizabeth, but not today, you still need to rest and to be honest I could do with some myself, I'm not as young as I used to be. Anyway, Kitty won't let us out of that door until she says you're fit and

134

ready."

"I'll agree not today, Gabriel, but I must go tomorrow, I must, don't you see?"

NOTHING remained of Willow Tree Cottage. Daniel paced around the site where the cottage had stood. Other than the foundation trenches and the stones which had been embedded in, there was no trace of their home, their furniture, their efforts to make the place into a loving family cottage, no possessions, no signs that only a day ago this had been a home. His home, more than a place to live or stay, the thing Daniel had wanted more than anything since Nathan had left and his Dad had died. And he'd had it for a brief moment in time. He'd had the home and the wife (where are you Elizabeth?). He'd had the roaring fire to keep the cold at bay, the animals and even a sense of a new family, a new community, a feeling of belonging and a place in society. For one precious week he'd had all of it.

The one thing above all else he regretted right now was storming off in a temper the previous morning. The pendant seemed worthless if it was too late. Daniel knew that the last words he'd exchanged with Elizabeth were harsh and meaningless. He knew that his wife was dead, there was no way she could have survived the flood. He'd seen the destruction wrought on the valley as he made his way up to Damflask, his previous buoyancy diminishing minute by minute as he had encountered the scenes of loss. Shaw Lodge had been wiped out, his wheel was now only a memory, the pubs, the stores, the houses were gone. There had been survivors and Daniel had questioned them, regardless of their own misery, from Malin Bridge right up to Damflask, and no-one who knew her had seen Elizabeth since well before the flood. Most people had been too distracted or dismissive to pay any attention to Daniel at first but he had insisted in a way that they were more intimidated by him than lost in their personal grief. The Ibbotsons from the Barrel had said that Gabriel had left the pub a bit worse for wear but had said that he was going to drop in on Elizabeth at the cottage just minutes before the flood came and took the pub with it. Gabriel was dead and nobody had seen Elizabeth. She too must be dead.

The pain in his body was irrelevant now, everything that he cherished had been taken away. There was no Elizabeth, no home, no family, no work, no nothing. He had nothing to live for yet he was alive and couldn't, wouldn't change that. If there had been some remnant of Willow Tree he could take with him... but there was no trace, no trace at all. Daniel, with his hand

135

clutched tightly around the pendant, carried on up the valley. Sheffield had no ties left for him, they'd all been washed away.

IT was late when Billy and Jim Nightingale finally got back to Bamford and sat scoffing bowls of their Mam's cherished stew. The two of them were beat: it had been one long day, what with all the death and digging and the trek across the hills, and the simple pleasure of sitting at home at the kitchen table in front of a fire roaring in the range was the perfect antidote.

"I told you nothing good would come of going over there," Our Mam boasted to Jim as she bustled about as if welcoming home none less than the prodigal son himself. "You might have been killed and what for? For the sake of a load of silly dreams that turned into nowt but a few shillings a week. Well be thankful you learned your lesson without drowning in the learning."

"You know, Our Mam," said Jim, chewing on a gristly chunk of meat and picking it in and out of his mouth with his fingers to inspect his progress, "it's a good job Billy boy and me were over there. We dug up a lot of bodies today, we did, both of us, we did our bit. You wouldn't believe what it's like, all that mud and stench and bits of people everywhere buried in it and all along the river men and women scratching through the puddle trying to find stuff, and to think it's all just the other side of these hills here. Pour us some more cider, Billy, will you."

"Shall I call in to see that Mr Gabriel bloke tonight, what do you think, Jim?" asked Billy, passing his brother his top-up.

"You can stay home." Ma Nightingale spoke sharply, betraying her relief at having her two sons home safely.

"Well he's probably feeling quite anxious," said Jim. "Just imagine it, Our Mam, if Billy hadn't come straight back here tonight to tell you I was okay, you wouldn't have been able to sleep with the worry would you? I reckon it would only be proper to go and let him know how things are, or aren't, as is the case in this case. Billy could just pop around to tell him and I'll go with him to make sure he doesn't get delayed. How does that seem, Our Mam? We won't be long and it does only seem right and proper."

"Well finish your dinner first," she said, unable to argue with her son's fine sentiments.

"You don't think we're going to leave our stew, do you? Not bloody likely."

"Watch your language, Jim Nightingale, you're not too old for a clip."

"Sorry Our Mam," said Jim, all humble but peeking up at his younger brother and winking. "It's the stress of the day, that's what it is."

The two finished their meal, put their jackets on and pulled their boots back on at the door. Promising to pass on Ma Nightingale's best wishes, they headed off to Mrs Scott's cottage. It was quite nippy outside and quiet but for the sound of men strolling off to the pub and women shouting for them not to have too much when they got there. The buzz of excitement that had enervated Bamford that morning had subsided with the day-trippers long since cosied up back in their parlours relating tales of hideous deaths and doomed villages to those who'd stayed behind.

"I'm not looking forward to this, Jim," said Billy when they arrived at Mrs Scott's door. The light was still burning inside and suddenly he felt nervous. "I didn't reckon on passing on bad news, I didn't bargain for that."

"Leave it to me if you like, Billy. It might come better from me anyway, being older and that. I'll perhaps be able to put it across more delicately."

"That's what I thought but I didn't like to ask, after all it was me who took on the job."

"That's settled then," said Jim. "Come on, the sooner we get there, the sooner we'll get it over and done with. Gabriel, you said his name was, right?" He knocked on the door and waved as Mrs Scott peered out from behind the curtain to see who was there. The door was opened immediately. "Good evening, Mrs Scott, we've come to see Mr Gabriel, if it's not too late."

The two brothers were welcomed in out of the night air but it was a sombre scene that greeted them. Jim was surprised to see a beautiful young woman sitting on the sofa and there was a man, obviously this Gabriel bloke, as well as Mrs Scott, but the young woman looked very unhappy and there seemed no inclination on the part of anyone there to talk.

"Mr Gabriel, I take it," Jim said, holding out his hand. "I'm Jim, young Billy here's brother."

"Ay, pleased to meet you," said Gabriel. "I'm Kitty's brother and this young lady is Miss Elizabeth, a friend, you might say. Sit yourselves down and tell us, what news is there from Malin Bridge?"

"Not good, I'm afraid," said Jim, pulling out one of the chairs round the table. Billy just hovered, fiddling with his cap. "You don't mind me speaking on behalf of Billy here, do you, but he's found the whole business quite upsetting and I am that much more familiar with the place, being as how I've been working over at one of the wheels at Low Matlock." He noticed the Miss Elizabeth woman suddenly start to listen. "Yes, I was working at Broadhead's Wheel, just up from Malin Bridge."

"Did you know anyone at Shaw's Wheel?" asked Elizabeth. "Did you know Daniel Fletcher? Have you any news of him?"

"I'm sorry, Miss, but I didn't know the gentleman," said Jim. "I've only been there a few weeks and hadn't got to know anyone from any of the other workshops along the river, apart from perhaps seeing some of them in the pub sometimes."

"And what about Malin Bridge, lad, what news?" said Gabriel.

"There's not much left of Malin Bridge, I'm afraid, Mr Gabriel. Young Billy here said you had particularly inquired as to a place called Shaw Lodge, opposite the old Cleakum pub. Well the pub's gone now, there's only a chimney left standing, which is a bit peculiar looking, and another gentleman I spoke to told me that Shaw Lodge had met a similar end, he'd seen it go himself, I'm sorry to have to tell you."

"Who was that? Who told you that?" pleaded Elizabeth.

"I didn't think to get the gentleman's name, Miss, but he was local alright, a short man, not much hair, I think he would agree, and a bit on the round side."

"Shaw Lodge was where Miss Elizabeth's parents lived," said Gabriel. "What did the man say about Shaw Lodge? You say he saw it go himself?" asked Gabriel, trying to signal Jim with his eyes not to be too unfeeling with his words.

"He only said that he saw the house knocked down and broken up by the water before it all floated away," said Jim. "I don't think your Mam and Dad would have known too much about it, Miss, he said there wasn't a light on in the place so it would seem they were carried away in their sleep, which is some sort of a blessing in the circumstances."

"Is there anything left?" asked Elizabeth, tears beginning to trickle down her cheeks.

"I'm afraid not, Miss, just a pile of stones, that sort of stuff. We did ask the man if there was any chance that whoever was in the house could have escaped but he just shook his head. I'm only sorry I can't give you any happier news."

"And what about Damflask, did you go anywhere near there?"

"We came back that way, Mr Gabriel," said Billy, feeling a bit left out of all the important conversation going on and it had been his bit of business with Mr Gabriel after all. "I let Jim ride the horse 'cause he'd been digging up bodies and limbs and things for hours before I even got there and he was plum done in."

"Alright, Billy," interrupted Jim quickly before taking charge again. "There was an awful lot of mess and destruction at Damflask, sir, it looked as if it took the full slam of the flood. You'd hardly know there'd even been a village there not twenty-four hours earlier. The stone bridge across the river was gone, vanished without so much as a side-support remaining, swept away along with everything else anywhere near the river. A terrible desperate thing to see, Mr Gabriel, terrible."

"That'll be enough, now," said Kitty. "I'm sure you two will be needing to get home after your trying day and we need to be left to think on what you've told us. This poor girl needs some peace and quiet, she's had more bad news today than can be expected for anyone to take in a lifetime let alone in one day. Off you go and thank you for all your help."

"You're welcome," said Jim, getting to his feet and moving towards the door. In truth he was ready to leave, it was all too sombre for him here. "I'm sorry to be the one to bring such bad tidings. Goodnight, everyone, goodnight."

"Our Mam sends her regards, Mrs Scott," said Billy, "told me not to forget."

"Thank you, Billy, say hello to her for me."

The brothers headed back up the street. "Have you still got that money in your pocket?" asked Jim. "We never did get that drink. Let's get one in before we go home, we've bloody well earned it. You and your 'digging up bodies and limbs'. You'll go far you will, Billy Nightingale, far."

"As far as the pub will do right now, Jim."

***

Part Four

"Come here you stupid fucking bugger and jump to it when I call you." Jack Quinn sat polishing a ten-inch knife. "Look at that, best you can buy in Sheffield," he said, "we certainly know how to make knives, eh, Briggsy, and what to do with them, slit through your bleedin' throat like a hot knife through butter so watch it. Tell me you've got summat good for me today or I might just have to put that little boast of mine to the test and try out the quality of this here blade."

"No need for that, Jack, I've never let you down before and I'm not going to, so go easy on the threats."

"Don't you 'go easy' me, you grovelling pipsqueak, I'll decide if and when you let me down. So, what's what today? Have you found me that cash yet?" Quinn carried on polishing, routinely holding the knife up to catch the light and swishing it through the air, stabbing it left and right and all the while keeping his eyes firmly fixed on the miserable wretch before him. Mick Briggs squirmed under the scrutiny. He was cowardly by nature, stayed with Quinn through fear and for the status it gave him with men even more pathetic than himself. No-one with any sense messed with Quinn or any of his lot and Briggs was at least wised up enough to know he had nothing else going for him: he'd put up with any abuse from Jack Quinn knowing it meant he'd get none from any other quarter. "I asked you a fucking question, have you found that cash yet?" yelled Quinn.

"No, Jack, but I know how we can," said Briggs. "Mind if I sit down, while I tell you what I found out?"

"Go on then pipsqueak but watch you don't spit at me across the table, I can't stand it when people cover me in their spittle when they talk. So what's what today?"

Briggs wiped his hand across his mouth. "Well I've been watching Hukin's place, like you told me to, and I seen more activity there than usual these last

141

couple of days. There's a kid living with him now, a boy, seems he was his cousin's lad, lost all his family in the flood and now he's living with Hukin. I thought he might come in very useful. I seen him already pinching the odd thing here and there. Thought I might be able to put the frighteners on him, what d'you say, Jack?"

"I say it's always worth a bit of beachcombing after a flood tide," said Quinn. "You've not done too badly, Briggsy," he said, pointedly stowing the knife away in its sheath. "Got to look after your tools, remember that, Briggsy. Now, what do we know? We know that Hukin bottled Pickens and pinched his wad, we're not sure how much but Pickens reckoned it was about two-hundred, give or take. We know that Hukin then talked to that whore, Melanie, but he didn't go in to her place he went round the pubs; he'll never amount to much that one, even without my help. Then he went home, so it's likely he stashed the wad somewhere, perhaps at home, that's what you've got to find out, Briggsy. Use the lad, get to know him, earn his trust and then, when the time comes, put the screws on, he'll soon squeal. There might even be a small bonus in it for you if you deliver."

"There's more Jack, there's more. I haven't seen her myself but I understand Hukin also has a young woman living with him now, another one who lost everything in the flood."

"What a real charitable soul our Mr John Hukin is turning out to be," said Quinn. "You've excelled yourself, Briggsy, here, get yourself a couple of drinks on me, let's call it an early bonus, while I figure out how we can turn this young lady to our advantage. Now piss off."

"YOU'VE got really pretty hair, do you know that Sally? If I had a daughter I'd want her to have hair like yours. I did have a baby once, a boy, but he didn't live no more than a couple of days so I never got to know him, poor bleeder. John tells me you had lots of brothers and sisters, that must have been nice. I know they're all gone now but at least you had them for a time. You'll have to show me your treasures one of these days and you can tell me all about them."

Melanie was brushing Sally's hair in her little parlour, the room she kept private for herself and let none of her customers in, even her regulars. John had been in there a couple of times but he was different, he actually had the makings of a good man for all his brawling and boozing and he never treated her like the cheap whore she was, not like the rest of the buggers, a quick in-and-out, cash on delivery, buttons up and off. He had a way of understanding that folks do what they have to to survive in this world and she carried her means of survival around with her, under her skirts. It was typical of him that he'd take in a couple of strays. John had taken Sally round to Melanie's place to see if she had any clothes that would fit the poor kid and it had taken a bit of a search to find something not too big but then Sally had the healthy build of a country lass anyway.

"I'd like that," Sally said after several minutes.

"You'd like what, love?" Melanie had lost track of what had gone before. She'd been warned that Sally had gone a bit do-lally after seeing what had happened to her folks.

"To show you my treasures and tell you all about them," said Sally. "I've got lots of precious things and I keep them safe in my bag, in this bag."

"I wondered what you kept in there, you never let it out of your sight, do you girl? All in your own good time, I'm not one to pry. I know how important it is to have private things that no-one is allowed to see so you hold on to them til you're good and ready to show me. Have you ever thought of having your hair tied up on top?"

"My Mam always says I'm too young for that, she says it might make the men in the pub think I'm older than I am."

"Well she does have a point. How long have you known John then love?"

"John Hukin, you mean. He's a flirt, he always flirts when he delivers the beer to Da's pub and I always laugh at him for his lack of schooling, he's only a brewery man, you know. And he's only looking after me temporarily until the pub is fixed up and Mam and Da get better. I'm not quite sure what's happened to them or why they didn't take me with them but John tells me not to worry because he knows where they are and he's got everything arranged. What do you think of Jimmy? I think he's funny yet he looks sad most of the time and I'm not sure why. Do you know?"

"The poor lad's just lost his home," said Melanie, "he's John's nephew and he has nowhere else to go."

"Fancy not having anywhere else to go but to John Hukin's poky little room," said Sally and Melanie couldn't help it but she deliberately gave a little tug with the hairbrush. "Ouch." "Sorry love." "I have my own room at the pub but it's not as pretty as this one. I've only got a small bed and a cupboard but I do have a nice cover on the bed, covered in little flowers which Mam helped me to sew on.. The cover's made out of some green cloth so it looks like a beautiful garden growing all over the bed. But I couldn't find it and I really looked very hard." Sally went quiet. She hugged her bag close and started rocking to and fro. "I did, I looked really hard but there was just so much mud around and everything was so dirty and wet and I just couldn't find it anywhere. You've got lots of pretty things, Melanie. Can I ask you something?"

"Go ahead, love, ask me anything you like."

"Am I like Jimmy ?"

"What do you mean are you like Jimmy?"

Sally turned and faced Melanie with tears coursing down her cheeks. "Sometimes I think I've lost my home too but I just can't remember. All I remember is the mud and looking for my treasures but I'm not even sure why they are treasures."

"Oh you poor girl," said Melanie, gathering Sally in her arms. "Your folks are all gone, I'm afraid, they died in the flood. You were visiting people at the time so you weren't there, thank God. John found you and brought you home with him."

"All gone," said Sally but then she suddenly pulled out of Melanie's arms and the tears stopped and the vacant, far-away look returned to her face. "That can't be right," she said, "how could you possibly know, you don't even know me, you don't even know where I live. I tell you what, though, when the pub's fixed up again I'll get John Hukin to take you out on his dray for a visit. Would you like that, Melanie, you could come to tea and I could show you my garden bedspread?"

"I'd love to come, Sally, thank you very much for the invitation. I don't get invited out of Sheffield very often, never, in fact."

"Then it's settled. I think Sunday would be best, we'll have to see when John Hukin has a day off. The boys always enjoy seeing him anyway, so he could play with Thomas and Hugh out in the yard while he has a few beers and we could sit like grand ladies in the parlour having tea. I have a best friend too, Elizabeth, she's just got married but I'm sure she'd love to meet you. I'm sure Mam won't mind you visiting."

"I'm looking forward to it," said Melanie. "Meanwhile I'd better get you back to John's, he'll be back from work by now and we don't want him worrying where you are."

It wasn't far to John's place and Sally spent the short trip finding out exactly what Melanie would like for tea on her trip to Malin Bridge. They got to the house just as John was arriving home and Sally went inside.

"I don't want to alarm you, John, but see who's over there," said Melanie.

"Where, I can't see anyone?"

"There, leaning on the bridge. It's one of Jack Quinn's runners, his name's Mick Briggs. Watch yourself."

"Thanks, and thanks for looking after Sally. I'll see you tomorrow." John stared at the man across the street and then followed Sally into the house.

FROM the ruined village of Damflask, Daniel had walked up the valley and on to Howden Moors. In March, the exposed highlands were a miserable place; either low clouds caused dense fog or the unhindered wind churned up the lingering snow into drifting swirling white-outs. Daniel trudged onwards, oblivious to the weather, oblivious to his slowly saturating clothes and boots and oblivious to the battering and injuries he had taken. His mind was a turmoil of anger and grief while his body just seemed to get on with the job of transporting him further away from the place where he had lost everything. In the early hours of Sunday morning he had crossed the peaks and moors and reached the small town of Glossop. He found sanctuary in a farmer's barn for a few hours before leaving as dawn broke. Walking through the fog-shrouded town, he caused quite a stir amongst the few people who were up, a ghostly figure emerging out of the gloom. His face was gaunt and weathered, his shabby clothes hung shapelessly off his lank frame, his beard had grown back unkempt and straggly and although he was aware of the locals he didn't really see them. He guessed he must have looked like some kind of mad prophet coming in from the wilderness. Glossop, Daniel had known from reputation, wasn't the kind of place where a strange face was common, or particularly welcome, but he hadn't been too concerned; he knew he was caught in some kind of delirium again, chilled spasms shook his body from time to time and his progress through the town was dream-like and unreal.

Once out of Glossop, he had carried on vaguely in the direction of the town of Stockport, stumbling along a rutted path. After a couple of hours he sat down to rest, realising that his body had no more energy to carry him on. As the morning progressed, the sun burnt off the remains of the fog and, sheltered now from the wind and the cold, Daniel watched as the colours of the landscape grew more vibrant in the clearing air. He felt some warmth radiating back from the rocks where he was sat and lay back to fully appreciate it. His dizzy fugue had started to wear off and although still desperately in need of food he began to feel a little better.

After a while Daniel sat up and studied where the path he was following led to. It meandered downhill to the bottom of a valley where it met with a small brook. At the junction where the road met the stream, a small encampment of gypsies or tinkers had been made. There were four colourful wagons parked up. In the distance Daniel could see a figure feeding the horses, another drawing water and another tending a fire. Gypsies had a bad reputation, Daniel knew that, but then folk from The Ponds had a bad reputation too. He had met a few travellers in his time and he knew they had their own language, customs and peculiar moral code. He also knew they could be incredibly hospitable, friendly and generous when the mood took them. Or they could be hostile and violent. Hunger prompted Daniel to approach them. He knew he wouldn't be able to survive out in the open for much longer: he had no knowledge about trapping or making fire, he was a city boy, so he got up and made his way down.

The path was deceptively long and it took nearly an hour for Daniel to reach the camp. By then he was sweating and weak again on his legs. He leant against one of the wagons and waited until the woman tending the fire noticed him. She was young, about sixteen or seventeen, Daniel reckoned. She was dressed in typical Romany style: a colourful dress filled out by layers of petticoats, a knitted shawl around her shoulders, dark hair pulled back in to a headscarf and arms garlanded with plenty of flamboyant bracelets. She was engrossed in keeping the fire alive, building up kindling with larger sticks as and when she could. Once the blaze was built up to her satisfaction, the girl placed a metal frame over the flames with a pot hanging off it and only then looked up and noticed Daniel. She looked at him quizzically but without fear and then called out: "Davy, Davy, get your arse over here." She turned towards a figure washing in the stream who gave no sign that he had heard anything. Then the girl addressed Daniel: "Sorry, my father is as deaf as a post and a daft old bugger to boot. Let me go and fetch him."

Daniel simply nodded and watched as the girl gathered up her skirts and hurried down to the water. He watched as an animated conversation ensued between the girl and the bather with many over-dramatic gesticulations from both parties. Then he felt his legs slowly give way and without resistance he slowly sank down until he was resting against the wheels of the wagon.

Eventually the girl's father relented and followed her up to the camp. When he got within a few feet of Daniel, he said: "What've we got here? Surely you must have somewhere better to go than an old tinkers' camp?"

"I've nowhere to go at all. No-one to go to anymore."

The old gypsy, hands on hips, huffed and puffed while shaking his head. "Well there's no place for you here, we can't take you in, we're struggling enough as it is."

"If you have any charity, just a little food, I'll be on my way. I just need a little food." Daniel tried to stand up, he didn't want to look weak in front of this grizzled, gruff man. He struggled to his feet but then collapsed back

146

down.

"Father, can't you see this man's ill and in need of help. You know we can't turn him away. We need to get him into bed and get some broth down him." The girl shoved the old man towards Daniel.

"We can't look after every misbegotten we find, girl. We need to look after our own first and foremost."

"You just pick him up and lay him down in our wagon, otherwise I'll see what mother has to say about it." The girl stared at her father.

"Okay, okay, I'll sort it out." Grumbling, the man helped Daniel to his feet and led him up the steps into the wagon. "You'd best lie down, believe me when the wife and daughter have gotten through with you, you'll wish you'd never turned up here."

Daniel sank into the comfort of the bed and fell asleep at once.

Over the next two days, Daniel remained in bed. He was nursed by the girl and her mother but having finally succumbed to the fever he had been barely aware of the care. It was only on the Wednesday morning that he awoke with a clear head. With his eyes still closed, he felt a cool cloth being laid on his brow and then a murmur of conversation.

"Let the man sleep Lorrie, he'll be up when he's good and ready."

"I'm just cooling him down Mother, you know he's been burning up."

"The fever's gone girl, let him sleep and then we can think about building his strength up. Lord, but he's as skinny as a skeleton, what he needs now is some grub to get him going again and get some meat on those bones. Leave him be til he wakes up and then we'll think about getting him on his feet again."

"I'm awake now, Mam," Daniel said and pushed himself up so that he was sitting against the bed head. The covers had slipped down revealing his torso and Daniel was shocked to see how thin he was. He had never been overweight but the years of hard graft and constant exercise, along with starchy meals to sustain him, had given Daniel a good few slabs of muscle and fat over his body. That had all started to disappear. He prodded at the top rib which had been giving him problems and though it felt tender it no longer hurt; he guessed the rib had started to knit together. He pulled the bed sheets up to cover himself: "I am hungry though, if you have anything to spare I'll eat it."

The girl, Lorrie, had gone bright red at the sight of Daniel's bare chest. "There's rabbit in the pot, I'll go fetch some." She dashed out of the caravan, skirts flying.

"Don't worry 'bout her lad, I think she's got a bit of a fancy for you. She's only young. I'm Josie, young Lorrie's mother. You're welcome to stay as long as you like, you're needing some rest and some feeding up. But I will warn you, we're moving on this morning, so if you live around these parts you might want to get off before we've put too many miles behind us. If your home's not too far I can get one of the lads to fetch someone to pick you up." Without warning Josie pulled Daniel's head forward and plumped up the pillows. "There, that'll make you more comfy. Now rest awhile til Lorrie comes back with some food."

Daniel was still slightly dazed. "Thanks, Mam, thanks for everything." The woman left the caravan, closing the door behind her. For the first time Daniel took in his surroundings. With the door shut, the only light coming in was through the windows but as they were covered by heavy curtains the interior of the caravan appeared quite gloomy. He was lying on a narrow cot which was hinged to the wall. The other beds were folded upright but it was obvious the entire family normally slept in here. There was a large wooden chest in the middle of the floor which acted as a table as well as for storage. Everything else in the caravan was stowed on shelves which bordered the whole of the cabin. Daniel felt quite guilty; it was obvious he had intruded into these people's home and disrupted their normal course of life. He didn't know whose bed he had usurped for the few days of his fever but suspected it was probably Lorrie who'd had to find somewhere else to sleep.

The door opened and the girl came in carrying a bowl of steaming food. Daniel felt his stomach lurch with hunger at the aroma.

"Here you go; Mother says I've got to make sure you eat the lot so you can start getting your strength back." The girl passed Daniel the bowl and gave him a wooden spoon.

"Thanks very much, it smells delicious."

"Well I'd taste if before you decide on that. Our Ruth's been on cooking this week and she's been a little preoccupied since she got married, seems she's got other things on her mind at the moment."

Daniel tried the stew, it was scalding and the meat was tough and stringy but it was food and to Daniel it did taste delicious. He finished quickly, licking the inside of the bowl, and then leant back with a sigh as Lorrie took away the bowl and spoon. "Well that was perfect, just what I needed. You can tell your Ruth that as far as I'm concerned she makes a fine cook."

The girl giggled and said: "Well I'll tell her but she'll only think that you're teasing. Anyway, I'm a much better cook than Ruth, everyone says so, whether it be rabbit or chicken or fish or even pheasant, everyone says that you can't beat my food." Lorrie looked up at Daniel coyly as if about to say something else and then with a tut of irritation realised that he'd fallen back into a deep sleep. She got up and marched out of the caravan muttering Romany oaths under her breath.

THE carriage pulled up outside Church Street Chambers amid the bustle and clatter of Sheffield traffic and despite herself Elizabeth stared at the scene with interest as if she had never seen such busy activity and crowds of people before. It had been just over a week since the flood had taken away everything of importance from her and the hurry of town life proved an irresistible diversion after the reverent pace of Bamford. The town streets thronged with noise and life. There were bread sellers offering stale crusts to the poor for a half-penny a loaf: barrow-boys barked their wares of warm peas, mutton pies, kidney puddings, boiled meat, stews of unknown pedigree, hot potatoes. There were paperboys, labourers, shoe-blacks, match sellers, all manner of street traders and all vying for space with the horse-buses and carriages and delivery carts and shoppers and strollers just walking about aimlessly here and there. Elizabeth looked up at the Chambers, where she had an appointment with her father's attorney-at-law, a Mr Samuel Bickerstaff, a man whom she had never met. It was Gabriel who had suggested the trip for he had frequently driven Mr Shaw into town whenever his employer needed to consult with his legal adviser.

"Would you wish me to come in with you, Miss Elizabeth?" asked Gabriel.

"No, Gabriel, it's so busy out here you might be best looking after the carriage. If this Mr Bickerstaff is as old a friend of my father's as you say then I can't imagine I'll have any difficulties. I can't imagine I'll be too long."

"Then let me help you down and I'll give George a drink while you see to your business."

Church Street Chambers was a rather grand building, several storeys high, with a dressed-stone façade, large windows and an impressive if compact portico. The main door opened on to an imposing entrance hall where fixed to the lobby wall was a large board listing which office was where. Elizabeth had to climb two flights of stairs and pass along a couple of mosaic-floored corridors to the back of the building before she found the correct door, with 'Bickerstaff & Son' scrolled in faded gold lettering on the frosted window. A dull brass doorknob was the only other adornment. She knocked, turned the knob and entered. Sitting at a large table scattered with piles of papers, blotters and a pot of pens was a youngish man hard at work.

"I'm looking for Mr Bickerstaff," said Elizabeth. "I'm the daughter of

Thomas Shaw, late of Malin Bridge."

"Would that be Mr Samuel Bickerstaff, the senior partner, or Mr Simon Bickerstaff, the junior partner?"

"I believe it was Mr Samuel Bickerstaff who dealt with my father's business."

"Ah well now, Miss Shaw, Mr Samuel Bickerstaff is rather busy right now with another client and he won't be available for another quarter of an hour, perhaps a bit sooner but I can't promise," said the clerk. "Would you wish to wait or to call back later?

"I'll wait if I may," said Elizabeth, looking around for a waiting room.

"As you wish. I'm sure I can find you a chair."

The clerk disappeared through one of the three doors which led from the outer office and, after the sound of clattering and scraping and a few murmured groans, reappeared carrying a straight-backed chair.
"There you are Miss Shaw. It was 'Miss Shaw' wasn't it?"

"Yes, thank you." Elizabeth sat down and took in her surroundings. On two doors were written the names of the two respective partners, the senior and the junior, the third, unmarked and through which the chair had been delivered, was obviously a storeroom. Facing her was a cupboard stretching the full length of the wall, corner to corner, glass-fronted and containing rows of books and rows of files. Over the clerk's desk was a framed embroidered sampler declaring: "All Men are Equal before God and the Law." Above the entrance door hung a clock, showing the time to be three minutes past twelve. At half-past the hour Elizabeth requested that the clerk go down to the street to explain her delay to Gabriel. It was not until the clock hands had moved round to ten minutes past one that Mr Bickerstaff senior's door opened and two men emerged.

"So we have an understanding, do we Mister Bickerstaff? I trust I won't be needing to call on you again too soon, I hope."

"No no that won't be necessary, I'll see to everything immediately, no fear on that account."

"Well it's 'that account' I'm a bit concerned about, your account, in fact. However, we're both men of business and we both know how some matters of business can take time, we both know how these things work, but 'time and tide' as they say and I can't wait forever either. Good day to you Mister Bickerstaff."

"Yes indeed, good day to you Mr Quinn. Open the door for Mr Quinn, Booth." Mr Bickerstaff waited for the man to leave before pulling the handkerchief out of his breast pocket and mopping it across his forehead. He was in a bit of a sweat and somewhat flushed.

"Everything alright, Mr Bickerstaff?" asked the clerk.

"Fine, Booth, fine. Is that son of mine back yet?"

"Fraid not, Mr Bickerstaff, but there is a young lady here waiting to see yourself, Mr Samuel, a Miss Shaw, daughter of Thomas Shaw, late of Malin Bridge. She has been here for quite some time, I'm sorry to say. I wasn't expecting Mr Quinn's business to take quite so long or I'd have advised her to come back later."

"Oh I do apologise Miss Shaw, I didn't notice you sitting there, you must think me terribly rude."

"Not at all," said Elizabeth.

"Thomas Shaw's daughter, you say, the late Thomas Shaw, did I hear correctly?"

"My father and mother were killed in the flood."

"Quite, quite, terrible thing. Well come in to my office and we'll see what we can do for you. Booth, two cups of tea, please, I'm sure Miss Shaw would appreciate it after her long wait."

The scene inside Mr Bickerstaff senior's office verged on chaos. The room itself was in keeping with the solid style of the Chambers building but its accoutrements had seen better days and a session by a good housekeeper wouldn't have gone amiss in sorting out the mess and getting rid of some of the steadily accumulating dust. Tied bundles of paper leaned against each other in staggering columns around the walls, there was a stack of yellowing newspapers building up in one corner and the hearth looked as if it hadn't been swept of ashes and cinders in weeks. "The cleaner hasn't been too well lately, poor woman," said the senior partner on noticing Elizabeth taking in the general state of untidiness. "I told her to take a couple of days off, the least I could do, she's been with the firm for years. Now sit yourself down and tell me what I can do for you."

"I understand you have dealt with my father's affairs for a number of years, Mr Bickerstaff. I know he had several small industrial properties up the valley which he rented out and of course there was Shaw Lodge itself, plus, I believe, a number of other investments in various concerns within Sheffield itself. I'm not entirely sure of the total value of his assets but I find myself in the position of being his sole surviving child and, of course, I am now on my own and unfortunately in the situation of needing to provide for myself."

"First of all let me say how sorry I am to hear about your father, it must have been a terrible shock for you. And to lose your mother too, that is most unfortunate, Miss Shaw. I know this must be upsetting for you but I need to ask you, exactly how and when did they die?"

"I told you, last Friday, they were swept away in the flood."

"In the flood, you say, awful business, awful. And have their bodies been recovered and formally identified?"

"No, not yet. One of their neighbours saw the house get knocked down and carried off by the water. I've been in touch with the authorities but I have had no news yet as to their bodies being found. I understand that some were recovered as far as Doncaster and that…" Elizabeth's eyes filled with tears "… that some bodies were too badly broken to be recognisable to anyone."

"Where is that tea? Booth, Booth," shouted Bickerstaff, "hurry with that tea, would you."

"And I'm not Miss Shaw any longer," said Elizabeth quietly, looking away from the man's gaze as she tried to control her feelings. "I was married a week before the flood, I am now Mrs Fletcher."

"I see, I see, and where would Mr Fletcher be right now?"

"I'm afraid he was drowned also."

"Most unfortunate," said Bickerstaff, almost audibly sighing with relief. "And did Mr Fletcher hold any properties? I expect he was a man of means, was he?"

"Daniel was a grinder, Mr Bickerstaff, he had nothing."

Booth came in with two cups of tea, nothing more, nothing less.

"A most unfortunate business all round," said Bickerstaff. "Booth, find the papers for Mr Thomas Shaw, they're in the outer office." He took a small bowl of sugar and a teaspoon from a desk drawer. "One spoon or two?" he asked.

"None, thank you," said Elizabeth.

"Well, Miss Shaw, sorry, Mrs Fletcher, but my immediate feelings are that there is very little I can do for you right now, on two counts. Firstly, there is no absolute proof that your father and mother are in fact dead: a witness saw the house disappear but we have no evidence as yet that anyone was indeed in the building when it collapsed into the water. Secondly, you have an elder brother, I recall: in the event of proof as to the demise of your parents being forthcoming, then the estate would naturally pass to your brother."

"But he too is dead," said Elizabeth, unnerved at the coldness of the advice being issued from across the desk.

"The flood also?" asked Bickerstaff.

"No, he was feared killed in the Indian Mutiny six years ago." Elizabeth was beginning to wonder just how well this attorney-at-law had actually known her father: surely a friend would have remembered about David.

"I see, even more tricky for you, Mrs Fletcher. Let me see; I tell you what I'll do," he said. "I will make some official inquiries of my own as to the fate of your parents and where we stand legally. Obviously you are not the only such case where death as a result of the flood cannot be proven absolutely. So leave it with me and I'll be in touch."

"But what should I do meanwhile?" asked Elizabeth. "I have no means, no income: I can't rely on the charity of others for much longer."

"Give me a few days, just a few days, Mrs Fletcher. As you can imagine, we legal men are quite busy at the moment with people in similar circumstances to your own after last week's unfortunate occurrence but I'll get on to your case immediately you leave this office. Where can I get in touch?"

Elizabeth noted down Mrs Scott's address and made to leave.

"Here are Mr Thomas Shaw's papers, as requested, and a note from Mr Bickerstaff junior to say he has been delayed with an important client and shan't be returning to the office today," said Booth entering Bickerstaff senior's office.

"Not now, not now, Booth. Open the door for Mrs Fletcher." "Mrs Fletcher?" said Booth. "Whatever you say, Mr Bickerstaff."

Samuel Bickerstaff gave his clerk instructions that he wasn't to be disturbed for any matter whatsoever and locked himself in his office with Thomas Shaw's file. He ran his eyes over the pages, totting up this property and that investment, this income and that bank account, making quick mental calculations matched only by the quickening grin on his face. "Mr Quinn," he sneered out loud, "I do believe 'that account' is about to be settled once and for all."

JOHN Gunson had not had a proper night's sleep since the Dale Dyke dam had burst, reliving that earlier nightmare over and over this time driven on by that awful helpless moment when he could only stand and watch as the embankment gave way, releasing nearly seven hundred million gallons in a wall of water crashing down at twenty miles per hour on everyone and everything in its path. Writhing around deliriously in his bed, the engineer was frantically sending out messengers to try to outrun the flood with warnings to people down the valley; he was rushing round Low Bradfield where the flood had already demonstrated its devastating power, washing away the bridge, a corn mill and schoolhouse and its first known victim, the two-day-old Dawson child not even yet named. Gunson cried out in his sleep as he heard the screams of the victims pierce his dreams. He woke again soaked with sweat from his subconscious drowning along with the hundreds of others. He would then lie awake re-examining his own actions to see if he could have done anything more, if he had missed something crucial on his first inspections, if the design had been at fault: he had stayed out at Bradfield for the whole of the Friday night and witnessed for himself the water's terrifying aftermath as he returned to Sheffield and images of torn bodies floated even now before his wide-awake eyes while processions of survivors made their way steadily and accusingly across his bedroom walls. Then he would fall asleep and the whole programme would begin again. Emotionally the man was a wreck; physically his face had shrunken into shadowed hollows while lack of sleep and no appetite for food had taken its toll on his whole body. On Wednesday next week, he would have to give evidence before the inquest at the Town Hall.

THE Mayor of Sheffield, Thomas Jessop, had established a relief fund immediately after the disaster and twenty three thousand pounds poured in from around the country in a matter of days; the great and the good and those of more modest means put their hands in their pockets while hundreds of workmen donated a day's pay. Red tape was cut to allow assistance to be given to the victims of the tragedy as soon as possible to alleviate their sufferings and at least provide them with food and shelter and clothing. In what was generally referred to as his head office, Jack Quinn tried to work out how to get his share.

Quinn had a few bases in Sheffield, just to be on the safe side, but he favoured this one on Campo Lane, figured it offered an air of respectability, being opposite the parish church as it was and just down from the Blue Coat Boys Charity School - a worthy establishment for a neighbour – but at the same time it afforded him plenty of opportunities to clear off sharpish if the peelers got too close: to his left he could scarper past Hartshead and melt away among the maze of narrow lanes and alleyways between Campo Lane and the market; to his right he could leg it down to Hawley Croft and go to earth among its hundreds of back-to-backs and decrepit workshops, a real slum nest, notorious, not somewhere any policeman would be likely to give chase for long on his own.

"Draw me up a list of the dead and the dying," Quinn instructed Will Pickens. "I want to know who lost what and who's still alive to tell their tale, especially if any of them are our customers," he said.

"Aw boss, that'll take me ages," moaned Pickens, "and I'm still not a well man after that bottling by Hukin," he said feeling for the scar.

"That was your own bloody fault, you sniveller, and you're not much other bloody use to me right now so you might as well earn your keep by doing summat useful. Get Porter to help you, we need to get on with this as quick as we can. Check with the Town Hall, have a look at their lists, then make enquiries at the Relief Committee, pretend you're asking on behalf of a friend, whatever, find out how to go about making a claim."

Pickens stood there, still caressing his scar.

"You still here?" snarled Quinn. "Get on with it, go on, before I start thinking too much on all that money you cost me acquiring your pathetic little scar."

"I will boss, I was just wondering where I might find Porter."

"In the Ruben's Head. Hey, Pickens, that was funny that was," chuckled Quinn. "'Where might I find porter?' 'In the Ruben's Head, of course'." The joke was lost on Pickens. "You miserable wretch," said Quinn, put out but feeling smart. "Porter is in the Ruben's Head, Pickens, taking care of a bit of business. And don't stop for any other sort of porter while you're there or you'll get another bottle where you don't want it. Go on out of here, let's find out what's what today. And if you see Peggy tell her I want to see her, sharpish."

Quinn sat back in his chair smirking. The flood had brought him an unexpected opportunity to make a bit of extra, a bonus on the back of clearing the town of some unwanted scum, and a way to get Hukin and get his money back at the same time. "Spring is in the air," he muttered. "Time for feathers to fly and bees to sting." He put his well-shod feet up on the table and leaned back on the legs of his chair. Jack Quinn wasn't a big man but he was wiry and strong and with a manner that broached no argument and a mouth in a permanently pursed pinch. He favoured natty dressing, expensive, a style that communicated an image of able authority and success to his many minions: he liked to tell them why he favoured red braces, because, he said, the colour reminded him of what could happen to customers and gang members who got out of line. But he also had his working clothes, for when he was on the job himself and didn't want to mess up his fine wardrobe: when his runners saw him in those, they were always afraid of the implications; sometimes he wore them just to keep the peasants on their toes. He was a cold, ruthless man but shrewd enough to drop a few crumbs now and then to his nearest and fearest. That's where the flood fund could come in very useful, he could drop a few crumbs without even slicing into his own loaf. He took his feet down when he heard a knock on the door.

155

"Who's that?

"It's me, Peg."

"Come in Peggy," called Quinn. "Sit yourself down. So what's what today?"

"Hello, Jack. Pickens said you wanted to see me. Got a job for me?"

"I might do, Peggy, I might do at that, all depends. How well do you know The Ponds?"

"The Ponds? Not that well to be honest though I do know one of the whores down there, Melanie I think she calls herself, we used to work neighbouring pitches before she went down in the world and I came up. Why?"

"You never cease to amaze me, Peggy, you're always reaffirming my faith in you as one of the most valuable members of my team. Would you believe that it's the very whore called Melanie who I'm interested in?"

"Come on now, Jack, there's nothing she can do for you that I can't," said Peggy, curling her lower lip in disappointment. She took it as a slight on her professionalism that one of her best free customers might be looking elsewhere for a bit. "And she hasn't got the tits I've got, you've said yourself many times how you 'appreciate my upholstery', your words, Jack. What do you want the Melanie cow for when you've got me?"

"Peggy, Peggy, would I look elsewhere for your sort of services when you're the best there is at providing them? Course not. No, I want you to renew your acquaintance with your old friend in arms, that's all. One of my spies tells me she's helping look after a young country girl, seems the girl lost her family and everything in the flood. Shame, I know. Depending on what you can find out, I might just be in a position to help the poor girl, that's all, and there could be a bit of a bonus in it for you."

"Of course, Jack," said Peggy, pushing out her breasts with rediscovered confidence. "Shall I start today?"

"Sooner you do, Peggy, sooner we can all help each other out, so to speak. Off you go. I'll expect a visit from you later, perhaps take care of a bit of business, perhaps follow up with a bit of pleasure. Now tuck your tits in and get to work, there's my girl."

Peggy sauntered to the door, turned to give Quinn what she thought was a real sexy look, then went out.

"It gets better and better," he murmured. "This calls for a drink." He took a small flask of whisky out of his pocket and raised it high: "Here's to me, Jack Quinn, the man who never looked a gift whore in the mouth."

IT was becoming a bit of a problem trying to control Jimmy. Let loose in

156

the town streets, the lad was finding there were too many temptations for a practised poacher, even if the prey were people rather than rabbits: they all had their way of sitting up and begging to be taken, all you needed was a more subtle sort of trap and, in the current climate, there was nothing like the fate of a poor young waif orphaned in the flood to set the spring: the excuse had served him well on several occasions when he'd got caught with his hands in someone else's pocket. John was sick of reading him the riot act or reminding Jimmy of how his mother had taught him the difference between right and wrong. In truth the man had a measure of sympathy for the boy and a good memory of his own carryings-on when he and Daniel were children working the same streets. Still, he had taken on responsibility for Jimmy and, even though he'd not seen eye to eye with the boy's father, John was determined to at least try to keep the youngster out of trouble. He'd had a word with the gaffer at the brewery and there was a chance the lad could get a bit of a job there, otherwise John would just have to take Jimmy with him on his delivery rounds and pay him a few coppers from his own pay but he knew it was no long-term answer, after all, his own meagre pay was now having to stretch to keep three of them in food. He'd even had to stop drinking so much, couldn't afford it any more. Even his rounds had been reduced because of the pubs lost.

"I suppose you can't read this, can you, John Hukin," sneered Sally.

"What's that?" asked John, miles away trying to figure out how he could manage everything. They couldn't carry on for much longer all living in one dingy room and, while he didn't mind giving up his bed to Sally, it didn't make going to work any easier when he'd spent the night on the floor, several nights, every night since the flood. He was not long home from work now and could have done with a drink and a snooze but those days were over.

"The Bible, of course. What's the point in having a book you can't even read."

"That was my mother's, that's what the point is," said John.

"Was she a nice woman, your Mam?"

"She was, although she never had much chance to buy us nice things and stuff. She did what she could. She gave us a warm home where we were always made to feel special."

"You special?" laughed Sally. "You're just a drayman."

"That's right," said John, "I'm just a drayman who can't read. That's me alright."

For the first time ever some of the hurt in his voice filtered through to the girl. She had always thought it a kind of game, teasing him, something she always did; she had always laughed at John Hukin, the beer man, the ignorant bear of a man who insisted on winking at her while flirting with her Mam and humping barrels for her Da. She looked around his miserable room, with a mattress on the floor where he slept so that she could have his bed and a curtain strung up on a length of string so that she could have some privacy, and there in the corner a few rags padded up for the Jimmy boy to sleep, whoever he was. She still wasn't quite sure why she was here; sometimes she thought she knew it was because she had no-one else and nowhere else but she was never able to make any final connection. What she was at last beginning to recognise was that John Hukin, the drayman who couldn't read, was taking care of her until she could make that final connection. "I could teach you, if you'd like," she said. "I've never done it before but I could have a go."

"Teach me what exactly?"

"I could teach you how to read."

John looked up at George Bisby's girl and saw that for a change there was no arrogance behind her offer. "I'd always meant to get Daniel to teach me," he said. "He was always offering but we never seemed to find the time and then he met Elizabeth and that was that."

Sally jumped at the signal. "Well I could teach you instead, we could start today, now if you like. I don't know how easy it would be with the Bible, though, the language is very peculiar, not how we talk at all any more, but perhaps we could find a newspaper or another book."

"I'd appreciate that," said John. "I'll look out for a paper tomorrow. I might not be a very good pupil, mind, you could have your work cut out."

"Where do you think they are now?" asked Sally.

"Who's that?"

"Daniel and Elizabeth."

"Best not to think about that right now," said John. "You mustn't trouble yourself with thinking too much Miss Bisby until you're proper well again."

"Miss Bisby," repeated Sally, "Miss Bisby." She started to drift. "What frightens me is that I'm not really sure who Miss Bisby is; I know it's me but then I reach a stop. My name is Sally Bisby. It's stupid but I have to keep telling myself that over and over or I'm frightened I'll lose that too."

"Do you remember how you got here, Sally, do you know why you're here?"

"I think I know why but I don't want to remember because I think it's because of something horrible. I keep seeing things and not seeing things and I'm scared of what I don't see." She looked at John. "What is it I don't want

158

to see, can you tell me?"

John didn't know what to say.

"Melanie told me that my parents are dead and that you've been looking after me," said Sally. "Is that true? There must be some reason why I'm here."

"There was a terrible flood up the valley and your parents and the pub and lots of other people and their homes were washed away," said John. "I went to look for Daniel and Elizabeth and I found you and brought you home with me, to here."

"And did you find Daniel and Elizabeth?"

"No, their village was washed away as well," said John.

"And who's the boy, Jimmy?"

"His parents were killed too and their cottage ruined by the flood."

"So you took him in as well. None of us has anyone left," said Sally. "It must have been an awful flood to kill so many people and take away their homes."

"It was," said John and for the first time he felt his body giving in to grief, for the fate of his friends, for Jimmy, for this poor deranged girl, for all the publicans mean and otherwise he'd seen and known every week for all these years, for the poor sods who'd lived along the river and whom he'd had a drink with on many an occasion. He had put on the strong act, he had collected up his bereaved strays and got on with his work to look after them as best he could and he'd not allowed himself any time to mourn or dwell on his own losses. Now he shook with the sheer scale and sadness of it all and at last he was able to shed his tears.

"John Hukin, you're a fine man," said Sally. She got up and cradled him in her arms, this man she had ridiculed for no good reason other than her own ignorance and stupidity.

The door burst open. "Quick, hide me."

It was Jimmy, breathless and shivering with fear. He'd noticed that man loitering across the street and had studied his habits and pounced when he thought the moment was right. He'd been wrong and he'd been caught in the act.

John rushed out the door to see who was following the lad and why but there was no-one there.

"What have you been up to?" he grilled Jimmy when he got back into the room. "Haven't we got enough problems without you bringing more."

"He won't be bringing any more problems, Jimmy is going to go to school," announced Sally. With a hint of her old know-all self, she took charge of the situation and relieved John of any further pointless preaching to the boy.

159

"Jimmy, you can't carry on thieving and dodging and making trouble for your Uncle John, it's not fair, you have to start learning how to behave and how to make your way in the world honestly or you'll end up in the workhouse or prison or worse. One of these days you'll pick on the wrong person and that'll be the end of you. School, that's the answer."

"What, Sally? But I hate school," he said.

"Miss Sally to you," said John.

"Miss or no Miss, I've decided," said Sally. "John, what schools are there in Sheffield for orphaned children?"

This wasn't something John had ever had to consider but on thinking about it he had noticed a school down by the Paradise Inn, where he delivered every Wednesday. "Hang on," he said, "there is one, in Campo Lane, I think, near the Paradise."

"School don't sound like no paradise to me," said Jimmy.

"That's it, the Blue Coat Boys Charity School, that's what it's called I think," said John. "It's behind St Peter's, that big parish church."

"Then it's settled, I shall take him there tomorrow," said Sally.

TWO days after her visit to Sheffield, Elizabeth received a telegraph from Samuel Bickerstaff containing mixed news. He had been able to establish that red tape had been suspended and that, where lives were believed to have been lost in the flood, survivors of the victims were able to claim some immediate compensation from the relief fund toward the loss of their homes and possessions. On the matter of any inheritance due from the demise of Thomas Shaw, the situation was, noted Mr Bickerstaff, less clear. He suggested that she return to Sheffield without delay so that she could be on hand to claim any relief compensation due and pending his formal investigations into her father's estate. He offered her a temporary position in his employment plus accommodation in his own home: this would ensure, he wrote, that she would be in receipt of some income until her father's affairs had been settled. Elizabeth showed the telegraph to Gabriel and Kitty.

"What do you make of it?" she asked.

"I don't really understand these things," said Gabriel. "On the face of it, it would seem to make sense for you to be in Sheffield to make sure everything gets sorted out but I'm not sure about you taking on work there, it's not what your father would have wished and you know you're welcome to stay here with us."

"I know, Gabriel, and I thank you and Kitty for that but I can't keep living

160

off you both: you've already done so much for me, giving me a home, feeding me, buying me clothes. And my father's not here any more, circumstances have changed a great deal and I know he wouldn't expect me not to at least try to make my own way. He was a proud man and he wouldn't want to think that his daughter was content to live on the charity of his own driver."

"We'll have no talk of charity, young lady," said Kitty. "This isn't an alms house yet, thank God. You're here because your family meant so much to my brother here and they looked after him, God rest their souls, provided him with work and a nice home all these years, and hasn't he told me often enough that in his own silly way he sometimes used to think of you as his own grandchild."

"I know," said Elizabeth. "Gabriel was always like part of the family but don't you see I can't just stay here and wait while other people fix up my life for me. I owe it to Father too not to sit back and let all his hard work go for nothing. Don't forget he'd already started teaching me some of his business, taking me along with him when he went calling at some of his properties to collect the rents and keep an eye on the state of the buildings. He wanted to make sure that I understood how it all worked so that I'd know for the future. Unfortunately that future is now and if it means I have to work for someone else for a time well then that's no great hardship. There's no shame in working. My Daniel was a grinder."

"But this Bickerstaff doesn't even say what sort of a position he's offering you," argued Kitty.

"I'm sure it will be fine and proper," said Elizabeth. "After all, he knew Father for many years, didn't he Gabriel?"

"Long as I can remember, Miss Elizabeth."

"Anyway, I've never been afraid of getting my hands dirty. So, I shall go to Sheffield first thing tomorrow. I'll be able to claim some compensation and earn some money and then I can begin to repay you for all your kindness. As soon as my inheritance is settled, as I'm sure it will be soon, I'll find a new home and send for you Gabriel. You're my last link to my family now, I couldn't imagine not having you around."

"You're certainly your father's daughter," said Gabriel. "Let's hope none of it takes too long. What time would you wish to set off tomorrow?"

"Early; the sooner I get there, the sooner all this will be behind us."

"As you're intent on going, would you have room for another passenger?" asked Kitty. "I understand Jim Nightingale is off back to Sheffield too tomorrow looking for work. That young man can't settle here in Bamford whatever his Mam says, though between you and me I think it's what 'Our

161

Mam' says about staying that makes him want to go. Can't say as I blame
the lad, God love him, and he reckons there'll be lots of work going trying to
build up the workshops and everything all over again."

"Is he going back to Low Matlock?"

"I believe he wants to start in the town first, see what's going on there. He's
always been an ambitious type, always talking about starting his own business
but never really knowing what type of business that might be. But he's a
chancer, right enough. You never know, that might make up for his lack of
formal education."

"Perhaps when we're both settled we could both go back up the valley. I've
not said my goodbyes properly yet and I'd like to see what's left of Willow
Tree Cottage, touch the stones, maybe keep a small one that perhaps Daniel
might have touched. I've nothing else left of him."

"You've his love in your heart, child," said Kitty, "and that will always be
there, so help me God."

"Tell Jim he can have a lift, Kitty, as long as you don't let Mrs Nightingale
blame me for his leaving. It will be good to know someone in Sheffield other
than Mr Bickerstaff. I might even persuade Master Nightingale to take me to
The Ponds, see if I can find Daniel's friend, John, if he is still alive."

"I've a feeling Mrs Nightingale won't blame you at all," said Kitty. "She'll
be only too pleased to think he'll have some responsibility in the town other
than his usual drinking and flirting. A young lady for him to look out for will
please her no end. And I do believe young Jim is a bit soft on you anyway."

"Soft on me?" Elizabeth laughed spontaneously. "I can't imagine why you
would think such a thing."

"You take an old woman's word for it," said Kitty. "You've fair turned his
head."

"Then perhaps I'd better unturn it."

JOSIE'S face creased into a frown and her plump hand rubbed her chin.
"Well that's up to Father. You'd have to check with him about that. You're
welcome to travel with us until you're fit and steady on your feet but after
that I don't think it'd be right. We're travelling folk and you're not. We aren't
like other people and I don't think you're like us. I don't think Father would
tolerate a gadgie for too long, it's bad luck, see."

"Who's 'Father'? Your father?" Daniel asked, slightly confused.

"Good Lord no!" Josie's many chins shook and rolled as she laughed
in hysterics, her vast bosom shaking up and down restrained only by her

waistcoat. Eventually she calmed down "'Father' is my Davy, my man, father of Lorrie and Ruth. My man is chief here. What he says goes."

"Well get him in here," Daniel said, "I'd like to talk to your Davy."

"Get him in here? I can see you don't know much about our ways. If you want to talk to him you'll have to go to him. When you're fit and steady on your feet you can go and talk to him but I'll tell you now it won't do you much good. While you're in need of care, you're more than welcome to our hospitality but once you're fit…"

"Yes I know, fit and steady on my feet," Daniel concluded for her.

"That's right, fit and steady on your feet. It's just our way, you know?" The big woman shrugged apologetically. "We haven't been made welcome around your folk for too long to remember, it works both ways I suppose. Anyway wait until you're…" she paused and grinned "you know, and then we'll see." She left the caravan and shut the door.

Daniel felt like banging his head against the wall in frustration. All he had asked was to travel with the gypsies to the next major town they were destined for, offering to do his fair share of the work to earn his passage, and all he had got was this superstitious gypsy mumbo-jumbo in return. He lay back in the cot and realised he was being unfair. The gypsies did get a hard deal wherever they went, he'd been as guilty as anyone in his time, blaming them for any trouble which occurred. He also knew that, if he'd ended up in The Ponds in the state he had been in, he would have been left for dead. These people on the contrary had taken him in without asking any questions, cared for him, fed him and even given up one of their beds for him. He didn't really know why he had asked Josie anyway, other than that he didn't know what else to do. There was an attraction to staying with the camp: a ready-made community to replace the one he had lost. It would also mean putting off making any decisions about what to do and where to go. In the end, Daniel regretted having brought the subject up, it had been a sign of weakness and dependency and it had been a long time since Daniel had been weak or dependant on anyone. He decided that the next day he would get up, thank everyone and move on. He didn't know where he would be moving on to but it would be under his own steam and on his own.

Daniel dosed on and off throughout the afternoon. Lorrie brought him another plate of food early in the evening and once again she chatted aimlessly while he ate and once again the heavy meal sent him to sleep. He woke up when he heard Josie and Davy coming to bed later on. He could hear their hushed whispers and creaks of the hinges as they folded down their cots but he feigned sleep, not wanting to intrude further into their lives. However, the mere fact that they were having to whisper to each other within their own home made Daniel more resolved to get out of their way early the next morning.

He woke before dawn. Josie and Davy were still asleep so he climbed out of his cot and dressed as quietly as possible. Outside it was dark, with only a steel-grey glimmer to the east hinting of the morning to come. It was chilly and his breath plumed out in white puffs as if he had been smoking his pipe. He was aware of how stiff he felt and how three days' lying in a bed had left him wobbly and unsteady on his feet. After stretching and massaging his shoulders and arms he realised that what he needed was some exercise, something to get his body active once more. The campfire in the middle of the site was almost dead, a hint of red embers glowing beneath the ashes was all that was left. Spurred by the sight of an axe propped up against the wheel of one of the wagons, Daniel decided to go and fetch some wood and build the fire up. The axe was satisfyingly weighty as he hefted and swung it from side to side. There was a small thicket off to the right of the encampment which he headed towards, looking forward to using his muscles again.

Once Daniel had left the clearing, any hint of the forthcoming sunrise was lost. Darkness and silence surrounded him and he felt totally alone. He quite liked the experience, the darkness and silence, as if within this small clump of trees he could be apart from all the shit that had happened; within this noiseless solitude Daniel felt almost as if he didn't really exist, as if losing Elizabeth, the flood, everything hadn't really happened to him but to some other man outside of this enclosure. But he wasn't here for escape. As his eyes grew accustomed to the gloom he began to make out the shapes of the trees and picked a likely looking one for felling, relatively young and not too tall. He rested the axe against his leg and spat into his hands, then after a couple of experimental swings he hacked low down into the trunk. The impact of the blade digging into the wood sent shockwaves through his body and he relished it. He chopped expertly, down then up, creating a wedge shape on one side. He then attacked the other side of the tree getting into a rhythm and building up momentum. It wasn't long before the sweat was pouring from his face and soaking his clothes but for the first time in what seemed like ages he felt vigorous and alive. He swung the axe up and down until the tree was supported by just a slim column of wood, then he pushed against the trunk sending it crashing down to the woodland floor. He dragged the felled tree around so it was lying flat on the ground then, with one foot steadying the trunk, he carried on with his chopping, slicing the tree into manageable sized logs. By the time he had finished, pale sunlight was streaming through the trees. Daniel took a rest and watched as the shafts of light penetrating the canopy of leaves highlighted the rising clouds of vapour from the dew-drenched plants nearer to the ground. Exhausted yet exhilarated from his exertions, he let the axe drop.

"Looks like you've chopped enough wood for a month. What're you planning, a huge bonfire?"

Daniel jumped, not having heard anyone approach. Davy, the old gypsy, came ambling through the trees. "So how come you need so much wood?" The old man got out a pipe and a pouch of tobacco and offered some to Daniel. They both lit up and sat down on the ground. Daniel said: "Thanks, I've been longing for a good smoke for some time now. The wood's for you, just a gesture for all that you've done for me. I'll be moving on today but I thought you can always do with more fuel."

"Josie was saying that you might want to stick around for a while. What happened to that idea?"

"Well that was just me mumbling, I wasn't thinking. No, I'll be leaving today. I need to make a decision about what to do and where to go." Daniel stretched out his legs and took a pull on his pipe.

Davy pulled out a couple of apples from his pocket and passed one to Daniel. "Well to be honest it would have been difficult. I'm fine with you tagging along but it would be hard to convince the rest of them. They're a rum lot, our folk, very superstitious, don't take kindly to strangers being around for too long."

"I'm beginning to understand that, I'm just sorry that I said what I did to Josie in the first place. I never wanted to impose myself on you but I think that's just what I ended up doing." Daniel tapped out his pipe and stood up.

"You haven't caused any problems, Son, and rather than be a burden you've been a breath of fresh air around here. There's nothing more my Josie likes than to be looking after a patient, gives her a chance to boss somebody around, and you've managed to turn our young Lorrie's head as well. When you leave I've no doubt she'll be mooning around like a lovesick fool for the next few days. Now help me up, Son, my legs ain't what they used to be." Daniel pulled Davy to his feet. "Leave the wood here, I'll get one of the young 'uns to fetch it later."

The two men walked back to the camp which was slowly stirring into life; the fire had been built up and a woman was cracking eggs into a pan. There were some kids running around down near the river, splashing in the shallows, a few dogs were milling around amongst them, yapping excitedly.

"Ruth, get a plate of breakfast for Daniel here," Davy called out. "Anyone who leaves here leaves on a full stomach." Then he shouted down to the river: "Rob, there's a pile of logs over in those trees yonder, go fetch them and stack 'em up on the back of my wagon."

One of the boys looked up and yelled back: "Ah come on, I did the wood yesterday, it ain't my turn, get someone else to do it."

"Don't make me come down there boy, trust me you'll live to regret it. Now do what you're told and get moving." Davy sat down in front of the fire and beckoned Daniel to join him. "Make yourself comfortable and get some food inside you."

Both of them were given breakfasts of eggs, bread, fried potatoes and some kind of meat. Daniel scooped up a mouthful of food and spent some time chewing. "What kind of meat is it?" he whispered to Davy.

"Don't know, don't want to know. What you don't know won't hurt you. My advice is to eat it and keep your peace, last thing you want to do is upset Ruth, she's a dab hand at curses and from what I understand you've already had your fill of bad luck of late." As if to demonstrate Davy shovelled a huge spoonful into his mouth with noisy relish; Daniel did likewise and they both ate in silence for a while.

After breakfast, the old gypsy gestured to Daniel to follow him and they went into Davy's caravan and sat down on what had been Daniel's bed for the last few days. "I've had Josie make up a small parcel for you, nothing much, just some food, a wad of tobacco, a jug of ale, some flints, a knife and a bit of money. There's a stout stick for you as well, you never know when that might come in handy. We know you came to us with nothing and I'm guessing that terrible flood in Sheffield has something to do with that but like I said we won't let you leave on an empty stomach and we won't let you leave empty-handed. It's just our way, you came to us needing help and we won't let anyone say that our hospitality is second rate. On the same note, I think it would be best if you left quietly and without fuss. If our Lorrie knew you were leaving, things could get noisy. The women will be down at the river washing clothes by now, so if you're happy to go now, you go with all our blessings, except Lorrie's I'm sure."

"Aye. Thanks for all your help and pass on my gratitude to Josie and Lorrie." Daniel stood up and stuck the knife in his belt and tied the rest up the bundle then picked up the walking stick. He shook Davy's hand. "You take care of yourself and the others, they're a good bunch of folk." The two men left the caravan and walked up the hill behind the camp.

Davy sighed: "If only everyone thought we weren't the troublemakers we're made out to be, then life would be a lot simpler. There aren't many people who have a high opinion of us and we have our fair share of troubles because of that, that's why we keep ourselves to ourselves." They reached the brow of the hill and Davy stopped. "Still, I think you're a good man, Daniel, and I think things will turn out alright for you in the end. In the meantime look out for yourself, a lone traveller around these parts can cause suspicion and worse. If I were you I'd steer clear of the small villages, people tend to strike first and ask questions later. Now you best be on your way, stay safe." With that Davy turned and went back to the camp.

The air was fresh and clear, any early morning mist having been burnt off by an unseasonably warm sun. Daniel headed west, walking leisurely, with the parcel from the gypsies slung over one shoulder and his stick striking the path in time with his strides. He was feeling alright with himself, more at peace than he had been since the flood, light on his feet, more rested than he could remember: in the last three days he had probably spent more time in bed than he had since he was a baby. He tried not to think about Elizabeth but he couldn't help it. She had been too good for him and he had lost her after a stupid argument. He'd made the pendant to give her by way of apology and now that was all he had left. He fished in his pocket to have a look at it, as if lingering over the token would bring him closer to her, but it was gone. Desperately Daniel patted down all his other pockets, still no luck. He knew he had it when leaving Damflask. Those bloody gypsies, he thought, then immediately regretted it; he knew them and knew that they wouldn't have picked his pockets. Maybe it had fallen out when he had been chopping the wood or lying on the cot in the caravan. He turned around and headed back to the camp; one thing he wouldn't live without was Elizabeth's pendant.

A gunshot brought Daniel out of his daydreaming. He had reached the top of the hill and could see the smoke rising from the camp. The report had echoed around the valley but Daniel couldn't understand why anyone would fire a gun, he couldn't even remember seeing one in the camp. He scrambled down the hill and came to a stop behind Davy and Josie's wagon. A voice was raised in anger, not one of the gypsies, the tone was too prissy and pampered.

"...have it out of you or you'll all hang. Who's been poaching on my father's land? Speak up and I'll let the rest of you scum go."

Daniel heard Davy speak: "Look sir, I don't know what's been killed but we've got nothing to do with it. All we've had to eat here is rabbit what we've trapped. There's been no game we've had at all."

"There's no point in denying it, I know you gypsy bastards, you'll take whatever you want. But this time you're not getting away with it. Either you produce the culprit or I'll have the sheriff arrest the lot of you."

The gypsies had all been hemmed in down by the river by an arc of six men on horses, one of whom wielded a pistol, still smoking from the shot. None of the gypsies gave any sign of seeing Daniel as he stalked into the central camp behind the horses. The first thing the riders knew about his arrival was when he knocked one of them out of the saddle with his stick. The man collapsed unconscious on the ground. The other mounted men wheeled around.

"What the...? Bastard, I'll see you swing for that." The man with the gun reined his horse around and rode at Daniel. The gypsies moved forward. One of the horsemen pulled his pistol and fired into the crowd to keep them back. Someone fell to the ground. Davy signalled to his family to stop where they were.

The other riders turned their mounts as the leader spurred his horse on towards Daniel, who stood his ground as the man approached. "I don't know why you're here," he said, "but I can tell you that these people haven't been poaching. They're good folk and don't deserve this rough treatment. Just leave them alone and go back to whatever you normally waste your time with."

The rider belted his pistol and raised his crop. "I don't know who you are but I think a good whipping would sort out your incivility." He took a swipe at Daniel with the crop but Daniel parried it with his stick, then yanked the man out of the saddle with one swift pull on his coat. The rider struggled to get to his feet, fumbling for his gun, but Daniel grabbed him by the throat and knocked the pistol out of reach. He pulled the man up with one arm in a choking hold around the neck and lifted the rider off his feet. The man's face started to turn blue as he fought for breath, his legs flailing in desperation.

"The thing I don't get about you milksops is that they train you in how to use a sword and a gun but at the end of the day you're as weak as a girl and yellow as the fucking Dutch." Daniel flung the man on to the ground and let him lie there gasping and wheezing. He walked up to the other riders who were shifting uneasily in their saddles: the situation wasn't turning out the way they had expected.

"Why don't you get on your way now," Daniel said, "and take these mummy's boys with you, otherwise you might find your guns and whips aren't enough to deal with what could go down here."

The horsemen, all young and nervous, looked to each other for leadership but there was none. "We'll take Charles and Roger away," said one, "we don't want any trouble."

"Then you shouldn't have come looking for it," said Daniel, "shouldn't have barged into this camp and shot someone. I suggest you ask these people if you can go." He gestured towards the gypsies grouped around the lad who had been shot. Daniel didn't hear anyone behind him, he just felt the pain as something sliced against his head and face. Blinded from the blood now flowing freely down his face, he turned and dropped to one knee, at the same time pulling the knife from his belt.

Charles Devonish had recovered enough to creep up on Daniel and slash at the man's head with his sabre. Devonish was the son of a major landowner in the area: his father's wealth had allowed for schooling in how to duel with pistol or sword and even to wrestle in the classic Grecian style, while his status had allowed him to bully freely and without consequence; he thought no-one could best him in a fight. Seeing Daniel on his knees, Devonish raised his sword once more to finish the fellow off with a few savage blows. But he had never encountered true, desperate violence and never been in a real fight. He yelped as much in surprise as pain as he felt Daniel's knife slice across his ribs once and then again. He passed out with an agonised look on his face.

Daniel turned to the riders, trying to wipe the blood from his face: "This is the end of this as far as I'm concerned. Now you can either leave and take your friends with you or we can suffer the consequences of something happening that we'll all regret."

Then Davy spoke out. "He's right, none of us wanted this and I'll say again, we haven't been poaching. We can end this now or you can kill some more of us gypsies and we can kill all of you. In the end there'll always be more gypsies and we don't forget."

Daniel still couldn't see anything but he heard horses mill around before cantering off. Then there seemed to be silence. He struggled to clear away the blood but still couldn't see anything. "What's going on? Who's there?" He suddenly felt hands raise him up and he instinctively lashed out with the knife but didn't hit anything.

"Easy, easy son. We aren't the enemy, calm down and let us have a look at that wound."

Daniel recognised Davy's voice and let the knife fall. "I can't see, that fool's blinded me."

"It's just the blood, he caught you with a good one, that posh fucker." Davy helped Daniel up and led him back to the camp. Daniel allowed himself to be lowered to the ground. He could feel the heat from the fire and a wet cloth being laid over his face.

"He's alive but there's a lot of blood, poor bugger," Davy said bitterly. "Ruth," he shouted, "come and clean Dan up."

"What about that man I knifed? I've landed you right in the shit haven't I?"

169

Daniel felt someone wiping away the blood.

"That's alright son, we can disappear if need be, we've done it before. The main thing is that you'll have to disappear with us."

Once the blood had been cleaned off, Ruth had a good look at the cut across Daniel's head. "I think you'll be okay. He got you round the side, over one eye and across the forehead," she said, tracing the slash with her finger, "but I think it'd be best if Mam had a look at it."

"Help him back into the wagon, girl. We'd best get the hell out of here."

MATTHEW Blagdon wasn't particularly looking forward to covering the reconvened inquest at the Town Hall for the Telegraph, all that detailed evidence to sit through and sift through about rock types and underground springs and whether the dam embankment was built properly and in the right place or not. It would be interesting to hear what the government inspector had to say, of course, that Robert Rawlinson chap, but the real meat of the story would be the verdict and who would get the blame for the collapse, somebody was bound to and not necessarily the right person. Still, all he had to do was report the matter.

What Blagdon really wanted was a good follow-up story, a survivor, one who had lost everything in the flood and whose story would touch the hearts of his readers and his editor. And he might have just the person, if he could find her, for stories about women suddenly left destitute, especially quite young women, always had more appeal than tales about young men, whom everyone expected to manage regardless of how tragic their circumstances. He flicked through his notebook and found the page he wanted: "Sally Bisby, that was her name. What does it say here?" He squinted to try to make out his scribbles. "That was it, gone a bit mad in the head after losing her whole family at their pub, what was it? The Cleakum. I remember now, just the chimneystack left. She was looking for souvenirs in the mud. That'd make a good picture for our artist. And what was that fellow's name with the dray, worked at Neepsend Brewery, I seem to remember?" Another flick through his notes produced the answer. "John Hukin, of course, grizzly sort of a man but quite caring, as I recall. Well, Miss Bisby and Mr Hukin, the search is on. I'm going to make you both famous."

THINGS were moving along nicely for Jack Quinn. Pickens had gotten his finger out and there wasn't much worth knowing about the Relief Committee that he and Porter hadn't reported back. So much so that Quinn already had his team filling out bogus claims for demolished houses, vanished workshops, household goods washed away, groceries and livestock all gone, lost workmen's tools – definitely worth a few claims, after all no-one wanted to see a working man without the means left to work, couldn't risk letting their comfortable employers suffer because of a minor mishap like a flood – and then there were those of his customers who owed him a bob or two and now seemed the ideal time to collect. "Yes, Jack my lad," he said, "things are moving along nicely. Jack is positively springing out of the box ready to deliver a few surprises or rather collect a few."

"What are you talking about, Jack?" asked Peggy.

"Don't you ever ask me what I'm talking about, woman," he growled. "If I'm talking something I want you to know then I'll tell you. Otherwise keep your mouth shut and your ears closed, understand?"

"Of course, Jack, I didn't mean no harm."

"Course you didn't, Peg, course you didn't. I've just got too much on my mind. So, what's what today?"

"Well I went to see the Melanie whore, like you asked. She was a bit funny at first, obviously, after not seeing me for so long, but I'd made out as if I'd bumped into her by accident, casually, like, and we went back to her place and soon got to talking about old times and about this and that."

"Never mind the this and that, get to the other," said Quinn. "What about the country girl? Who is she?"

"Her name's Sally, she called in to Mel's while I was there, nice kid, a bit dotty though, seems her family ran a pub out at Malin Bridge that was washed away while she was off visiting relatives. She's staying with John Hukin."

"She is indeed." Quinn rubbed his hands together. "Staying with John Hukin and lost all her folks. It just gets better; today it just keeps on getting better."

"There's a lad there with them too, a nephew of Hukin's, goes by the name of Jimmy, but I didn't see him."

"I've told you before, Peggy, you're a wonder. Now make us both a nice cup of tea and perhaps I'll find something a bit stronger to spice it up a bit."

Peggy went over to the sink in the corner of the room and filled the kettle. She always liked it when she'd done well for Jack because otherwise he could be such a bastard. She was never sure what she really thought of him but she knew which side her bread was buttered: Peggy had been a no-hope street tart when she'd been picked up by Quinn, one of the town's most feared gang bosses but at least he'd given her a regular living, a proper place to live and protection on the streets. She didn't love him, not at all, but she did have a bit of feeling for him, after all, she knew him when he was stark naked, when he was breathless and excited by their love-making and all his defences were down: okay sometimes afterwards he'd smack her about a bit but he never really hurt her and she always smiled to herself then anyway because his willy looked so silly and floppy while he was hitting her.

"My God, come here quick, Jack," she said. "Just look out there, talk about coincidence. That's her, that's the girl."

Quinn rushed over to the window and gazed down on Campo Lane. It was busy. "Which one you stupid cunt? There's loads of girls down there."

"That one, her, her," said Peggy pointing through the glass. "Her with long dark hair, with the little boy. I bet that's the Jimmy kid."

"The one in the blue skirts?"

"That's her, I'd swear to it."

"My, she's not in bad shape, a real country lass, ripe for the picking."

"That's not what you're after her for is it Jack? I thought you had her figured for a claim."

"She's well enough figured to claim my attention. However, Peggy, business is business. Where do you think they're off to?"

"Looks like they're going in to that school place. Perhaps they're trying to get the kid in there."

"Better and better." Quinn stood looking out of the window long enough to make sure that Sally and the boy were indeed going into the Blue Coat School. "Hold the tea, Peggy, one more little job for you to do and then you can get your tits back here. I want you to go down and hang around until they come out of the school, then I want you to make yourself known to the two of them, the girl will be okay because she's seen you at the Melanie place, and just get friendly like, find out what's what and make sure you introduce yourself to the kid. Off you go."

Peggy clonked down the stairs from head office muttering to herself about how she was supposed to be a fucking whore not a bleedin' spy. That tickled her: "A fucking whore? Well what else would a whore do." She laughed as she made her way slowly down Campo Lane, not sure whether or not Quinn would be watching her just to see how she performed, she wouldn't put it past him. She decided not to cross the road just yet, just to make him have to crane his neck if he was watching. She sauntered up and down, looking in shop windows, then staying on the same side of the street she turned around and strolled back again as far as the Paradise Inn. Then she crossed over and strolled back along the railings of the Parish Church. She pretended to have caught her boot in the hem of her skirt and snuck a glance up at Quinn's window: she was right, the bugger was watching her, so she straightened up, stuck out her chest and gave a girlish little wave up to the window without actually looking over. "Silly bugger, Quinn." She liked to make comments about him when he was out of earshot; she'd nearly been caught a few times but that only added to the fun. Next time she managed to glance up at the office he'd gone. She was so busy with her little game that she almost missed the girl and boy coming out of the Blue Coat and had to hurry along to catch up. As if she was just passing by, she managed to knock into the kid.

"Hey missus watch where you're going," snapped Jimmy, none too happy that the stupid school had agreed to take him in.

"Jimmy, that's enough," said Sally and she was about to apologise to the woman when she recognised her as Melanie's friend. "Hello, remember me? We met at Melanie's, over in The Ponds?"

"Did we?" said Peggy, pretending to study the girl's face. "You do look a little familiar. Yes, I remember now, Sally, isn't it? You popped in to Melanie's when I was visiting last week. We go way back, Melanie and me, too far really, I don't know where time goes any more."

"Yesterday, we met yesterday."

"Was it only yesterday? Goodness, see what I mean, I am hopeless."

"Come on," said Jimmy, "let's go home."

Sally ignored him. "I'm sorry but I don't remember your name."

"I'm Peggy. And who's this little scamp who gets so cross with people?"

"This is Jimmy. We've just managed to get him a place in the school here, he starts next week."

"Won't that be nice," Peggy said. "I bet you're looking forward to that, Jimmy, a bit of schooling's no bad thing. One of my regrets that, I never got to go to school."

"Well you can go instead of me," he said. "I don't want to go to no school and I don't want to wear no stupid school uniform neither."

"It's a very smart uniform," said Sally. "You're just annoyed because you'd rather carry on roaming the streets."

"There can be plenty of fun in that, Jimmy, I'd agree with you there," said Peggy. "I bet you're good at dodging about, are you, getting into lots of mischief?"

"I only play," said Jimmy. "I don't get into no mischief."

"Course not," said Peggy. "Best of luck then. Perhaps I'll bump into you again soon, Jimmy, when you start school. I'd best be off now, bye, Sally, and best of luck to you too trying to get him to school. Cheerio to you both. Say hello to Melanie for me."

Peggy crossed back over Campo Lane and disappeared round the corner at Hartshead without looking back. She hurried round the block and went back to head office with her information.

NOW that she was back in Sheffield, Elizabeth wasn't feeling quite so determined, too many awful things had happened which she could scarcely cope with and yet here she was deliberately choosing to leave the comfort of Bamford to live instead with a family whom she didn't even know and to do a job - she didn't even know what job. She had asked Gabriel to set her down a few minutes' walk from Bickerstaff's office; to part with her old friend there, however temporary, would have seemed too final somehow.

"Is this the place, Church Street Chambers? Looks quite the grand place," said Jim Nightingale. Elizabeth was glad of his company. He had chattered away during their ride across the hills, pointing out different sights to her, telling her the names of the hills and the streams, what his plans were, where he would start looking for work, and he had escorted her to Church Street so that he'd know where she was. Kitty and his mother had insisted, he told her.

"Yes, this is it. It's not quite so grand inside, believe me." She stood there, not moving, Jim waiting patiently holding on to her travel bag. "You know what, I'm a bit scared," she said at last. "I don't feel brave at all now I'm here."

"Well don't you worry none, Miss Lizzie, because I'll never be more than a call away. And I'm coming up to the office with you whether you want me to or not, just to let this Bicker bloke see that you're not on your own in town. Us country bumpkins have got to stick together, we have. Not that I'm saying you're a bumpkin, or course, nor am I myself, for that matter, but that's what some townfolks think of anyone from the country, think they can lord it over us. Lead the way."

The two of them made their way up the stairs and along the corridors to Bickerstaff's door, the sound of their feet echoing around them and drawing attention to their self-consciousness. Jim stopped Elizabeth's hand on the doorknob. "Before we go in I want to just fix up a few things, Miss Lizzie, I'll say it now because I don't want to give these people any cause for relaxing; they are more or less strangers after all and if they know I'm not established here yet they might try to take advantage. So here's the arrangement: as soon as I've got myself a place to stay I'll call back to see you, I'll come right up here to the office, and then I can give you my address. Then I'll know where you are and you'll know where I am. There's no need for you to be nervous, see, Jim Nightingale's got you covered. In we go."

Booth was on duty at his desk, still surrounded by stacks of papers. "Miss Shaw, I don't believe the Mr Bickerstaffs were expecting you quite so soon. I'll just have a word." He knocked quietly on Bickerstaff senior's door, waited for the instruction and entered, closing the door behind him.

"He looks as if he's never seen daylight," said Jim. "I wouldn't want to work in a place like this, give me the fresh air any time."

"And how much fresh air was there when you were working at Broadhead's Wheel?" Elizabeth smiled at her companion but the throwaway comment suddenly reminded her of Daniel at work and brought back unbearable memories of how the last time she had seen him had been in the middle of a stupid row. Jim noticed her face cloud over.

"As much as I could breath in whenever I went outside," he said. "Course most of the time I was inside and there weren't much of anything fresh in there, not even me." He decided to shut up: he had been told that Elizabeth's husband had been a grinder. He was saved by Booth's return.

"And who are you?" Booth addressed Jim. "Mr Bickerstaff was wondering."

"Was he now," said Jim. "Well I'm a very close family friend of Miss Lizzie and I'm here to make sure she settles in to her new position alright and that no-one takes advantage of her, in that position."

"I can assure you, sir, that you are in a respectable attorney-at-law's office and that no-one here is planning on taking advantage of anyone, least of all of Miss Shaw, daughter of one of our very valued clients, late clients, er late client."

"So long as we all understand that," said Jim.

"Mr Bickerstaff senior will see you now, Miss Shaw, alone, if you please."

"My name is Mrs Fletcher, if you please."

Elizabeth walked to the door with Jim. "Don't forget our arrangement," he said. "I won't," she said, "and thank you for helping, I'm feeling much better. I look forward to seeing you again soon." Jim left the office through the door with the gold lettering on to find himself a place in town while Elizabeth was led through the senior partner's door to find out what her place would be in the town. "Says he's a family friend, Mr Bickerstaff."

"Right. Come in, come in, you've taken us a bit by surprise by arriving so soon, Mrs Fletcher, but no matter. I'm pleased you could see the sense in our little arrangement," said Samuel Bickerstaff.

"You didn't tell me exactly what the arrangement is to be," said Elizabeth. "What position it is you're offering me?"

"No need to worry about that yet, Mrs Fletcher, first things first." Bickerstaff senior shouted to Booth for tea then stood up and walked over to the window and stood with his back to her. "Marvellous church that, don't you think," he said looking out over St Peter's, "although I've never been entirely taken with the idea of having an office overlooking quite so many gravestones, seems a bit close to home, really, what with all the wills business we have to conduct. Hmmh. Unfortunately, Mrs Fletcher, it seems that all you can claim from the flood relief fund is about fifty pounds. The going rate for awards on household claims in the town seems to be hovering round the seventy five per cent mark. I understand that you were no longer living in Shaw Lodge at the time of the inundation but had moved to a small cottage at Damflask, where you had resided for no more than a week following your marriage to Mr Daniel Fletcher. It would be ridiculous to suppose, I fear, that a small cottage, newly inhabited by a young couple newly wed, would have contained much in the way of furniture and so on. Am I right? Booth, tea." Bickerstaff turned to face Elizabeth. "Am I right, Mrs Fletcher?"

"We did have a few things, basic, I suppose. We hadn't had time to fix the place up as we wanted."

"Of course not, my point entirely and hence my arrival at a figure in the region of fifty pounds. Of course I have obtained the necessary details of how to submit your claim and I will be more than happy to assist you in drawing one up. However, I'm afraid any fifty pounds you may be awarded would of necessity have to be left with me, to cover expenses and investigations relating to your father's estate and any inheritance rights you might have in that regard. Where is that Booth?" There was a slight kick on the bottom of the door. "Get that, won't you, Mrs Fletcher."

"What? Oh, yes."

"Ah good, Booth, tea." Bickerstaff went through the ritual of getting out his small sugar-bowl and teaspoon from his desk drawer. "You don't, if I recall correctly," he said, waving it at Elizabeth. "Now where was I? I've no reason to expect it to take too long to sort out your father's affairs, Mrs Fletcher, especially as you yourself will be on hand to answer any queries that might crop up. Meanwhile I have requested Mrs Bickerstaff to prepare a room for you at our home in Broomhall. No doubt you're tired from your journey today and not much in the mood for work so your duties won't start until tomorrow. Mrs Bickerstaff will instruct you in the ways of the household and she will assign you your daily tasks. However, as you must remain in the office today until I am ready to take you to Broomhall, you may start by doing a bit of cleaning in the office here. Booth will show you where everything is. You can begin by washing the tea cups."

"I wasn't expecting to become your cleaner, Mr Bickerstaff," said Elizabeth. "I often helped my father with his business matters so I am used to book work."

"Be that as it may, Mrs Fletcher, I can only provide you with work that is there to be done."

"And what shall I be paid for doing this work?"

"We'll discuss that later. Right now I have more pressing matters to attend to, legal matters, including your own, my dear girl; as you can see your father's file is still on my desk awaiting attention." Bickerstaff shouted for Booth to come in. "Instruct Mrs Fletcher on where everything is in the office, she'll be helping out here, dusting, tidying and so on. Is Mr Simon back yet?"

"Not yet, Mr Bickerstaff, in fact I haven't seen him all day, sir. Shall I go out looking for him? I am familiar with one or two of the places he likes to frequent."

"That won't be necessary, Booth, just let me know when he does arrive." The clerk led Elizabeth back out to the front office. "If he arrives," muttered Bickerstaff senior. Young Simon hadn't turned out to be the hard-working son his father had hoped, quite the opposite: it had been a terrible mistake making him a partner in the firm; not only was his work found to be wanting (what little he ever did) but his gambling debts were beginning to drain his father dry and now they'd brought that Quinn character down on him. "Poor Mrs Fletcher," mumbled Bickerstaff, "I'm afraid my need is greater than yours at the moment. Right you are, Mr Thomas Shaw," he addressed the file, "let's see how I can access your money."

Meanwhile Elizabeth was accessing Bickerstaff's brooms and buckets and dusters. None of this was what she'd had in mind coming to Sheffield and it served to make her loneliness even more acute.

AFTER the altercation with the horsemen the gypsies had broken camp and moved on immediately. Rob, the lad who had been shot, had been laid up in one of the caravans. Fortunately the wound looked far worse than it was: the bullet had grazed the side of his head, causing a lot of blood and a severe headache for the boy but, once Josie had stopped the bleeding and left him to sleep for the rest of the day, he had been up the next morning revelling in his new status as one of the walking wounded. Daniel had not been so lucky: he had regained the sight in his right eye but the gash across his left was deep and, although Josie had cleaned, treated and bandaged the wound, it was far too early to tell whether or not he would see through that eye again.

From Glossop the group had headed north on to Saddleworth Moor, hoping that anyone trying to find them would assume they would continue westwards towards Manchester. When they were sure that no-one had followed them, they had turned west and by the Monday evening had made camp just south of the town of Leigh. Now, with the horses watered and fed, the wood collected and a fire set, the air of panic had subsided.

Davy poured out some beer and sat down with Daniel and the two other men, Angelo and Marcus. They all lit up their pipes and idly watched as the women prepared the food. All told, there were sixteen in the camp including Daniel, made up of three families: Davy's; his cousin Angelo with his wife Megan and four kids and then Angelo's brother Marcus, married to Julie, and their three children. In the intervening days since the incident, Daniel had got to know all of them to varying degrees and whatever superstitions they had held about his being within the camp seemed to have gone.

"I know you might not realise it but you're lucky with that eye, I've seen plenty who've died from a wound like that," Davy said.

"I'm just lucky Josie was around to treat it. If it hadn't been for her I'm sure I'd be dead." Daniel crossed himself and fingered Elizabeth's medallion which now hung around his neck: after finding it in the grass after the fight, he wanted to make sure he never lost it again. "For a while I wouldn't have minded being dead but now I just feel lucky to be alive."

"Aye you must have a way with Lady Luck, Dan," Angelo said. He was a burly man with a thick black beard. He habitually wore a bandana and plenty of gold and looked more pirate than gypsy. "From what I hear about that there flood in Sheffield, the fact that you were caught up in the full of it and survived is a miracle. And like our Davy says, there's plenty who die from the poison of a sabre wound. If I didn't know you better, I'd have said that was the luck of the devil."

"Ain't nowt wrong with having a bit of the devil in you," Marcus piped up, a slight man who always managed to find something to laugh about. He spat into the fire: "So long as old Nick is checked by Our Lady if you know what I mean, you might as well take luck wherever you can find it. Now, Dan, you're a good man, that's obvious, but there's a touch of the devil in you too and that's no bad thing."

The four men were served bowls of steaming stew and got down to it with gusto. The meat had a different taste to it than usual, far stronger and more gamey.

"What's this? Doesn't taste like rabbit." Daniel asked.

Marcus laughed around his mouthful. "That's rabbit alright to anyone who asks, a winged one, that's all. Other people call it pheasant. Comes courtesy of our Lord Muck, the guy you knifed. Just had to let it hang for a few days."

Daniel was amused, he really had believed the gypsies hadn't been poaching. But so what? The food tasted too good to bother about where it came from. The conversation died as they all concentrated on the food. Daniel seized the opportunity: "I think I'll be leaving tomorrow, I need to find a place to work, a town or city somewhere. At the end of the day I'm no traveller, I need to settle some place." The fire cracked and snapped sending a shower of glowing embers into the night air like an explosion of fireflies suddenly appearing and then slowly fading away. Daniel looked around at his companions.

Davy didn't look too surprised. He wiped his mouth with the back of his hand and belched. "Well you know you're welcome to stay here with us a bit longer but if you're sure you want to go then Liverpool is probably your best bet. It's a big city and a big port and easy to lose yourself in, just in case there's any comeback from that bastard as clobbered you. Also I've got kin there who'll put you up 'til you've found your feet. My brother Eddie married a local girl and stayed there; they've a son, Paul, who works at the docks, he should be able to sort you out with work." Davy bent forward and warmed his hands by the spitting flames. "It'll be a shame to see you go but I know the travelling life isn't so easy for one not born into it."

"I'll be sorry to leave too but I've got to get on with my life and that means earning a wage somehow. The flood took everything I had and I need to start again." Daniel felt that somehow he was letting everyone down until Marcus said: "Well it's one less mouth to feed and one less person to get us into trouble. Anyway, Dan, if you don't leave now I reckon Lorrie will have you talked into marriage before you know what's hit you and I don't think you're quite ready for that."

Davy laughed: "I don't think anyone would be quite ready for that. I love the lass but to be honest I don't know how she finds time to draw a breath with all that yapping she does."

"She's just young and full of life, that's all." Daniel felt inclined to defend the girl.

"Pah! Young and not so young lad," Davy said. "You haven't many years on her and in some ways she's far older than you. That's the way women work, sometimes I think they're born old."

"Well then I think it is best that I'm off. No offence Davy but I don't think I'm ready for marriage just yet either." Daniel tried to sound light-hearted but the last thing on his mind was Lorrie when the first thing on his mind was still

Elizabeth.

"I know, son, but best you don't sneak off like a thief this time, Lorrie would never forgive me that again. I'll have a word with her and if things don't work out in Liverpool then you know you're always welcome back here." Davy passed the flagon of beer around and they all refilled their mugs.

Daniel was touched and having the fallback of Davy's offer gave him a lift. Liverpool didn't sound too bad, there was obviously opportunity and it was a big port. If things didn't work out there and he didn't fancy returning to the gypsies, he could always find a berth or work his ticket on a ship and move on to the Americas.

Davy lit up another pipe. "I don't think we need worry about that fight with the squire, any repercussions would have happened by now. I think you'll be fine so long as you keep your head down. Now, enough has been said on that subject so let's return to the more serious matter of getting drunk."

"I'll drink to that," Angelo spluttered and drained his mug.

The following morning Daniel felt dog-rough. The drinking had gone on late and there had been much singing and dancing, only marred by the fact that Lorrie had refused to speak to him. It was obvious Davy had had his little chat with her and the news hadn't gone down well. It had been the one sour note of the evening. Although his mouth felt thick and his head banged and throbbed, Daniel managed to stumble down to the river and fall into the icy water. Feeling more refreshed, he was able to stomach some cold stew that had been left in the pot. Only Davy and Angelo were already up and they had brewed some strong bitter coffee.

"Lord knows how you found your way to bed last night Dan, I mean we were all blind drunk but with your one eye it must have been twice as hard," Davy said as he passed him a mug.

"My head for drink isn't what it used to be. I can't even remember when I stopped being able to remember. I think it was just after I was dancing, or maybe singing, God knows."

Angelo hawked up, a guttural, phlegmy, throaty sound which went on for ages before finally he released a huge glob into the dying flames. "My advice to you lad is this: whatever you choose to do in this new life of yours, make sure it ain't nothing to do with music. I've heard cat fights sound better than your singing."

Davy laughed loudly: "Now that's the truth. No, I'd stick to doing something with my hands if I was you." He tossed the dregs from his mug into the fire and, groaning, stood up stiffly. "Gods, these bones aren't getting any easier to live with. Right, let's get things packed up."

"What about the others?" Daniel asked, getting to his feet.

"Let them sleep in for now they'll come to sooner or later,"

By the time everything was cleared away, an unsteady Marcus had emerged along with Angelo's oldest son. They broke camp, Daniel riding up front with Davy and the rest of the wagons rolling behind in convoy. Once they turned on to a main road, with the sun already bright, it was clear they were now travelling in a more southerly direction. Davy clicked his horse into a quicker walk.

"Best thing for you to do is leave us at Warrington," he said. "After that we'll be going out of your way. We'll be passing through there in a couple of hours. Then it's no more than twenty miles to Liverpool, probably less. You might not make it before nightfall but you can always get some lodgings or sleep rough for the night and have a easy walk in the morning."

"Where are you heading?" Daniel suddenly felt unsure of himself now that they were so close to parting company: all at once Liverpool sounded like another country to Sheffield. He had never seen a port and couldn't imagine a place where there was so much water that ships all the way from America could dock there. Even the image of so much water made him uneasy, he had no idea how he would react to that.

"We'll be moving down into Wales for the summer, do some trading and whatnot."

Daniel grinned. "Oh aye, I can guess what the whatnot might be."

"It's a living Danny boy," the old gypsy chuckled. "What some people call thieving others call a redistribution of wealth."

"Fair dues, can't say I've ever had much wealth to redistribute but if those bastards who shot Rob are any example of the rich then redistribute away."

"Speaking of Rob," Davy said, "When we get to Warrington and that idle layabout gets up, I'll get him to take Dobbs and tell Eddie to be expecting you." Dobbs was the old horse who trailed behind Davy's wagon. Davy kept him for sentimental reasons, although he would never admit it, and it was the only horse not hitched to one of the vans.

"Why Rob? Surely he's too weak to go?"

"That lad's plenty strong enough. Besides, he's the only who's old enough to ride that far on his own and light enough for old Dobbs to take him."

Daniel felt guilty. "Why don't you just tell me where your brother lives and I'll find him?"

Davy scratched his head. "Trouble is I've never known where he lives, apart from Liverpool. I've never been there myself, all I do know is that he and his lad are regulars at a boozer called the Cracke. Rob can leave word there about you coming."

"I'm sure I can find the pub without sending the boy all the way there."

Davy laughed: "They might be city folk now but they're still gypsies. Without word from one of us he'd soon as spit on you as help you out."

It wasn't long before the group arrived in Warrington and the others were waking up. Daniel was ready to leave, just waiting to say his goodbyes. Josie came bustling over: "Let me take a look at that eye of yours before you go." She expertly unfastened the bandage and peered closely at the wound. "It's scabbed up nicely that has, I don't think you need worry about it going bad."

"Will the sight come back in it?"

"It's too early to tell, love, but I wouldn't raise your hopes too high. Still I don't think it'll need another dressing."

Davy put his arm round Josie's shoulder. "Now then woman, haven't you had enough at playing nurse?" He pushed a small money-pouch into Daniel's hands.

"I can't take this. You've already given me enough, too much." Daniel protested.

Davy became more serious: "Look, what I gave you before wouldn't even get you to Liverpool. You'll need this to get by until you find my brother. Liverpool's an expensive place compared to the country and there's no rabbits to catch. If you're really bothered pay it back to Eddie when you've got a job. Besides, Josie won't allow you to go if you don't take it."

"Certainly not, I won't have anyone saying they weren't treated right and proper by us," Josie cackled. "Anyway, with your face looking like that you'll need all the help you can get."

Daniel reluctantly pocketed the pouch. The others drifted up to say farewell. Finally Lorrie slowly walked up to him. "I'm sorry to see you go Daniel and I can't see no sense in it at all. But if you're decided then you're decided. I've made you this." She handed him a small cloth and leather bundle. He unfolded it to find an eye-patch. "It might make you slightly less ugly, you great oaf, so tie it on."

Feeling a little foolish, he tied it over his left eye. "What do you think?"

Lorrie inspected him with an exaggerated scrutiny. "Well you ain't no oil painting but I suppose it's an improvement." Suddenly she leant in and kissed him on the cheek. "Take care Daniel and maybe I'll see you around one day." With that she ran back and ducked into one of the caravans.

Embarrassed and a little flustered Daniel turned to see Davy and Rob looking on with great amusement, even Dobbs seemed to be quite taken. Davy pulled a scarf from around his neck and gave it to him. "Take this, these are our colour see? Eddie will recognise that even if he's as pissed as a lord." He turned to Rob who was still grinning from ear to ear. "Now you listen to me, go to the Cracke and let Eddie know to expect a big scary looking bloke with an eye-patch and one of our neckerchiefs. Tell him to look after him as he would one of ours. You know where we'll be when you've done."

Rob clambered on to Dobbs and they ambled away.

"You'd best be off now, Dan, we aren't the type for long goodbyes," Davy said and clouted Daniel round the back so that he staggered forward in the road. "Take care now and remember, if you can find us you'll always be welcome." With that the old man turned and went back to the wagons. Daniel took one last look and then turned in the direction of Liverpool.

"IT'S just not right, not fair, Martha, they're treating John like a criminal, like he personally went up there and started the flood all by himself." Charlotte Gunson put her untouched cup of tea back on its saucer, conscious of how her hand was trembling. She'd had as little sleep as her husband since the Dale Dyke Dam burst ten days ago and the strain was wreaking havoc with her health and appearance: she had lost weight along with her appetite, her eyes were red and raw from crying and lack of sleep, and she hadn't dressed her hair for so long that it hung limply on her shoulders. Martha Treaton, a neighbour from two houses down, was the first visitor she had entertained since that awful night and even then it had been the guest who had made and poured the tea.

Martha reached over and held Charlotte's hand. "It'll blow over sooner or later love, folk are just angry now and blaming anyone. They'll get to the bottom of it at this inquest today and then your John will be in the clear, you'll see."

"But don't you understand? They've got to blame someone and John's the easiest target. The company won't stand by him, they'll be covering their own backs and that Mr Leather will just deny any involvement. Mark me, they've got it in for John, this thing will kill us both." Charlotte picked up her cup again, stared absently at the tea, then put it back down. "You should see what they're saying in the papers. There's even a reporter come down from Newcastle, who actually called John blind and ignorant, actually wrote those words down in black and white."

"Well that's pure nonsense, John's just about the cleverest man I've met. Who'd write a damn fool thing like that?"

"It's true, and even the people who work with John are treating him like some kind of leper. And after all he's done. Why on the Sunday straight after the flood he was back there, showing inspectors what had happened, and he's been back and forth more times in the last week then I can count. And then he's been stuck in meetings with that government inspector, Mr Rawlinson, until all hours of the night." Charlotte began shaking and crying, she dabbed at her eyes with her hankie. "John was nearly killed himself, he was up there when it happened. How could anyone blame him? But do you know what they're saying? They're saying he's no more than a local engineer, not half as competent as the man from London."

"Don't worry, love, things will turn out alright, you'll see. Once they have this meeting they'll get to the bottom of it." Martha knew she was just repeating meaningless platitudes but didn't know what else to say. The truth was that she wasn't all that confident herself that John wouldn't be blamed for the whole tragedy.

Upstairs Gunson straightened his bow-tie for the countless time, adjusted his waistcoat and pulled his sleeves down. His palms were clammy and perspiration beaded on his brow and upper lip despite the coolness of the morning. He took his brushes and smoothed out his hair again. Looking in the mirror at his stranger's face, he knew he was just putting off leaving for the inquest. "Well, time and tide waits for no man," Gunson muttered to his reflection. "Quite literally, unfortunately," he added somewhat grimly. He went downstairs and could hear Charlotte talking to someone in the kitchen . As he pulled on his overcoat he put his head round the door and said: "Right I'm off love, I'll see you later. Wish me luck."

Charlotte Gunson sprang to her feet and hurried out into the hallway, there were still tears in her eyes as she hugged her husband. "You take care, darling, don't let them bully you. Just come home as soon as you can."

"I will, now don't you fret love, whatever happens we'll get through this, things will be okay again."

"Are you sure you don't want me to come with you?"

Gunson wasn't sure of much at the time but of this he was certain; he didn't think the inquest would be very easy, in fact he thought it would be incredibly gruelling and he didn't want to put Charlotte through something like that. "I'm sure love, I'll be happier if I know you're at home. Tell you what, let's push the boat out tonight, have a fine meal: go and buy a chicken or something and we'll open that bottle of port Frederick gave us. There's been enough misery in this house lately. We need to start putting this thing behind us." He gave his wife another hug and a kiss. "Thank you for being you, my love. Now chin up and go make Martha some more tea."

Gunson walked briskly down Division Street, just in case Charlotte was watching from the window. Once he was sure he was out of sight, his pace slowed to little more than a trudge. The fact was that it was very possible he could be indicted for manslaughter as a result of this inquest. He had never let Charlotte know this, it would have been too much, but it had been dwelling on his mind for the last few days now. Gunson was angry but exhausted. He knew he wasn't at fault regarding the dam but he also knew that wouldn't be enough if John Webster thought differently. Webster was the coroner for the inquest and Gunson knew of him by reputation only but the reputation didn't fill the engineer with any confidence. Apparently the man could be very blunt and forthright and had the tenacity of a bulldog worrying a rat. If the man got some notion in his head that Gunson was to blame, then it would be very difficult to shake him off. Gunson didn't know what had happened at Dale Dyke, didn't know why the dam had failed. He suspected that there had been some internal landslide beneath and within the structure; he also thought that, in hindsight, the outlet pipes should have been bigger, able to release more water, but as far as he was concerned the specifications had been good enough for seven or eight previous dams, none of which had failed so far. Gunson was aware that in practice the specifications had varied slightly for each project depending on the local conditions - the geology, the water table, things like that - but they had varied in order to make each individual project as safe as possible.

What really infuriated Gunson were the reports that had been in the press. There had been the uninformed, ignorant article in the Newcastle paper, there had been the speculative and stupidly biased feature in The Times that had called his dam nothing more than a 'light screen'. And then there had been that letter, published in most of the papers, from Mr Bloody Rawlinson himself to somebody in Dublin, inferring that their dams were not subject to the same structural weaknesses as Dale Dyke had been. Gunson felt like a man being judged guilty before being allowed to prove his innocence.

The inquest was due to be held at the Town Hall at ten-o'-clock. Gunson had left home just after nine and it was only a five-minute walk. He arrived to see that already the steps were crowded with reporters, barristers, officials and members of the public. Rawlinson was nowhere to be seen, the only person Gunson did recognise was Mr John Towlerton Leather, the consultant on the dam project. The man was hob-nobbing with some self-important looking people, engrossed in conversation. The doors were open to the entrance hall so Gunson made his way through the throng and found a place of refuge behind one of the pillars. He thought he'd just stay there until the inquest was opened.

"Alright Mr Gunson? How you doing?"

Gunson looked up to see George Swindon approaching him. "George, what are you doing here?"

"Well I thought they might want to have a talk with me, seeing I was building the bleedin' thing." The Londoner came up close. "And also I wanted to make sure they didn't fuck you up the arse over all this shit, 'cos I've read the papers and from what I can see they've already put you through the mill over this flood thing."

Gunson was genuinely moved, he'd always got on quite well with George but hadn't expected this show of support. "Well thanks George, I appreciate it, but I can't see there'll be any problem; whatever caused the flood wasn't through the fault of the company."

George squinted and rubbed his head. "I don't know about that guv'nor, they got that cunt Leather giving evidence ain't they? That fucker will stitch you up good and proper if he thinks it'll save his own skin."

Gunson actually thought the same but said: "Why do you think that? He was the consultant engineer. If he tries to place the blame on me it will reflect back on him."

"I'll tell you why, 'cos he's one of them, ain't he, one of the boys, one of them fucking toffs. They look out for each other. But don't you worry Mr Gunson sir, if he lands you in the fucking shit, I know enough lads that'll take care of that toffee-nosed wanker."

Gunson was tempted by the idea, to see John Leather trussed up or tarred and feathered, or even a brutal beating would be quite a sight. But in the end Gunson was Gunson: "I'm sure that won't be necessary, George, we're here to get to the truth of the matter and that's what counts. I don't think violence would solve anything."

"Well guv'nor if you change your mind, just let me know." George gave him a wink. "I'd best fuck off, get me a decent seat in the gallery. I'll see you later mate." With that the small cockney walked off.

"Will all those who have business pertaining to the inquest on the bodies of Thomas Elston and others, please make their way into chambers, the hearing is about to commence," an usher announced loudly and swung open the double doors. Gunson straightened his tie once more, adjusted his waistcoat and pulled down his sleeves. "Well, this is it," he said to himself and headed through the doors.

WITH the country's leading newspaper reporters and some from even further afield gathered in Sheffield, Matthew Blagdon felt at once knowing and provincial, the former because many of his more esteemed colleagues were forced to ask him about who was who, what were people saying in the town and so on, the latter because they did so from such a superior stance that they just got up his nose. He had watched a few of them question some of the crowd hanging around outside the Town Hall and scribbling in the same sort of notebooks he used. To the people in the street, his credentials as a newspaperman were just as impressive as the outsiders' but inside the hall it was a different matter. The inquest assemblage comprised councillors, directors of Sheffield Water Company and potential witnesses, professional and otherwise, who may or may not be called to give evidence, and the well-known titles of the various national newspapers provided sufficient oil to loosen their collective tongue. Whatever, thought Blagdon, his words would appear in the local paper, that's where his name counted, for now.

At exactly ten-o'-clock the district coroner, John Webster, strode into the room and took his place on the bench in between Robert Rawlinson, the Home Office's appointed engineer, and Nathaniel Beardmore, a second engineer engaged by the government to assist Rawlinson. Blagdon looked across the room at Gunson and noted that the sight of the triumvirate had already made its mark: the poor man had looked dreadful enough before, now a cold pallor had completely drained his facial palette. Everyone sat down and a reverential silence took over the room.

The first witness called was John Towlerton Leather, introduced as the water company's consultant engineer. He marched confidently to the stand. He detailed the excavations of the trench, how subsequently the trench had filled with water which had constantly to be pumped out again; he explained that the embankment wall was made of stone, clay, shale and earth; he emphasised that he was an experienced engineer who had built many dams and that the plans for the Bradfield reservoir were his own, not Gunson's, delivering all this evidence in a confident, professional manner. Blagdon was getting restless, trying to concentrate on all the dry technical data, then Webster started. He wanted to know about valves and pipes which shook when a group of strong men tried to open those same valves and pipes just before the flood: what did all that imply? He wanted to know why there was no way of checking those same pipes for any possible fractures and why the design, which had the pipes buried under puddle and water, didn't allow for inspection: what did that imply? All the time doubt was being cast on Leather's ability as an engineer and his blustering professionalism began to wilt under the relentless onslaught. In the end, thanks to deft and persistent probing by the coroner, Leather was forced to admit that a landslip under the side of the bank could have led to the embankment giving way: it was possible, he said, that water from underground springs could have seeped in between the rock base and the bed of clay sitting on it, causing that bed of clay to slip. It was a relieved John Towlerton Leather who slipped out of the stand and back to his place in the hall: he wanted to mop his face but felt it would look too much as if he had been under undue pressure. At least his grilling was over.

John Gunson was summoned next, the engineer figured by lots of the gossip in the town to be the fall-guy. He outlined the methods of construction, particularly referring to the pipes, and read out the statistics of the rainfall in the area and how all this had been taken into account in building the dam. Webster was then on the attack again, on the question of water seeping out of the rocks, on the inaccessibility of the pipes for safety checks, and he refused to accept Gunson's assertions that the dangers supposed by the coroner were not real. Webster visibly rose in stature on the bench: "It would be better to construct the dam on the assumption of every conceivable danger and to take precautions against these dangers." An audible gasp went round the room at the coroner's directness and the reporters scribbled furiously.

Then, with the proceedings apparently promising more good copy for the papers, the inquest was adjourned until the following day. Blagdon and the rest of the reporters were the first out, all rushing to get their stories written. Gunson stayed seated for a time, alone in the crowded room, all around him voices speculating on the outcome of the hearing and shaking their heads: Webster might be a bit forthright in his approach for a coroner but he wasn't afraid to speak his mind, he was a well-respected member of society, an Alderman, and many admired his determination not to be bamboozled into accepting technical generalisations.

THE chatting had stopped and the two of them were reduced to silence. It was the first time John and Jimmy had been back up the valley since the flood and they had struggled to put the horror of it all to the back of their minds as they tried to establish some sort of normality as best they could with three of them living in one room, two not even townsfolk, let alone used to a shit-hole like The Ponds. John had felt guilty about not arranging the funeral for Jimmy's Mam and Dad as he'd promised. The lad had not let him forget, using the broken word as a bitter reproach whenever John tried to keep him in check.

Jimmy was too young to appreciate that there mightn't be much left of his parents to bury, if anything, and John had avoided confronting the boy with the reality. In the end he had told Jimmy that a friend had said the old home had totally collapsed and buried his parents underneath the rubble. John said that that was the best possible grave ever, their own home, a place Jimmy would never forget. As they got nearer and nearer to the site, John hoped they'd find ruins that at least lent some truth to his story.

"Let's stop here and pick some flowers, shall we," said John, pulling the dray horse to a halt. "It wouldn't do not to leave something to mark the spot."

"Don't forget you said we could make a wooden cross."

"We will, I brought a couple of tools for that very purpose."

It wasn't easy finding any wild flowers amid the ruins: the swathe of destruction along the path of the flood was still utterly, overwhelmingly shocking and the two companions were sucked into their thoughts of that awful night and the hysterical screams of the dying.

"Look over there," said John, turning away so Jimmy wouldn't see his moistening eyes. While he had gained a couple of dependents in Sally and Jimmy, John had lost his oldest friend and, with him, all John had to sustain his memories of childhood and family. "There's a few daffodils, let's get them, they're a lovely sunny colour, I'm sure your Mam would love those."

"Yellow was her favourite colour," said Jimmy, rushing off to collect the prize. "I think it might be mine too from now on."

They scrambled over a straight line of rocks, obviously once a garden wall for the precious flowers stood regularly along the row and didn't grow anywhere else in the plot. "You know, Uncle John, maybe some people were buried here too, just like my Mam and Dad were, so we shouldn't take them all, we should leave some for this grave too."

"That's a very kind thought, Jimmy. Your Mam will be proud of you now she's up in heaven."

"Do you think she will be in heaven, and my Dad?"

"I've told you before, there's no doubt about that whatsoever. They were good people, your folks, and I'm sure Jesus would have welcomed them into heaven as soon as they got there."

"I want to go to heaven when I die, then I'll see them again and we'll be together again. Perhaps there's rabbits up there too, what do you think?"

"Maybe little fluffy white ones. I can't imagine any of the mangy things you caught being up there, that's if there's any left down here after your efforts."

"Perhaps my poaching will stop me going to heaven, perhaps it's already too late and I'll never see Mam and Dad again."

"It's never too late, Jimmy, never too late. Come on, I think we've got enough now."

They found the ruins of the house through trial and error and instinct. It was difficult to recognise any pointers, only a few humps of ground and odd stumps where tall trees used to stand were left, but, by standing and taking in the views all around, views that were once as familiar to Jimmy as his own kitchen, they managed to work out exactly where they needed.

"Look, there's my Mam's mangle. I know it's hers because my Dad had to put a new roller on once and the wood never matched and Mam always said it never worked properly. Look, you can see where my Dad bent one of the nails in the end when he was hammering it in, used to drive my Mam mad that did, it was always pulling little bits of threads in the clothes." The contraption was half-buried in a large, irregular mound of stones. "I don't suppose she'll be doing any washing in heaven," said Jimmy. "And look, here's our teapot. You know what I can't understand, Uncle John, is why people who are big and strong and can move out of the way get killed but something like a stupid teapot can survive. And all you have to do to break them normally is drop them on the floor."

"It is strange that, Jimmy. Do you want to keep it?"

"No, it's a sad teapot now."

"We could put the daffodils in it, what do you think?"

"Okay."

John started fashioning a cross while Jimmy went to fetch water from the Loxley but when he filled the teapot he poured the water away again quickly; it seemed a bit peculiar to be putting water from the Loxley on to his parents' grave when that's what made their house fall down in the first place. He ran back to John with the empty teapot. "I think we'll let the rain fill it instead, Uncle John."

"Good idea, then the water will be nice and clean. Where shall we put it?"

"In front of the cross, right on the top of the stones so everyone will know not to touch them cause this is someone's grave."

"Another good idea, Jimmy lad, you're a clever one, no mistake, you'll do well in school."

"No I won't," said Jimmy, "cause I'm not going."

"But think how proud your Mam would be."

"I don't care. She never went to no school and neither did Dad. And you're always saying you've done alright without worrying about no schooling."

"Well I've been wrong," said John. "I'm sorry now, even got Sally to start teaching me how to read properly."

"I don't see no point in reading."

"Just think about it, Jimmy. Say you didn't go to school, then you'd perhaps spend your life like me, just delivering beer barrels all day, or working in one of them factories where you can't breath for dust. On the other hand, say, think about this grave here and what happened to your Mam and Dad: they died because the dam up the river broke; say you went to school and started learning stuff, you could grow up to be an engineer making dams that wouldn't burst and kill people. It's worth thinking about, lad. Now let's put up this cross, show me where."

The two mourners stood back quietly looking at the simple marker and bright daffodils that had turned a pile of rubble into a humble monument to Jimmy's folks. It was a grey day with a gentle breeze blowing, dancing the sunny flowers about in the pot.

"Would you like to talk about your Mam and Dad, Jimmy?

"I'm feeling a bit too sad now, Uncle John."

"Okay, then we'll just stand here a bit longer and say a couple of prayers."

"Won't you speak a few words, Uncle John, isn't that what's supposed to be done at funerals?"

"Well, I'll try. Let's see. Here lies Molly and Stephen Urmston, Mam and Dad of young Jimmy Urmston here. They were good people and good parents to Jimmy. They worked hard and didn't do any harm to their neighbours. They went to church as regularly as most and Molly I know was keen on her Bible. It's true that Stephen and me didn't always see eye to eye, he was a proud man and I'm a stubborn one, but he nevertheless made me as welcome as he could into their home and Molly was always on hand to keep the visit warm and friendly. They tried to bring up young Jimmy to be a good lad and I'm sure he won't let them down. May they rest in peace with Jesus in heaven, amen."

"Amen," said Jimmy.

"Tell you what, lad," said John, "when you're ready, I brought us a bit of snap. Fancy going and having a bit of a picnic?"

"Ay, let's go now. I don't want to keep feeling too sad. I reckon that was a proper funeral, do you?"

"I think we both did a good job, Jimmy."

"But I'm still not going to no school."

THE smell was the first thing to hit him, a very distinctive saltiness in the air that you could actually feel clammy on your skin and taste drying in your mouth. Then the noise: the cries of gulls shrieking and cawing as they

191

swooped, minding neither feet nor wheels in their ceaseless foraging for food; the sound of ships' riggings creaking and groaning their background confusion amid the shouts of sailors and dockers humping and loading bales and boxes carrying all manner of cargoes; the whish and slosh of the water as it slapped persistently against the huge wooden hulls, washing bits of rubbish backwards and forwards on its choppy surface with every nuance of the tide. The strange sights and sensations would grab anyone by the throat who had never strayed more than twelve miles from Sheffield before. Then there was the size and scale of the city and its buildings, a feeling of space and vastness which had always been denied Sheffield by its intruding hills. Strangely, it was the familiarity of sights that made things appear so peculiarly alien to him: wretchedly poor housing made life no different here to what it was in The Ponds; factories belched noxious fumes here just as they did in the steelworks of his home town; city noises, from the clatter of machinery to the bustle of street traffic, was the same all-pervading din as he had always known from childhood. The differences within that familiarity were what stood out far more than the complete foreignness of the townscape and architecture and even the smell of the atmosphere. For it was just as likely to be a Chinaman or a Negro sat on the doorstep of one of the slums chatting to his neighbour. The factories didn't manufacture steel or fashion cutlery; here they built equipment and fittings for ships. The same rowdy banter could be heard in the streets but the accents were not the broad measured vowels of a Yorkshireman instead a bewildering array of different types, from the city's own clipped nasal sound to the Welsh sing-song, the Scottish guttural, the Irish brogue and the dozens of other languages spat freely wherever he went. Even the names were not the solid reassuring Yorkshire names but somehow sharper and more exotic. Despite the strange sights and sounds, Daniel thought he would like Liverpool.

The Mersey River was by far the largest Daniel had seen; the rivers of Sheffield by comparison were mere streams. It was so wide that the buildings on the far bank were distant, seemingly miles away, while in between huge slow ships manoeuvred up and down, some pulled by small boats attached by long hawsers. Yet the presence of so much moving water roused his spirits rather than discomforted him, despite his painful memories of the flood, and the sense of far-away oceans and high-adventures were borne on the air as effortlessly as the circling, diving birds. It was an exciting place, where journeys started and new-lives were made. Daniel knew he had made the right decision. Liverpool was a place where maybe, given time, he could put the miseries of the past to rest.

IT didn't take long for the full range of Elizabeth's duties at the Bickerstaffs' residence to become only too clear. After arriving at Broomhall the previous evening, her office chores done, Elizabeth had been shown to her room in the top of the house; it was pleasant enough if fairly basic, with a small cupboard in which to hang her clothes, a simple bed, table and chair and a small chest of drawers. The woman of the house, Mrs Bickerstaff, was one of those people who have the knack of expressing sympathy and concern but at the same time surreptitiously weaving in their own demands. She fussed over Elizabeth, full of condolences for her great misfortune, offered a shoulder to cry on whenever the poor girl needed comforting, gently hinted that she could provide the wise mother figure whom Elizabeth had so tragically lost – she herself had only a son and would dearly have loved a daughter – all the while managing to explain to the recipient of all this attention exactly which part of the cleaning rota she would be expected to cover and which kitchen responsibilities she was expected to take on. When Elizabeth finally managed to mention that she hadn't eaten since leaving Bamford that morning, the good Mrs Bickerstaff had swept her up to her new bedroom, declaring that the girl must surely be too weary to eat much supper and that a tray would be sent up later when she was settled in. It must have been two hours before there was a gentle tap on the door. Elizabeth jumped to answer it.

"Hello, you must be Elizabeth, I'm Mary, the cook. I'm sorry you've had to wait so long but her ladyship downstairs was on the warpath. You must be starving, poor thing. I've brought you some broth and a few vegetables, not much, I'm afraid, but I did manage to sneak a piece of cake for you when Mrs B wasn't looking. She guards that larder like it held the crown jewels."

"Thank you, Mary. I'm really hungry but I didn't know what to do, whether to go downstairs to the kitchen or not. I got the impression Mrs Bickerstaff wanted me to stay in my room."

"She probably did, the old trout. You'll get used to her, she's not really all that bad compared to some as I've worked for. As long as you look like you're listening to what she says and you don't get caught idling she'll not bother you too much. It's that son of hers you have to watch, Master Simon, a real waster, not that he's home much, he's out gambling away his inheritance most of the time. I feel sorry for his father, must be a real disappointment to him. Anyway, you get on and eat. Tell you what, you bring your tray down to the kitchen when you've finished and we can have a bit of a chat. If her ladyship says anything, I'll tell her I asked you to so I could show you what's what in the kitchen. She'll not argue with that."

When the cook had left the room, Elizabeth took her tray over to the small table which she had moved to the window so she could look out over the lights of the town in the distance. The supper was modest but delicious, the broth was well seasoned and even the vegetables had been enlivened with herbs and peppered butter, Mary was certainly a good cook.

Despite Mary's assurances that her tray excuse would cover any questions about the newcomer being downstairs, Elizabeth was relieved not to meet Mrs Bickerstaff on her way down to the kitchen. She was also relieved to remember which door led to the kitchen, no good avoiding her ladyship and then bursting into her parlour. She found Mary sitting enjoying a cup of cocoa.

"Feeling better now?" asked the cook, getting up from the table and pouring Elizabeth a cocoa too.

"Much, you're a really good cook, Mary. Does Mrs Bickerstaff know how lucky she is?"

"Reckon she does in her own uppity way. They treat me quite well, really, like I said, I've worked for worse. Now, tell me about yourself. I understand you lost your family in that awful flood."

"I lost everything," said Elizabeth, "my parents and my husband."

"Your husband? I didn't know as you were married."

"Only for one week. Then I saw Daniel being washed away, he was on the other side of the river coming home, he was a grinder, he'd been working very late, he had a big order on he had to get finished. A few minutes sooner and he'd still…"

"Oh you poor love, I'd no idea."

"I miss him all the time, every minute. We were fixing up our own little house, we called it Willow Tree Cottage because there was a big willow tree in the front garden. Daniel made a plaque for it and hung it on the door."

"Sounds very pretty."

"It was, right by the river."

"And your folks, you lost them too?"

"They lived further down the valley, at Malin Bridge. The house was swept away while they were in bed asleep."

"That's some blessing, then, Liz. Do you mind if I call you Liz?"

"Not at all, new life, new name. I suppose I'd better get used to it."

"Well you won't have too bad a life here, I'll make sure of that. Like I said, her ladyship isn't as bad as she'd like you to think and Mr Bickerstaff, well, he's a hard worker that one and he had high hopes for the firm when young Simon, that's the son, was persuaded into the same line of business, the law and that, but I'm afraid he's a bad'un. He had to do important exams and all that to get his piece of paper and all that but I think he barely scraped together

194

enough marks to get through. Now his name's painted in fancy letters on a door and I get the distinct impression that that's as far as his legal work goes now. It's hard not to hear the rows that go on sometimes. Master Simon comes back here at all hours and sometimes his father's still up waiting for him and, well, it wouldn't be right for me to repeat what I've heard them shout at each other. No doubt you'll hear it soon enough yourself anyway. Now, young lady, I think you should get up to that bed of yours and get some sleep. I'll try to let you have a bit of a lie-in tomorrow but it depends on her ladyship. Has she told you what you're to do in the morning?"

"Cleaning the silverware, I think."

"Well at least you'll be able to do that in the kitchen so we can chat some more then."

THERE were almost too many quotable comments for the assembled press reporters made at the inquest when it reconvened the following day. The scribblers expected to lead their stories on the verdict and any scapegoat who might get the blame for the dam bursting but the coroner, Webster, let off so many fireworks from the bench that even his learned companions were forced to try to rein him in. Blagdon himself found he was getting quite enthralled by what he had assumed would be quite dull proceedings until the final summing up.

It was the water company's legal adviser, Ralph Blakelock Smith, who sparked Webster's most dramatic declaration: Leather, the company's consultant engineer, could, warned the district coroner, face very serious consequences. "We could find Mr Leather guilty of manslaughter," he announced to a shocked assembly and the excited gasps of astonished reporters, before retracting the threat and causing further amazement by pre-empting the verdict and declaring that the jury had in fact already made up their minds to find no-one guilty of manslaughter. Gunson as well as Leather were pleased to hear it but several of m'learned friends were unhappy with such procedural carelessness and a general buzz of whispers spread around the room. They were silenced by Gunson being recalled to the stand.

Webster set to once more, pillorying the witness for his assertion that it was common practice for engineering specifications such as those drawn up for the Bradfield reservoir to be used as a guide only. Gunson tried to explain that conditions on the ground had to be taken into account but it was no use, the coroner was on the attack. He wanted to know if the reservoir the company was building further north of Sheffield at Agden was being constructed on the same principle, with the specification being "a mere guide". It was, said Gunson, whereupon Webster turned to the jury: "You will remember, gentlemen, that Agden is made in precisely the same was as the one that is broken." Then he turned his vitriol full on poor Gunson, describing him as an engineer "of bad judgement". Despite his professional standing, his years of experience and his persistent high regard for safety on all his projects, Gunson now found himself battered in open court. "I'm sorry," Webster addressed him, "that you have so little knowledge." Once again turning to the jury, Webster did not mince his words: "They have not constructed the work in a workmanlike manner, they have destroyed nearly three hundred of our fellow citizens."

Finally the Home Office engineer, Rawlinson, was called to give evidence. Point by point he demolished the arguments about the dam construction put forward by Leather and Gunson. The outlet pipes were inadequate, they were built in the wrong place, they were unsupported; for some reason the water company's engineers had seen fit to blow the trench used to drain water from the reservoir during construction, when indeed it should have been left to carry away any overflow; he had heard that Gunson had seen water lipping over the embankment and seeping into the wall, therefore the wall must have been porous; he had examined the situation at Agden and found that the tips of in-fill had been too deep and consequently had not been compacted properly, therefore that wall too must be porous.

The jury retired to consider their verdict. Gunson sank lower and lower in his chair: of course they would believe Rawlinson, he thought. He barely heard the verdict delivered by the jury foreman; he knew he was not named personally and that no criminal charges were to be made but the words which he carried home with him were damning enough: "…that, in our opinion, there has not been that engineering skill and that attention to the construction of the works which their magnitude and importance demanded…"

On the way out of the Town Hall, Gunson declined to give any comment to the newspapers.

"MY God, Peggy, I don't see you for years and the next minute I'm seeing you every bleeding day. Come in then now you're here."

"I didn't think you'd mind, Melanie. I've got a new regular over this way and I thought I couldn't not call in and say hello. I enjoyed bumping into you the other day and it got me to thinking that we none of us should ever lose touch with old friends."

"We were never that close, as I remember," said Melanie, "and I'm not too sure about the 'old' bit but sit yourself down anyway. Who's the new punter then? You're not poaching on my territory, I hope."

"Would I?" said Peggy. "No, he's not so much a new client as an old one but he's moved over this way and as he's one of them good payers who doesn't expect too much and never gets his fists out I thought I'd oblige when he asked me to keep him on the list. I must say you haven't got a bad place here, considering where we are and all that."

"Could be worse. What about you?"

"Well I've got someone special, looks after me properly; he likes to get his pleasures in a nice place so he fixed me up with one. You seem to have a good few friends here too judging by the comings and goings last time I was here. That Sally seems a nice kid. She's not in our line of work is she?"

"No, tell you the truth I'm not even sure she even knows what line of work I'm in. She's a simple country girl, in fact sometimes she's a bit too simple, goes off somewhere in her head every time she thinks of her folks and what happened. Only natural, I suppose."

"You said she's staying down the street with a friend, I seem to remember."

"Ay, with John Hukin, he's a drayman over at Neepsend. It must be a real struggle for him now with two extras to feed."

"But you help out, don't you, must be something between you and him then, is there?"

"Me and John? Never. I look after him and all that sometimes, least I used to, but we got to be friends and now that seems to be how it is," said Melanie.

"And what about Sally? Hasn't she got any money and that, to help John out like?"

"How could she, she's lost everything, poor kid. Anyway, what's with all the questions?"

"Just catching up. Don't want to put my foot in it if anyone should come in." Peggy gave what she thought was a knowing wink and then changed tack, putting in a bit more concern into her voice. "What about the relief fund they've set up in the town for victims of the flood and people who lost all their stuff, hasn't Sally tried them for any money, surely she'd qualify for something, being orphaned and everything?"

"Not as far as I know but you could have a point there, Peggy, perhaps that's not a bad idea."

"If good folks are good enough to give money to help those in need, then those in need should benefit, that's what I say. This friend of mine, the one I was telling you about, the special friend, well he understands all that relief fund business, he's done claims for quite a few people I know, successful ones at that. I could ask him to help the girl with the paperwork, what do you think?"

"No harm, I suppose. I'll mention it to John."

"No need to bother John about it yet, Melanie, sounds as if he's got enough on his plate right now and he might feel a bit guilty for not having done anything himself or, worse, he might be afraid young Sally will think she's in the way and he sounds too kind-hearted for that. Let me ask this friend of mine first then I'll get word to you or, better still, I'll call over myself and tell you."

"Well I can't say as a bit of money wouldn't come in handy right now. Apart from putting food in her mouth John's having to get clothes for the lass, hers having all been lost. I've given her a couple of my own cast-offs but they're pretty old, I don't throw anything away that's still fit enough to pull a few tricks."

"You always had an eye for nice clothes, Mel, and you always knew how to wear them to their best advantage, still do, looking at you,," said Peggy, steering the conversation away before the relief fund ended up back at John's door. "And look at this place, like I said, you've got it looking really pretty. Ever fancy moving right back into town again?"

"No, Peggy, I'll probably see my days out here. Always thought I'd meet some nice man who'd look after me and give me a nice home – every whore's dream, I suppose, but it seldom happens."

"This John bloke sounds like he could be that nice man, sure there's nothing more to it than being friends?"

"I can't say as I've never thought about it but no, John will make some lucky woman a great husband when he sobers up a bit but it won't be me, he'll be looking for someone more like his Mam, not some worn-out whore like me."

As the two women sat chatting, Mick Briggs still kept watch across the street. He varied his spot and made sure he spoke to enough of the locals hanging about so he'd be taken for one of them but he was getting right fed up with this sentry duty. He'd seen Peggy going in to the whore's place and the two of them had deliberately ignored each other: so far her visit was the only thing he'd have to report to Quinn but then Quinn liked his runners to keep an eye on each other and no doubt Peggy would report back on him too. At least he was where he should be. Briggs was getting a bit nervous over what he could tell Quinn because so far he had nothing much of anything to tell and he wasn't looking forward to the boss' vicious humour. Still, he'd had an idea and an idea was something to talk to Quinn about and maybe it wasn't a bad idea at that. Standing here all this time had given him a gaffer's knowledge of Hukin's comings and goings, when he left for work and when he got home from work, and, with the lad off to school and out of the way soon, that would only leave the girl to worry about. Briggs was about to leave and report back to head office when he saw Peggy come out of the whore's house and make her way off down the street. He decided he'd best stand his ground. If Peggy had something good to pass on to Quinn, Briggs didn't want to be the one to interrupt any celebrating they might get going.

JIM Nightingale walked straight in through Bickerstaff & Son's fancy door without even knocking. He was in high spirits; he'd got himself a job at one of the big factories in the town, much more his cup of tea than stuck out in a village in the middle of nowhere, and some decent lodgings even Our Mam would approve of, not too dear on the old pocket either, and he wanted to tell Elizabeth his good news and keep his promise to come and check she was alright. That idiot-looking Booth was there, of course, looking as if he hadn't moved at all these last few days, probably couldn't with that silly collar sticking up round his neck and a nose so long and pointed it was likely pinned into the pile of papers on his desk to keep them from blowing off.

"I've come to see Miss Lizzie," Jim announced. "If she's not here, I want to know where I can find her, thank you."

"Really," sneered Booth, "'thank you'," sneered Booth. "Well I'll thank you not to come barging in here demanding to know anything, let alone the address of one of Mr Samuel Bickerstaff's clients. Don't you know the word 'confidential'? No, I suppose your type wouldn't."

"I know right enough what 'confidential' means you rude little toady. No wonder you're stuck in a dead-and-alive place like this. I want to know where she is and I'm not leaving here until you or your Bickerstaff boss tells me."

"You'd better stand over there in the corner then 'cause you could be in for a long wait."

"The corner's the place for you, you dunce. And I don't aim to wait all that long at all." Jim strode across the office to the senior partner's door when it opened suddenly in front of him and Samuel Bickerstaff filled the frame.

"What on earth is going on out here? What's all the shouting about?" he demanded. "This office is dedicated to the noble practice of the law and I will not tolerate such behaviour on these premises."

Jim got in quick. "I'm a trusted and close family friend of Elizabeth Shaw, I knew her father well and had his full confidence over various business

199

concerns at and around Malin Bridge, though I was more involved with Broadhead's myself, Low Matlock, no doubt you know it, Mr Bickerstaff, a man of your position no doubt makes a point of keeping up with business matters in the area. Knew it, I should say, I'm afraid I lost the wheel to the flood. As to the shouting you mentioned, I'm afraid your clerk here was being a bit over enthusiastic in his work, seems to have taken one look at my gear and assumed I was some common type." Jim turned to Booth: "I think 'type' was the word you used, young man, wasn't it?." He looked back at Bickerstaff: "But a man such as yourself would understand that even us business people sometimes have to put on some dirty clothes when the occasion demands. Nightingale's, the name, James Nightingale, we met the other day when Miss Elizabeth arrived." Jim shook hands with Bickerstaff and went on in to his private office without waiting for an invitation. (He could hear Bickerstaff muttering under his breath at the hapless Booth: "You idiot, you nincompoop, I hope you haven't cost me a potential client.") Then Bickerstaff bustled in behind Jim.

"Most unfortunate, Mr Nightingale, do sit down. A friend of Thomas Shaw, you said?"

"That's right. Our two families have always been close and I always promised Mr Shaw that I'd take care of his daughter if anything ever happened. Now I'm here to do just that. I only called in on the off-chance to find out where she is but, to be straight with you, Bickerstaff, I'm beginning to wonder if anything's going on. First of all the clerk there refuses to tell me where Miss Elizabeth is, then he tells me to go and stand in the corner. Not what I expected from the firm of Bickerstaff & Son, especially after the way Mr Shaw spoke so highly of you."

"I can only apologise again for Booth. He's not usually so rude but I will have strong words with him, I can promise you. As for Miss Shaw, that's to say Mrs Fletcher, she is now living in my home so she is quite safe and is being well looked after."

"And where exactly is your home?" persisted Jim. "I need to know where she is so I can go see her. I need to make sure she gets what's coming to her."

"No worries on that account," said Bickerstaff. "Here, I've written down the address, it's in Broomhall, shall I tell her when to expect you?"

"Well I can't make it today. Like I said, I called in on the off-chance. Just tell her I called and I'll be in touch." Jim stood to leave. "I know Mr Shaw had great faith in you, Bickerstaff, I'm sure you won't abuse that faith and let his daughter down."

"You can rely on it," said the senior partner. "But there is a small matter of establishing whether or not her brother David is alive or dead: as the elder son he is the immediate beneficiary of Mr Shaw's estate."

"Her brother? David, yes of course," said Jim, trying to cover his momentary confusion. "And what exactly have you done in that regard?"

"Oh, well, er, I need to write to his regiment, find out what proof there was of his death in India."

"Right, well, I'll be checking with Miss Elizabeth to see how your enquiries are going. Cheerio."

Jim smirked at Booth as they passed on the way out. Once in the corridor, Jim shut the door behind him and moved slightly to the side to listen at the crack. He was right. "Get that Thomas Shaw file out again," he heard Bickerstaff. "Find out the name of the son's regiment and get a letter off to them right away. I want to know if the bugger's dead or not. Today, Booth, today." Jim left Church Street Chambers in higher spirits than when he'd arrived. He was also sweating like a pig; fancy Jim Nightingale getting one over on some fancy bloody attorney.

THE Cracke was one of the oldest pubs in Liverpool, a dark poky place in a narrow back street just off the edge of the city centre, with partitioned corners and tiny rooms perfectly suited to the particular whispered conversations some of the less salubrious types of customers might want to hold. It hadn't been too hard to find, the pub's reputation went before it. Daniel had sought it out as soon as he got to the city, hoping to meet Davy's cousin sooner rather than later and perhaps get his help in finding work but this was his third night propping up the bar and there'd been no sign of the man. Meanwhile the need to get a job was getting critical: Daniel had been more than grateful for the money the gypsies gave him but it was disappearing quickly and having to buy drinks on the off-chance of meeting someone he didn't even know didn't help. Davy had told Daniel that his cousin worked on the docks and should be able to fix him up with some work but there was a limit to how long a man with little money could wait. Perhaps he ought to go back to his original plan and work his passage on a ship to America. It was already Friday night but the shipping offices were bound to be open the following day so he could at least make some enquiries. He made up his mind, that's what he'd do first thing the next day. He ordered another beer by way of a small celebration at having come to a decision. The pub was filling up now with men on their way home from their shift at the docks but Daniel was lost in a world of his own, images of the valley back home intruding on his imagination every time he tried to picture his new life in the New World. Leaving the country wouldn't be much of a wrench but severing that last connection to Elizabeth would be heart-breaking; their cottage was gone and their lives had been destroyed but the site of their home and happiness and history was still there up the Loxley valley and Daniel couldn't help feeling a sense of betrayal by deliberately turning his back on it all and England forever. He poured half his beer down his throat quickly as if to wash away what he knew was a completely irrational guilt before the glass was almost knocked out of his hand by a total stranger.

"'Ere y'are mate, you must be Dan."

Daniel was shaken from his dreaming by the greeting and slap on the back. He turned to meet the owner of the voice, a small man, whose face was smeared with dirt while his soiled clothes looked like they should have been burnt months ago. The man was only shoulder height to Daniel, he had a tanned friendly face and sharp blue eyes, brown receding cropped hair covered a maze of white-ridged scar tissue and one half of his left ear was missing.

"Yeah I'm Daniel, who wants to know?"

"Calm down feller, word is you're looking for work."

"And whose word might that be?" Daniel was immediately cautious, he didn't know anyone in Liverpool and wondered how this man knew his name.

"Davy Lee's, he's my uncle, says he owes you one and said I'd find you down here. Told me there'd be a big scary-looking bloke waiting in the Cracke with an eye-patch and wearing one of his blue neckerchiefs. I just finished me shift and I was going home when I thought I'd better just pop in and see if you was here like. Fuck me, I said to meself when I saw you at the bar, you're the spit of what Uncle Davy described so I came over to say hello."

"Davy Lee? You mean Gypsy Dave?"

"I suppose so. That's not what I call him but he is a gypsy alright, like me Dad, though Dad's settled down here now with me Mum. Me, I'm scouse born and bred but family's family see. Cousin Rob dropped by the other day with Uncle Davy's message and told us how you'd all met like and said you'd be here looking for work. Said if I saw you I should take you home and make sure I saw you were sorted at the docks." The small man straightened up with pride: "I've got a bit of influence at the docks and I know they're looking for labourers at the moment. If you want work, I can get you some." He turned his head to look at the barmaid. "I'll have the usual, Polly, thanks."

"Gypsy Dave eh?" Daniel smiled and stuck his hand out when the young man finally stopped talking. "I'm Dan and who are you?"

"Paul. Like I said, if Davy owes you one, we all owe you one." They shook hands. "If it's docker's work you want I can get it. It's not easy work but from what I hear you can take care of yourself, pretty clever with your fists and strong as a fucking ox I understand. You should do fine."

"Well if you can get me a job I'd really appreciate it and if you can put me up for a couple of days until I get sorted, that'd be even better. I'm in a boarding house up the road but to be honest money's tight."

"No problem." Paul blushed slightly. "Fact is I still live at home but there's plenty of room and I know everyone would like to meet you. Tell you what, stay here a minute while I go and have a quick word with someone, won't be long."

"Alright." Daniel watched Paul approach a big gruff of a man sitting in one of the corner chairs and looking for all the world as if he was holding court. Paul spoke a few words, the man nodded his head, Paul gestured over towards Daniel, the man's eyes followed the direction of the thumb and Daniel was given the once-over. More words were exchanged, Paul returned to the bar, fetched a drink for the big gruff of a man and then took his place again next to Daniel. "Two more here Polly when you're ready."

Gypsy Dave. A chance encounter that he had already put behind him. It would seem the old traveller had kept his word after all.

"You're in," said Paul. "Turn up tomorrow at five, that's in the morning, and have a word with Ernie McGovern. Tell Ernie that Joe McCarrell sent you, that's him over there, and you'll be sorted. You might start off with some shitty jobs but stick with it and you'll find it works out alright." Paul clinked his glass against Daniel's. "Slavery!" he said and they drank a toast.

Daniel turned to him and laid a hand on his shoulder. "Thanks, pal, and don't worry about me, I've done my share of shitty jobs and no doubt I'll do a lot more of them. Thanks. I'll be there first thing in the morning."

"Good, that's that sorted. Now we'll finish these up and get off home and get our tea, me Mum sets a good spread. Have you got anything to collect from your digs?"

"Just a small bag."

"Where is the place?"

"Just off Mount Pleasant."

"Good, that's on our way."

They walked along Hope Street with Daniel only half-listening to Paul, who didn't stop talking, even for breath, as far as Daniel could tell, but he loved the sing-song voice, which seemed to sound exactly the right note to go with this good turn of fortune.

"THE main thing is, Charlotte, there were no criminal charges, no-one has been named personally responsible and I have got the full support of the company." John and Charlotte Gunson were taking a Sunday afternoon stroll in the Botanical Gardens a few days after the conclusion of the inquest. Gunson was relieved to see that his wife seemed to be slowly recovering from the ordeal, she still seemed frail and unsteady but the colour had returned to her cheeks somewhat and she had begun to take care over her appearance once again. He was still suffering nightmares of the flood and felt an inherent sense of guilt merely through association with the collapsed dam but the results of the inquest hadn't been as bad as he had expected.

He felt that the judgment of inadequate engineering skill and lack of attention to construction was unjustified, he knew that in the end the flood was the result of a collaboration of factors and events far too complicated and involved for any jury of laymen to be able to fathom the exact cause. To understand why the Dale Dyke dam had burst would require a comprehension of not just dam structure but the entire history of dam construction, a knowledge of geology, meteorology, physics, architecture and engineering as well as witnessing the process of building the Dale Dyke itself. Events as tragic as the flood couldn't be put down to one cause, same as in life; they were an amalgam of natural and human intervention. In hindsight it was easy for Gunson to see where he might have included more safeguards or had a tighter control on the construction and he would personally grieve and repent for it til he died. However, he was pragmatic enough to know that it was only through hindsight that these facts were apparent: the likelihood of any of the precautions he'd identified actually succeeding in preventing the dam from breaking was small. Gunson was more relieved that Charlotte's health was returning than worried over what damage had been done to his reputation. He had been amazed to receive a communication from Samuel Roberts and George Housefield, two of the company's directors, stating that they fully backed and appreciated his position as resident engineer. So long as Charlotte was recovering, Gunson was happy to shoulder the burden of remorse on his own.

Gunson took his wife's hand and together they walked around the park. He felt her squeeze his hand every now and again as if in affirmation that they were together and happy again.

"Let's put this behind us now and get on with our lives," Gunson said.

"Frederick will have completed his studies this summer and will be back with us. The company has already said there'll be a position for him, you never know, he might end up as my boss."

Charlotte laughed at this and Gunson was filled with simple happiness at the sound of it. "I hardly think so John, he's only just graduated."

"I know but they're being taught all sorts of stuff nowadays, things which were just not known in my day." Gunson was aware that science was progressing at such a rate that nearly every month new theories were being proposed and old ones being debunked.

They reached the top of the gardens and turned right on to Clarkehouse Road and headed back home.

"There's someone outside the house John," Charlotte said and Gunson could feel her hand grip his a little tighter. Gunson peered ahead but his eyesight wasn't what it used to be and his spectacles were at home. It was only as they got within twenty yards that he could make out who it was.

"Nothing to worry about, Charlotte, it's George Swindon, you know, I told you about him. Someone I now consider a true friend." Gunson quickened his pace and called out: "George, wait up, don't go."

The grizzled little cockney looked up and smiled as he saw the couple hurrying to meet him. "Alright Mr Gunson? I just thought I'd call in and say hello. Seems like things didn't turn out so bad after all."

"Quite right, well you must come in and take some refreshment."

"No, no that's okay, you've only just got back, I don't want to inconvenience you in anyway."

Charlotte took control. "Nonsense Mr Swindon, John says that you're a friend of his and after all this trouble any friend of his is more than welcome in our home." She took George by the arm and ushered him into the house. "Now, a nice cup of tea?"

"That'd be lovely, Mam." George hovered in the hallway, uncertain as to what to do next. Gunson came to the rescue: "I think George might prefer something a little stronger love, how about a drop of scotch, George?"

"Well you know me, Mr Gunson, normally I don't touch the stuff but seeing as we've got something of a little celebration going, I won't say no." George took off his hat and ruffled his grey, frizzy hair. "Yes, I'll be happy to join you in a drop."

Gunson took the Londoner into his study where he kept his books and his hard liquor. "Have a seat George, and please call me John." Gunson poured two generous measures and passed one over. "I'd just like to say thank you for turning up last Wednesday. You don't know how much it meant to me to see a friendly face that day. I was more than a little anxious, let me tell you."

"Can't say that I blame you guv', you was all set up for the fall-guy and I wanted to make sure that if you was I was there, just in case I could help out in any way. You don't work with a geezer for a while without knowing if he's a good bloke or a complete wanker. Me and the boys may be a bit rougher than what you're used to but we're not idiots. We always thought you was a good bloke. We was just looking out for you." George swallowed the whisky in two gulps. "That's good stuff, don't seem to burn like the rotgut I have."

Gunson smiled and refilled George's glass. "I don't think anything burns quite like the stuff you used to serve in the tea up at the dam."

The two men fell silent at the memory of the dam and the works hut where George used to brew up his special. Gunson downed his drink and poured another. In the end George broke the silence: "A fucking shame that. All them people killed, who'd have thought it? Still, when you start fucking around with Mother Nature sometimes she don't like it and fucks you right back. And then there ain't nothing you can do about it."

Gunson laughed despite himself and said: "I think you've just put it more succinctly than any of the coroners or expert witnesses did at the inquest."

George's wrinkled face creased into a grin. "Sometimes you don't need no education or nothing to know that. I've seen enough in my life to know that there's nothing more powerful than nature and in the end you're either lucky or you ain't. I guess Sheffield wasn't lucky this time."

"So what are your plans now?" Gunson opened up his cigar box and offered it to George. Once they were both puffing and their glasses replenished, George said: "I don't think I'm hanging around Sheffield no longer, too many bad memories. I thought I might clear off over to Manchester or Liverpool, there's plenty of work for a geezer like me over there."

By the time George left a couple of hours later, both the men were quite drunk and promising that they'd keep in touch whatever. Gunson swayed into the parlour where Charlotte sat embroidering.

"Well Mr Swindon seemed like a nice man. You seemed to be having a good time with him."

"A true friend my love, they broke the mould when they made him." Gunson slurred and then slumped into an armchair.

"He seemed to know some interesting songs at any rate. And you seemed to be quite the enthusiastic pupil." She couldn't help enjoying the moment, it was the first time she had seen her husband relaxed and unworried for the first time since the flood.

"Well you know I've always had a good voice," John mumbled and then his eyes closed and all that could be heard were his deep rolling snores.

IF it was one thing Jimmy had always hated it was having his face rubbed hard with a wet flannel. He preferred to keep his dirt on. It had served him well when he used to hide in the bushes or down on the ground in the grass, it helped him to blend in and made it much easier to catch rabbits, so he didn't see why he had to have a clean face now, it was just something else awful about going to school.

"You'll thank us in the end when you're able to read and write and you get yourself a job in an office or somewhere where not everything's covered in muck and grime," said Sally. "Just think, you'll be a proper man about town."

"I'd rather be a mucky boy in the country," said Jimmy, making gruesome faces as the flannel did its worst. "It's better in the country than here. My Dad was always saying he couldn't understand why Uncle John lived in such a filthy hole when he could have lived in our barn, we'd have made it comfortable for him and he could have worked in the fields with us and gone out catching rabbits and things with me."

"I don't think you should be so mean about your Uncle John, I've told you before, he's working very hard for all of us. And if you go to school you won't have to live in a barn or a room like this, Jimmy, you'll be able to get yourself a nice big house in the country and maybe John could go and live with you there."

"But I don't want a big house, I want one just like my Mam and Dad's and I want one next to where theirs was. I think you're mean sending me to school when I don't want to go. Why don't you bloody well go yourself."

"Don't use such language, Jimmy, I bet you never spoke like that when you lived in the country, your Mam would have given you a thick ear, same as mine would've, so don't start cussing like that now just 'cause she's not here to hear you. You're talking silly anyway, I'm too old to go to school, besides, I used to go to school, up at Malin Bridge. It was fun, you'll have fun and there'll be lots of other boys your age to play with, you'll be able to tell them all about how to catch rabbits and they'll think you're really clever."

"No they won't," said Jimmy. "I won't know anyone and they'll all hate me and think I'm some stupid little boy. Do I really have to go, really?"

"Yes you do," said Sally, drying the lad down with a towel. "Now come on and get dressed. We don't want to be late, what sort of an impression would that make."

"What's 'impression' mean?"

207

"It means you don't want them to think you're not interested enough or polite enough to get to school on time after they were good enough to offer you a place."

"They'd be right then, I'm not interested."

"Just stop moaning, Jimmy, you're going to school whether you like it or not."

After Jimmy had passed Sally's inspection, the two of them set off to Campo Lane. All the time Jimmy was trying to persuade Sally he'd go to school the next day without moaning, just as long as he didn't have to go this day, but it didn't work. No matter how logical he thought his arguments, Sally was determined.

"And just think, you'll have a nice comfy bed to sleep in instead of lying on a pile of rags on the floor," she said.

Jimmy stopped in his tracks. "You mean I'll have to sleep there as well and not go home to Uncle John's anymore?" His lips trembled and Sally had to look away from the misery and fear in the boy's face.

"On Sundays you'll come home, we'll come down to fetch you and we'll have some treats waiting for you."

Jimmy just stared at her, drained white. He didn't speak for the rest of the walk into town and when they arrived at the Blue Coat School he rushed on in without even waiting for Sally. She reported his arrival to a rather severe looking woman in the office and was instructed to take Jimmy into a side room where he could take off his old clothes and put on his new uniform. All the time the boy refused to speak.

"You look very smart in your new clothes," said Sally, adjusting the cap on Jimmy's head.

"They're not my clothes and they're not new neither," he said.

"Jimmy please, don't be so upset, I did tell you you'd be staying here. You'll be sleeping in a big room with lots of other boys and you'll be able to tell each stories when the lights go out."

"I don't want to hear their stories," he said, still curling his lower lip.

Sally was feeling really guilty but the matron took charge. "That's enough now we haven't got all day," said the woman. "Come along boy and I'll take you to the assembly hall. You may go, Miss Bisby. You may collect the boy on Sunday morning at eight-o'-clock sharp." Sally watched as Jimmy slunk away under the watchful eye of the matron. Jimmy refused to look back.

He was taken into a large room with lots of wood panelling and big windows. "That's the headmaster, Mr Bagshaw," said the matron, "you will wait here until he speaks to you." Before Jimmy was a large, pot-bellied figure of a man, standing so straight up that his belly stuck out even more "like some huge boil", thought Jimmy, "or some big barrel of stale beer", and he smirked trying to imagine the big belly crawling with puss inside or sloshing about full of ale. The whack of a belt on the table in front of him wiped the smile off his face.

"The purpose of Blue Coats is to educate those of you who have been orphaned in the ways of punctuality, of good manners and language, of cleanliness and neatness. You will regard us, in time, as your Alma Mater and Pater and will learn the importance of cheerful obedience to duty, of consideration and respect for others, of honour and truthfulness in word and act. You will learn basic reading, writing and arithmetic and above all you will learn your position in society and how to respect your betters."

Jimmy had no idea what the stiff old misery-guts standing on the podium in front of him was talking about. He'd heard about alms in the Bible but as regards all the other stuff, especially about respecting your betters, personally he thought it sounded like a complete load of bollocks. The uniform he'd been forced to put on was uncomfortable and looked daft. His collar was high and starched to the point of choking him; the blue coat, from which, for some bizarre reason, the school seemed to be named, was heavy and constricting with stupid yellow braiding and brass buttons as if they were playing soldiers; the corduroy trousers were thick and cumbersome and, to top it all, there was a poncey cap shaped like a muffin. If I wanted a fucking muffin on me head I'd become a fucking baker, Jimmy had thought to himself when he had first put it on. He'd heard John use the word 'fuck' and was suitably impressed by it to use the word as liberally as he could, regardless of what Sally might say.

There were five other kids stood in a row next to him in front of this Mr Bagshaw, the you-can-call-me-Sir headmaster. Jimmy was already figuring out how soon he'd be able to get out of the place. He already hated the school, the other kids who looked like complete sops and the man who was still droning on.

"You will find us harsh but fair. Step out of line and we'll beat you severely but behave yourself and you should emerge from Blue Coats better people. All of you here have suffered a loss from the terrible flood we have just experienced but you have to put that behind you and move on and improve yourselves so that you may serve society as well as you can within the station that has been allotted to you." The headmaster surveyed the six children in front of him, sizing each one up as if to read their characters and spot any potential troublemakers; his gaze halted on Jimmy who was slouching with a bored sneer on his face. In a practised smooth motion the man launched a missile which struck the boy just above his left eye. Jimmy recoiled from the stinging impact and saw a spray of tiny specks of chalk bouncing off the floor. He felt more shock than pain and, startled, looked up at his attacker.

"You boy, you'd better smarten up your attitude before it lands you in a whole lot of trouble," Mr Bagshaw bellowed.

Anger filled Jimmy and without thinking he shouted back at the man. "Fuck this for a game of soldiers, you can stuff your fucking chalk, your fucking rules and your fucking precious uniform right up your fucking arse." Without waiting to see the results of his outburst, Jimmy pelted back down the hall they'd been standing in, out through the doors, over the yard and off through the gates. He found himself out on Campo Lane and sprinted off down the road, not knowing where he was going but just determined to put as much distance between him and the school. He'd gone about two hundred yards when he heard someone shout his name. He stopped, looking around fearfully, but couldn't believe anyone from the school could have chased after him quite so quickly.

"Hey Jimmy, ain't you meant to be at school. Don't tell me you've run away already?"

Jimmy looked in the direction of the voice and recognised the woman leaning out of a window across the road, the same one who had known Sally and met them the first time he had been taken to the Blue Coat. Jimmy had forgotten what the woman's name was but remembered that she had seemed alright. He looked back to see if there were any pursuers from the school but could see no-one. He rushed over the street to where the woman was and said: "Ey up Mam, if you could see your way to putting me up for a couple of hours, I'd owe you one."

The woman laughed: "Lor', you have run away. Well Jimmy lad, if education doesn't suit you, I'll not be the one to force you into it. Wait at the door to the left and I'll come down and let you in."

"Well can you hurry up? Otherwise I'll have those fucking bastards on to me in no time at all." Jimmy jigged around nervously, constantly looking back towards the school.

The woman who had disappeared from the window suddenly returned. "Here, you watch your bleeding language when talking to a lady or I'll shop you as soon as blink."

"Sorry Mam, it's just that I think they'll be coming for me pretty soon."

"Wait at the door."

Jimmy scuttled up the steps and waited. The door finally opened and the woman ushered him in.

"Come upstairs lad and get yourself some grub. You don't remember my name do you? It's Peggy, Sally's friend."

"'Course I remember your name, Mam, it's just that I've been brought up properly."

"In that case I'm not sure your parents would approve of that colourful language you used earlier." Peggy pushed open a door into a kitchen and bustled around preparing something for the lad to eat.

"My Mam and Dad are dead, got flooded. We had a funeral though, a proper funeral." Jimmy grabbed a slice of buttered bread which Peggy handed him.

"Well that's a bleedin' shame. No-one your age should lose their folks that young."

"I'm ten," Jimmy said defensively.

"Ten eh? Well, if it's not education you want, maybe you'd be wanting to find a job?" Peggy sat the boy down on a stool. "I happen to know someone who can always use a young lad who's as quick with his wits as he is on his feet."

"A job? A job for me? That'd be smashing." Jimmy could hardly believe his luck: escaping from the school into a job.

"Well let me see what I can do, there's somebody I'd like you to meet Jimmy. You wait there and I'll go and see if he's got time for us to pop in." Peggy turned and opened the door.

"Who is it, who's the man?" Jimmy demanded through mouthfuls of the doughy bread.

"Someone called Jack. I think he could find a place for you in his business." Peggy left, leaving Jimmy munching and wondering what sort of a job he'd landed.

THE brewery had directed Matthew Blagdon to Bungay Street. He'd never ventured too far into The Ponds before and as he walked along the pavement he seemed to develop a nervous facial tic as he constantly fought to keep the stink out of his nostrils. And it was some stinking place. He thought his nose had suffered the worst it could encounter when he'd followed the trail of the flood water but this was altogether more depressing; this was the stink of the living, not the dead. He actually caught himself starting to feel some sympathy for the poor blighters who had to face this every day and every night. "There but for the grace of God, as somebody or other once said," he told himself, all the time concentrating on where he put his feet, couldn't be too careful with so much muck everywhere. When he found the house at last, he wasn't sure it would be any better inside than out on the street. "All in the line of duty," he told himself then went on in. He found John Hukin's room on the first floor. The door was already open. "Must be to let the fresh air in," Blagdon thought, amused at his wit, "here goes."

Hukin was sitting with his back to the door at a table bare but for a tattered magazine. The girl, Sally, was perched on a chair next to him patiently going through letters and words with the man. Blagdon felt a flicker of shame at his own arrogance before the simple sight of a big, working man trying to learn how to read. "Excuse me, may I come in? I don't want to interrupt your lesson. Sounds as if it's going well."

John immediately shoved the magazine to one side with a flicker of a different kind of shame. It wasn't lost on the reporter.

"Do we know you?" asked Sally.

"We know him," said John, now hunched, staring out of the window.

"I got your address from the brewery. I hope you don't mind. I was hoping to talk to you about how things are with you both now. It's already a few weeks since the flood and I was wondering how you're both managing." He looked around the room taking all the poverty in with a glance.

"We're managing," said John. "I don't know what it's got to do with you, though."

"John, don't be like that. It's very kind of..."

"Matthew Blagdon, Miss."

"...very kind of Mr Blagdon to call to see how we are."

"He's not interested in us, he only wants a bloody story for his bloody newspaper," said John.

"Are you a reporter, Mr Blagdon?"

"Yes, I work for the paper here in Sheffield. We met before, actually, at Malin Bridge. Your name is Sally Bisby, as I recall. I was with John here when he found you after the flood, you were searching for mementos of your family."

"My treasures," said Sally. "They're my treasures. I remember looking for them in the mud but I don't remember you."

Blagdon was about to say something else but he noticed the girl had gone into some sort of a daze. He turned his attention to John. "Is she alright?" he asked.

"Oh yes, she lost her family, her home, everything, and now you bloody well come round here making her think about it all over again – of course she's not alright, you bloody fool."

"I'm sorry, genuinely," said Blagdon, looking back at Sally and seeing her rifling through a scruffy old bag.

"Ay, well, we're all sorry," growled John. "Sit yourself down," he said, relenting, glad of some change of company. "What do you want to know? How we're doing? Well, we're three in a poky room, as you can see, one on the bed, that's Sally of course, and two of us on the floor; we've just got my drayman's pay to live on and we're surrounded by squalor and little hope of anything better turning up. You can fill in the details yourself with your fancy newspaper words. As you've already seen, I won't be able to read them anyway."

"Can nothing be done?" asked Blagdon. "What about the relief fund, surely Sally would be entitled to some compensation, after all her family owned a pub."

"Owned? You daft bugger, they rented it. People like us don't own pubs."

"Well there must have been things in there that they did own, furniture, carpets, clothes, the usual stuff."

"What's the point in getting a few pounds when you've lost everything that matters," said John. "Anyway, I'm too busy working and doing as much overtime as I can get just to hold on to this heap of shit, I don't have any time to even think about Sally putting in a claim. You've seen how she's gone off in a dream now; she couldn't do any claim thing by herself and I couldn't write out a damned claim anyway. Reading and writing's not my strong point, as you've already observed."

"I could help," said Blagdon. "You helped me when I needed a ride up the valley, let me help Sally now."

"You do want your bloody report, don't you." John glared at the intruder.

"Of course I do, that's my job, but it doesn't mean I can't help you while I'm getting it. I could take Sally down to the Town Hall and register her losses, she might get something. I can write about how easy or difficult it is for people. I really could help, you know."

"I'd not got you marked down for a Good Samaritan," said John. "Anyway, isn't it a bit late now to claim relief?"

"Not really. And I do know the people in charge so I could help explain the delay if there was any problem." John didn't reply, just carried on looking around aimlessly but with a scowl on his face. "Come on, John," Blagdon persevered. "Don't be so bloody stubborn. You look worn out, man, and the girl could do with some assistance, you both could. You might not like me very much but that's no reason not to accept a genuine offer of help."

"And what do you want by way of return?" asked John, reluctant to soften his mood even though he knew the reporter was talking sense.

"I just want to know all about Sally; who lived at the pub, how she escaped, why she's here with you, how you're coping, that sort of stuff."

"I suppose there'd be no real harm in that," said John at last, "but it depends on you helping like you said you would."

"You can rest assured. Shall I come here to fetch you both or do you want to meet me somewhere?"

"Well I'll have to try to get off work early but it might not be too much of a problem tomorrow. That's the day I used to deliver to the pubs up the valley. Not that many of them left now wanting beer."

"Tomorrow's good for me," said Blagdon. "Why don't I call here for Sally and we can meet you near the Town Hall when you've finished work."

"Alright, about half-two," said John. He stood up and went over to Sally, gently taking the bag of treasures out of her hand and squatting down on the floor in front of her. "Sally, listen girl, I want you to remember Mr Blagdon's face because he's coming here to see you tomorrow and then you're both going to meet me in town. Remember we talked about your Mam and Dad and all the others being lost in the flood and how it was something that you knew but didn't want to think about? Well Mr Blagdon here is going to see if he can get us some money from the Town Hall, just to help us out like til we get things organised. So take a good look at his face so you recognise him tomorrow."

Sally looked long and hard at Blagdon's face. "You've got a nice face," she said. "I like your face. Are you going to get the pub back for us?"

"Not entirely," said Blagdon, "but hopefully we'll be able to get you something. I'll see you tomorrow, then Miss Bisby. And by the way, I think you've got a very nice face too." Sally blushed.

John took the reporter down to the street and they went over the arrangements for the following day again. "God it would be good if we could get her back the pub," said John. "I don't think poor Sally's ever going to get better while she's stuck in this hell hole. She needs the country and the country air, that's what's she's used to."

"I nearly suggested you give her the money yourself, John, but I realised that would be an unforgivably cruel joke. See you tomorrow."

John watched Blagdon walk off down the street and realised something had been triggered by the reporter's remark but he couldn't quite grasp what exactly. "'Give her the money yourself'," he kept repeating in his head, "'a cruel joke'." Then he had it, then he grasped the missing something: he had money, Quinn's money, and he'd completely forgotten all about it.

THE head office had been a hive of activity all morning and it was doing Jack Quinn's head in. Runners were lining up to see him, scribblers were busy trying to squeeze the last dregs they could from the relief fund before the coppers got too suspicious (there was already talk in the Town Hall of chancers conning money out of the fund and the number of beggars on the streets had multiplied, all giving the same hard-up flood stories) and Quinn was thirsting for a shot. "Here you lot," he shouted, pulling some coins out of his pocket, "you've earned this, go get yourselves a couple of drinks, the noise in here is worse than in a bloody steel factory and it's hammering my head flat. Clear off and enjoy yourselves for a bit and I'll see you all later. Well done everyone," He threw the money across his desk and the grovellings of gratitude brought a smile to his wallet. After all, it was only a couple of glasses of ale they'd got themselves, stupid buggers. "Peggy, you stay here. Briggs, you wait outside til I call you. You can have your drink later."

The room was quickly emptied and the sound of the chattering gobs of small fry let off the hook for a bit gradually died down. Quinn visibly relaxed and turned his attention to Peggy; he could concentrate now.

"That's better," he said. "I thought my head was going to burst open like a whore's fanny ready to do business. Peggy, well, so what's what today?"

"Couple of things to report, Jack. I went to see the Melanie whore and it turns out that Sally, the girl staying with Hukin, hasn't even thought about claiming from the fund yet so I got Mel to agree I'd have a word with you so you could help the girl and she's not going to mention it to Hukin; I told her he's too tired to bother right now when you're here only too willing to help her out. And just now I've left the snivelling kid waiting upstairs in my room. He's ran off from the school already, little bleeder's only started there today, and I told him you might have a job for him."

"Oh yeah?"

"And his little thief's face lit up like a beacon. Want me to call him in or what?"

"Mmh," said Quinn, swivelling round in his chair a few times while he thought. "Not right now, Peggy, because Briggsy's outside and the kid might have seem him down The Ponds hanging around Hukin's place. Don't want to frighten him off now after all your good work. Tell you what, take him for a bit of a walk, here's a few coppers, buy him some cake and lemonade in the street or whatever it is kids like – make sure you go to one of our own carts, no point in giving money away - and then call back here in about half an hour. Won't do any harm for him to get to know you a bit better, Peggy, it's all an investment. Never too young to get friendly with a whore."

"Right you are Jack. What's the plan for him?"

"I've told you before, don't ask questions that don't concern you until I say they do, haven't I told you that before? Haven't I?"

Peggy hated the way his mood would change as quick as a punter's dick: up one minute, down the next. "Yes, Jack, it's just that as I made contact with the lad..."

"Don't go thinking you've done anything particular, slag, you only do what I tell you, remember that, and if you do alright it's up to me to say so, alright?"

"Alright, Jack, just don't get so nasty, I'm doing everything you ask."

Quinn swiped the back of his hand across Peggy's face. "Everything except mind your own business when I tell you to, now clear off and I'll see you later. And wipe your face, no need to scare the kid with a bit of blood. A bird showing the back of my hand isn't worth nowt in the bush. And tell Briggs to come in."

Outside the door, Briggs saw Peggy wiping her mouth and cleaning the cut with spittle. "That's the sort of mood he's in then?" he commented. "I fell, that's all," said Peggy. "Oh ay? Funny you only cut your lip then, Peg." Quinn was clever: he had worked all his runners so none would ever admit to any of the others that they weren't important enough to escape the back of the boss' hand. "Thanks for the warning, girl, I know to watch my step."

"Bugger off, Briggs," said Peggy and she went up to find Jimmy, still trying to ease the sting, right in the corner where her lips met, it was. "Bastard, you bastard," she was muttering when she walked in on the boy.

"Who, me?" asked Jimmy, not knowing what he could possibly have done just by sitting in a kitchen.

"Not you, lad, not you. Come on, let's go get ourselves a treat."

In the office, Mick Briggs was trying to sell his plan to Quinn. "I can't see as how it can go wrong, boss," he said. "I know exactly what time Hukin goes out to work and what time he comes back home again; the kid's away at school now so there's only the girl to worry about. Soon as I see her go out, soon as I'm in to Hukin's room to find the money. What do you think?"

"I think, Mr Briggs, that that's not a bad idea, not a bad idea at all. And it has the advantage of being quick; I've been waiting too long to get my hands on that money since that bloody idiot Pickens lost it. Why not do it tomorrow? The man's at work on Tuesdays isn't he?"

"Sure is, Jack, tomorrow it is then."

"So what's what today?" asked Quinn. "Anything else to report?"

"Only that I saw Peggy going into the whore's house but I assumed that was on your business. There was one other bloke called to see Hukin but I don't know who he was, he was just arriving as I was leaving." As soon as he had said it Briggs was sorry but it was too late: he nearly stuttered a lame explanation but stopped, experience told him it was never a good idea to try to pull the wool over Quinn's eyes.

"Someone arrived but you were leaving?" repeated Quinn. "Are you telling me that someone arrived as you were leaving and yet you carried on leaving, is that what you're telling me?"

"Well I'd been standing there all bloody day, boss," said Briggs, momentarily showing his impatience.

"Poor you, poor fucking you," shouted Quinn, in an instant grabbing a cane from behind his desk and raising it over the cowering Briggs' head. He stopped mid swing but held the stick aloft. "Don't you ever complain to me about having to stand in the street all bloody day, scum. All bloody day and all bloody night if I say so, get it?"

"Sure, sure, I'm tired, that's all," Briggs stammered. "And I wanted to make sure I was fresh for the break-in, if you were to give the go-ahead, like, like you have given."

"Good work, Briggs," said Quinn laughing. "Just thought I'd keep you on your toes, especially if they're feeling a bit numb from all that standing. What was he like this bloke who visited Hukin?"

"Quite smartly dressed, boss, not the usual sort you see round The Ponds, looked as if he had a couple of bob."

"Find out who he was and we'll see if he's got a couple of bob he doesn't need," said Quinn. He got up and joined Briggs on the other side of the desk. "We'll discuss any finer points of your plan later. I might have a way of making sure the girl's not around. Now, you go and enjoy that drink I promised. No doubt the others are in the Paradise. We'll talk later."

Briggs stood up to leave, relieved to be leaving; Quinn's temper wasn't one to suffer too long if you didn't have to. "Thanks, boss," he said and headed for the door but before he got there Quinn slashed the cane across the backs of his legs. "What the hell was that for?" Briggs cried.

"Just joking," cackled Quinn. "On your toes, man, on your toes."

Quinn made a point of slamming the door behind Briggs, enjoying the sound of the noise and the knowledge that it would have made the runner wince and charge down the stairs double-quick. Once on his own, the gang boss went through some fancy posturing, swishing and whipping and jabbing the cane through the air as if he was a swordsman in the middle of a fight-to-the-death encounter on the ramparts of some mediaeval castle. "I am Sir

217

Quinn de Sheffield," he informed his imaginary opponent, "and I will not have any other pissing noble knight muscling in on my battleground. Take that, you dog," he said, lunging in the general direction of the tea-pot and managing to spear the handle, picking up the pot and swirling it through the air like a skewered victim. Dregs of old brew splashed around the room. "Fucking bloody tea-pot," he shouted, hurling it to the floor. "Why don't no-one ever empty the bloody thing properly. Peggy, Peggy," he yelled. "Where is that bleeding whore?" Quinn went back behind his desk and had a shot of cheap brandy: it was his turn to wince but he had a second measure despite the bite. He threw back another one when he heard Peggy's voice on the stairs. "Come in Peggy, my love, come in." He was certainly feeling warmer now.

"Jack," she said, peering round the door before opening it fully, trying to gauge the man's mood, whether or not he had calmed down, "I'm got someone here who's quite anxious to meet you. Shall we come in?"

"Do, do, get your arses in here."

Peggy shepherded Jimmy through into the office. Quinn liked the look of the lad straight off even in his pathetic uniform: here was a kid who wasn't afraid, he stood his ground, no hiding behind the woman's skirts like some weaselly little wimp, he could already teach some of Quinn's other runners a thing or two on how to create the right sort of impression.

"And who are you that you're so anxious to meet me?" asked Quinn. Peggy opened her mouth to speak but Quinn raised his hand. "He looks like a lad who can talk for himself. Are you, Son?"

"Well I'm not your son and of course I can talk," snapped Jimmy. "I'm here for a job. Peggy told me you might have one for me."

"All in good time, Son, all in good time. I don't even know your name."

"Jimmy."

"Jimmy, is it? And where is Jimmy from exactly?"

"I'm from out Hillsborough way but I'm in town now because our house got washed away."

"And can you read and write, Jimmy? I'm told you go to school," said Quinn, curling his upper lip at the corner in what he assumed would pass as a smile.

"I don't go to no school, I only went this morning and that was enough for me, I was out of there quick as."

"Well, young Jimmy, as it happens I could offer you a little job but I do like my people to be able to read and write so part of our arrangement would be that you'd have to go back to school to learn, even if you weren't there all day every day, like."

Jimmy turned on Peggy. "You didn't say anything about me having to keep going to school, you said I could just get a job."

"Peggy's not the boss, see," said Quinn, "are you Peggy? Tell him."

"No, I'm not the boss, Jimmy, and if Jack here says it would be a good idea to learn how to read and write then he's no doubt right. He's a clever man is Jack."

"I don't need to go to school for that. My Uncle John's learning on the table at home."

"Well that's interesting to know. Do you get on well with your Uncle John, Jimmy?" asked Quinn, tickled at the titbit of information about Hukin.

"Course I do, he's my uncle isn't he."

"But let's just say I did give you a few little jobs to do, Jimmy, I wouldn't want you to go telling your uncle about them, see, he might not understand our little arrangement. Do you think you could keep it to yourself?"

"Course I could," said Jimmy laughing. "I was always keeping stuff from my Mam."

"Good, then I think we're going to get on very well. Your job here will be our secret but you will have to go to school or your Uncle John might start wondering what you're up to."

"But I can't go back now, I ran away."

"Peggy will take you back and she'll make up some excuse for you, it'll be fine. Then what I want you to do is to nip out tomorrow and come over here to head office to see me. Meanwhile make sure you have a good look around that school of yours, find out where everything is, where the office is, who does what and when, that sort of thing."

"Why?"

"One of the things you have to learn, lad, is that everything you get to know can come in useful, that's why. It pays to keep your eyes and ears open always, always, then, when you need to know stuff, it's surprising what stuff you actually already know. And make sure you keep your nose clean: one of the other things you have to learn in our line of business is when it pays to keep a low profile."

"What's that mean, 'keep a low profile'?" asked Jimmy.

"It means make sure you behave yourself and don't stand out, just melt into the background, like, then no-one will be keeping an eye on you and you'll be able to poke around the place without anyone realising what you're up to."

"Okay, Mr Quinn."

"And one more thing, Jimmy, and it's very important so don't you go forgetting: when you do come here, any time you come here, knock before you come in, otherwise you might get the odd knock yourself, understand?"

"Not sure," said Jimmy. "I'm to knock on the door every time I come here, I understood that much."

"You'll get the rest soon enough. Off you go now with Peggy and pay attention in those lessons. Peggy, you brought me a good 'un. Why don't you come back later and I'll try to make that lip of yours better."

Peggy took Jimmy by the hand and flounced out but at the door she turned to Quinn and licked her lips til they gleamed wet. "Right you are, Mister Quinn."

SAMUEL Bickerstaff was on his way home nursing a copy of the telegraph he had sent to David Shaw's last known regiment straight after the visit by that chap Nightingale. "It pays to be careful," he thought, immediately regretting that such an adage obviously struck his own son as an irrelevant inconvenience. It was because of Bickerstaff junior and his total lack of care that Samuel himself had been forced to start acting at the blurred margins of the law, leastwise he had recently persuaded himself that there were blurred areas, in which the established line between what was right and what was wrong could be, let's say, fainter than well drawn. The man had always prided himself on his professionalism and good standing within the legal circles of Sheffield: he had built up a good practice, with a good reputation; perhaps he had never shone, never performed as a great orator addressing a packed courtroom in some landmark case, but he had worked hard and honestly. Then his son had started gambling and opened the door to Jack Quinn, whose threats of blackmail and extortionate interest payments on Simon's debts had forced Samuel to chip away at his own high ethical standards. Mrs Bickerstaff was unaware of the situation, of course; she knew that their son stayed out late nearly every night and that he would come home in a drunken temper but she always managed to persuade herself that it was just a passing phase and that he would mature into a man as fine as his father. Dora Bickerstaff hadn't had much education herself, coming from a very traditional background in which she was groomed to be a good housewife to a good husband and then a good mother to his children. She worked hard at presenting an image of herself as an able manager of the home but really she found it all very difficult and, apart from the occasional heavy-handed approach with the servants for the sake of face, she was much happier when she was in the background providing gentle, encouraging support for Samuel while getting on with her embroidery. "All very well," said Samuel to himself, "meanwhile

I'm left to sort everything out." He had already worked out how to pay the nasty Quinn character two hundred pounds out of Thomas Shaw's estate but, with the appearance of James Nightingale on the scene, he was nervous at going too far: there was only so much he could put down to defendable legal fees, otherwise that fine line definitely blurred all the way to embezzlement. Bickerstaff senior shuddered as he opened the door to his house.

"Dora, I'm home," he called as usual. He put his hat and gloves on the rack and his umbrella in the stand. He patted his top pocket where the telegraph was stored, the piece of paper that should provide proof of him trying to sort out Mrs Fletcher's affairs should it ever be necessary.

Mrs Bickerstaff hurried into the hall to greet her husband. "Thank goodness the rain stopped when it did," she said, "I feared for you getting a good soaking on the way back from the office. I really do wish you would take the carriage."

"I enjoy the walk, my dear. Don't forget I'm sitting at a desk most of the day. Is Simon at home?"

"No, the poor boy really wanted a night in with us but he had some tedious dinner engagement to keep."

"Really," said Samuel. "And what about Elizabeth, is she here?"

"I believe she's in the kitchen with cook. I'll say this for her, Dear, she's a very hard worker. It doesn't seem to matter how many tasks I give her to perform, she just gets on with it, although I have noticed a certain coldness comes across her face sometimes, as if she wasn't properly grateful for the position you've given her. She perhaps doesn't realise how much she's in your debt for all your help."

"Perhaps," said Samuel. "Indeed perhaps you should go a little easy on her, Dora, give her time to settle in more."

"Actually Simon invited her to accompany him to his dinner engagement but she even turned her nose up at that. Shall I pour you a sherry?"

"Yes, thank you. I'll have a sit for a bit and then I'll have a talk to her. Let's go into the drawing room and you can tell me all about your day."

"Well I got Elizabeth to build up the fire for you coming home so it should be nice and cosy. I'll just tell Mary you're home. We'll eat in an hour, will that be fine with you? We've got a nice roast as it's been such a miserable day. Perhaps you could leave your chat with Elizabeth until after dinner."

The rich smells of the beef and potatoes roasting in the range filled the kitchen with smells which reminded Elizabeth of her old home at Malin Bridge and of Mrs Trickett's farm kitchen. She could picture the boys there playing while their Mum got on with the cooking and washing. Her own mother's kitchen was always quieter, less frantic, more a place for relaxed conversation than for noisy gossiping.

"You're miles away, Liz," said Mary. "Thinking of home, are you Love?"

"It's difficult to accept sometimes that all that life is over now, completely gone," said Elizabeth. "One minute people and places are just there, part of what you see and do and hear every single day without ever stopping to think about it all, about how wonderful it all is, then suddenly they're gone, you're alone, suddenly you realise that whatever was left unsaid will never now be said, it's too late, too late to put right bad moods or cross words."

"Is there something like that niggling you at the back of your mind?"

Elizabeth started folding up the laundry so she had an excuse to be looking at something anonymous. "Daniel and I had a terrible row when he was leaving for work that morning and that was the last time we spoke to each other. I kept looking forward all day long to his coming home so we could put everything right again, so I could hug him and see him smile with the row all forgotten. We'd sit in front of the fire together, just chatting; he'd tell me about what he'd been doing at work, whether or not he had managed to finish the big order he had on, and I'd tell him about what I'd been up to, who I'd seen, what Pebble had been up to, chasing the chickens or barking at the stupid goat or whatever – Pebble was a lovely puppy, Mary, really funny and mischievous, he was a present from my Mam when Daniel and I got married, I even tied a red ribbon round his neck and he looked really nice, silly but nice – but none of that was allowed to happen. You really shouldn't be unkind to people, ever, or have stupid arguments about nothing, because you might not be able to put it right again."

"Yes, Love, but we're only people aren't we and that's the way of things, none of us can live as if the next minute was to be our last, no matter what they teach you in Sunday School. You just have to get on with things and sometimes that means you're in a bad mood and you get cross. Makes the good times better, too."

"And right now we'd better get on with serving the dinner."

"Just think, you could have been going out with Master Simon this evening instead of dishing up the meat and veg," said Mary.

"I wish he'd leave me alone," said Elizabeth. "He's beginning to get on my nerves the way he hovers around. He's like one of those persistent flies you get round fresh cow dung."

"You mean he keeps sniffing around?" laughed Mary. "Come on, let's get this meal dished up and on to the table; the sooner their lordships get it eaten, the sooner we'll be off duty."

Elizabeth carried the terrines through into the dining room followed by Mary bearing the tray of roast beef for Samuel Bickerstaff to carve, a tradition he upheld even on weekday evenings. The Bickerstaffs were already seated and waiting.

"By the way, Mrs Fletcher, I had a visit today from one of your father's friends, a James Nightingale," said Samuel.

"You mean Jim?" Elizabeth was surprised to hear the quite respectful tone in the senior partner's voice.

"I suppose that probably you would call him by a more familiar term, him being an old family friend and so on. Yes, he called in to the office today looking for you and we had a very interesting chat. I understand he was a business associate of the late Mr Shaw and a very good one, I've no doubt; a man not afraid to get his hands dirty by the looks of things; he actually came into the office in his work clothes, explained that he had been carrying out some maintenance or other at one of his shops. He was most concerned over your well-being, Mrs Fletcher, and I was pleased to inform him that yours and your father's affairs had been left in good hands. I passed on this address to Mr Nightingale so you may expect a visit. I'm sure it would be very pleasurable for you to have a visitor related through friendship to your family."

"Did he say when he might call?"

"He didn't but I got the impression it would be quite soon, rest assured on that point. Do take him into the parlour when he calls, I'm sure a man of his standing would feel more at home there than chatting with you in the kitchen."

"Of course," said Elizabeth, not a little bemused.

"You may tell him when he does call that I have already set in motion my enquiries into your brother's regiment for proof of death," said Samuel, slicing the beef. "There you are Dora, your favourite bits," he said, serving his wife the seared outside slices.

"My brother's regiment?" Elizabeth seemed to be hearing all sorts of bits of diverse information.

"As I explained to you some weeks ago and to Mr Nightingale on your behalf, it will be impossible for me to declare you as rightful beneficiary of your father's estate until I have the necessary legal documents relating to your brother and his last known whereabouts. All in good time, Mrs Fletcher, all in good time."

"May we eat now, Mr Bickerstaff," said Dora, always choosing to refer to her husband formally in front of the servants. "It would be a shame for cook's lovely dinner to get cold while you discuss business that would be best kept to the office."

"I don't see any point in getting Mrs Fletcher to come in specially to the office when I can speak to her here without any bother," said Samuel, sounding brisker than intended. "However, you're right, Dora, let's eat. I'm sure Mrs Fletcher doesn't want constant reminders anyway about her tragic losses." He picked up his knife and fork and began to eat. Elizabeth took this as a signal to leave and she was glad of it, she had things to think on; Mr James Nightingale, indeed; business associate of her father; old family friend; what was Jim up to? And telegraphs to David's regiment when everyone knew he had been killed years ago in the war in India. Back in the kitchen, there was none other than Jim Nightingale himself.

"Hello Miss Lizzie, I bet I'm a sight for sore eyes," he said. "By the way, best if old Bickers doesn't know I'm here, certainly not in the kitchen. I've already primed Mary, though I thought it best not to go into details."

"Your secret's safe with me don't you worry. I suppose the kitchen's not really the place you'd expect to find a successful businessman, is it?" Elizabeth was pleased to see Jim. "I was surprised to hear you were on such close terms with my father, Mr Nightingale, but then I imagine you're the sort of man who's always full of surprises."

"I like to keep a couple of cards up my sleeve, Miss Lizzie, you never know when you'll need to play the joker."

They both laughed out loud.

"It is good to see you Jim. You've made an impression with Mr Bickerstaff senior."

"Ay, well it came about by accident really. That Booth character was so snotty I wanted to put him in his place and before I knew where I was I was in a different place, I'd gone from being told to stand in the corner by the little turd of a clerk to being invited to take a seat in the inner office by Mr Bickers himself. I couldn't believe it when he believed every daft word I said. Good job you went along with it when you found out."

"He's just told me now, before I was dismissed silently while they eat their dinner. But I have been instructed to invite Mr James Nightingale into the parlour when he does visit me. 'A man of standing' is they way your were described."

"You didn't realise that when you gave me a mug of tea did you, Mary, that I was a man of standing."

Mary was a bit confused: Jim hadn't filled her in on any details at all: he'd only just met the woman and she did work for Bickers; for all Jim knew at that stage, Mary could have been just another toady who'd go ratting to the boss. "I don't know what you two are talking about but if there's a joke on his lordship in there then that's fine with me," she said. "I gather Jim's a friend from Bamford, Liz," she said.

"A new friend but a true friend," said Elizabeth.

"I think it best for now if old Bickers carries on believing all the guff I told him," said Jim. "It might keep him on his toes. What I can't really understand is how he can have you cleaning and cooking and all that if he was such a trusted friend of your Dad. Might not be a bad idea if he knows I'm looking out for you, girl."

"I don't know if they were friends, Gabriel only told me that my father had been dealing with Samuel Bickerstaff for years. I have to believe that my father trusted him. And do you know what, Jim, you've already had quite an affect with all your story-telling," said Elizabeth and she told him about the telegraph to her brother's regiment.

"Goes to show, then doesn't it, you young women of today still need a good man to get things moving for you and I've always had a bit of name for moving things on when it comes to young women."

"I'll bet you have, you saucy young pup," said Mary. "Have you eaten anything yet, Jim? There's food ready if you'd like some home cooking. Liz and I were about to eat and I doubt you get much wholesome food in your digs."

"I'd love to, Mary, but I'd be a bit nervous of his lordship coming in unexpectedly, wouldn't want to have to play the joker when there's a proper ace up my sleeve. And to be honest, Mary, I fancy a beer in the pub. I wouldn't say no to something to take with me, though."

"No problem, lad." Cook started packing up what looked like enough food to feed the whole of Jim's boarding house, especially taking into account the servings his landlady dished out. "There," she said, "that'll keep things moving in the right direction."

"And you're the one called me saucy," said Jim.

"When will I see you again?" asked Elizabeth.

"I'm going to call round proper on Sunday afternoon and you can invite me into the parlour then but I'll give you my address in case you need me beforehand."

"Have you heard any news from Bamford at all?"

"Not yet. I'm thinking of going over there for the day quite soon, maybe you could come too. I'll tell Bickers there's a family matter needs settling with the Bamford branch of the family and that it wouldn't do for Thomas Shaw's daughter to miss it just because she had to stay here and wash his lordship's drawers."

They all pictured his lordship's drawers and his lordship in his lordship's drawers before Jim snuck away through the back door. "Keep your noses clean, ladies," he said on his way out, "and keep them out of those drawers."

"He's a right card that one," said Mary when he'd gone. "You're lucky to have found him."

"I know," said Elizabeth. "Funny how dreadful things can happen but out of them you meet such good new people. In that sense I am lucky."

THE whole idea had been going through his head over and over; John could think of nothing but the money he'd taken from Will Pickens, money that he knew belonged to Jack Quinn. How could he have forgotten about it? Easily, he told himself; nearly 250 people had been drowned in the town in less time than it takes to down a few pints, not the sort of occasion to be thinking of money, especially as he'd known some of those people very well. He'd lost his best friend, Daniel, and gained two kids who depended on him. And if it hadn't been for Blagdon he wouldn't be thinking about the money now. But it had set him thinking, right enough, trying to work things out. Quinn wouldn't have forgotten the money no matter how many poor buggers were killed and he'd want it back. He'd probably guess it was still at John's place and he'd be figuring out how to get at it. So what would a crook like Quinn do? "Of course," said John out loud: he suddenly remembered the bloke who had appeared out of nowhere in Bungay Street doing nothing but hang around all the time, hang around directly opposite the house where John's room was. The thought made him chuckle to himself. "Well you're too late, Quinn, so you can call off your lapdog. The money's gone."

John had decided to move the cash as soon as he'd remembered it. It was Tuesday so his round took him out of town and back up the Loxley valley. The money was now well hidden, buried deep under some stones at the Urmstons' grave. What he was trying to sort out now was the best thing to do with it because Blagdon's suggestion had certainly hit home; Sally had lost everything; he could at least make sure she got something for all her pain. He hated to see her wasting away and drifting off into her own sad memories; now and then she said she knew she had to accept what had happened, other times it was as if she just couldn't face it. But she was getting better, slowly, and teaching him how to read seemed to be helping. He was quite enjoying it too, if he was honest, and it had let him see a different side to the Sally

Bisby who used to make cruel comments about his lack of schooling. He remembered how she used to run out to skit him every Tuesday without fail when he got to the Cleakum on the dray. "Funny that," he said to himself.

John had finished his deliveries for the day before going off to meet Sally and Blagdon. He had stabled George at the brewery yard and was going to go straight to the Town Hall but it was only just gone one-o'-clock so he was a bit early: he decided to rush home and have a quick wash.. He heard himself whistling on the way home and caught himself feeling fairly happy for the first time in weeks. "Funny that."

When he got to Bungay Street he noticed that Quinn's runner was nowhere to be seen. "Must have realised I'd got him worked out," thought John, sauntering along the pavement. Melanie was standing on her doorstep and she greeted him with a peculiarly smirky smile.

"Who's the fancy man then?" she asked.

"What fancy man?" asked John, still thinking about the missing runner and wondering if that was one way to describe Quinn's poodle.

"The one in the fine suit and polished shoes," said Melanie, "the one who turned up at your place an hour or so ago and left ten minutes later with young Sally. She obviously thought he was quite fancy too, judging by the way she'd tarted herself up. She introduced him on the way past, all chirpy, as you might say, said his name was Blaggers or something and that he was taking her out for something to eat. Quite handsome, he was, I wouldn't have minded a nibble of his desserts myself."

John felt himself get hot and bothered in a totally unfamiliar way. "He's a reporter from the local paper," he said. "He's taking Sally to the Town Hall to find out if she can get any money from that relief fund they set up after the flood. I'm supposed to be meeting them."

"Well they didn't look as if they needed anyone else along," said Melanie. She noticed John's face redden, not something she'd ever seen in the man before other than when he was beetrooted with drink and she knew he'd been off the ale for weeks. "Not bothered, are you, John? You look a little upset."

"Why would I be bothered?"

"Funny but there seems to be quite a few men only too ready to help your pretty young lodger with her claim," said Melanie, enjoying seeing her friend flushed. "Only the other day an old whore I know even offered the services of her bleedin' pimp to help Sally get her hands on some relief money, persuaded me not to bother yourself with it, you being so busy working and that, she said."

"What whore? What pimp?" John was suddenly all attention. "Come on," he said smartly, "what whore, what's her name?"

"Hold on there, only an old tart as used to work the pitch alongside mine a few years back," said Melanie. "Her name's Peggy, don't know the pimp, all she told me was that he's set her up in her own place in town somewhere. He smacks her round a bit, she says, but then what pimp doesn't treat his whores like animals. Why the questions?"

"What else do you know about her? I've never heard you mention anyone called Peggy before."

"Well you wouldn't have, you daft bugger, I'd not seen her in years and then she suddenly turned up a couple of weeks ago out of the blue like a bad penny, said she had an important regular client moved into The Ponds and thought she'd look me up. Whoever important would want to move in round here, I wondered, present company excepted, of course, Mr Hukin. I was quite surprised to see her to say the least, Peggy and me were never what you'd call friends, like, if you know what I mean, but it was pleasant enough talking about old times and old punters and their little preferences, and little everything elses half the time. She's been here a couple of times since then, that's how she knew about Sally, 'cause Sally called in when Peggy was here."

"What about that bloke who's been hanging around over the road, the one you said was one of Quinn's men, Briggs, have you ever seen this Peggy one talking to him?"

"Not as I've noticed but then I don't see Peggy to the door. What's up, John? You've gone from being quite a softie to being all serious?"

"Has he been here today?"

"I think I saw him earlier, why?"

"Well, he is one of Quinn's men, one of his runners, and I'm now wondering if this Peggy one's pimp is none other than the same Jack Quinn. Seems a bit of a coincidence that they all suddenly turn up here after that Pickens business."

"No, I couldn't imagine Peggy'd get mixed up with someone like Quinn. Even us whores have our standards, you know."

"Well perhaps you're right, you know her better than I do, Mel. I'll see you later, I'm supposed to be meeting Sally and that reporter at half-two at the Town Hall."

Melanie watched as John disappeared down the street and in through the door. She liked his back, strong and square and manly, the sort that suggested comfort and protection; she liked the way he walked, with proper strides like he had somewhere to go, except when he was drunk and stumbling about like a dieing ox and the only place he was going was in and out of the gutter, if he could decide which; she liked his worrying over people he cared for and, whatever she may have said to Peggy to the contrary, she wouldn't have minded a bit more of that worry for herself. "Stupid whore," she said to herself. The next minute the door to John's house burst open and two men fell out into the street, John and Briggs. The whole length of the street came to a standstill as everyone stopped to watch the fun – John Hukin had become very boring lately and the loungers and ne'er-do-wells who congregated in Bungay Street were pleased to see he hadn't completely reformed, they'd missed his brawls. The two men staggered and sweated as their punches landed and fists hit home. They stumbled awkwardly trying to keep their balance as shins cracked under the force of boots put in and kicks connected but it was Mick Briggs who went down first and ended up rolling around in agony in the dirt. John was on him like a demented bear.

"Right you bastard, what were you doing in my room, eh?" John had Briggs pinned across the throat with his left arm, leaving his fisted right hand ready to crash down into the man's jaw. "Come on you fucking scumbag, who are you, Quinn sent you didn't he?"

"I don't know no Quinn," gasped Briggs, "honest. I didn't know it was your room, I was looking for a friend. I haven't taken owt, I swear."

"You've been hanging around here long enough to know where everyone lives, you lying bastard. I know you work for Quinn. Well you can tell him from me to keep you and him out of my way, get it?" John snarled. "Get it, I asked?" he shouted, raising his right arm as if about to inflict even more punishment on the lump of battered flesh cowering beneath the threat.

"I get it, I get it."

John let the man up off the ground but kept his fists clenched and his arms braced in case the runner wanted a second round. He needn't have worried, Briggs was off as fast as he could run, he might work for Quinn but he was no fighter, not unless he was the one holding the knife and the victim was tied to a post. "You'll be sorry for that," he yelled back at John. "Quinn's not going to like what I've got to tell him."

"Best of luck in the telling then," shouted John, "you'll need it more than me."

Melanie appeared with a bowl of water and a towel to clean the cuts on John's face. "Didn't think I'd ever have to do this again," she said. "Then just as I think you've gone all soft on me, you come up again fighting like a champ. Looks as if you were right about him."

"I found him rummaging around in my room," said John.

"What could he be looking for in your room?"

"No idea," said John, "there's nothing in my room worth pinching. Ouch!" He pulled back sharply as the cold water stung one of the cuts by his mouth.

"Well he must be after something, my lad, and my advice to you is to get rid of whatever it is, quick. Quinn's obviously got you right high on his list."

"I'm not bothered about that bastard," said John. "Anyway leave off now, woman, I've got to get into town by half-two."

"Keep your shirt on, Hukin." Melanie finished stemming the last cut. "Your face looks a right mess," she said. "It's still a nice face, though."

"That's what Sally said to Blagdon," said John.

"Did she now?" commented Melanie. "I told you, the man's got something."

"I'd best be off."

John went back home leaving Melanie holding the basin of water. She looked around Bungay Street: "What the hell," she said and emptied the bowl in the gutter. The bloodied spill didn't make much difference, the gutter ran with foul water as a matter of course.

IT was only his second day at school and Jimmy was itching to get out and over to see his new boss at head office. He liked the sound of working at a head office. It made up for having to wear stupid clothes and having to say yes-sir-no-sir all the bleedin' time in this place. He didn't like sleeping in no big room with lots of other snotty boys he didn't even know neither. All that talk of Sally's about telling each other stories when the lights went out was just stupid too; anyone who even opened their mouth got a belt if one of the older boys heard them, prefects, they called themselves, bloody toffy-nosed snitchers, Jimmy called them. He'd done like Mr Quinn told him, though; he'd kept a low profile so he could have a good look round and he paid attention to who was who and what they did; he'd even listened in some of the lessons, didn't want to lose his new job just because of jumbles of letters, he might as well learn how to sort the jumbles into proper words. And the silly old bugger who was teaching him actually thought it was because Jimmy was interested. Funny how Mr Quinn had made it sound like a good idea to go to school when John and Sally only made it sound like something they thought he ought to do. Now he just looked at being in school as part of his job.

Jimmy's excuse to get out of the classroom came from an unexpected quarter. "Urmston, you took your beating like a Blue Coat boy yesterday and I have high hopes for you. As you've worked very hard and behaved yourself since that little incident, Urmston," said the headmaster, "I'm going to send you out on an errand for me by way of a reward. I want you to run up to the stationer's shop in Church Street and get me some envelopes. I am going to trust you with the money, let's call it a little test, and I'm going to trust you to come straight back. Do you know the shop I mean?"

"I'll find it, Sir, one that sells envelopes, Sir, thank you, Sir, your money will be safe with me, Sir."

"Alright, Urmston, off you go."

The boy was gone before the headmaster had even finished speaking. Once outside he turned left round the corner and headed up to Church Street, running as fast as he could: he wanted to get the envelopes quick as he could so he'd have time to nip in to head office before going back to school. On his way out of the shop he passed someone he vaguely recognised crossing the road and going into an office a bit further down the street but he didn't have time to stop. It wasn't someone he knew himself, it was the woman who'd married John's best friend, lived out Malin Bridge way, as far as he remembered, he used to see her about sometimes when he went to the village with his Mam who knew her Mam. Jimmy legged it back to Campo Lane on the far side of St Peter's church, just in case any nosy buggers were looking out of one of the school windows. He reckoned he could manage ten minutes at head office before having to get back with Mr Bagshaw's stupid bloody envelopes. He legged it over Campo Lane, charged in through the street door and took the stairs two at a time: he just managed to stop in time before charging in through the office door and remembered to knock.

"Come on, come on, I haven't got much time," he muttered to himself.

Jimmy could hear raised voices coming through from the office but he couldn't make out what was being said. He could make out that they weren't happy voices and he was beginning to think he'd better leave when Quinn shouted out: "Who's that knocking?" "It's me, Jimmy, from the school." "Jimmy, come on in lad."

There was a weedy-looking man sitting in the office, he seemed to be squirming in his seat.

"This here's Will Pickens, Jimmy, he works for me too but I don't think he's feeling too good today, are you Will?" Pickens pulled a face but remained silent. "So what's what today, Jimmy?" said Quinn.

"You told me to call in today, remember, boss?"

"Oh yes. And how's that school of yours?"

"I did like you said, Mr Quinn, I've had a good look around and I'm keeping a... a... a low profile," said Jimmy, grinning from ear to ear.

"See, Pickens, all you have to do is what I say, like young Jimmy here, then there'd be no trouble and I wouldn't be forced to get angry. I don't like getting angry, Pickens, makes me go all sweaty and I don't like being sweaty, makes me feel like a common type. Now, what was it you were telling me, Pickens?"

"What," said Pickens, "in front of the lad?"

"Jimmy's one of us now - isn't that right Jimmy? - so you can speak freely, not mentioning too many names, of course, no point in complicating matters for the lad. So what happened, Pickens, where is the bleeder?"

"I don't know, Jack, I thought he'd be coming straight back here to see you. Said he was coming straight here after he'd had a pint in the Paradise. Perhaps he wanted to clean up a bit, he looked as if he'd taken a right hammering."

"Well you've been on the receiving end of the same fists so you should know, you pathetic little squirt, you're all pathetic, no good any of you in a fight."

"Has there been a fight, Mr Quinn?" asked Jimmy, "I wish I'd seen it."

"None of your business, kid," snapped Quinn. "You speak when I speak to you, understand?" Quinn saw Jimmy bristle. "I saw that look, Jimmy, you're a good kid, won't take any nonsense, I can see that, you're going to be one of my best crew." He turned back to Pickens: "Now get out there and find the bastard, I want to know everything that happened, don't forget all this is your fault and I'm running out of patience; they say it's a virtue but it's not one I'm over-familiar with. Go on, clear off. Now, Jimmy, let me find some paper and a pencil 'cause there's something important I want you to draw and perhaps you and I might have a bit of a treat at the same time."

Quinn crossed the office to an old cupboard which he started to unlock with a key he kept in one of his trouser pockets. While Quinn had his back turned, Pickens skulked out of the office, sneering at Jimmy as he went. "Bloody John Hukin," he mouthed to the boy under his breath, "you just tell him to fucking well wait."

"Still here, Pickens? Want to make me angry, do you?" said Quinn. Pickens rushed on out.

Quinn handed the pencil and paper to Jimmy and poured him a drop of cheap scotch, not too well watered down. He handed the cup to Jimmy and chinked a toast: "Down the hatch, lad," he said.

Jimmy drank the whisky and burst into a fit of coughing and wheezing. "I've never had none of this before," he said.

"Better start getting used to it, lad. Now, draw me a plan of where the main office is in the school and where the other rooms are."

"I'll have to be quick though, Mr Quinn, I'm supposed to be out on a message."

"A quick sketch will do, Jimmy, then I can study it and you can explain anything I don't understand when you come tomorrow."

"Okay." Jimmy drew a map of the ground floor of the Blue Coat School. "There you are, Mr Quinn, but I don't know what you want it for, you're not thinking of going back to school are you?"

"Perhaps I could get a job there as a teacher," said Quinn. "Imagine all the things I could teach those lost boys. I'd be a teacher with more pet poodles than the queen."

"What's a poodle?" asked Jimmy.

"A dog," said Quinn, "a silly little yapping dog. Now be off with you, I've a business appointment to keep with my lawyer."

Jimmy had to race along Campo Lane and he was well out of breath when he got back to the classroom. "Sorry I was such a long time, Sir," he said to the headmaster, "but I had to stop to help a woman whose pet poodle was stuck in the railings by the church and it kept yapping and yapping. I hope I'm not in any trouble, Sir."

"Not at all, Urmston, I'm pleased to note that in future the lady in question will regard the Blue Coat uniform as a sign of good manners and generous Christian spirit. You did very well, young man, very well. From a very poor start you show indications of becoming a fine example of what the Blue Coat can achieve." Mr Bagshaw sniffed the air around Jimmy. "What's that I can smell?"

"The woman gave me a boiled sweet to suck after I'd helped her, she said they were special ones, Sir."

"My, you did make a good impression. Well done, Urmston."

"Thank you, Sir," said Jimmy. He took his place back on the bench in the class-room but he couldn't concentrate any more on his lesson: it had been a funny afternoon; people kept telling him how good he was and how good he was going to be and then there was that Will Pickens business, why had he given Jimmy a warning for his Uncle John?

THEY missed each other by minutes. While Jimmy was rushing back into his schoolroom, John was going in the other direction, home. He'd hurried down to the Town Hall but his skirmish with Quinn's man had made him late, half an hour late, and there was no sign of Sally and Blagdon, either inside the Town Hall or out. Some flunky behind the desk in the entrance lobby seemed to think he'd seen the two of them but said they had long since left the building. John had no option but to go home, feeling his stomach tied in unfamiliar knots and trying to figure out why. When he passed the Paradise, the temptation to drown his inexplicable sorrows proved too much: he decided to go in for a drink, his first in weeks.

The pub wasn't one he'd been in before. It was a gloomy place, with high-backed booths stood all the way down the wall and most of the windows hidden behind heavy curtains which looked as if one shake would free enough dust to make a thick fog. The back door was open to let some much-needed air in while the front door was kept shut to keep out prying busy-bodies. The customers in there seemed to adopt the same attitude: when John got his pint, he decided to move down to the booth nearest the open door, it was obviously the least popular seat.

The scene on the outside was no more inspiring than the one behind him on the inside. Hawley Croft around behind the Paradise was a warren of filthy narrow streets and snickets rotten with rubbish, where scruffy urchins played in the dirt and washing was optimistically strung across the street from one row of terraces to the opposite. The skyline was streamered with smoke trails rising up from the stacks of the back-to-backs. All in all not much better than The Ponds but without the river views.

John's pint hit the spot, alright, the rough beer racing through his veins and hitting his brain cells with a good-to-be-back slap, but Melanie's remarks about Sally and Blagdon wouldn't stop echoing round his head and he realised he was beginning to resent the newspaperman's appearance, in more ways than one. He found himself revisiting various scenes involving Sally; the way she would rush out of the Cleakum just to treat him like a dolt; the way she always dismissed him as "just a drayman"; the way she offered to teach him to read and how precious those moments had become to him, private moments, moments in which he felt important for the first time since his father had died; he remembered the day she had told him he was a fine man for taking care of her and Jimmy and how she had held him close when tears had finally got the better of him and he'd wept for the people lost in the flood. He was so lost in thought that it took a while for the noise from the booth behind him to register. When it did, John didn't need to turn or stand up to take a look; he recognised the voice.

"I'm getting right sick of the whole bloody thing, I can tell you. I've had enough, Peggy, it's not my bleeding fault Briggs copped it from Hukin and it looks as if the bastard's scarpered, the stupid bugger. He's only gone and left me here to put up with bloody Quinn's fucking temper." It was Will Pickens talking and John could guess what he was talking about.

"What did Quinn have to say about it?" said the woman quietly.

"His bleedin' bloody majesty's only told me I've got to find Briggs, or else."
"Or else what?"
"Or else I'm fucking well in for it, that's or else what. I've had enough of Quinn, I'll tell you that much for nowt. I know you and him's close, Peggy, but I aim to put some distance between me and Sheffield and Quinn and sharpish. For once Briggs 'as shown some bleedin' sense." There was an abrupt change in Picken's tone. "You won't go and bloody well tell him will you?"

"We're not that close, Will. We're as close as it suits me to be, that's all, and when it stops suiting me then Mr Jack Quinn can go fuck himself." At that Peggy burst out laughing. "Hey, d'you get it, Will, I'll finish with him and then he can go fuck himself. I think that's real funny that, don't you?"

"Nothing about him's funny," said Pickens. "Anyway, I'm off. If you see him tell him I'm out looking for Briggs."

"Are you leaving town now, Will?"

"Not sure," said Pickens. "I'll need to get some money together first. You never know, I might find Briggs and then get one of Quinn's pathetic bonuses. You never know, perhaps Briggs managed to find the money at Hukin's before he took the beating and he's run off with a tidy little packet himself. Bastard, I bet that's what happened."

"I wouldn't like to be in his shoes no matter where he is if Jack finds out. The boss's not one to let a small fortune slip through his fingers. How much did you reckon there was?"

"There must have been about two hundred quid. Now if Briggs hasn't got it and I could get my hands on it, I'd be out of Sheffield faster than it would take the time to count it."

"You and me both," said Peggy.

"What do you say I go back to Hukin's to take a look, Peggy?"

"I don't know, Will, whatever you say about Briggs he's always been sharp when it comes to finding money. I don't reckon it's there. But I tell you what, I bet I know someone who'll have a good idea, that Melanie one, her and Hukin are quite thick, I bet she knows. It might be time I paid her another social visit. Drink up and don't you do anything daft yet. Stay out of Quinn's way but hang around a bit longer. I'll cover for you if I have to and then we'll see if you and I can't sort something out between us. Maybe it's time we both cleared off."

John listened to the two of them slide out of the booth and their voices fade towards the door. A sudden brief intrusion of light suggested they'd just left the Paradise. He finished his drink and left through the back door, then threaded his way out through Hawley Croft. He didn't know whether to be angry or to find the whole thing just too funny. Quinn had had one of his thugs on duty in Bungay Street for weeks, he had even set one of his whores on to get to John through Melanie and all for a bundle of notes that John had actually forgotten existed until yesterday. Thank God Blagdon made that comment about helping Sally when he did, otherwise the money might have ended up back in Quinn's pocket.

When he got back to The Ponds, John went straight to Melanie's to warn her about her so-called old friend but Peggy had beaten him to it, she was already there.

"John," said Melanie, "there's someone here I'd like you to meet: this is Peggy, the old friend I was telling you about the other day."

"Hello, John," said Peggy. "I've heard lots of nice things about you from Melanie. I told her she was very lucky to have such a good man in her life and living on the doorstep, too."

The visitor stuck out her hand for John to shake: he decided to play ignorant. "Peggy, did you say? Oh yes, I remember now, you used to work the same pitch as Melanie years ago. What a coincidence you got a client near here after all these years."

"A lucky coincidence," said Peggy, "otherwise I might never have looked up Melanie and I always say you shouldn't let go of your old friends."

"You never know when you might need them, do you Peggy," said John.

"How's that face of yours?" asked Melanie, moving close to John and turning his head towards the window to get some better light.

"Been in a fight have you love?" asked Peggy.

"Bit of a scrap, that's all, found some waster in my room rummaging around."

"Seems to be mending fine," said Melanie, leaning in on John to examine his cuts.

"And what happened to the other feller?" asked Peggy. "I bet you got a few punches in, you look like a man as can take care of himself," said Peggy.

"Cleared off right sharpish, nursing a few bruised ribs, I'd imagine," said Melanie.

"What was he looking for anyway?" said Peggy. "I can't imagine anyone having anything worth pinching around here."

"He was looking for trouble," said John, "and he got it. I tell you what though, ladies, all that fisticuffs gave me a right thirst. I even went into a pub in town I've never been to before, I was that parched I couldn't even make it to my own local so I popped in for a quick one in Campo Lane, place called the Paradise. Can't imagine either of you two knowing it though, bit of a rough dive even for women of your profession."

"Not one I ever go into," said Melanie.

"No, nor me," said Peggy, trying to read any recognition in John's face.

"No, nor me, not again," said John. "Well, best get home now. Can I have a quick word, Melanie, outside; you and me need to fix up for a bit of, you know, later." He turned to Peggy as he was leaving. "I think that fight's sharpened all my appetites," he said before giving her a cheery wave. "We'll no doubt bump into each other again, Peggy, now that you're round here quite often. Funny that, after all this time; like you say, though, a lucky coincidence."

Once in the street he pulled Melanie to one side and whispered. "She does work for fucking Quinn. Watch what you say to her and I'll call back when she's gone."

"Works for Quinn?" Melanie was livid. "I'll teach that bloody whore…"

"Leave it," said John, "I'll do the teaching, you just keep chatting, casual, I've not made up my mind what sort of a lesson to give her yet."

John carried on home and rushed in to find out how Sally had got on with the relief fund and to tell her he had come into a bit of money that would take them all out of The Ponds but he found the room empty. There was no sign that Sally had even been back. He pottered around for a bit and then decided he needed some food, not that there was much: Sally seemed able to conjure meals out of nothing but, left alone, John just slapped some lard on a thick slice of bread and made do. He wiped away the crumbs and decided to impress Sally by doing some reading practice but he couldn't settle: it had been a long, hard and tiring day - he'd been working, he'd been in a fight with one of Quinn's lackeys who was trying to rob him, he'd been spied on - and he needed someone to talk to, someone to take his mind off brawls and gangs and all the rest of the shit that seemed to be piling up right now. But she wasn't here and he was alone. His empty room was too quiet, too empty, it was as if all he had to look forward to was more of the same. He laughed at himself for getting sentimental about Sally; for thinking he could take her out of this place, for thinking she'd gone all gentle on him; the girl was off with the first well-shod man she'd met. John clattered his chair backwards across the floor as he stood up, put his coat back on and went off to get drunk.

ELIZABETH was cleaning the offices of Bickerstaff & Son under the constant gaze of Booth. She welcomed the change of scenery from the house in Broomhall but she got more and more uncomfortable providing a change of

237

scenery for the clerk.

"Look," she said when the staring was suddenly accompanied by the growing sounds of very deliberate smacking lips and deep sighs, "if you don't stop looking at me I might be tempted to tell Mr Bickerstaff senior that he has a waster on his hands. If you have so little work to do, I'll suggest that I go back to the house to help Mrs Bickerstaff with her menu-planning and you can carry on cleaning. I'll be appreciated for being conscientious; you, on the other hand, will find yourself with a mop and bucket in your hands instead of pen and paper. It's entirely up to you."

"Aren't we the snooty one," said Booth. "Who do you think you are, anyway? Think you 're better than me just because you think you've got some money due? Well, my girl, think again."

"What do you mean, 'think again'?" asked Elizabeth.

"God, you don't know anything, do you. Who do you think that was who went in to see the boss?"

The sound of Samuel Bickerstaff's door opening brought a wry smile to Booth's face as he turned his attention back to his desk. Quinn emerged, patting his top pocket.

"Trouble is, quick as you pay one lot off, he works up another," said Quinn to the attorney. "I think you and I might be in for a long and prosperous relationship, Mister Bickerstaff. It's an ill wind and all that, more like a howling gale really, but it's fair weather for some."

"Good day to you, Mr Quinn," said Bickerstaff, looking decidedly gloomy. "I'll bring in the fresh markers next week."

"No need to discuss business in front of the staff."

"I see you've got yourself a new one, Mister Bickerstaff, and who's this pretty little wench?"

"I'm no wench," said Elizabeth.

"Now, Elizabeth," said Bickerstaff, "Mr Quinn is a client."

"As am I," she said.

"Really?" remarked Quinn. "You must be one of Master Simon's if you're forced to do a bit of cleaning on the side. Another of your son's business associates, eh," he said, turning to Bickerstaff, "payment in kind, as they say. No wonder he can't stump up his own debts."

"I suggest that you watch your tone, Mr Quinn," snapped Bickerstaff, trembling; he was torn between his natural good manners in the face of such ungentlemanly insinuations, his fear of the man and his need to keep Elizabeth sweet so he could pay the bastard off. "Mrs Fletcher is one of my clients, temporarily fallen on hard times since the flood."

Quinn trembled too but with temper. "And I suggest that you watch your tone when you're talking to me, Bickerstaff," he said. "One word from me and you won't have any bloody clients and it won't be temporary hard times either." He glared at the attorney and then broke into an ugly smile. "So, what's what? Same time next week then," he said, again patting his top pocket, and was gone.

"What an awful man," said Elizabeth. "He must be a very valued client for you to put up with such unpleasant behaviour."

Booth involuntarily sniggered and quickly had to disguise it as a bit of a cough. "That reminds me, Mr Bickerstaff, a telegraph arrived while you were dealing with Mr Quinn. From London."

"I'll take it in my office," said Bickerstaff. "Why don't you have a break, Mrs Fletcher. In fact, why don't you finish for the day and go home. I'm sure you must be feeling quite upset after Mr Quinn's affrontery."

"Thank you," said Elizabeth. "perhaps Mrs Bickerstaff would enjoy a stroll in the Botanical Gardens with me later, unless of course she has some chores for me to do."

"Good idea, tell Mrs Bickerstaff that I insist on you both having a walk, forget the chores, they can wait, and tell Dora to wrap up well."

Once inside his office, safely hidden by the closed door, Samuel sat down heavily, closed his eyes, leaned back on the legs of his chair and let out a long gasp of air. He could see no solution to the problem of Simon and his gambling debts. No amount of trying to reason with his son had worked, meanwhile business at the firm was sliding because the '& Son' partner was more sleeping than silent, meaning that money to pay for Simon's habit was in shorter and shorter supply. That unfortunately did not mean the demand was going down, on the contrary, Quinn's threats were getting increasingly expensive to fend off. At one time Samuel and Dora had hoped their wayward son might marry into a good family, with a wife who would bring to the marriage sufficient financial security to take the burden away from her in-laws and sufficient influence to keep her husband at home and out of the gambling dens. But, for all his mixing with people he referred to as 'the elite of the town, people of influence', so far none seemed interested in pursuing Simon Bickerstaff for anything other than his wagers. Samuel suspected that even Simon's many pressing dinner engagements were little more than visits to dens with more than a hand of cards on offer. Thank God, he thought, Elizabeth Fletcher had turned down Simon's invitation. And thank God Elizabeth Fletcher had come along when she did: her father's money had provided a useful 'loan' account on which Samuel could draw.

He fully intended to pay back every penny he had borrowed as soon as the situation improved. Unfortunately at the moment that seemed more and more unlikely. Had it not been for the fact that Thomas Shaw's daughter was only very recently widowed, he might even have thought of pushing her towards Simon, that would have solved all his problems. Samuel rubbed the palms of his hands over his face and concentrated his gaze on the telegraph lying on his desk. Perhaps that was the answer after all, he thought, a marriage between Elizabeth and Simon: then Simon himself could play the attorney, make sure that he freed up Shaw's estate for Elizabeth to inherit legally as Shaw's only surviving heir and Samuel would be freed of responsibility. The girl might even prove an effective foil against Quinn. It might even prove one line of reasoning young Simon might actually appreciate – a rich young widow who was pleasing on the eye too. Samuel allowed himself a hint of a smile and decided to arrange a sociable outing for the three Bickerstaffs plus their young lodger. Then he turned his mind back to business. He took up the telegraph and opened the envelope. It was from David Shaw's regiment.

"David Shaw was reported missing, feared dead, in India. He was found several months later, badly disabled but fit and well then honourably discharged. Whereabouts unknown: last heard of in America."

Samuel Bickerstaff folded the paper and stowed it away in his desk drawer, under lock and key. Then he poured himself a large brandy.

***

Part Five

It had been a bad crossing and Oonagh had spent most of the night in the cabin fending off nausea and drifting in and out of sleep, the rhythmic groaning of the ship at once lulling her into fitful sleep and waking her again with its reminder of the heavy seas immediately beyond the porthole. The Irish Sea could be notoriously rough between Dublin and Liverpool: to the south, the Atlantic rushed up the channel between Ireland and Wales; to the north, the ocean poured down the breach between Ireland and Scotland, forking out around the Isle of Man and then colliding again at Manx's southern tip; the competing currents met head on in the middle, right in the path of the Dublin-Liverpool passage. Depending on the weather, the meeting of the waters was a mere jostling for supremacy or a crashing battle between insistent fronts. It was March and the weather had paid heed to the old adage and been decidedly windy. Oonagh Shaw felt as if she had personally ridden every heaving wave. She was relieved to be told by the steward that the ship was at last approaching the calmer waters of the Mersey estuary and would be docking in a couple of hours. She did her ablutions, dressed, packed everything away in the overnight bag and finally hurried to join her husband on deck. He was standing at the handrail looking out at the shoreline, a stretch of sand traced along the tidal edge with black and bitty webs of flotsam and jetsam and backed with marram-tufted sand-hills which gradually gave way to grassy wasteland. Oonagh slipped her arm around his waist and snuggled in close.

"My first glimpse of England in seven years," he said, "but not to the homecoming I'd always dreamt about."

"Not many people are lucky enough to get what they dream of, David," said Oonagh.

"I was lucky enough when it came to finding you," he said. "How are you feeling? Has your stomach settled down at all?"

"I'll be glad to sleep in a proper bed that doesn't lurch from side to side all night. I do believe last night was worse than anything we went through coming over from America and that was six weeks of open sea. Was I really disgusting last night, getting sick and everything all the time? It's not really how a new wife wants her husband to see her, I thought I could keep the romance going a little longer."

"You were pretty disgusting, yes," he laughed. "For a minute I thought I was back in the sick ward in Hyderabad. I kept waiting for the wallah to come round to empty your slops."

"David Shaw, you are not being very gallant. Perhaps I should have stayed at home in Dublin."

"I'm very glad you didn't, Mrs Shaw," said David, turning to kiss his wife on the cheek, "after all, what's a bit of sick between husband and wife."

"It's a nasty, smelly mess, that's what it is," said Oonagh.

The ship was still rising and dipping in the sea but now it was in a gentle swell, accompanied by the swish of the water as the prow cut its way through. In the distance they could see the port of Liverpool growing ever more prominent.

"I suppose I've only myself to blame," said David. "I could have come home sooner, when I still had people to come home to, but that's always been my problem, pig-headedness: I didn't want to go home until everything was just right and now it doesn't matter, everything else is so wrong."

"You weren't to know what would happen."

"Perhaps not but it's my fault that my parents died believing their only son to be dead."

"You had your reasons, David."

"They just don't seem like very good ones any more, perhaps they never were, perhaps I was too busy leading my own life to be bothered with a simple thing like a letter."

"A letter can be one of the hardest things to do and the longer you leave it the more difficult it gets. I don't think you should torment yourself. And don't forget you were on your way home when you read about the dam bursting."

"I know," said David. "In a way that makes it even harder. A few weeks earlier and I would have been home in time."

"And you might be dead now too," said Oonagh. "Is that what your parents would have wanted? I don't think so. You being there wouldn't have prevented what happened, it wouldn't have made any difference other than perhaps you being killed too."

"I know you're right and I know I just keep going round in circles," said

David. "and what good would a one-armed man have been anyway? I'd hardly have been able to save anyone, would I?"

"Well you could have waved your stump up in the air so everyone would know it was you going down," said Oonagh, then regretted it. "I'm sorry," she said, "it was my stupid attempt to try to snap you out of your guilty thoughts."

"No need to apologise, it would have been a funny sight right enough," said David. "Do you know, Mrs Shaw, I do wish my parents had met you. Actually, Oonagh O'Connell, you were to be the ace up my sleeve, that's why I married you, so that Mother and Father would have been so delighted to meet you that I would have been forgiven anything. And I'm sure you would have gotten on well with my sister. Elizabeth was a child when I left home but she had the makings of a lively young woman. Anyway, enough; here we are about to land in England and all I can do is talk about sad things."

"Isn't that only to be expected," said Oonagh. "You put up with me and all my melancholia when we got back to Ireland and I didn't even have such awful news to go home to."

The tugboats were now attached to the ship and guiding her up the River Mersey to the landing stage at Liverpool. The deck was a hive of activity: crewmen were busy at the ropes ready to throw them ashore for the ship to be tied up; stewards were rushing around collecting blankets and clearing the deck for landing while down below others were humping trunks and baggage out of the cabins to be hauled up the gangways for disembarkation. The passengers themselves were full of animated conversation and a cheer went up when the ship finally docked; it had been a rough crossing.

The quay was a chaos of people, every individual bustling about with a purpose. The ship was tied fast, then the sound of straining rope and creaking wood attracted all eyes upward as the gangplank was lowered down to the wharf, its clatter to the ground greeted by cries of relief from both passengers and the waiting crowd alike. Porters darted about, eagle-eyed for a paying customer and touting their terms as the ship's hands began off-loading cargo from the hold and baggage from the deck. Insistent shouts, and the calling of names added to the cacophony, turning to delighted screams as passengers emerged down the gangplank and were spotted by kinsfolk and friends who'd had a two-hour wait for the boat after its longer-than-scheduled crossing from Dublin. A ship's safe arrival was always an occasion.

"Isn't it wonderful to watch?" said Oonagh, still leaning over the handrail on deck. "Not quite the same as landing in Cobh, I suppose, after all that time coming over from America, but it's grand all the same. Just look at the faces on all these people. You know my favourite bit of the journey was sailing into

Cork harbour to Cobh, I just loved it, I loved that feeling of arriving home and getting that first smell of home up my nostrils, but this has a different sort of excitement, David, it's like the end and the beginning all rolled into one and we can be tumbled this way or that, depending on what happens from now on in."

"Well it seems to me that from now on in we start our life together properly," said David. "We'll go back to Sheffield and sort out whatever needs doing, then we'll be free to decide what we want to do and where we want to do it. How does that sound to you, Mrs Shaw?"

"That sounds very acceptable to me, Mr Shaw."

"Come on then, let's get off this floating sick-bed and get our feet on solid ground."

The chief steward on board had advised David that the best hotel in Liverpool was the Adelphi and, with all their luggage stowed away on the back of a hire-carriage, that was where he directed the driver. It wasn't a warm day but it was dry and David asked the driver to put the hood down on the carriage.

"We've been stuck in a somewhat smelly cabin since yesterday evening and need some fresh air," he said.

"Did one of you get sea-sick?" asked the driver, attending to the hood.

"I'm afraid I did, I confess it," said Oonagh. "In fact at one stage I felt so sea-sick I thought I was sicking up the whole of the Irish Sea."

"My wife's exactly the same," said the driver. "We've never been on a long trip, not overnight or anything like that, but we've been on the paddle-boats in the park and as soon as my wife gets in she's off. It doesn't stop her, though; every time we get a chance to go to the park she wants to go on the boats, says she might live in a port but the island in the middle of the lake is the furthest she's ever likely to get. Would the Missus like a blanket to put over her knees before we set off?" the driver asked David.

"I don't know, you'd better ask her."

"That would be very welcome," said Oonagh. "Perhaps you could show us something of the town on the way to the hotel."

"There's lots to see here if you've never been anywhere else," said the driver, pulling out a blanket from under his seat. "I don't know what Dublin's like but I'd imagine it's pretty similar to here."

"We've actually come across from America a few weeks ago," said Oonagh.

"America? In that case there's probably nothing to show you here at all, just a load of people and buildings, same as every other city. Mind you, they do say that the only place in England bigger than Liverpool now is London, at least I think that's what they say, not that I ever really know who 'they' are when people say that."

"What happens in Liverpool apart from the shipping business?" asked David.

"There isn't anything much apart from the shipping business, most of what happens here is to do with ships or the goods and people coming and going in them. That's why we're here, the crossroads of the world, with enough cross words when the pubs shut to sink the whole damned lot. Pardon me, Missus. If you're safely on board then, I'll get you to your hotel."

The carriage headed inland away from the river, bumping over the cobbles of the dock road and threading its way through streets lined with warehouses and taverns before heading off into the town, with its busy shopping streets choked with horse-trams and thronging with all manner of pedestrians of every shape and colour.

"It's like all our travels rolled into one place," said David. "Everyone's come here, I don't know why anyone bothers to leave."

"Look, David, over there on that bit of waste ground." Oonagh pointed to a man all bound up in chains. "Why on earth is he chained up in the street? My God, they're putting a filthy big sack over him now. Jesus, they're tying it up. Oh that poor man."

"That poor man is probably making quite a few shillings for his trouble," said David. "Driver, can you stop for a minute," he shouted. "You watch now, Oonagh, he'll be out of that in no time and the chains will be slipped."

The stuffed sack writhed around in the dirt, with lumps and bumps sticking out and subsiding again, and in less than a minute the prisoner had shrugged his hessian cell to the ground and was holding a jangle of empty chains high in the air. The small crowd gathered around him applauded and some threw pennies into his cap.

"You see," said David, "that's what he does for a living, he escapes from things."

"Well fancy that, I've never seen anything like that before," said Oonagh. "What a strange talent to discover you have, and even stranger exactly how you discover you have such a talent in the first place. Shall we get out and give him something, what do you think driver?"

"I think you may well find him in that very same spot tomorrow and the next day doing that very same trick, Missus," said the driver. "Always put off til tomorrow what you don't have to do today, especially when it comes to parting with money. Come back later in the week if you must."

He flicked the reins and the horse walked on, pulling the coach slightly uphill now. They passed a huge indoor market, the traders spilling out on to surrounding pavements and gutters and cluttering them with stalls and carts selling everything from ribbons to knives. The whole place was bustling with people.

"My God will you look at that," said Oonagh. Across the road was a huge classical building with formal gardens laid out along its length. As the carriage rounded the bend, the visitors could see a colonnade of tall pillars atop a sweeping flight of stone steps. "Sure that's grand enough to grace any city in the world," she said.

"You sound like someone who's just left their back-to-back," said David.

"I could be," said Oonagh, "except that I don't know what a back-to-back is; it sounds like a couple in bed who aren't talking."

"Back-to-backs are houses which are built immediately back on to one another, so each one has only one door, at the front. They're very small."

"Being that close to the neighbours and in such a small house, it would be no surprise if a couple didn't do any talking in bed, or anything else for that matter. It wouldn't do me to live in one of those, David. Keep that in mind when you're looking for somewhere for us to live."

"I doubt if we'll have any such problems here," said David as the carriage pulled into a short driveway and came to a halt outside a very imposing portico. The Adelphi was said to have a good reputation throughout England and Europe and, judging by its size, there would certainly be no question of hearing the neighbours in the next room.

A uniformed commissionaire opened the carriage door for the new arrivals and instructed a couple of hotel porters to retrieve the luggage and carry it into the foyer. David paid off the driver and went to the reception desk to register for the best double room available. He ordered some champagne to be sent up to the room immediately, plus a box of chocolates and tea for two. Then he crossed the hall to Oonagh who was already engrossed in conversation with the doorman. "May I have my wife back?" David whispered, then he dangled the key to their room in front of her. "Your proper bed awaits, madam," he said. "Would you like to join me upstairs?"

IT was a long time since John Hukin had woken with such a bad head and it was a struggle to get up off the palliasse on the floor and get ready for work. Sally had been asleep in bed when he finally arrived home the previous night but she had left a simple note written in large letters for him on the table: "What happened to you yesterday? I missed you at the Town Hall." He had pulled the curtain back quietly and looked down on the girl as she lay asleep, her sister's old doll on the pillow beside her. Then he'd stumbled over to his corner of the room and collapsed into a dream-riddled sleep: recurring images of Sally surrounded by water and crying out for help while he was busy fighting Matthew Blagdon, transformed into one of Quinn's men, kept swimming around in his head, all mixed up with scenes of his room floating down the Sheaf while he fended off the dead dogs and cats in the stream and tried to grab a hold of his home and pull it in to the side and up the riverbank to put it back in the building where it belonged. John felt hung-over and sick, sick with yesterday's booze still sloshing around inside him and sick of squalor, sick of a life which seemed to get more and more pointless, sick of living in a place where people like Jack Quinn could and did get away with murder. He thought about his mother and how she'd gone to her grave feeling guilty that she hadn't been able to give her sons a better life and what had this son done about it since? Nothing, hadn't even tried to better himself. He thought of how he always used to kid around with Daniel when his friend encouraged him to find a good woman: "I don't need any wife, thank you very much," he'd say, "I'm quite happy looking after myself and enjoying a few jars without some woman in the background nagging me all the time." Happy enjoying a few jars? He'd been kidding himself: where was the happiness in getting blind drunk every night, there was no life in that. "And look where a good woman got Daniel," John thought to himself, "into a watery grave. He'd have been back home in The bleeding Ponds if he hadn't got married and moved to Damflask." John looked at himself in the chipped mirror on the wall and hated himself for the thought.

"Is that you, John?" He heard Sally call, her voice far-away with sleepiness.

"No, I've gone," he said.

John walked to the brewery in a daze, hunched over and looking neither right nor left as he figured out what to do with his life. First things first; if Sally was going to take up with Blagdon, then John himself wouldn't have the responsibility of looking after her for much longer. Secondly, he had to decide what to do about Jack Quinn, if anything: he believed that Quinn could been involved in his Dad's murder but he had no proof and perhaps it was time to let go of all that; he could take Quinn's money and clear off somewhere, make that better life that his Mam had wanted for him, he could imagine her smiling in heaven as she looked down and saw him put all that brawling and hatred to one side and get himself out of The Ponds. The third factor was young Jimmy: well, he was at school now and the lessons should see him right and get him a good job at the end; on the other hand, Jimmy was the last of John's family

247

and John wouldn't like to lose contact with the boy, didn't want to think of himself as being totally alone in the world without any blood-ties left. As for his job with Neepsend Brewery, Sally had told him often enough that it was a nothing job and maybe she was right. His problem now was to come up with a plan that took all of these factors into account.

He got to the brewery, harnessed up Stanley and set off on his rounds. The streets of the town were returning to some sort of normality and even Neepsend, which had suffered terrible losses in the flood, was clear of most of the mud and debris left behind by the terrible tide, though the skeletons of.partly destroyed houses still stood uncertainly. The smell remained but it had turned sickly sweet after the sour stench that seemed to cloy like a tangible fog in the days immediately after the water had gone. Gangs of labourers were at work in the area so the pubs and taverns were building up business again. At least it meant John was busy. His day passed in a series of idle chatter as barrels were delivered and collected and, before he knew it, it was time to go home again.

John decided to walk back via Campo Lane on the off-chance of seeing Jimmy. A rough plan had started to take shape in his head and he wouldn't have minded a quick chat with the lad to find out how things were going at the Blue Coat School. Jimmy was due home for the day on Sunday so John felt no urgency in his detour. He was in no hurry.

He saw the boy, alright, in the distance, talking to the Peggy woman outside the school entrance. John saw Jimmy run back inside while the woman turned round and walked back up Campo Lane. She crossed the street and disappeared into one of the buildings opposite the parish church. John bought a pie from a street cart and strolled calmly into the churchyard, chose a shrub-shaded spot between the gravestones and sat down on the grass facing the building as if he was just sitting down for a break. But he wasn't feeling calm, he was boiling up inside at the realisation that Quinn had spread his tentacles and drawn even young Jimmy into his fold. John had no reason to rush home and every reason to see what was going on here. It didn't take long. Minutes later Quinn himself appeared briefly at the window of one of the upstairs rooms and, judging by his face, Peggy had given him some welcome information. There were obviously a couple of new factors for John to take into account. He finished his pie and headed off back to The Ponds, trying to figure out what the hell was happening with Jimmy and if Quinn was the pimp Melanie was told was anxious to help Sally get her hands on some relief fund. At least he now knew where to find the bastard.

248

"WHY don't you come in and wait, I'd be glad of the company. I'll make a brew and tell you what happened at the Town Hall yesterday."

Melanie had called round to see if John's cuts and bruises were on the mend but he was late home from work. "I'd forgotten you were going there yesterday, Sally, how did it go? Are they going to give you any money?"

"I'm hoping so. It was very upsetting, though; I had to write out a list of everything that had been lost at the Cleakum and how much I thought it would cost to replace it all. It was hard having to remember what we had at home, picturing all the rooms where we lived and what was in them, all the memories I've been trying not to face. It was horrible having to turn them into pounds, shillings and pence. I'm afraid I got very sad and burst out crying. My tears fell on to the paper and all the ink ran so it had to be done all over again. Fortunately Matthew was there and he copied it out for me so all I had to do was sign my name at the bottom."

"That's not a bad young feller you've got yourself, Sally, he seems a right gentleman," said Melanie.

"What?" asked Sally, somewhat puzzled.

"Well the two of you seem to get on very well together."

"Me and Matthew?"

"Yes, you and Matthew, who else are we talking about? You could do worse than take up with a newspaper reporter, I bet he's not on bad money and he looks like a decent bloke. You wouldn't have to worry about living in a place like this shit-hole if you stuck with him; look at him, he's clean enough to eat off, good looking too. And he's certainly taken a shine to you, I'd say."

"But I'm not interested in Matthew Blagdon, not in that way," said Sally. "You must be seeing things."

"I look and I know what I see," said Melanie. "You take it from me, Sally, he's got your best interests at heart, his heart."

"He's been very kind, that's all, and in return he wants my story for his newspaper. Anyway, why would he be interested in me? Just think of all the fashionable young women he must meet all the time."

"Why he would be interested in you, my girl, is that you're a sweet person, very pretty, healthy country shape to you. And you're a damsel in distress and some men go for that, brings out the protective side of them. Mind you, that's one side I've only ever heard about, I've never experienced it for myself." Melanie went a bit quiet then: "Well I have, in a way; that's how John's always been with me, protective like."

"John? And you?"

"There's no 'and' girl, there's John and there's me; all I mean is he's always

249

been right good to me, taken care of me and that. I reckon he's the protective sort, except he's thinks no-one would ever want him."

"Do you want him?" asked Sally.

"Me? I don't really want any man, not for keeps, though sometimes I do look at John and wonder how it would be if we got together. I imagine it could be a warm, happy life. I could see myself looking after him, like yesterday, after that bleeding fight."

Sally stopped short. "I didn't know John had been in a fight yesterday. Is he alright? I know he didn't come home last night, not until really late, I gave up waiting and went to bed. When did it happen?"

"Round about the time he was going into town to meet you, as I remember."

"And is he alright, was he hurt?"

"Few scratches and bruises, not much, the other feller came off worse but then they usually do if they end up in a brawl with John Hukin. He's always been handy with them fists of his."

"That would explain why he didn't turn up at the Town Hall," said Sally. "I thought perhaps he'd forgotten or changed his mind."

"Oh he hadn't forgotten. But I told him you looked in safe hands so perhaps as he was late already he ended up going for a drink instead. He did call back here for a bit, late afternoon, but I didn't see him after that."

Melanie suddenly remembered that Peggy had been there when John called back and felt angry with herself that she'd forgotten his warning. "By the way, Sally, remember that woman you've met here a couple of times, a so-called old friend of mine, name of Peggy?"

"Yes, she's very friendly. Did I tell you I met her in the street last week when I took Jimmy to have a look at the Blue Coat School?"

"And did she meet Jimmy?"

"Yes, we had a little chat before going in to the school. Why?"

"Well Peggy my old friend isn't what she seems. I've found out she's actually not a very nice person to know so it'd be best if you didn't bother with her, just ignore her next time."

"Wouldn't that seem a bit rude?"

"She's a lot worse than rude, as it turns out. All that time I thought she just wanted to renew an old acquaintance, she was actually here to spy on us, the bleeding cow. She works for a bleeding crook, so be careful, young girl, and don't go near her, and don't let Jimmy go near her either. John would do his nut if he found out she'd met Jimmy."

"I have found out," blurted John as he pushed through the door. "Saw her outside the school with the lad today and then she rushed off back to Quinn."

"John are you alright? Melanie told me you were in a fight yesterday."

"I'm alright, don't fuss," said John, unexpectedly abrupt and keeping his eyes away from Sally.

"She's not fussing, she was worried about you, that's all. Mind your manners John Hukin, there's no need to come growling in here just because Quinn's got you all riled up."

"How did he meet Jimmy, that's what I'd like to know?"

Sally didn't speak and looked at Melanie for support.

"Peggy met him in the street with Sally when they went down to the school," said Melanie. "It was no-one's fault, we didn't know she had anything to do with Quinn."

"Well she has and now Jimmy's involved.," said John. "God knows what he's doing with the lad."

"I'm so sorry," said Sally, her eyes filling up with tears.

"Don't you start crying again for God's sake," said John harshly. "It's a bit late to be sorry."

Sally could only stare at him, silent, hurt by such sudden aggression from the man she had come to regard as her only real friend. Then she turned and left.

"You stupid, mean bastard," said Melanie. "It wasn't her fault, she's just a young lass from the country who's just lost her whole bleeding family, you stupid bugger, you're the only person she's got left in the world who had anything to do with her own life and all you can do is lay into her. Why?"

"She introduced that whore to Jimmy, didn't she?"

"Ay, she did, because she's a straightforward kid who didn't see any harm in saying hello to someone in the street who she'd met here. What else would she do?"

John sat down in one of Melanie's armchairs, lolled his head back on the cushions and closed his eyes.

"Here," said Melanie, handing him a stiff drink, "you obviously need this." He took the drink, swirled it around and gazed at the liquid running down the inside of the glass. He took a mouthful and let the burn of the cheap liquor hit him.

"What's happened to you, John? I've never known you so closed in on yourself."

"I've had enough of it all, Melanie, that's all."

"Had enough of all what?"

John took another swig. "Everything," he said.

"What 'everything'?" asked Melanie.

"Just everything."

"John Hukin, you're going to tell me what's wrong or else."

John downed the rest of his drink in one gulp. "There you are, you see," he said, opening his eyes wide and slitting his face with a sneery smile, "that's more like me, isn't it, that's the John Hukin we all know and love, the one who spends his life looking into the bottom of a glass, or a jar, or a mug or a bottle, anything as long as there's a drop of booze in it. God, I even deliver the stuff for a living. Give us another one, Mel. I'm getting back to my old self, my real self."

"You're not having another one here until you tell me what's up," she said, "and you can take that awful look off your face, it won't wash with me. You're talking a load of nonsense. This bleeding Quinn business has got you all tied in knots. Ever since that bloody flood and Sally and Jimmy came to live with you, it's as if you've gone and drowned yourself in it all. Well you'd better pull yourself together, my man, because they both still need you and if Quinn's really got his hooks into Jimmy then you'd better figure out how to deal with it. Getting drunk here isn't going to help anyone."

"Maybe I'll just take Jimmy and we'll clear off somewhere."

"And what about Sally? You can't just go and leave her here."

"Oh yes Sally, what about Sally?" John hiccupped. "Well, Sally's got her fancy man, Mr 'I'm-alright' bloody Blagdon, Mr 'I'm-a-reporter' Blagdon, Mr 'you've-got-a-nice-face' Blagdon. Sally doesn't need a drunken idiot like me getting in the way. Give me a bloody drink, woman."

"Oh, so that's it," said Melanie. "One minute you're off the booze, you're working all the hours God sends you, you're learning how to read and you're holding things together. Then Matthew Blagdon comes along, shows an interest in Sally, and you fall to pieces. Aren't I the stupid one, not realising it earlier, and I thought I knew men. Well love a duck."

"You know nothing," said John. "I'm going to the pub. You can come if you like or stay here, I don't give a shit." He stood up and lurched over to the door.

"And what about Sally? Don't you think you should go say you're sorry first?"

"Miss Bisby can join me in the pub if she wants an apology."

Melanie was left alone. "You silly cow," she said to herself. She put on her working finery, fixed her hair on top and shaped bright red lipstick round her mouth, pouting her lips together as she looked in the mirror. She looked at herself in the glass: "And here's you thinking you might have found a good man for yourself." Then she left the room and set off to earn a few tricks.

THERE had been a marked change in Elizabeth's duties for the Bickerstaffs, even Mary the cook had commented on how the number of chores the girl was expected to do had tailed off. Mary put it down to Jim Nightingale's visit to the office, figured his lordship had gotten a bit nervous about treating Elizabeth like a skivvy now he thought there was a respected old family friend in the picture. He was a laugh, that Jim, and Mary had been only too pleased to cover for Elizabeth when he had called round unexpectedly that afternoon to take the girl out for a few hours. Not that it was difficult, now that even Mrs Bickerstaff was watching her bossy attitude to someone who was, after all, a client. "She deserves a bit of fun," the old biddy had joked lightly when Mary said she had given Elizabeth the rest of the day off. Before Jim Nightingale's visit Mary would have been told in no uncertain terms that it wasn't her place to give anyone any time off. They'd have a good giggle about it in the kitchen when Elizabeth got home.

Jim had decided it was time that Elizabeth went back to Malin Bridge, told her it would lay a few ghosts to rest and help her to start looking forwards instead of revisiting the past all the time in her head. She had wanted to go to The Ponds to look for one of her dead husband's old friends but Jim convinced her that a day in the fresh air would do her more good right now than breathing in the stench of that place. He didn't know Sheffield all that well yet but you didn't need to, everyone knew The Ponds by reputation.

The start of their journey out of Sheffield was accompanied by lots of idle chatter: Jim told Elizabeth about growing up in Bamford, how his brother Billy idolised him, how he himself had always wanted to live in a big town where there were lots of people and lots of things to do, how he was a bit of a chancer but had his head screwed on and wanted to do things with his life. Elizabeth told him about her life before the flood had washed it all away, how she had often visited Sheffield but preferred the ways of the country and hoped to move back there one day, when she felt able to cope with the memories.

"I always loved living by the river, looking up the valley and seeing the hills, or across over the fields. Do you know I even used to love it in bad weather, watching the trees bend in the wind and then spring up again and the rain making all the stones look shiny and new. Everything looks much greener after the rain, like having a good wash," she said. "Even now, after all that's happened, the countryside is coming back to life."

"It'll struggle through all this mud," said Jim. "No disrespect, mind, but to me the trouble with the country is that a lot of the people living there are green too. Give them a patch to grow a few scrawny vegetables and they're set for life. I'm looking for lots of red in my life, swirls of colour and excitement and lots of money in my pocket to spend on nice clothes and a nice house, maybe a family."

"Lots of red?" said Elizabeth. "Swirls of colour? I don't see much sign of red in Sheffield, it's all dirty and black."

"Ah but that's only on the surface," argued Jim. "There's life there."

"There's death everywhere."

That's when the idle chatter stopped. Jim was left concentrating on trying to think of something to say to lift the occasion again. Elizabeth stared around at the destruction all around her; she was glad she hadn't come up the valley sooner to be confronted with the full horror of what had happened to Daniel and her family and so many of their friends. Gangs of workmen were still cleaning up the mess left by the torrent but the worst of the debris – the bodies, the dead animals, the personal belongings and the huge millstones deposited by the tide - had been carted away leaving the ruins of what were once homes, bridges, workshops, and the piles of shovelled, sifted mud still to be cleared.

Elizabeth couldn't figure out where Daniel's workshop used to be; most of the buildings along the river running in front of Holme Lane had been flattened. At Malin Bridge, the bridge itself had disappeared and Jim had to help her clamber over the rocks and boulders left by the flood to get across the river and over the Rivelin to look for the ruins of Shaw Lodge. There was no sign that a house had ever stood on the spot. Elizabeth kicked over bits of rubble and sometimes bent down to pick up what she thought might be something of her old home left behind but there was nothing. Across the way, all that remained of the Tricketts' farm was, bizarrely, the barn, as if the flood had had a murderous, twisted sense of humour in deciding to leave an old empty barn standing while claiming the houses and the people living in them. All that was left of the Cleakum was a ragged-edged chimneystack.

On the way up to Damflask, they saw a huge boiler, some eighteen feet long, that had been ripped out of a mill and then dumped in the middle of the stream, but it was difficult to see much else; the force of the flood had altered the course of the river so that land on which once had stood villagers' houses was now under water, part of the new river bed, while all around were what looked like large craters scooped out as the flood had angrily eddied and whirled around anything in its path. As for the Barrel Inn, that too was gone.

"Whereabouts was your cottage?" asked Jim.

"Willow Tree Cottage was over there across the river," said Elizabeth. "It was just up from the bank in a small clearing in the trees."

"Do you want to go over and take a look?"

"I'm not sure," she said.

"Shall I go and take a look, see if there's anything lying around?" said Jim.

"It's up to you."

"Jim, I don't think I can move."

"Come and sit down for a bit then, there's no hurry, we've a couple of hours of daylight left."

"Why do these things happen, Jim? Why did such a terrible thing have to happen?"

"You've got me there, Lizzie. Even with all the Sunday School teaching Our Mam insisted on and that, I've never understood why bad things go on and people are left with nothing. I learned in school that in some countries there are things like mountains that blow their tops off and rain down fire and in other places there are winds that twist around so fast that nothing can stay standing in their way. I know we're all supposed to get down on our knees and pray and thank God for our own safety and everything but that always struck me as being selfish, and pretty useless, if I'm honest, although I'd never dare say that to Our Mam."

"Don't you believe in saying prayers, Jim?"

"Not really. Sometimes I can look at a beautiful sky, perhaps, and I say a kind of thank-you in my head then but I'm not entirely sure who I'm thanking, only that I'm glad there's a beautiful sky for me to look at, however it got there."

"A bit like how I feel when I see the trees bending in the wind."

"Perhaps you and I have got something in common."

"I say my prayers," said Elizabeth. "Every day and every night I pray for Daniel and hope he died quickly when the water took him away right in front of me. Sometimes I'm even stupid enough to think that maybe, if I pray hard enough, God will give him back to me, but that is being stupid."

"I think there'll be a lot of people feeling exactly the same round here."

"Do you think we are all being stupid?"

"Nothing's stupid if it helps," said Jim. "Anyway, who am I to talk, I've done enough pretty stupid things in my time."

"You're not stupid, Jim Nightingale, you're funny."

"Well before you start laughing out loud I'm going to cross the river and see what's left of your old house. With a bit of luck I'll find you something to keep as a reminder."

Jim waded through the stream and scrambled up the bank to the ruins of Willow Tree Cottage, leaving Elizabeth lost in thought and reliving the happy moments of her life spent in those very ruins when they formed the foundation stones of her life with Daniel. "I don't need any souvenirs to remind me of what I had," she thought. She watched her new friend shifting stones and shuffling his feet around in the dried mud, picking up the odd mangled chicken feather and waving it over at her, standing every now and then to straighten his back before bending to resume the search. Behind her, what was left of what had been a friendly community was a desolate sight with just a few people still scratching around and trying to sort out piles of stones into new building materials.

"Found something!" shouted Jim and he sloshed back through the water in a hurry to give Elizabeth a piece of old board. It was smoothed out of shape around the edges and was velveted green with river slime but she recognised it immediately. "I thought you'd appreciate that," said Jim and he read out the inscription: "Willow Tree Cottage, D&EF."

Elizabeth stared hard at the plaque and then hugged it to her heart and rocked gently back and forth with her eyes closed tightly.

"It had got lodged between some rocks," said Jim. "I noticed the bit of green paint."

"We made it almost as soon as we moved in and Daniel hung it by the door," said Elizabeth. "There was a beautiful willow tree draped across the front garden and it seemed like the perfect name. Daniel burned in the letters and I painted the leaves on. I'd forgotten all about it. Just a scrap of wood and how precious it is now."

"I couldn't see anything else over there but I'll keep on looking if you like."

"No, Jim, this is perfect. Thank you. Thank you so much."

Elizabeth stood and hugged her friend, then she buried her head in his chest and let the tears flow. Jim wasn't quite sure what to do but in the end he hugged her back, not quite sure whether he was glad or not to have found such a potent reminder of Elizabeth's past, something he had hoped to help her forget.

They were still standing there when someone shouted over to them.

"Hello, is that Elizabeth?" said a woman's voice. "Is that you Elizabeth? I can't believe it, is it really you?"

Elizabeth turned round and there in front of her, hurrying over the waste ground, grinning from ear to ear, was Mary Ibbotson, the landlady from the Barrel who had readied the cottage on Elizabeth and Daniel's wedding day.

"Well thank the Lord, it is you," said Mary. "I thought you'd been drowned."

"And I thought you must have been killed too when I saw the pub had gone."

The two women threw their arms around each other, relief and pleasure bursting out of them with laughter.

"What happened here? How did you manage to escape? Are the rest of the family safe too?" asked Elizabeth, questions spilling over each other in the need-to-know.

"We were lucky," said Mary. "An hour or so before the dam broke a young man was sent to Sheffield to fetch the engineer to have a look at a crack in the embankment but the girth on his horse snapped, so he stopped off at the Barrel to get it fixed and he told us what was going on. Most of the people in the village decided not to take any chances. We all went up the hill to spend the night with neighbours, thank God. And thank God for that broken girth. Mind you, the poor neighbours who took us in - we're still there while we sort out somewhere to live. But what about you? Did you see Gabriel? I didn't think we'd ever get him out of the bar that night, you know what the man's like, he gets all confused and dithery."

"Gabriel is safe and well. He got me out of Willow Tree Cottage moments before the water came and he took me to stay with his sister in Bamford. He's there now but I'm working in Sheffield. This is Jim Nightingale, he's from Bamford, and he brought me out here today. I've not been back since that night. Jim, this is Mary Ibbotson."

"Hello Jim Nightingale," said Mary, shaking the young man's hand.

"I'm pleased to meet you," said Jim. "It looks as if the village didn't fare well."

"Not at all but at least most of us survived even if the village didn't. Are you just visiting from Bamford?"

"No, I'm living in Sheffield too."

"Jim was working down at Low Matlock when the dam burst and he spent the following day helping to dig out bodies from the mud and look for anyone still alive," said Elizabeth.

"Not too many of those, unfortunately," said Jim.

"Not at all down-river. And your parents, Elizabeth, and that lovely family, the Tricketts, all gone."

"Are you going to rebuild the pub?" asked Jim.

"We don't know what to do," said Mary. "We're getting a bit too long in the tooth to start out again, in fact start out even further back than we did last time; then we did actually have a pub to start out in. At least we're all alive while many others aren't."

The three of them stood there quietly before Elizabeth broke the silence.

"Look what Jim found for me," she said, showing Mary the plaque from Willow Tree.

"Well would you believe something like that would still be there," said Mary. "Millstones and houses and everything floated away and that little bit of wood stayed where it was. You'll be able to use it on your next home."

"I don't think it would be the same."

"And why not? It would be a good reminder of God smiling down on you both."

"I mean it wouldn't be the same without Daniel," said Elizabeth.

"Daniel? Why, what's happened to him?" said Mary.

"I saw him swept off his feet and taken away by the flood just as he was coming home across the river," said Elizabeth.

"And you've not seen him since?"

"No." Elizabeth bit into her bottom lip and tried to hold on, trying not to burst into tears again.

"Then I've got news for you, my girl. We saw Daniel a day or so after the flood. He'd been dragged along by the water as far as Rotherham and he woke up in the mud at the side of the river there. He came back here to look for you."

"Daniel's alive, he's alive? Mary, are you sure?"

"Certainly I'm sure."

Elizabeth started shaking from head to foot, her eyes wide open but not seeing and her mouth hanging open in disbelief. "Daniel's alive," she kept saying, over and over. "Daniel's alive." She had become totally lost within herself, unaware of where she was, what she was doing, what was going on around her. All she could think of was Daniel, his face, his hands, his body, his voice, his rushing home to find her. And all these past weeks she had thought he was dead. She turned away from the others and stood quietly looking over at the site of their old home. Somehow it looked less ruined.

"Poor girl, I thought she must know," said Mary.

"She didn't," said Jim. "But I tell you what, Mary, I'm going to start saying my prayers again just like Our Mam told me to."

"You're going to start saying your prayers? That's a peculiar thing to say."

"You don't know how peculiar," said Jim. "Do you know where he is now, Daniel?"

"No, I assumed he'd be in Sheffield," said Mary. "Although he was in a dreadful state and he seemed to set off... Oh my God."

"What's the matter?"

"I told Daniel that Elizabeth was dead. I thought she and Gabriel had been killed. It was so late when Gabriel left the pub and he didn't seem to take it in when we warned him to get Elizabeth to high ground and then we saw the cottage had been destroyed and I just assumed... Oh my God. I don't know where Daniel is but he doesn't think he has any reason to come back here."

"You were saying something about him setting off," Jim prompted.

"Yes, he set off over the hills, in the opposite direction to Sheffield."

DAVID and Oonagh had had a relaxing day in Liverpool. They had strolled around the formal gardens in front of the magnificent St George's Hall and had bought several items of fresh clothing in the shops to save having to open up their trunks but mainly they had enjoyed just resting in their suite in the Adelphi Hotel. Their journey wasn't yet over: they'd had weeks at sea and then the crossing over from Ireland but, despite their break in Dublin visiting Oonagh's family, both felt they'd been on the go for long enough and needed to stay put in Liverpool for a few days at least before carrying on by train to Sheffield.

It had also given David the chance to send a telegraph to his old regiment. He wanted to find out if any of his friends from his India days were back in England. It had been six years since he had seen any of his comrades from India, he'd been left for dead in Kashmir when he'd been shot. Weeks later after being cared for by some villagers he'd made his way back to the nearest garrison. The regimental surgeon had identified gangrene as soon as David had entered the camp, the smell was nauseatingly apparent to everyone apart from David. The arm had come off just below the elbow and his military career had ended with the saw.

"I'm sure you'd enjoy a trip to London, Oonagh."

"I'm sure I'd enjoy spending a few days there," she said. "In fact I'm going to stop spending in Liverpool so there'll be plenty left in your wallet." They had just got back to their hotel room after a visit to the telegraph office and were taking off their heavy outdoor clothes.

"You're very fond of my wallet, aren't you, Mrs Shaw?"

"There are a few well-stuffed features about your person that I am even more fond of, Mr Shaw," said Oonagh, helping undo the buttons on David's overcoat.

"If you're not careful I'll hit you with my stump, Mrs Shaw," he said, lifting high what remained of his left arm.

"Please do, Mr Shaw."

"I'll have you know that this stump was acquired in the service of Her

Majesty the Queen, Mrs Shaw, and I'll thank you not to be so disrespectful. This stump is a lasting memorial to Britain's glorious success in battle in India and my own acclaimed heroism on the field."

"I am more than respectful of your stump, Mr Shaw, but prefer its role in my own service rather than Her Majesty's. Now let's get out of these things and you can give me a personal demonstration of your heroism in action."

AGAINST his better judgement Jimmy had actually begun to enjoy school. Of course he hated having to stay there and wear such silly clothes but he felt quite proud of learning how to read and write. He could put his name down on paper now and it seemed to give him a sort of status that he didn't quite understand. And he loved being told all about the different places in the world, geography it was called. All those pink bits on the map belonged to England and he was English, wasn't he, so in a way they all belonged to him too. Sometimes he imagined what it would be like to go and see some of those places and he'd be treated special because he was a part-owner. Despite being at something called 'a charity school', Jimmy began to feel quite rich. After all his moaning about the Blue Coat, he now regretted having agreed to help rob the place for Jack Quinn.

The break-in was set for Thursday night and, with a sense of alarm, Jimmy had realised that that was tonight. The boss had ordered him to call in to head office during the day for his last minute instructions and Jimmy couldn't put it off any longer no matter how much he might want to. He asked the teacher for permission to go to the toilet and then legged it out of the building and down Campo Lane to see Quinn.

Jimmy was about to rush in through the door when he remembered Quinn's strict orders: he stopped, knocked on the door and waited to be called in.

"It's the lad himself," said Quinn when finally he summoned Jimmy in from waiting outside. All the time Jimmy was composing an excuse for the teacher as to why he was in the toilet for so long: he didn't want to say he just couldn't poo because the last time he'd used that excuse he was dosed with some foul-tasting liquid that made him go quicker than a bullet from a gun. "So, Jimmy, what's what today?" said Quinn. "All set for tonight, your big night, when you become a full member of the crew?"

"Yes, Mr Quinn, though I'm a bit nervous. I've never done owt like this before. What if we get caught?"

"You make sure we don't get caught, lad, that's part of your job, we're all relying on you, aren't we gentlemen?" said Quinn, addressing Pickens and

Porter: Mick Briggs still hadn't been seen since the fight with John and even Quinn's spies hadn't been able to turn up any clues as to where he'd gone. "And lady, of course," he said, looking at Peggy. "Now, Jimmy, run through these drawings of yours so we all know exactly where we're going. When you know what you're doing, see, there's no need to be nervous. It's when you don't know what you're doing that things go wrong. And if they go wrong tonight, Jimmy lad, then you will need to be nervous because I'll be after you for cocking it up."

Jimmy's plan of the ground floor of the Blue Coat School was spread out on the table. He traced the map with his finger, trying not to shake, and for the third or fourth time talked them through where the side-door with the weak lock was positioned on York Street, what the corridor lay-out was just inside the door, which way to turn after going straight ahead down the corridor to get to the main entrance hall, which door in the hall led into the headmaster's office: the locked cupboard in which the school's funds were kept was to the right, tucked into a corner between a couple of tall bookshelves. The cupboard was just an ordinary cupboard but it did have a strong padlock on it. Jimmy had seen the headmaster fumbling around in it once and had spotted him putting a wad of notes into a black metal box stored inside. The headmaster had then conveniently dropped the key into a draw in the desk. Jimmy felt embarrassed at the obvious trust shown in him by the head.

"Looks good, looks good," said Quinn. "Now, Jimmy, remind me what you're going to do for us."

"At eleven-o'-clock I'm going to sneak downstairs and hide under the stairs in the entrance hall until you come. Then I'll show you where the key is in the desk and you can get the money out of the cupboard."

"Very good, very good," said Quinn. "Now, the thing is, Jimmy, there's been a bit of a change of plan. You see the more I thought about this job the more something was bugging me, not quite right. Then I figured it: what's the point in any of us here risking breaking in to the place when you could do the whole thing yourself, on the inside. You sneak down the stairs at eleven, just like we planned, but instead of meeting us in the hall you get the money yourself, take it to the side door and slip it out to Pickens here, then you lock up again, go back to bed, tuck down for the night and then we all have sweet dreams. What do you say, lad?"

Jimmy's insides started turning upside down and inside out. Now he couldn't hide the shakes. "I don't know, Mr Quinn. Like I said, I've not done owt like this before. I'd rather someone was there to help."

"Would you now," said Quinn. "You see, Jimmy, what you don't understand yet is that what you'd rather happen doesn't come into it, it's what I say that matters. I'm the boss, you're a kid, I tell you what to do and by God you do it, understand? Tell him what happens if I get cross, Will."

Pickens had gone through his own gamut of full concentration on the planned job, through relief that he didn't have to do much except stand outside a door and now to amusement at someone else being on the receiving end of Quinn's attention, the sort of Quinn's attention no-one wanted to be on the end of. "Well, Jack," he said, looking at Jimmy with an ugly sneer, "you don't like to get cross, it makes you not just cross but very angry and you don't like to get very angry. Sometimes when someone makes you very angry, Jack, you like to teach them a bit of a lesson, a bit like a teacher passing on the benefit of their knowledge and experience to a naughty schoolboy who won't pay proper heed. So, Sir, you might opt for a slap, only it would be a hard slap across the face. Then again you might opt for the cane, only not just a cane, probably a leather strap across anywhere it might happen to land – back, legs, arse. Then again if you're really angry, you might get mad enough to pay a visit to the lad's friends in The Ponds and take it out on…"

"I think young Jimmy gets the picture," interrupted Quinn. "So, Jimmy, what's what?"

Jimmy was fixed to the spot, couldn't even shake now. "I come downstairs at eleven, get the money box out of the cupboard, sneak along to the side-door and hand it over to Mr Pickens. Then I go back to bed and we all have sweet dreams."

"There you are," said Quinn, "how easy is that? Where's all your worry coming from? There's no need, we're all one big team here, lad, we all work together, for each other. There's honour among thieves, haven't you ever heard that? After tonight, you'll be one of us thieves, good and proper. Now get back to school and the next time I see you will be to give you your share of the takings. Look on this as a little test and, if it goes really well, I'll think about bringing you in on a really big job. Go on, off you go."

"Yes, Mr Quinn," said Jimmy, sneaking a pleading look at the kindly Peggy but realising he'd get no support from that direction. He ran back to school already smarting from the imagined slap across the face and hurting from the leather strap. He wanted his Uncle John.

"Do you think he'll sort it?" asked Peggy.

"No question," said Quinn. "I'm not sure about him having any sweet dreams, though."

"How much do you think we'll get, boss?" asked Pickens.

"The lad mentioned a big wad of notes being stashed away so, however much there is, it shouldn't be a bad haul for us in return for taking no risks. It's a charity school so perhaps they've just done a collection from all the mugs who keep it going with their big hearts and big wallets," said Quinn. "So, Pickens, you be outside that side-door from eleven on and you, Peggy, you go with him; that way if anyone starts nosing around you can pretend you've just left the pub and stopped for a bit of slap-and-tickle."

THE nightmares of seeing Daniel being washed away by the flood had been replaced by different but still grotesque images of separation that kept Elizabeth agitated while she was sleeping and lost in a dreamworld while she was awake. In these new horrors she found herself rooted to the spot and screaming soundlessly while, striding away into a strange distance, Daniel marched unheeding away from her and out of reach. The landscape would change between two constant personalities: sometimes Daniel was heading for a tangle of trees and strangling branches, his feet sinking into soggy marshland, but each time he would manage to shake off the clinging tentacles and clogging ground and fight his way forward; other times he would be disappearing into crowds of people in busy city streets, their arms outstretched in welcome to the exciting bustle, and he would have a spring in his step as he hurried into the throng: whatever the scene, Elizabeth was always left alone, invisible and helpless to alter his course.

The news which Mary Ibbotson had passed on had thrown Elizabeth into a hysteria of indecision. She didn't know what to do. She didn't know where to look. She didn't know how even to begin deciding what to do or where to look. When she had returned late to Broomhall that evening after her trip up the valley, she had gone straight to bed, hardly managing a simple goodnight to the cook. She had stayed in bed the following day, prompting fears in the household that she was unwell. Bickerstaff had had words with his wife, suggesting that she must have overworked the girl despite his warnings; Mary had ventured up to Elizabeth's room from the kitchen with some food, only to be greeted by the patient sitting there silently by the window, oblivious to all talk. When at last Elizabeth had regained full consciousness, she determined to pull herself together and work out what if anything she could do.

John Hukin! In the delirium of finding out that Daniel was still alive somewhere, she had forgotten about John, ridiculously, because that was where she had wanted to go when Jim Nightingale persuaded her that a trip up the valley would be better. For the first time in days she smiled. Thank God for Jim, she thought, what a lucky friend for her to have made. If it hadn't been for him… She might not know where Daniel was but at least she knew he was alive.

It was already too late in the evening to venture out to The Ponds to find Bungay Street, especially on a Friday, when she knew there would be more people going in and out of the pubs, so she decided that early the next morning she would start her search.

JIMMY hadn't carried out the robbery. He was scared of Jack Quinn but more scared of getting caught and put in jail. He didn't know how young you had to be to go to jail but he didn't want to take any chances. He had lain awake in bed watching the clock, nervous every time one of the other boys coughed or used the toilet, convinced that somehow they knew what he was about. He had even gotten out of bed himself just before eleven and shivered in his bare feet on the cold floor: he had sat on the side of his cot thinking about Quinn's fist, Quinn's leather strap, Quinn's threats to John and Sally, but still he had sat for a good half hour, not moving but for his shivering, picturing Pickens and Peggy still waiting at the back door, everyone getting angrier by the minute. How long would they wait, he wondered, before giving up?

The answer was that they had waited until well after midnight. Neither looked forward to telling the boss the next day and agreed to go together to break the bad news.

Peggy crept down from her rooms above the head office the following morning, trying to tiptoe without making a sound as she passed Quinn's door. Safely past, she hurried down to the street, stopped to peer from behind the door frame, ready to rush back upstairs if she saw Quinn coming, then she scuttled along Campo Lane to the Paradise to meet Pickens. They tried to plan what they were going to say but, whichever way round they organised the words, the facts remained unchanged and weren't going to please the boss. After a couple of quick gins, they lingered their way back up the street.

Quinn greeted them with his usual, "So, what's what?" beaming at the thoughts of getting his hands on some cash. He might have had a happy look on his face but he didn't like the look on theirs. "Hand it over then," he ordered, deliberately keeping hold of his smile.

"There's nothing to hand over, boss," said Pickens.

"The kid didn't show," said Peggy.

"What do you mean 'didn't show'?"

"We waited at the side-door as planned but the kid didn't turn up," said

Pickens.

"He let you down, Jack, let us all down, left us standing there in the street waiting for nothing."

The smile was abandoned. It took a few minutes of heavy breathing and finger drumming for the news to sink in then it hit him like a plumb. Quinn wasn't a happy man. "That bastard kid," he snarled, leaping out of his seat and storming round the office, kicking furniture and hammering his fists into whatever wouldn't move out of the way with the first kick. "All that bloody money. I'll get that little runt, double-crossing me. The snivelling bastard, the fucking bastard little creep. Didn't neither of you have any idea about this, any hint, any anything?" he said, suddenly turning on the other two and pausing mid-outburst. "How do I know you're not holding out on me and blaming the boy? How do I know you've not stashed the money away yourselves somewhere?" Quinn bent over Pickens, his face just inches away and fuming sour breath. "Are you double-dealing me? For all I know you even kept that money and only pretended Hukin had taken it."

"No, boss," said Pickens. "Would I have come back here if I'd kept the money? We waited for well over an hour last night, how could we have had any idea what the boy was up to?"

"The problem is you never have any idea, you pathetic toad. Perhaps you should've waited a bit longer, perhaps the kid was delayed and you cleared off too soon," Quinn yelled, swiping Pickens across the face and booting him in the shin with the underside of his foot so hard that Pickens was sent sprawling across the floor.

"We waited as long as we could, there was a policeman on the corner already starting to watch us," said Peggy. "There's only so long we could be snogging in the street without looking as if something else was going on, Jack."

"Don't you 'Jack' me, you cheap whore, you make your fucking living snogging. You waited as long as you could?" shouted Quinn. "It's up to me how long is long enough and I don't think you bloody well waited long enough. What's a bloody hour when my money's at stake?" He leapt at Peggy and grabbed her by the throat, squeezing until her eyes began to pop and she was gasping for air before he flung her against the wall. "I bet you didn't wait long at all, you stupid bitch. I bet the kid did the job, went to find you two, you weren't there so he decided to hold on to the money for safekeeping until today, that's what I think. Little Jimmy wouldn't let Jack Quinn down," he said, his anger subsiding into a hideous grin, "he'd be too bloody scared."

Quinn walked over to the window and strained to see the Blue Coat School down on the corner. "Tell you what, Peggy love," he said, "why don't you just call in to the school now and ask to see Jimmy. Tell them you're his auntie or something, buy him some sweets before you go, here's a few coppers, and tell them you've got a treat for the lad. Then we can get to the bottom of all this. I'm sure he'll have the money safe somewhere and we can all forget about this business with a good night out on the proceeds. Clean yourself up a bit first, you don't want them thinking you're a whore. Go with her, Will, just to keep an eye on things. I'll have the glasses filled ready for you when you get back."

Peggy's neck was red raw and she tried to sooth the burn with the fingers of one hand while she rubbed the back of her head with the other: her eyes were wet from the pain of the assault. As for Pickens, he was barely able to stand: a blood stain spread through his trousers where Quinn's boot had riven a deep gash in the man's leg while his foot had twisted under him in the sudden violence of his fall.

"Come on Will, Peggy, just a little misunderstanding," said Quinn, putting on that he might have gone a bit too far. "So what's what? Perhaps I was a bit sharp with you both but it doesn't mean anything, you know I rely on you both, I'd be lost without you and you'd be lost without me, I always look after you, don't I? It's just that you know and I know that you both need a bit of a quick reminder now and then of how things are, of how I'm the one who knows how to get things done, how to bring the money in. It's a big responsibility, I feel responsible for you both and I have to bear the burden of that responsibility, that's something you might not fully understand. Now take Briggs, you see he never fully understood my position either; I had to teach him the odd lesson too, show him the way things work, but unfortunately he never did quite get it so the last lesson I taught him was his last. Understand what I'm saying?"

"Has Briggs been around?" asked Pickens.

"Well," said Quinn, "they say that what goes around comes around but let me just say that Briggs won't be coming around any more, ever, in any sense." Quinn changed his sickly smiling smirk into an expression of out-and-out hatred. "Now get going the two of you and bring me back that money. I'm off to see a man about a debt but it won't take long so I'll be waiting for you when you get back."

Peggy and Pickens stumbled out of the room, glad to get out of Quinn's reach, shaken by his brutal attack and shaken by what Quinn had said about Briggs. They thought Briggs had scarpered out of Sheffield: they hadn't figured on Quinn having killed the poor bastard.

Neither of them spoke as they walked down Campo Lane to the school, each of them nervous of putting into words what they were both thinking. The perks of working for Jack Quinn had long since evaporated; status among the town's pimps, whores and thieves, a roof over their heads in a safe address and a few so-called bonuses awarded according to the man's whims were no compensation for suffering the constant ordeal of his mood swings and violent temper. Briggs had put up with his share and look where it had landed him, crumpled in a back alley somewhere, probably, with his throat slit, that was Quinn's favourite method of despatch - he never used the word 'murder'. What had happened to Briggs could as easily happen to them.

The entrance to the Blue Coat School was in front of them and Peggy turned to look at Pickens. She hitched up her skirt ready to climb the few steps and turned to look at Pickens again. "Let him bloody well do it himself," she said. Then the two of them walked past the school, rounded the corner and were gone.

THE smoky fug inside the pub hung in layers like a heavy mist on a still day; it rolled and undulated without actually going anywhere. The noisy clamour of voices was still something Daniel was finding hard to get used to. In Sheffield, pub conversation tended to be muted and sparse with plenty of time to contemplate what had just been said. Scouse drinkers were a different lot, no-one seemed to stop talking and the only way to be heard was to speak louder and faster than your companions. This inevitably led to an ever-increasing level of volume and confusion of voices.

Daniel sat on his own, tucked away in a gloomy corner, staring into his pint glass and trying to ignore the din. His eye under the patch was itching infernally and he wanted nothing more than to give it a good rub. He resisted purely because he thought leaving it alone was the only possible way he might regain his sight. It was strange only having the one eye to look through. Daniel found his perspective had entirely changed: every view he had was now framed by the profile of his nose. He didn't have a particularly large nose but still it remained an ever-constant presence to every image and scene he met, protruding in and blocking things off. He had begun to loathe his nose.

He hadn't seen Paul in the four days since he had started working at the docks, they were on different shifts and by the time Paul had finished Daniel was fast asleep only a couple of hours from waking and going back off to work. It was hard graft and Daniel ached in places he never knew existed before. Being a grinder meant that he had developed great strength in his arms and shoulders just through keeping the wheel in place but the work at the docks required a different type of strength, always on the move shifting bales and bundles from here to there, loading and unloading, dragging crates and clambering on to piles of cargo to start demolishing the piles and moving the cargo somewhere else. His back, legs and feet were being sorely tested by this new regime and although Daniel knew he'd get used to it if he carried on it wasn't much comfort for the time being. He never felt any of these aches and pains while he was working, it was as if his body did what it had to do and only protested once he had finished and started to relax.

Daniel got on well with Davy's brother Eddie. Neither of the brothers could read but word always seemed to get back as to where the travelling gypsies were. They were now camped just south of the town of Caernarfon. Martha, Eddie's wife, a Liverpuddlian born and bred, fixed up meals for Daniel and generally fussed over him like he was one of her own. But Daniel felt himself falling into a routine he didn't want to fall into: he got up at four in the morning, went to work, finished at five in the afternoon and went to the Cracke for a couple of drinks, went back to the house, had a meal, then went to bed. It had only been four days but Daniel could see it could easily extend into years unless he made a decision about what to do. The more ships he witnessed coming in and going out, the more he wondered about working a berth over to America and starting afresh all over again. There must be a call for experienced grinders over there. The problem was he didn't know where or how to start getting a job. Working in Liverpool gave him an idea of the wider world. Everyone he worked with and everyone he met seemed to have links with some other place, whether it'd be the Irish down at the docks, the Chinese living down the road, the Negros from the Caribbean or Africa whom he passed in the street or the varying Europeans working the ships that docked each day at the port. Everyone came from some place else and was full of stories of that other place. Seventy miles east to Sheffield just didn't sound too far away when others were talking about the other side of the globe.

"So how you finding the job Dan?" The huge figure of Joe McCarrell settled itself into the chair opposite. Daniel hadn't seen or heard the big man enter.

"Christ! Where did you spring from Joe?"

"I guess I caught you on your blind side." Joe drained his pint in one go and waved over to a man stood at the bar. "You want another?"

Daniel nodded. "Yeah, why not, it's not bad ale here."

Joe shouted at his man: "Two more Des." He hunkered down on the table and lit a cigar. "The reason why I ask is that I know you're not from around these parts and I know you have no real ties here."

268

Daniel raised his eyebrows. "So what does that have to do with anything?"

"All I'm saying is that you're the new boy and I need a new face. Someone who can work with me and someone who can take care of my business. I think you might be that man." The two pints of beer arrived at their table. "Cheers," Joe said and took a mouthful.

"I thought your business was at the docks. I thought that was where you worked and who paid you." Daniel had his suspicions where this was going but thought he might as well string it out for what it was worth.

"I do work for the docks and I do a good job there, it's just that I have more to consider nowadays. I've two kids growing up and a wife who doesn't stop spending. I can't afford to be just another foreman, I need extra income, more money coming in."

"And where do I come in?"

"It's just a case of getting some things past the customs men. They hardly ever check anything anyway, their presence is usually enough to stop things getting through that shouldn't."

"If that's the case, why don't you do it yourself?"

"Because I can afford to pay somebody else." Joe smiled and raised his glass. "There is a risk, I'd be lying if I said there wasn't, but the rewards are handsome enough."

"So what are you smuggling in?" Daniel asked.

Joe raised his hand in protest. "I'm not smuggling anything in Dan, heaven forbid that I ever do. All I'm asking is that you bring a few things through that aren't at the scrutiny of the excise men. I'm just avoiding a few over-zealous taxes, that's all."

"Like what? What would I be bringing in and what is it worth to me?" Now they were getting down to the nitty gritty.

"A few cases of spirits, maybe some perfume, maybe some tobacco. It's worth an extra pound a day, not that it's every day of course."

Daniel knew he could be in an impossible position. "What can I say? If I say no, you'll have me out of a job. If I say yes and then get caught, well, I don't think you're likely to come down and say I was working for you."

"You won't get caught, no-one ever does. It's a piece of piss, all you do is load the cargo on to the pallets labelled custom-checked and then bring it through."

"If no-one gets caught, how come you need someone else to do it in the first place? Surely you must have people doing it for you already."

"Well I won't tell a lie, some men have been caught. But I take care of them Dan, I really do. If you're sent down I will make sure your job's kept open and pay you for taking the fall. A pound a day every day that you're inside. But it won't come to that, trust me, the only reason I need someone else now is that one of my men died the other week and left me a man down."

"Oh aye, and what did he die from?"

"Old age, he was over sixty. For God's sake, this isn't a dangerous job, even if you did get caught, chances are you'd be able to say you'd just made a mistake, you're new on the job after all. The maximum you'd get is two years and that's worth over six hundred pounds. You can't lose." The big figure loomed over the table casting even more of a shadow over Daniel. "So what's it to be?"

Daniel resisted the urge to rub his bad eye, itching more than ever now. Nothing was ever simple, even the simplest of jobs seemed to bring complications with it. He knew that many would jump at the chance of earning a couple of quid more, even someone like John would probably have taken the opportunity, but Daniel had spent his entire life trying to avoid all that shit. From his earliest days in Bungay Street when the local gangster, Jack Quinn, had tried to enrol the street boys to do his bidding through to when he was trying to steer Nathan away from that kind of life, he'd always avoided any trouble with the law. The closest he'd come was the occasional pub brawl or when he was with the gypsies. "I'm going to have say no," he said finally. "No disrespect Joe, but I may not be here much longer, I'm thinking of working my way over to America, I think I've had enough of England."

Joe's face darkened. He was already leaning over close to Daniel's face but managed to move in closer, one hand resting on Daniel's. "I won't tell a lie, Dan, your answer disappoints me. I'll give you a day or two to re-think your position."

Daniel clasped McCarrell's hand and lifted it up. "I won't tell a lie either Joe, I don't like being threatened. I won't say anything about this if you don't but if you take this further you'll have more than your fingers to worry about."

"What do you mean?"

Daniel tightened his grasp around the big man's hand, crushing his fingers until he heard the bones crack.

"Jesus, Mary and Joseph, fucking stop it." Joe McCarrell's eyes began to water.

Daniel kept his grip on the man's hand. "Let me tell you now Joe, I've had enough shit to last me a lifetime. All I want now is a quiet life, do my work and get the fuck out of here. Do we agree that this will be the last of this business?"

"Yes, yes, whatever. Just give me back my hand for God's sake."

Daniel released the man's hand. "I've no quarrel with you Joe, please don't make it worse than it could be."

Joe McCarrell stood up. Once he was sure he had enough distance he poked his finger towards Daniel. "This isn't the end of things, I'll sort you. Things can get a lot worse, believe you me."

DAVID linked his arm through Oonagh's. "So how did you like the show?"

"It was fun but I didn't think they showed stuff like that anymore." She flicked at an imaginary spot on her sleeve. "It seemed terribly old-fashioned in some ways and quite risqué in others." The couple were walking out of the Neptune Theatre.

David laughed. "Well believe it or not that show had the best reviews in town, I asked the man at the desk. I suppose it'll take some time to get used to being back in the old country again. I think their culture is somewhat different to what we're used to in the States. Now which way back to the hotel?" They stopped in the street, which was bustling with the throng of a late Friday night.

"I'm pretty sure we came from up there, I remember that stall selling chestnuts on the corner." Oonagh pointed along the road to the left.

"Well you've always had a better sense of direction than me. I couldn't even find my way out of India for years." David, seeing a space in the traffic, steered his wife across the road.

"I think we can cut down there and come out just by the hotel," Oonagh said when they reached a side street.

"I'm not sure about that darling, it looks a bit dark. Maybe we should keep to the main road."

"Nonsense, look there are lamps all along and I can see the other end. We'll be fine and it'd be nice to get away from all these people." She guided her husband down the street.

As they walked the noise from the road behind them seemed to be swallowed by the surrounding buildings which suddenly appeared to loom up from either side. The glow from the lamps was meagre and flickered in a way that caused all sorts of moving shadows. The other end of the street didn't seem to be getting any closer.

"I think we should go back to the main road, I'm not really convinced about this place."

"Maybe you're right David," Oonagh said in an unsteady voice and made to turn round but she was shunted into the wall.

"Now then mate, couldn't see your way to lending me a bob or two?" A shuffling figure emerged from the darkness.

David tensed, it had been a long time since he had encountered anyone remotely threatening. His wealth and position had kept him clear of the waifs and strays in America. "I don't have any spare money and I wouldn't give you any if I did."

"David," Oonagh said anxiously, "give the man some money."

"All I'm asking for is the price of a cup of tea." The man walked further into the light. As he did he pulled out a blade which gleamed in the shimmer of the street lights. "But on the other hand, I don't like your tone. Maybe I should just lighten your wallet by the full amount. Come on, don't be shy now."

David pushed Oonagh behind him and looked to defend himself. All he had was his umbrella which he brandished and immediately felt foolish.

"Come on pal, we can make this easy or hard, you've only got one arm and a brolly ain't gonna make a difference either way. Give up the money and we'll all be on our way." The man came into the light, the gleam of the knife now weaving from side to side. "You make it easy for me and we're all said and done. Make it tricky and we've a whole lot of shit to go through, primarily you getting gutted."

"David." Oonagh's voice plaintively called out from behind him.

DANIEL had had a bad day. He had gone to work that morning after his brush with McCarrell and almost got a tonne weight from one of the cranes on his head for thanks. After recognising the threat, he had just walked off the docks and gone to the Cracke. He'd had a few pints and then left: the only place McCarrell's lot would look for him would be the Cracke. He walked out and went down to the George's Hall gardens and sat down on one of the public benches. Things weren't turning out how they should have. By now he was meant to be sorted out: a job, a plan, a future. But all he had was a crap job, no plan and no future; he'd even made a few more enemies. He'd sat in the gardens until he was moved on by a warden and had then just wandered the streets lost in his thoughts.

By the time he decided to go back to Parliament Street it had been dark for some time. He decided to cut down a side street to take the long way home, making sure he didn't pass the Cracke again. He didn't know if McCarrell would have anyone looking for him but he'd just as soon not find out the hard way. He walked down the poorly lit road thinking about whether it would even be safe to go back to the house. Joe knew where he was staying and the other obvious place to find him was at Eddie and Martha's, maybe he should find some other digs for the night.

He didn't notice the scene until he was almost on top of it. It would have been funny if it hadn't been so serious: a one-armed man was trying to fend off some knife-wielding thug with an umbrella while trying to protect a woman at the same time. Daniel launched himself at the thief, tackled him from behind and then grabbed the arm holding the knife, twisting it til the blade fell to the street with a dull clatter. He pushed the man against the wall and punched him hard, three times in the face, each time the man's head struck the wall behind him until he collapsed unconscious to the ground. Daniel caught his breath and turned to the couple. "Are you alright?" he asked. "Did he hurt either of you?"

"No, thank God. And thank you, I wasn't sure how I was going to get out of that one. I'm a bit handicapped as you can see." The one-armed man peered down at the man out cold. "You must have one hell of a punch, he doesn't look like he'll be waking up for quite a while but just in case he's got any friends I suggest we head back to the main road."

"Aye, that's probably a good idea, these kind often have some sort of look-out or back-up." The three of them hurried back down the street and into the now welcoming crowds. "So where were you heading? This isn't really the place to take a young lady."

"Young lady? Hear that David?" said Oonagh.

"We kind of got lost, to be honest neither of us is really used to Liverpool and one street looks pretty much the same as another. We left the theatre and were headed back to our hotel, I thought we were going in the right direction but I think we made a few wrong turns." David turned to Oonagh. "Are you alright Love?"

"I'll be fine, just a little shaken that's all. I think I'd just like to get back to the Adelphi and have a small brandy to settle my nerves." She rested her hand on David's arm which was still brandishing the umbrella like a sword. "Here, I'll take that darling."

David handed over the brolly and looked up and down the road. "No, I've absolutely no idea where we are, we'll have to hail a cab."

"If it's the Adelphi you're wanting, there's no need to waste money on a cab. It's not far from here and I'd be more than happy to take you, I know how hard it is to find your way around this town, I haven't been here that long myself." Daniel gestured that they should follow him.

"Thanks, you've been very kind. Here, let me offer you something in return." David fumbled awkwardly in his jacket pocket and pulled out his wallet.

Daniel laughed. "Good God man, put your money away. I only did what most people would do and I certainly wouldn't accept payment for it."

"Well just the price of the cab fare you saved us then. That's only fair."

"No, I mean it. I don't want any money, now please put your wallet away before someone else tries to pinch it."

Oonagh took David's wallet out of his hand and put it in her bag. "Listen to the man David and stop embarrassing him. However, I'm sure the gentleman would appreciate a drink back at our hotel as much as we would." She looked at Daniel questioningly. "We'd like it if you would join us, Sir."

"Now that's the kind of thanks I will agree to," Daniel grinned, "a tot of brandy would be nice to keep the chill out on a night like this." The three of them started off down the road. "So, where do you come from? I can't place either of your accents. I'm Daniel by the way."

"I'm David and this is my wife Oonagh. I don't think you would recognise our accents; mine comes by way of England, India and America and my wife's from Ireland via America, so there's a fair mixed-bag of influences. You, on the other hand, come from Sheffield if I'm not very much mistaken."

Daniel stopped abruptly, suspicion apparent on his face. David and Oonagh turned in surprise.

"How do you know where I'm from? Who sent you? Was it McCarrell? That squire bloke? Who sent you?"

David uncoupled his arm from Oonagh's and raised his hand. "Easy Daniel, no-one sent us. You saved us remember. I only know where you're from because I'm a Sheffield lad too and it's nice to hear a good Yorkshire accent again. We're only here because I've come to settle my family's estate, they were all killed in the flood you see. We only arrived in Liverpool a couple of days ago."

Daniel didn't relax: things had been happening too fast recently and he wasn't prepared to let his guard down overly soon. "So you don't know Joe McCarrell?"

"Don't know any McCarrell or any squire. Look Daniel, I was on my way from America to visit my family but they were all lost in the flood and I'm on my way now to sort things out. We're leaving for Sheffield tomorrow. I give you my word that nobody has sent us. Come on, think about it: you saved us from a thief in the street, you just happened upon us. I've only got one arm and I'm with my wife, what threat could we possibly pose to you?" When Daniel didn't say anything, David continued: "You're welcome to go about your business, we can find the hotel without you, but we would like to thank you and it is possible that if you're in some kind of trouble with someone then maybe I can help. I'm not without a certain amount of influence."

Daniel calmed down. What David said made sense and, as it happened, he liked their faces. "I'm sorry, it's just that I've had a hard few weeks and I'm a little on edge. I am sorry and I will join you for that drink if the invitation still stands."

Oonagh put her hand on Daniel's shoulder. "Of course, we're in your debt. Come on, let's all get back to the hotel."

They carried on, at first in an uneasy silence but after a while they started to chat again.

"I lost my wife in the flood. It was a terrible, terrible thing. Almost got killed myself."

"What part of Sheffield are you from?"

"From The Ponds originally but more recently I'd moved into a little place up the Loxley valley, at Damflask. Ah, here we are." He stopped at the entrance to the Adelphi. "I'll let you go in first," said Daniel. "Look at the state of me, you make sure it's okay first. I don't want to cause you any unpleasantness."

David went in first and Oonagh followed immediately behind with Daniel. He felt slightly over-awed by the grandeur of the place, it was all a bit different to the Cracke.

"Let's find a table in the bar and order some drinks, I think we could all do with a large stiff one." David led the way, ignoring the outraged faces on some of the guests and the staff, and found a quiet corner where Daniel would be a little less conspicuous. Once the drinks were ordered Daniel pulled out his pipe. "Will this bother you?" he asked Oonagh.

"Goodness no, I much prefer a pipe to what David smokes. He has these foul-smelling cheroot things."

"So you managed to escape from The Ponds? From what I remember that's a pretty tough part of town."

Daniel shrugged. "It certainly wasn't the best part of town, I was lucky to get out but then I was lucky to find my wife, Elizabeth. She was from Malin Bridge and was the reason we moved to Damflask, her father had an old cottage there and when we married he very kindly gave it to us as a wedding present. Of course it's all gone now."

David had gone very still and pale but neither of the other two noticed. Oonagh was busy speaking directly to Daniel. "It was a tragic disaster, the flood. I think David's family were from that place, Malin Bridge. Such a tragedy really, because David hadn't spoken to them in years, they thought

275

he was dead you see? And his sister, Lizzie, she was really quite young, only seventeen, far too young for anyone to..." Oonagh noticed the faces of the two men and her voice trailed off.

"What was your wife's maiden name?" David asked in a choked voice.

"Shaw," Daniel said, equally hoarse.

"Lizzie Shaw, my God."

Oonagh left the two men sat in the bar by a dwindling fire at two-o'-clock in the morning. They showed no sign of stopping talking and only absently acknowledged her departure.

MOST of the household was still in bed with only Mary the cook already up and about when Elizabeth put her coat on to head off to The Ponds. It was a miserable, showery day and, judging by the puddles on the ground, it had been raining for most of the night.

"Are you sure you should be going down there on your own?" said Mary. "Wouldn't it be better to wait for Jim to go with you? I know you're anxious to find Daniel's friend but you really should take care."

"Jim's already done enough for me," said Elizabeth. "Besides, he's at work and I just can't sit here and wait for him to finish. I've got to start looking for Daniel, find out if John has any news. I've been lying awake for hours as it is waiting for daylight, Mary, I can't sit watching the clock any more."

"Shall I come with you? I can always leave a note for her ladyship, tell her I've gone shopping early. I could leave their breakfast ready if you hang on for a bit."

"Thank you but I want to go right now. I'm too excited and too desperate to wait. My stomach's churning upside down and inside out and I can't concentrate on anything but finding Daniel. I've already lost too much time. All these weeks have past with Daniel thinking I'm dead, he could be anywhere, he could be getting further away by the minute. I don't think I can wait even just a few minutes more."

"I understand," said Mary. "At least tell me the name of the street you're looking for, just in case."

"John lives in Bungay Street, that's all I know," said Elizabeth. "I don't know which house or whether he's still alive himself. If I can't find him there, I'll go to the brewery at Neepsend where he used to work. He was best man at our wedding and he helped us move our things up to Willow Tree Cottage in his beer dray."

"Well you take care, my girl, and don't do anything stupid. I'll see you when you get back, I'll keep some supper for you."

Elizabeth set off in the rain. It was just getting light and the only people about were the men and women trudging to work and the lamplighters putting out the street lamps. She wasn't sure exactly where she was going so she headed into the town first and then headed off in the rough direction of The Ponds. She couldn't miss it in the end, the streets gradually got filthier and totally unloved and the stench was overwhelming. It was worse than anything she had ever imagined and her heart swelled for Daniel as she thought of him growing up in such an awful place and how much of a change Damflask must have been for him. She was aware that even in her mean circumstances she was so much better dressed than anyone else she saw and she was self-conscious when she had to ask a woman if she knew where Bungay Street was.

"It's just down there on the right," said the woman, "and you be careful, Love, this is no place for a young lady to be wondering around on her own."

"Thank you," said Elizabeth, "I'm sure you're as much of a lady as I am."

At that the woman cackled with laughter and Elizabeth noticed that she only had a few brown teeth left at the sides of her mouth, all the front ones, top and bottom, were missing. "A lady? Me? Of course I am, Love, that's why I'm off to spend the day in the bleedin' cutlery works," she said. Elizabeth could hear her still laughing and muttering to herself as she walked off down the road.

It had taken best part of an hour to get to The Ponds from Broomhall and by the time Elizabeth found Bungay Street the pavements and roads were filling with people and horse-drawn carts. There were children playing in the gutters and elderly people standing in doorways watching the world go by. She approached one of them, an old man enjoying a cigarette and chatting to anyone who'd listen as they went by, and asked which house belonged to John Hukin.

"Well now, Miss, it's like this" he said, "there's none of these here houses as belongs to John Hukin, these here houses all belongs to landlords, see, and you can be damned sure they don't live in any of 'em theyselves. Oh no, they live in right posh places, like places like Broomhall and Broomhill, that's where theys live, cleanin' up here to live in all the Brooms. I've always thought that quite a funny idea, really, don't you?"

Elizabeth wasn't quite sure what to reply so she nodded her head a few times and pretended to grin by way of agreement. "Do you know John Hukin?" she asked.

"Do I know John Hukin?" said the old man, taking a drag on his cigarette and making a big show of exhaling the smoke: Elizabeth noticed he had no teeth at all. "I knows everyone here, Miss, everyone. Been here all my life, I have, and I'm not shy of tellin' you that it's gone right downhill, it has, it's not what it used to be. It used to be a right good place to live, with right good neighbours and everything; now it's all pimps and ne'er-do-wells. Most of these people you see now going past I seen grow up from being little'uns and they just don't have the same respect any more, not as it was in my day. And that John Hukin's no better, I don't know what you're lookin' for 'im for. His father was a waster, spent all his money on gambling while his poor wife had to manage best she could, no wonder the lad grew up the way he did, fightin' and cussin' all the time and getting drunk every bloody night. I wasn't surprised when he took up with the local whore, not surprised in the least. But then it takes a lot to surprise me. I sees a lot and keeps me mouth shut. Well you've got to aint yer?"

"Where does he live, I really need to find John Hukin, if you could tell me, please," said Elizabeth.

"He lives six doors down on this side Love, upstairs," said the old man. "You'd better knock before you go in, though, he's got some young slip of a lass moved in with him and you wouldn't want to disturb owt." He finished off with a pantomime wink and started sniggering so uncontrollably that he ended up having a terrible coughing fit. Elizabeth left him to it. When she'd gone he managed to start sniggering again: "I meant to tell you," he said, "Hukin's already left for work."

The street was mainly red-brick terrace houses, dingy looking, with paint peeling, cracks in some of the window panes and clumps of straggly pale weeds growing out between the walls and the pavement, but quite a few of the tenants seemed determined to put up a fight and there were white nets and patterned curtains hanging in some of the windows in defiance of the dirty squalor of the place.

The door to the house John was said to live in was wide open. Inside was a hallway with two doors leading off and the stairs rising up the side wall. The oilcloth on the floor was worn so thin that only hints of the original multi-coloured design remained. Elizabeth stood looking in and up, hoping some sign of life would show her she was in the right place. She could hear muffled voices from behind the two doors but none that she recognised. She climbed the stairs to the next floor. The landing was dismal; there was light coming in from a window on to the street but the glass wasn't very clean and the weather outside didn't help. She stopped again outside the closed door in front of her, not really knowing what to do. She pressed her ear to the wood and strained to listen but couldn't hear any voices coming from the other side, only quiet

278

sorts of sounds, as if someone was moving around. "Daniel, Daniel," she muttered to herself and gained the courage to knock on the door. There was no answer and the sounds of movement inside didn't stop. "Oh God, I hope the old man wasn't right and I'm not disturbing anything." She knocked again, harder. This time she heard someone walk over to the door. It opened and standing in front of her was Sally.

The two girls stared at each other in amazement. It was Sally who managed to speak first. "I thought you were dead, everyone said you were dead." Then her face drained and a look of fear took over as she reached out her hand to touch Elizabeth's arm. "You're not a ghost are you? I couldn't stand it if you were a ghost."

"Oh Sally, no, I'm not a ghost, I'm here, I'm alive, you're alive," said Elizabeth and she opened her arms and hugged her friend, the two of them laughing and weeping at the same time. "My God, how pleased I am to see you, I thought I'd lost everyone and suddenly I haven't. I can't believe it, I just can't believe that I've knocked on the door of a place I've never ever been to before in my life and who should open it but you."

"And here I was just tidying up the breakfast dishes and wondering how to fill my day and suddenly here you are," said Sally. "Lizzie, Lizzie, Lizzie, let me look at you, I just can't believe my dearest old friend is standing here in front of me. Come in, come in, we've got so much missing time to fill in."

There wasn't much to take in in the room but Elizabeth did notice the mattress on the floor. So much for the old gossip down the street: Sally must be John Hukin's 'young slip of a lass'.

"So you're living with John?" she said.

"Yes, he's at work now. Lizzie if it hadn't been for John I'm sure I'd be dead too now, like everyone else. Anyway take off your wet coat and bonnet and I'll build up the fire so we get nice and warm. Remember when we used to sit in front of the fire at home: the last time we did that you'd just got married and you were telling me all about your wedding night and not wearing any nightie." In an instant Sally regretted voicing the memory. "Oh Lizzie I am so sorry to bring that up. I was so busy chattering I wasn't thinking properly. You must be so unhappy losing Daniel after just one wonderful blissful week. How awful the way everything we ever knew has gone."

"But he hasn't gone, he's alive," said Elizabeth. "Mary Ibbotson at Damflask told me that she saw Daniel the day after the flood. Do you remember Mary, she used to run the Barrel."

"Is that still there?" asked Sally, clouding over slightly. "The Cleakum was taken by the flood, all but the chimney, and my Mam and Father and all my sisters and brothers were drowned. There's not much left up at Malin Bridge, it's mostly all gone."

"I know, I went up there a couple of days ago. You can scarcely even tell where Shaw Lodge used to be. It's as if none of it ever really existed. All that's left of the Tricketts' farm is the barn. Remember their beautiful garden?"

"What a wonderful setting that was for your wedding," said Sally, at once realising what Elizabeth had just told her. "You say Daniel's still alive?" she said, her face beaming with happiness for her friend.

"Yes but no-one knows where he is. He saw our cottage had been destroyed and thought I'd been killed too. Mary said he had set off across the hills away from Sheffield and that was the last anyone at Damflask has seen of him. That's partly why I came looking for John, I thought he might have some news."

"As far as John's concerned Daniel is dead, Lizzie. He went up to your old cottage at Damflask after the flood and saw it had been washed completely away and he hasn't heard from Daniel since." Sally saw her friend's expression change from hope to despair. "But it's possible he might have some ideas," she said quickly. "Perhaps they used to talk about other things and places they'd like to do and see and there could be somewhere Daniel always said he'd like to go. Perhaps that's what he decided to do when he thought you had been killed. I'm sure John will have a few good ideas."

Elizabeth brightened. "He will, won't he, friends talk about things like that don't they, we used to."

"We used to talk about that sort of thing all the time. Remember when we planned all the different places in the world we were going to visit and then you went and got married instead and just moved up the road."

The mood lightened and Elizabeth began to feel hopeful again. "I suppose I didn't get very far, did I?"

"And here I am in The Ponds," said Sally, "how much of a change of destination is that."

"Tell me, how come you did end up here?"

"I went back to Malin Bridge as soon as I heard about the dam breaking and John found me scrabbling about in the mud where the Cleakum used to be. I was in a right mess, I think I lost my mind for a few days, I couldn't believe my whole family had gone so suddenly and unexpectedly, even now I know I sometimes get lost in awful black thoughts and I persuade myself they're all still alive and I get all confused and mixed up. John brought me back here to live: I'd nowhere else to go and I was too muddled in my head to tell him where my relatives lived in Oughtibridge. And I'm still here, as you see."

"I'd forgotten that you weren't at home when the dam burst," said Elizabeth. "I've been too caught up in my own worries to even think properly. I heard that your pub had gone and I think as far as I was concerned that was that. It makes me feel so selfish."

"Don't be ridiculous, Lizzie, we've all had more than our share of loss to start worrying about how we've behaved with it all. I haven't even been up the valley since. Maybe I should have gone back to see if there was anything I could do to help but I haven't and I don't feel selfish about that. Tell me what happened to you anyway, how did you escape?"

"I was on the hill just above the cottage and I saw Daniel on his way home on the other side of the river, then the huge wall of water suddenly crashed down on top of everything and I saw him being swept away and I passed out. Gabriel – remember Gabriel? our driver? – he took me to his sister's house in Bamford and I was in bed with a fever for days. I came back to Sheffield to see my father's attorney and I'm living in his house until he sorts out my father's affairs. I only found out two days ago that Daniel survived the flood and had been back up to Damflask looking for me. Now I don't know where to start looking for him."

"John will know what to do," said Sally, full of optimism. "I know he misses Daniel too and he'll be so happy to know that he's still alive."

"It is funny you being here with John, don't you think, the way you used to skit him for not being able to read?"

"I can't believe I was so mean to him, Lizzie, you should have told me."

"I did, you were so hard on him but I was amused to see how you made sure you went outside when he was making a delivery. I take it you've changed your attitude."

"He is such a good man. He really looks after me and Jimmy, that's his little cousin, he's at school now. John took Jimmy in after the flood because the boy lost his home and family too so John's having to work long hours to earn enough money to keep us all. His has a big heart, Lizzie, I should have recognised that from the way he used to play with Thomas and Hugh. I'm teaching him to read now and he's not stupid at all. But I do worry about him because lately he seems to be feeling quite down. He stopped drinking, you know, so that we'd have more money to live on, but he's come home drunk a couple of times this week and I can't get him to tell me what's wrong. I wish he would. I hope it's nothing to do with me, maybe I've become too much of a burden, after all he only took me in because he felt sorry for me and I'm still here all these weeks later. Perhaps I should try to find a job and help out, I could clean or something."

"That's what I've been doing," said Elizabeth.

"Cleaning, as a job?"

"Yes, for Mr Bickerstaff and his wife – he's my father's attorney. I have a room in their house in Broomhall and I help around the house and in the kitchen and sometimes I have to go to his office in town to clean there."

"What's it like?"

"It's no different to when we used to do it at home, there's just more of it and her ladyship – that's what we all call Mrs Bickerstaff – is a lot fussier than my mother ever was," said Elizabeth. "You and I didn't exactly lead privileged lives at Malin Bridge, did we, Sally? We all had our share of the chores to do."

"We weren't rich but we had rich lives."

The two young women drifted into quiet memories again, tinged with sadness but dominated more by happy recollections of life before the flood.

"I used to love helping out at the Tricketts' farm," said Elizabeth. "Wouldn't it be wonderful if we could all go back up the valley to live?"

"How I've thought about that over and over again," said Sally. "I'd find it hard to leave John now, though, he's been kind to me and I don't think I could just leave him."

"My, you have changed your attitude, Sally. Are we talking about the same John who is only a brewery delivery man?"

"We are but I'm going to take out the word 'only'," said Sally. "Wasn't I such a prig?" she said smiling with embarrassment. "I thought I was so high and mighty because I could read and he couldn't and it turns out he's a much kinder person than I could ever be."

"Yet you did look forward to him coming every week, admit it."

"I suppose I did. Strange really."

"Perhaps not so strange," said Elizabeth, pulling a knowing face. "Will John be home from work soon?"

"Not for hours yet."

"Well then I suggest we stroll into town and go to a tea shop. We could both do with a treat."

"I was actually taken out for a treat recently, to a posh café in town for something to eat with a reporter from the newspaper."

"Well you won't be going to a posh one today," said Elizabeth. "Get your coat on and we'll go."

"Agreed." Sally stood up, tied her hair back and put on her boots. "Look at the state of these old things," she said. "I've had them for years."

"Who knows, one of these days you might be able to afford a new pair," said Elizabeth.

"Ay, after six months' skivvying, maybe," said Sally. "By then my hands will be so raw I won't even be able to do the laces up. Perhaps I'll be like Cinderella and my Prince Charming will come along. Can you imagine a Fairy Godmother coming to The Ponds?"

"To be honest I can't imagine anyone choosing to come to The Ponds."

"Perhaps I've already met my Fairy Godmother, it's John," laughed Sally.

"No but he could be your Prince Charming."

"John is someone else's Prince Charming," said Sally. "He's well in with a woman down the street, she's actually really nice, Melanie's her name, she's been like a friend to me. She's a prostitute."

The two young women burst out laughing and headed out into the rain for their treat. "Do you know what's so great about seeing you again, Sally?" said Elizabeth. "Until now I'd forgotten who I was."

JACK Quinn was champing at the bit. It had slowly but surely dawned on him that Pickens and Peggy might have scarpered, that he might have perhaps over-reacted to the school job not going as planned and had let his temper get just a little the better of him. He'd waited all day yesterday for them to come back from the school with news of his money, he'd even organised a bit of uncustomary gentle persuasion to bring them back into the fold and had had a few drinks lined up for them and a bit of a bonus by way of warming things up again with a down-payment on the takings he was still confident of snatching. He had even lowered his own personal standards and sense of status by eventually calling in to the Paradise for a drink: it had cost him a few bob, too, with drinks all round for those of his runners who were there but he still didn't hear a whisper about Pickens and Peggy. Not that he'd told anyone he was looking for them, of course, then they'd know there was money at stake and trouble brewing, but he'd hinted sourly enough that it would be in everyone's best interests if they told him where the two bastards were holding up. Now it was well over twenty-four hours since he'd last seen them and the missing money was burning a hole in his brain. He figured he had two courses open to him: he could forget all about it – not an option, he had never let a job go undone, ever, and, if he did and word got out, he'd lose his authority– or he could sort the bloody kid out himself. He sat behind his desk nursing a large gin and drumming his fingers; he always thought better with a drink and some concentrated physical activity, confined, limited activity but aggressive, he enjoyed the dull repetitive thud, it kept his fingers toned, in practice, made perfect. It worked. He shot out of his chair, locked his office and rushed out.

His destination was the Blue Coat School. After all, what was a good plan using Peggy was just as good using himself only this time he wouldn't have to share the takings. "I'd make a good uncle," he joked to himself as he stepped lightly down Campo Lane, buoyed with the thoughts of his eagerly awaited easy pickings: "I'd have the kid's best interests at heart, close to my heart, right next to my heart, in my inside top pocket, in fact."

It was relatively quiet in the school's entrance hall, with just the hum of something indistinct being recited over and over again drifting in from behind closed doors. Remembering the directions Jimmy had provided, Quinn headed over to what he knew was the headmaster's office and marched straight through the door.

"I beg your pardon," bellowed the headmaster. "Don't you know how to knock?"

The suddenness of the rebuke was as unexpected as it was fearless. This wasn't the sort of reaction Jack Quinn expected from anybody, least of all a snotty-nosed headmaster, yet he felt himself redden like a naughty schoolboy caught in the act.

"I asked you a question," Mr Bagshaw repeated in no-less authoritative tones. "Don't you know how to knock or do you always just burst in through the door when you feel like it? Just who do you think you are?"

Quinn was too flustered to reply but he stared at the man on the other side of the desk as a growing sense of rage welled up inside him.

"I beg your pardon," he managed at last, slicing through the comment with as sharp a tongue as he could muster, leaving the head not knowing whether or not he had just heard an apology or an insolence. "I'm looking for my nephew, Jimmy."

"Jimmy who, exactly?"

"Jimmy, my nephew, Jimmy." This wasn't something Quinn had reckoned on, not knowing the brat's name, and for all his stature in Sheffield's seedier quarters he found himself being carpeted by a stupid bloody schoolteacher.

"If he is your nephew I assume you at least know his surname."

"It's just bloody 'Jimmy'," snapped Quinn.

"Well we don't have any boys here by the name of Bloody Jimmy," said Mr Bagshaw, "so I suggest you leave right now before I summon the police to find out what you're after."

"There's no need for that, you pompous old fart," said Quinn regaining his edge. "I'm looking for a boy called Jimmy who joined your school about a week ago. He came here with his aunt, my cousin, Sally, and I need to speak to him right away, about some important family business."

"I don't like your attitude, sir, and your tone is quite inappropriate for this establishment," said the headmaster. "If indeed you are young Jimmy's uncle and there is some important family matter to discuss, then I suggest you wait until tomorrow, when his aunt, your cousin, collects him to take him home for the day. Now leave before I do call the police." Mr Bagshaw stood up behind his desk, brandishing a very long, very thick stick. "I'm not having some ill-mannered oaf barging into the school and disrupting the boys' lessons. Good day to you, sir."

Quinn glared at the headmaster, looked at the stick and then back at the man's face. "Not a good idea, that," he said, "not a good idea. You don't know who you're dealing with, you stupid git, but you will." Quinn leaned across the desk and cackled just inches from the headmaster's face, suddenly jerking his own chin forward abruptly so that the head almost stumbled backwards at the implicit threat. "Tomorrow, you say, and what time would that be, may I ask, please, Sir."

"Eight-o'-clock in the morning, sharp."

Quinn stood back and adopted a more conciliatory expression. "Right, eight-o'-clock tomorrow it is then, sharp, thank you very much, most helpful." He turned and headed back out of the office but paused in the doorway and turned to face the head again. "Not a bad est-a-blish-ment you've got here," he spat out, mimicking the teacher. "But you might be advised to watch your own manners in this part of town," he said. "There's some dangerous characters around here and they carry a lot worse with 'em than that pathetic big stick of yours. Some wouldn't be as forgiving as I am to have it shoved in their face but you're lucky there, Mr Headmaster-whatever-your-name-is, because in future I'll be keeping a close eye on you myself, a very close eye."

As he stalked his way back down Campo Lane, Quinn felt as if the money from the old fart's office was already in his pocket. There was no way young Jimmy was going to put up with that sort of school carry-on; the boy would have taken the money just for the hell of it. "Money is the route of all evil," Quinn joked with himself, "and I'll be back along this route tomorrow, eight-o'-clock, sharp."

IT was very late in the afternoon when Elizabeth got back to the Bickerstaffs' house. By the time she and Sally had strolled around town and had their treat in the tea-shop, enjoying simple girlie conversation again after all the misery of the last couple of months, it was already getting too dark to go back to Bungay Street with her friend to wait for John to get home from work. Both had agreed that John would insist that Elizabeth couldn't walk back to Broomhall on her own and felt that accompanying her wouldn't be fair on him after his day's work. Anyway, Sally would be able to give him the news about Daniel and see if he had any suggestions to make as to how to find him.

Elizabeth went straight into the kitchen to find Mary. Everything seemed to be in a state of mild panic. "What on earth's going on?" she asked the cook, who was busy stirring and doctoring a steaming potion on the hob.

"You wouldn't believe it," said Mary, "it's more than I've ever seen in this house before. It's his lordship."

"Nothing's happened to him has it?" asked Elizabeth. "Is he alright?"

"Oh he's alright, alright," said Mary, "he's blind drunk."

"What? Not Mr Bickerstaff senior?"

"The very one," said Mary. "I'm just trying to make him something to calm him down a bit. He started drinking quite early then he had a terrible row with Master Simon, said he was at the end of his tether and would no longer be bailing out the – now what did he say? – 'the worst son ever to drain a hard-working father dry'. He said he'd had enough of paying huge gambling debts to some local crook when" (Mary put on a serious but slurred voice) "'I haven't even had the pleasure of the gaming tables myself, I've been so busy working hard to cover my burdensome offspring'. Then he said it was all over, enough was enough, and that Master Simon would in future either pull his weight in the office or find himself a new job and a new home."

"And what did Master Simon say?"

"He called his father 'a silly old buffer' and said that it was thanks to his gambling associates that the firm of Bickerstaff & Son had any clients left to work for. He said everyone in Sheffield knew the old man was past it and that it was a miracle the firm hadn't closed down years ago. Then her ladyship started sobbing and screaming at the two of them and then his lordship called me to fetch him another bottle from the cellar and had me open it right then and there and pour him another glassful. Then he started accusing Master Simon of leaving the family open to threats of violence from 'one of the worst types ever to come up from the mud'. Said the man even kept calling in to the office demanding more and more money and that he'd run out of legal ways to pay the man off and refused to do it any longer. Then he said that it was a good job you had come along when you did, as well. What do you make of that Liz? That was a funny thing to say, don't you think? Oh I tell you, it was a right to-do."

"Poor Mr Bickerstaff," said Elizabeth.

"Poor? I don't know about that."

"Well if he's had to start doing something not entirely right then I do feel sorry for him, Mary. Imagine if he has been forced into doing something illegal, then his whole business could collapse."

"I see what you mean," said Mary. "I could lose my job here. I told you it was a right to-do. Why do you think he mentioned you?"

"I've no idea, probably because otherwise he couldn't afford to pay an office cleaner or for more help in the household."

"I wonder what's brought it all to a head now?"

"Did he mention the name of the crook?".

"I'm sure I heard him say the name Jack Quinn."

"Of course," said Elizabeth. "That would make sense. He's an awful man. I've seen him in the office a few times and the way he talks to Mr Bickerstaff is really nasty and unpleasant but I didn't realise he was a crook. The clerk made an odd comment about him but I can't remember what, only that it seemed odd. Actually the last time Mr Quinn was in I did hear him mention debts and something about markers. What are markers?"

"I think it's gambling debts. Perhaps this Jack Quinn's been in again then. Maybe he was in yesterday, when you weren't there."

"Do you think I should go in and ask if I can be of any help?"

"No, keep out of it girl. Her ladyship was put out that you disappeared for the day. Leave it to me. I'll take in this hot toddy and see how things are going in there. You help yourself to some tea and I'll report back."

Mary was only gone a minute. "My God he's in a bad way," she said walking back into the kitchen. "He's crying now, Liz. All he keeps saying is 'what have I done?'. You go on up to your room and I'll call you down later and you can tell me all about your day. Did you see your friend?"

"No but I saw my best ever friend, Sally, who I thought had died in the flood. She's staying with Daniel's friend, John, the one I went to find. They don't know where Daniel is but perhaps John will have some ideas on where to look. He was out at work today but I'll see him tomorrow."

Just then Mr Bickerstaff stumbled into the kitchen and slumped in a chair as soon as he saw Elizabeth. "I'm so sorry, Miss Shaw, so sorry," he cried.

"Sorry for what, Mr Bickerstaff?"

"I'm so sorry, so sorry, and you but an orphan." That was all he could manage. The next moment he was fast asleep with his head on the kitchen table.

***

Part Six

L ightness of spirit had lifted the gloom at Bungay Street. John normally slept in late on Sunday morning but the news the previous evening that Daniel was still alive, somewhere, had him up and about early after a restless night exploring ideas on how to find his missing friend. He had imagined all sorts of situations, trying to piece together what Daniel might have done in the wake of the flood: John knew that Elizabeth had seen Daniel being washed away, that his friend had then been seen at Damflask, where he was told that his wife had been killed, and had then been seen heading off west over the hills. Was he heading for Glossop or Manchester, where he might look for work in one of the mills? Or was he so heartbroken that he would go further afield, Liverpool perhaps, with plans to put everything behind him and leave the country? John opted for the latter. He knew Daniel, he knew that his friend would be so sick at heart at losing Elizabeth that he would choose to just go, once and for all.

"I think I might ask Matthew Blagdon for his help," John said to Sally, who was cleaning the room to make it look nice for Jimmy's day at home.

"Help doing what?"

"Well I thought maybe Daniel might have decided to go to Liverpool to catch a boat somewhere and I can't think of any other way of reaching him than perhaps through the newspaper."

"Do you think he'd have money to buy a ticket somewhere?" asked Sally. "After all, everything was lost in the flood and he wasn't a rich man anyway, it's not as if he'd have money hidden away anywhere."

"Mmh, you're probably right," said John. He sat there mulling it all over again. Sally meanwhile was making up the bed on the floor for Jimmy.

"I do miss having Jimmy around, don't you?" she said, stopping to stare at the pile of torn blankets she had tried to make cosy in the corner. "I know it's important that he goes to school and he was starting to run a bit wild but seeing his bed all laid out again makes me wish he was still here with us. It

289

was like having our own little family when he was here."

"He could get work on the docks or even try to work his passage somewhere," said John.

"Jimmy?"

"No, Daniel. I think I'll get in touch with Blagdon tomorrow, see if he can draft out a notice or something to put in the Liverpool and Manchester papers. There's a chance Daniel might see it."

"He might," said Sally. "More importantly Elizabeth will feel that something is being done to find him. I think that's a really good idea, John, a good start. I knew you'd come up with an idea."

"It's not much of an idea really and it's only based on what I think Daniel might have done."

"You know him as well as anyone," said Sally.

"It's hard to know what anyone would do after losing everything," said John, turning to face Sally and sounding almost wistful. "I've not had to face that. I lived in this room before the flood and I live here still, only you're here now too."

"And you've got Melanie just down the road," said Sally, suddenly busy busy again. "I'd better be off. I've to be at the school at eight-o'-clock to collect Jimmy and I wouldn't like to get on the wrong side of the matron or whoever she is. I'm so looking forward to him coming home I'd hate to be late and the old bag tell me I was too late."

"'Old bag' eh?" said John. "Perhaps you've been in The Ponds too long, Miss Bisby."

"Know what, John?" she said, stopping to look at him in the middle of putting her coat on. "I know it sounds really silly but I love the way you say 'Miss Bisby'. It makes me feel right important, in a nice, simple sort of way."

"Well you are important."

"I'm a snooty Miss, that's all," said Sally.

"Not as snooty as you used to be," said John. "I think Bungay Street has rubbed off a few of the old sharp corners."

"No," she said, "you've done that. Bye, see you later."

JUST the two of them should be enough, one each for the girl and the boy. If the boy gave any trouble, then the two of them would just grab hold of him and the girl was bound to follow. The odd threat would make her follow silently without kicking up much of a fuss in the relatively quiet hours of Sunday morning. Anyone going in to the church would think it was just some

290

kid getting a well-deserved slap around the ear from his father, they wouldn't interfere, not with a family row in this edge of the town. Porter was lined up to help. Quinn had lost an ace up his sleeve with Peggy clearing off, what with both the boy and the girl knowing her, and Porter wasn't the sharpest tool in the box but Quinn wasn't left with too many options right now, not with his other runners out collecting much-needed readies; he'd have to build up his team again and make some head office promotions and the cash haul from this little outing would see to that. He'd buy back his reputation as the gang boss everyone wanted to work for, no mistake.

"There'll be a good bonus for you today, young Porter," said Quinn. He was standing at the window looking out, anxious to get going, waiting to see the Sally one appear on her way to the school to fetch Jimmy. "Pull this one off and I'll be looking on you as my number one runner. I've kept you a bit protected so far, breaking you in gradually like, but I reckon you're ready for a bit more hands-on responsibility."

"D'you reckon boss?" said Porter, flattered by the promise of moving up in the gang. It made getting up early on his normal lie-in day worthwhile.

"Have you got the rope ready like I asked?"

"Yes, boss."

"Well leave it handy on the table so we can grab it as soon as we get back."

"Yes, boss."

"They should be here soon."

"I thought you said eight-o'-clock, boss? It's only quarter to."

"You're not here to question my methods, Porter," said Quinn suddenly swinging around to face the young man. His instinct was to lash out with his belt but he decided against it: he couldn't afford to lose Porter as well right now. He turned back to the window. "I know it's only quarter to but it's important to be ready, remember that if you're going to move up in the world. What if they're a bit early? Then what would you do? You'd be rushing and that's not good. I need someone I can rely on to remain calm."

"Right, boss. I can stay calm."

"Right."

ELIZABETH was laughing to herself as she strolled into town to meet Sally. She was picturing the normally sedate Mr Bickerstaff sprawled across the kitchen table fast asleep and snoring his head off and the smell of stale alcohol pulsing out of his gaping mouth and souring across the room. She still didn't understand why he had kept apologising to her and was none the wiser this

291

morning: he was still in bed when she left the house, sleeping it off. She was looking forward to seeing John Hukin again after all this time but was a bit sorry she wouldn't be around in the Broomhall household to see Mr Bickerstaff emerge from his room, no doubt highly embarrassed by the whole episode the previous night. Even better would be the look on her ladyship's face, trying to maintain her loftiness in front of the staff. Jim Nightingale was going to love the story when he got back from visiting Bamford. Elizabeth had given him a letter for Gabriel and Kitty and was looking forward to hearing all the news when he got back to Sheffield. So much seemed to have happened since her few days in Bamford that she'd hardly had time to think about her father's old driver and his sister but she remembered her few days with them fondly, the knowledge that Daniel was alive somehow eclipsing the fact that she had spent much of her time at their cottage either in tears or in bed. Jim Nightingale had really come to her rescue, managing to be sympathetic but lifting her spirits at the same time. Thinking of Jim reminded Elizabeth that she was about to meet another Jim, John's young nephew Jimmy. She had arranged to meet Sally outside the Blue Coat School to take him home for the day and she decided to call in to a corner shop to buy him some sweets by way of saying hello. From what Sally had said about the boy, some gob-stoppers would go down well.

"IT'S not quite the Adelphi but at least the bed was comfortable enough," said Oonagh Shaw, tucking into a big breakfast of sausages and eggs and black pudding. "I don't know about you, David, but I'm ravenous. This is hitting just the right spot," she said, piling up another forkful and shoving it in her mouth.

"Anyone would think you hadn't eaten in days," said David.

"That's just how I feel, don't ask me why. Just wait until I get started on the toast and marmalade," said Oonagh.

"Perhaps the clean fresh air of Sheffield has sharpened your appetite."

"Somehow I don't think that's what it is. Don't you want that sausage?"

"You take it, you greedy witch," said David. "Would you like this pudding as well?"

"No, I don't mind leaving you something. Actually you should eat more, have the sausage back, it could be quite a long day. Do you know the area where Daniel's friend lives?"

"The Ponds? Only by name and not a very good one at that," said David. "Will you please take that sausage back, I don't want you accusing me of half-starving you."

"Thank you. Mmm."

"Do you want to come with us? I can't really see the point but if you'd rather not stay in on your own…"

"I'm looking forward to staying in on my own," said Oonagh. "Much as I love you, my dear husband, I haven't had a break from you since we were in Ireland. I intend to curl up on the sofa and read."

"Probably just as well," said David. "After all that food you'll have a fair bit of extra weight to carry around."

"Charming as ever."

"I doubt if it'll take all day anyway. We should be back early afternoon, at least I will be, after all I'm only going with Daniel to keep him company and take a look at Sheffield again. He'll probably stay with his friend, they've a lot of catching up to do."

"Where are you meeting up, in Daniel's room?"

"No, I said I'd see him in the lobby."

"At what time?"

"Well, just about now, to be honest."

"You'd better go then and leave me to enjoy my toast without every mouthful being chewed over."

"Very funny, Mrs Shaw. I'll deal with you later."

DANIEL had already been out for a walk. He hadn't bothered with breakfast, being back in Sheffield was too much of a shock to the system and he'd been wandering around the streets of the town centre half-dazed, half-amazed. The last time he had been here the streets were stinking and wretched, piled high with thick mud and rotting rubbish and pathetic carcasses deposited by the Dale Dyke dam burst, and people were clambering about desperately trying to rescue family and belongings from the fetid sludge. Now the place was cleaned up and much of the rubble removed. Sheffield was pulling itself together again and in a strange way he was glad to be home. In a strange way also he was looking forward to going up the valley again with David and Oonagh later in the week: after all that had happened - his time with the gypsies and his brief time in Liverpool - he felt he could even return to the site of Willow Tree Cottage and grieve properly for Elizabeth, the way she deserved, and not via anger and raging despair. Had he not met David and Oonagh he would have been on a ship heading for America right now but he was glad he wasn't. For all the tragedy of the flood, this was where he belonged.

"There you are, Daniel. Ready for the off?"

Daniel turned to see David Shaw approaching him across the hotel lobby. Suddenly, the way the light fell across David's face, Daniel could see an echo of Elizabeth in her elder brother's features and was filled with a great warmth for the man. "What a pair we are," he said quickly, realising he'd been somewhat scrutinising his brother-in-law, "you with your one good arm and me with my one good eye."

"We're a team alright," said David. "Between my one arm and your one eye, we certainly saw off that thug in Liverpool, if you'll forgive the use of the word 'saw'."

"Well I did 'saw', this one good eye of mine is all-seeing, I can tell you."

"Especially when there's a chance of a good brawl. Isn't that how you lost that eye in the first place?"

"Aye," said Daniel and both men smiled at the pun and the rapport already established between them.

"I can see Elizabeth would have had her work cut out with you," said David. "I'm sorry; that wasn't very sensitive of me."

"Don't worry about it. You can't keep watching what you say because of what's happened to people, otherwise you'd end up talking in silence."

"I see," said David, "one-armed, partially blind and now potentially mute."

"I think we'd better go, don't you. I'm not convinced this conversation is getting very far," said David. "Come on, I'll show you the delights of The Ponds and I'll hopefully introduce you to my best mate, John Hukin, always assuming he survived the flood."

"Is that likely? I'm not sure exactly where the water flooded."

"Knowing John he slept through the whole thing in a drunken stupor. Is Oonagh joining us?"

"No, she says she needs some time off from my company and wants to curl up with a book."

"It's probably just as well, The Ponds is no place for a gentlewoman."

"Let me tell you," said David, "Oonagh is not always that gentle."

They laughed together and left the hotel like a couple of old friends.

"It's going to be a good day today," said Daniel. "I don't know what's in the air but it smells good."

"Don't tell me your nose is playing up now," said David. "I don't think anyone has ever accused Sheffield air of smelling good."

THERE was a constant procession of boys walking single-file along the Blue Coat's highly-polished corridors and across the lobby to be escorted to church for the morning service and a lucky few being collected by their kin to go home for the day. Sally had been so anxious not to upset the dragon of a matron that she had arrived half-an-hour early to collect Jimmy. What greeted her had come as a complete surprise. She had been whisked in to see the headmaster and then treated to a whole catalogue of praise for the boy.

"He hasn't been here long but he's already turning into one of our brightest and keenest pupils," said Mr Bagshaw.

"What, Jimmy?" Sally couldn't hide her amazement.

"Yes indeed," said the head. "He didn't get off to a very good start and I thought we might have a real troublemaker on our hands but young Urmston has acquitted himself well in the classroom and shows a strong inclination for learning. I wanted to assure you that he is doing very well, that's why I called you into my office. We'll certainly be glad to keep him here and perhaps, at some point in the future, try to arrange a scholarship for him to continue his studies at a higher level, that's if you agree, of course."

"Well it would be up to his uncle but I'm sure that would be wonderful for Jimmy. Thank you, Sir."

"I also thought that you might like to take some time while you're here to have a look at some of the work he's been doing. He certainly shows a natural aptitude for geography. He has a great interest in the world and the Empire in particular."

"I'd love to see his work, if it's not taking up too much of your time," said Sally. "Your comments have really given me something to be pleased about today, we'll be able to ask Jimmy all about school without worrying about him complaining like he did before he started here. You've no idea what a struggle it was to get him to come, you'd have thought we were bundling him off to prison or the workhouse or somewhere."

"That's only natural, really," said Mr Bagshaw. "Unfortunately there are still too many people about who are living in the past. Their attitude to schooling is that it's a complete waste of time. Fortunately Jimmy's not like his uncle in that respect and has quickly realised what riches of the spirit are there for the taking just by opening a book. He is a very bright lad."

Sally wondered what the man could mean about Jimmy not being like his uncle, after all, as far as she knew John had never even been to the school. She decided to let it pass as the headmaster led her into one of the classrooms and pointed out all the examples of Jimmy's handiwork that had been judged good enough to be pinned up on the wall. There were drawings, maps and short sentences written in a neat but boyish hand. Jimmy was sitting quietly on one of the benches, glowing with innocent pride and trying to be well behaved and not leap up at the excitement of seeing Sally.

"I've been hearing some very good things about you, young man," she said to him. "Your Uncle John is going to be very pleased with you."

"Jimmy's uncle did actually call into the school yesterday," said the headmaster quietly to Sally. "I must say he seemed like a rather unpleasant character. He said he'd be back this morning but, I have to be honest, I'm not sorry he hasn't appeared."

"John wasn't here yesterday, I'm sure of it," said Sally, totally perplexed, "and I certainly don't think you'd describe him as unpleasant. He said nothing about coming with me this morning, I've just left him at home getting the place ready for Jimmy's visit."

"Well then I don't know who this character was," said Mr Bagshaw. "Perhaps you'd be advised to keep your eyes open when you leave. Anyway, I'm glad we've had a chance to talk. Jimmy, I'll see you tomorrow, bright and early."

Jimmy was at last free of the classroom discipline and jumped up to hug Sally. "I might like it better than I thought I would but let's get out of here quick," he said. "I want to go home and see Uncle John."

THE church clock was only just ringing out the hour but Quinn's patience was already spent. He'd seen a young woman walk up Campo Lane on the other side of the street a few minutes ago and thought it might be the Sally one but it wasn't, although she did look vaguely familiar. In fact she was waiting outside the school herself; perhaps she had a kid to fetch as well. A snake of boys had left the building and gone to the church.

"Poor bleeders," said Quinn. "Still, time for us to get going," he said to Porter. "We don't want to miss the buggers after waiting all this time."

Quinn picked up his knife and tucked it down his boot, just in case things got a big rougher than expected. Then he and Porter headed for the Blue Coat, varying their pace so as not to get there too soon but ready to hurry if Jimmy and the girl suddenly came out of the building. They sauntered along like two friends chatting during a casual stroll but kept their eyes peeled and their minds alert. When they were just yards from the school, Sally and Jimmy emerged through the door, turned left in the direction of the church and, as their faces lit up at seeing someone they knew waiting, Quinn and Porter pounced. Quinn grabbed Sally by the arm, digging his fingers in and almost

296

dragging her off her feet with the suddenness of the pain and force: Porter back-handed Jimmy to the ground then grabbed hold of his arms, twisting them behind his back and in one quick movement he lifted the groggy boy up and started to frogmarch him back to head office. What they hadn't reckoned on was Elizabeth. When she saw Quinn approaching she knew there'd be trouble. She had no idea why Sally was mixed up with the man but as soon as he grabbed her friend she launched herself at him, scratching and clawing, kicking and thumping and all the while screeching and screaming for help. Quinn knocked Elizabeth to the ground with an elbow to the face, panting heavily but still clutching Sally with a vice-like grip: "One more word from you, bitch, one more fucking scream, scratch, kick or thump and your friend's dead."

The few passers-by looked on in disgust at such an uncouth display, drunks from the night before brawling and scrapping right outside the parish church and just before morning service: the Sunday-best women tutted at the unladylike behaviour of the two young girls while the be-suited men admired Quinn for his no-nonsense approach to his disorderly family. They didn't see Quinn pull out the knife.

THE fire was built up, the kettle was simmering and there was a plate of scones and jam on the table. There was also a small package on the table, wrapped in tissue paper and tied with string with a label attached: "To Jimmy, welcome home." John was sitting in the armchair with a contented smile on his face. The last twenty four hours hadn't been too bad, considering: he'd discovered that Daniel was still alive, he knew that Elizabeth was coming and he was looking forward to seeing that young scalliwag Jimmy again. He had also liked the banter he'd had with Sally before she'd rushed off to the school, liked the way she'd talked about 'their own little family' and the way there seemed to be quite a nice warmth between them. He looked up at the clock on the wall, realised the big hand had only moved a short distance since he had last looked, and burst into a silly grin. They'd be back soon enough without him counting out the minutes, he thought. He started to plan a nice day for them all: perhaps they could go for a walk up to the Botanical Gardens, take some sandwiches with them, maybe, and some lemonade and cakes; or they could go to Youdan's variety hall in town, they'd all enjoy having a laugh and a sing-song there, though he wasn't sure whether or not they'd let Jimmy in because of his age. John looked up at the clock again and then stood up and paced around the room. "Where are they?" he said out loud as he looked out

297

of the window. There was no sign of them. He sat down again, tapping his foot up and down impatiently on the floor.

QUINN was in a right good mood for the first time in days. He was sprawled in his usual fashion behind his desk in head office, feet up, drink poured. He was nursing his shiny ten-inch blade and waving it round in the air. As soon as he and Porter had got back to the office with their three captives, they had been joined by a couple of Quinn's older runners, Whitey and Bassett, two big brawny blokes, men on whom he called regularly when he needed a bit of extra muscle. They were a bit like a double act: they always worked together and took it in turns to do the dirty work, not because they hated it, on the contrary, because they enjoyed inflicting pain so much that they had to share out the pleasure equally. In the corner of the room tethered up in a couple of chairs were Elizabeth and Sally, bound with thick ropes and with grubby scarves tied round their mouths to keep them quiet. Jimmy stood freely in front of the boss. Everyone had been waiting several minutes for Quinn to talk.

"So, Jimmy," he said at last, "what's what?"

"What's what, Mr Quinn?" asked Jimmy.

Quinn lurched over the desktop at the boy and slapped him hard across the face. "Don't you 'what's what' me, you little tyke." Jimmy collapsed on to the floor under the weight of the blow. The two girls' eyes were bulging with fear and helplessness as Quinn followed up the slap with a good kick into Jimmy's stomach. Whitey and Bassett loved every groan of pain and fidgeted to join in; Porter tittered nervously, feeling a bit out of his depth. Quinn pressed his foot down on Jimmy's head: "Where's my fucking money?" he bellowed just inches away from the lad's ear.

"I couldn't get it, Mr Quinn, honest, I did try but the office was all locked up and I couldn't get the door to open no matter how much I tried, honest Mr Quinn."

"'Honest Mr Quinn'," the boss repeated, looking at his runners and laughing at the joke, "I don't think so." He turned back to the boy on the floor. "Know what, Jimmy my old son, I don't believe you," said Quinn and he ground the bottom of his boot into Jimmy's face.

"Let us have a go, boss," said Bassett, "go on, we can do that for you, you take it easy and just watch."

"You'll get your go, alright, don't worry about that," said Quinn. Then he turned his attention to Elizabeth and Sally. "It's like this, you see, young

Jimmy here owes me and I mean to make him pay up. You might think this here innocent looking waif is a right little goody goody but let me tell you he's part of my team, the Quinn team, and no-one in the Quinn team messes with Quinn. He agreed to rob that bloody school of his for me and I intend to get what's due. What you also don't know is that bloody Hukin also has money belonging to me and I want it back. Oh yes, I can see your eyes, you don't believe a word of it but, let me tell you, Hukin's not shy when it comes to taking other people's money." Quinn started laughing. "I'd say 'ask him next time you see him' but then there's every chance you won't be seeing him, ever again." Quinn left Jimmy cowering on the floor and went back behind his desk to take a slug of his drink. "I'm working up quite a thirst," he said and shoved the bottle towards Whitey. "Here, pour some out for yourselves and join me."

Whitey fetched three glasses out of the cupboard, poured out the rough spirit and handed drinks to Bassett and Porter. "Your health, boss," he said, raising his glass. Whitey and Bassett knocked back the spirit in one go, Porter tried to follow suit but ended up spluttering at the too-much burn in his throat. "What do you want us to do, boss?" asked Bassett.

"Porter, I want you to go to Bungay Street and tell John Hukin we've got his people here and that if he doesn't produce that money he stole from Pickens there won't be none of his people left no more. Do you know which house it is?"

"Yes, boss," said Porter, "I kept watch there once with Briggs."

"Good," said Quinn. "Tell Mister Hukin that I'll meet him in the churchyard across the road in one hour, let's make it ten-o-clock, allow you time to get there and back. He will hand me the money, I'll hand over these lot."

"Right you are, boss," said Porter. He stepped over Jimmy and for bravado's sake aimed a kick at the boy's back.

"Like your style," said Bassett.

"Be as quick as you can," said Quinn. "As soon as you get back we'll sort out who's going to be where. I'd like to make Mr Hukin feel welcome in our part of town and I know just who to choose for the welcoming committee." He sneered in the direction of his two heavies.

"You can count on us," said Whitey. "It's about time we had some relaxation on our day of rest."

"You'll have fun, alright," said Quinn. "Hukin needs teaching a lesson or two. Now tie this lad up and let's relax a bit before we go to work. Here's to profit, lads."

Quinn sat back in his chair smirking while Whitey and Bassett had the most fun they could out of trussing Jimmy up like a turkey.

HE was trying not to get too agitated but John couldn't keep his eyes off the clock for worrying about why Sally and Jimmy were so late. It was already gone nine and there was still no sign of them. They must have decided to stop off somewhere for breakfast, he thought, then decided against that idea; Sally knew that there were some treats waiting for the lad when he got home. He was about to grab his hat and coat and go off to look for them when he heard the sound of footsteps climbing the stairs and he rushed to open the door full of eagerness. It wasn't Sally and Jimmy as he'd expected. There in front of him was his old friend, Daniel.

"My God," was all he could say, then the two men hugged each other until they were both nearly out of breath and there were tears in their eyes. Real sobs came from both of them; all their history of a shared childhood, their closeness over the years, the tragedy of the flood - memories welled up to the surface in the emotion of their reunion and the two grown men blubbered like babies. "My God you're alive." "My God just look at you with your eye patch." "Even my one eye can see you still live in this hell-hole." "I thought you'd be half way round the world by now."

The two of them broke apart and stared at each other through glowing faces, grinning like Cheshire cats.

"I'd like you to meet someone," said Daniel wiping his tears and turning his attention to David. "This is David Shaw, Elizabeth's brother, we met in Liverpool."

"Elizabeth's brother? Pleased to meet you, David, does she know you're back?" said John shaking hands eagerly with the tall stranger.

"Elizabeth's dead, John. She was drowned when the dam burst, I saw it happen." Daniel turned away: he had been determined to maintain the happy mood of being here with John again but the first mention of Elizabeth was enough to break down his reserve. No matter how good it was to rediscover his old friend, seeing John again only made Daniel remember his wedding day vividly when John was his best man.

"Why don't you sit down, you big brute of a man," said John kindly. "I've something to tell you. David, you sit down too." The two visitors sat opposite each other on either side of the fire and John offered them a smoke. "I'm sure there's a right good fancy way of making a speech on this sort of occasion but I'm no fancy man and I'm no good at speeches and that sort of thing, either right good or otherwise, so I'll just have to tell you both straight: Elizabeth isn't dead, she's alive and she's in Sheffield and she's due here in this very hell-hole any minute now." He finished with a sudden burst of laughter and watched with the idiotic look of a fairy godmother on his face as the news sank in. David's expression changed slowly from sadness to a beam of contentment, as if all along he had expected his spirited little sister to have come through it all. Daniel just stared hard at John, his mouth hanging open in disbelief and all the muscles round his eyes twitching and flexing and then suddenly his look of total despair had gone and he too took on the ridiculous helpless grin of the simple but honest fool. He stood up and all the hugging started all over again.

"Elizabeth's alive," he informed John. "Elizabeth's alive," he repeated emphatically to David. Then he threw back his head and shouted to the ceiling: "Elizabeth's alive."

"As you can see this man is devoted to your sister," said John.

"I'm getting the message," said David, "loud and clear, and to think if we hadn't met in Liverpool he might have been on his way to America by now and never have known she had survived. Do you know what happened?"

"I've not seen her yet myself. She suddenly turned up here yesterday and then went out with Sally. Do you know Sally, Sally Bisby, her family ran the Cleakum pub near your father's house? The pub was all but demolished by the flood and all her folks were killed. She's been staying here since that God-awful night."

"I remember the pub and that Elizabeth had a friend from there, the name 'Sally' vaguely rings a bell, but I'm afraid I was the big brother then and not, I'm afraid, too interested in what a couple of little girls might get up to. So it was Sally."

"Sally is alive too?" asked Daniel suddenly aware of conversation going on around him. "My God, I thought there'd be no-one left up there."

"Aye, well, there's not many left. I'm afraid Mr and Mrs Shaw - your parents, David – have all gone and the Tricketts, remember them, Daniel? Where you had the wedding?"

"As if I'm ever likely to forget my own wedding," said Daniel, "though God knows these last few weeks I've tried to put all thoughts of it right to the back of my head. It wasn't something I could remember without terrible pain."

"From what Sally tells me Elizabeth was saved by Gabriel, her father's driver. They saw you across the river just as the flood arrived and saw you swept away in the water and Elizabeth believed you to be dead right up to a few days ago when she went back up to Damflask. She was sitting by the ruins of your old cottage when one of the villagers told her you'd been back there the following day. That's how she came to be here looking for me, in case I had any news. It seems the villagers had told you that Elizabeth was dead so there were the two of you each thinking the other had gone."

"And now we each of us know we're both still around," said Daniel "What a wonderful day. I have to say I'm right glad to see you, John, but even more glad at your news. And you say Elizabeth's due here any minute?"

"She was to meet Sally in town and then come back here. That's why I was so quick to answer the door when you arrived, I thought it was them back. They were collecting my little nephew from a school in town to bring him home for the day but that was at eight-o-clock and to be honest I don't understand why they're not back yet."

"Shall we walk in to meet them on the way?" asked David.

"I thought of that but then I thought they might have stopped off somewhere for breakfast, as a treat for the boy, like," said John.

"What shall we do? I'm in your hands."

"Well it's a day for celebration so, although it's early, I suggest we have a drink," said Daniel. "No doubt they'll all arrive home as soon as the beer's in the glass and they'll think we've been boozing all morning with no heed to them," he said. "Sometimes that's the best way to make something happen, isn't it, by starting on something else."

"Agreed," said John. "And if they haven't got back by the time we empty our glasses, we'll off out to look for them. I'll nip out and buy a few bottles."

"I'll come with you, take more of a look round the old neighbourhood. You might as well wait here, David, we'll not be long."

John and Daniel set off to find something for their celebratory toast, both animated and talking and interrupting each other as they caught up on what had happened over recent weeks, in which their lives, like those of many of the people of Sheffield, had been veered off in totally unexpected directions.

"David seems like a nice bloke," said John. "How did you two meet up?"

"In a street incident worthy of the great John Hukin," said Daniel.

"He wasn't brawling? He doesn't strike me as the type."

"He was attacked in the street with his wife and I just happened along at the right moment."

"So of course you had to help out."

"Of course. It's not often you see a one-armed man with his wife getting threatened in the street with a knife."

"Good job you turned up, then."

"It was. David's no coward but, let's face it, even a man with two good arms would find it tricky fighting off an armed thug with just an umbrella while at the same time trying to keep his wife out of harm's way."

"An umbrella?"

"An umbrella," stressed Daniel. "But he did wield it like a true swordsman."

"I like the sound of your brother-in-law."

"He was a true find, in more ways than one."

The brother-in-law had meanwhile settled down in the chair back in John's room, trying not to feel too mentally uncomfortable as he relaxed in an environment far removed from his usual standard. David was impressed by the simple attempts to give the place a real homely feel and he picked out what he decided were obviously Sally's touches. He noticed the table set and the small neat package addressed to a Jimmy – that must be John's nephew, he thought. The homely feeling in the place was tangible and David's mind wandered back through the years to his own childhood home, where he had always felt protected and loved but from where ultimately he had decided to set off from the easy comfort to find his own way in the world. Feelings of guilt threatened to take over again as he thought about his parents: he had failed to repay their love with even a short letter in all the years since the war in India and in the end his return home was too late. At least he would soon be seeing Elizabeth: how was his little sister? what sort of a young woman had she become? How surprised she was going to be to find him here in The Ponds. He stretched out in front of the fire and began to relax as the humble room enfolded him but the cosy atmosphere was broken suddenly by a jarring rap on the door.

"Hello," said David, opening the door to a young man who was clearly out of breath. "Take your time," said David kindly. "Are you a friend of John's? He's not here right now but he'll be back soon. Would you like to come in?"

"I'm no friend of Hukin's and no, I don't want to come in. I've got a message for him, that's all. You tell him this: Jack Quinn said he'd better get himself down to the back of the churchyard in Campo Lane with the money if he wants to see the nipper and the lass again. Ten-o'-clock."

David grabbed the youth by the collar. "Just a minute," he said, "who's Jack Quinn?"

"Mr Quinn's the boss and he wants the money back that John Hukin stole from him," said Porter. "Hukin has to bring the money with him to the churchyard and Mr Quinn'll let the boy and the woman go. And Hukin'd best be on his own, Mr Quinn said."

"What boy? What woman?"

"Hukin'll know," said Porter, kicking his captor sharply in the shin. He managed to wriggle free and made a dash for it down the stairs and out into the street. He ran back to Campo Lane as fast as he could, quite pleased with himself that he'd managed to deliver the boss's message so easily.

David was left nursing his leg and his pride. "Do you know what I've just done?" he said to Daniel and John as they chattered in with the beers. "Me, a grown man and veteran of the Indian mutiny, I've just let some snotty youth get the better of me. And worse than that, it was some snotty youth with what I assume was supposed to be a threatening message for you, John."

"What sort of a threat?" said John, all trace of smiles now evaporated.

"I didn't take it too seriously, the messenger wasn't much more than a boy," said David.

"Tell me exactly what he said."

"That you had stolen money from someone called Quinn and that he wants it back this morning and in return he'll let the boy and girl go, whoever they are." As soon as he'd said it, David realised this was no silly threat. The youth was obviously talking about Sally and Jimmy. "I'm sorry," said David, "I'm even more of an idiot than I thought."

"What's going on, John?" asked Daniel. "I didn't realise you'd become mixed up with Quinn."

"I haven't, not really," said John. "I took some of his crooked money off one of his runners in a street fight, months ago, and I forgot all about it until a couple of weeks ago. Then I found out he'd managed to draw little Jimmy into his web and he sent one of his whores down here snooping around Sally. He must have them. He must have grabbed them this morning outside the school, that's why they're not back."

"Chances are Elizabeth's with them too then," said Daniel.

"The message only mentioned one young woman," said David.

"Knowing Elizabeth she'll have got involved somehow, she wouldn't have just stood back and watched if her friend was in trouble."

"Where's the money now?" asked David.

"Not here, that's for sure," said John. "One of Quinn's men has already tried breaking into the place to take a look. And now I've put Sally in danger, just over a few bloody pounds. I'll get that bastard. If he touches her…" John made to rush out of the room.

"Hang on, let's figure out what to do," said David blocking his way. "We don't want anyone getting hurt here. It doesn't sound as if this Quinn character is likely to keep his word about letting them go so easily."

"David's right," said Daniel. "We need to work out the best way to handle it."

"The meeting place is the churchyard, what's it like there for a start?" asked

David.

"It's not much, just gravestones and a few trees."

"Is it quite open then?"

"Yes, open enough, there's not many places to hide," said Daniel.

"Where's this Quinn likely to be holding them?" asked David.

John's face shed a little of its gloom. "Quinn's office is right opposite the churchyard," he said, almost grinning, "and he doesn't know that I know that. I bet that's where they're being kept."

"That's it then," said David, immediately working out the tactics. "You meet Quinn as arranged while Daniel and I go to his office and rescue them all. The message said ten-o-clock. If we go now, Daniel and I will have time to work a flanker while you, John, take up position ready in the churchyard."

"Quinn's not likely to be alone though," said Daniel. "Your plan means John will be left on his own to deal with them."

"I can look after myself," said John. "I've had enough set-tos with Quinn's men to know what to expect. And don't forget, Quinn wants this money back and I'm the one who knows where it is."

"Right then, we'll save the beers til later."

THE ropes were getting tighter and tighter around their wrists and ankles as Elizabeth and Sally strained helplessly watching Whitey and Bassett having fun with Jimmy. He had been untrussed and then stood up and twisted around and spun back again over and over and over until he fell to the floor but each time he fell the two thugs would kick the boy up again with their huge booted feet. The lad was already battered and bruised from the game. His head was dizzy, his body was reeling, he couldn't stand up even when kicked up. There was blood pouring from his left eye. Quinn wasn't bothered or particularly interested, instead he kept watch at the window, looking out for anyone who might have volunteered to help Hukin. The girls were left alone other than for the odd reminder visits from Whitey or Bassett: Whitey liked to leer up to them, to rub their thighs and breasts with his hands as he gasped rhythmically inches from their faces, all the time laughing; Bassett liked to tweak on the ropes, putting in a stick and twisting it like a tourniquet while he licked inside their ears. Jimmy saw what was happening and cried with his lack of strength. Porter sat nervously in the corner: he wished he was some place else but here; from what he'd heard whispered, Quinn could turn on anyone at any moment and instead of that being some other lad on the floor it could just as easily be Porter himself.

"There he is now."

Quinn pulled back to the side of the window as he saw John enter the churchyard. He looked alone and Quinn couldn't see anyone else hanging around but that didn't mean anything; Hukin was no fool, he wouldn't show all his cards at once.

"The fun's over, you two," he said to the two thugs. "Porter, you stay here and watch these two. Whitey, Bassett, you two come with me. I want one of you on either side of me so Hukin can see you but keep a few yards away, I don't want him too scared until I've got the money. Jimmy, you get over here now."

"Are you going to hand over the kid and the women, boss?" asked Porter.

"You just concentrate on doing what you're told," said Quinn. "I'll do what I decide to do. You just stay here until you hear from me." Then he yelled at Jimmy. "I said get over here now, you little bleeder."

Jimmy struggled to his knees but could only stay like that through holding himself up by his hands on the floor. Quinn yanked him to his feet and the boy yelped with pain as he was dragged by the collar out of the office and down the stairs. Whitey and Bassett left the building first, crossed the road ahead of Quinn and took up position inside the churchyard with their backs to the perimeter wall.

DANIEL and David had left John on Church Street so he could walk across the grounds of St Peter's on his own for his appointment with Quinn and had then hurried down a side street further along to take up position just off Campo Lane round the corner next to the Paradise. It was a good vantage point: they could see along to the door of Quinn's office and into the churchyard where John was already in place, braced for whatever might happen.

"There's Quinn now," whispered Daniel, ducking back out of sight. "The one dragging the boy, see him?"

David casually looked in Quinn's direction. "Got him," he said behind his hand. "Two heavy-looking blokes have gone into the churchyard ahead of him, did you recognise them?"

"No," said Daniel, "but I'm sure Quinn wouldn't be doing this on his own. We'd best be as quick as we can getting the girls out. Two big men like that - the odds aren't that good even for a brawler like John."

"Let's just hang on a minute until they get into the churchyard," said David. "There's no point in risking Quinn seeing you now just in case he recognises you. He must have seen you around enough times with John."

"Right. What's happening now?"

"The two men have split up and gone one on either side of the gate. Quinn's moved towards John, he's still got the boy. They've started talking. I think we should go now," said David. "I'll set off first then you follow a few feet behind."

ELIZABETH and Sally had started trying to bump their chairs around in an attempt to loosen the ropes as soon as Quinn and his men had left. Porter didn't know what to do: he'd grown up in the warrens of Hawley Croft round the back of the Paradise pub and had heard the other kids talk about Jack Quinn as if he was some sort of local hero, so when Porter started working for the boss he'd felt a swagger of naïve pride. He'd heard the stories, alright, Quinn's ruthlessness was legendary, but it was the idea of working for the big bad man that had appealed to Porter, while the cruel reality was too scarey, too raw. He could hear the two women straining and mmm-ing behind the tightness of their gags and he was frightened. "Stop that, please," he said weakly. "Mr Quinn will be back soon. I don't want to see no-one else getting hurt." The women carried on struggling to get free.

DAVID strolled as anonymously as he could along Campo Lane, keeping a careful eye on what was going on in the church grounds. He signalled to Daniel that it was safe to follow and, one by one, the two men slipped unnoticed into the building which housed Quinn's head office. All they had to do was find the right room.

"I SEE you're showing what a big mighty gang boss you are by torturing little boys now, Mister Quinn," said John, fighting off all his natural instincts to lay into Quinn and pound him to death with his fists when he saw the bloodied figure of poor Jimmy. "So much for your reputation. And here was me thinking all this time that you were a hard man."

"And here was me thinking all this time that the drunken brawler John Hukin was basically an honest man," said Quinn. "But what do I find? You robbed me of legitimate business proceeds when you picked on poor old Pickens, a slight, some might say pathetic, figure of a man, little bigger than a child himself when you come to think about it."

"You've never made any money legitimately in your life," said John.

"Them was gambling debts that you took, Hukin, gambling debts, earned legally by me and lost stupidly by people like your old man who couldn't resist putting on a bet even when he didn't have the money to cover it. Do you know he'd plead with me, your father? He'd beg me to give him time to pay off what he owed me, said he needed the money to feed his family, but he never learned, just kept on gambling and owing me more and more. In the end, of course, I had to do something about it. What a sad man he was, your dad. Miss him, do you?"

John's fisted were clenched so tightly that the palms of his hands started to bleed under the sharpness of the nails digging in. "What do you mean you had to do something about it?" he asked.

"Well," said Quinn, glancing round the churchyard with a tired-looking grimace on his face and then staring back at John, "like you say, I've a reputation in this town and it wouldn't have done to let some loser from The Ponds get away with owing me money, now, would it. What do you think, deep down, that I mean by 'doing something about it'?"

"You bastard."

"Probably," said Quinn, "but that's of no consequence now. Let's get down to business, shall we. Where's my money?"

"I don't have any money of yours," said John. Beyond Quinn he saw Daniel and David had gone into Quinn's place.

"Let's cut the crap, Hukin," said Quinn, making a show of tightening his arm around Jimmy's neck. "Pretty little thing, Sally, wouldn't you say? The other one's not a bad looker either. Whitey and Bassett here have taken quite a fancy to them both."

"Alright," said John. "So I do have some money which you claim is yours but I'm not stupid enough to have brought it with me. I knew you'd have a bit of help with you so why don't you cut the crap and then we'll talk properly about how to work this deal."

FROM what John had said Quinn's office was on the first floor of the building, overlooking Campo Lane, and the sounds coming from behind the first door they came to were a giveaway. It was obvious that inside someone was moving around in some sort of panic. Daniel and David looked at each other in silence and then carefully tried the door. It wasn't locked. They readied themselves, opened the door and charged in. Two pairs of eyes looked at them above the gags, changing instantly from fear to joy. A third pair just

308

looked petrified. "My God Quinn's just left this messenger lad in charge," said David. "We meet again," he said to Porter.

David held on to the youth as Daniel rushed to remove the gags off the women. "Elizabeth I thought I'd never see you again," he said, trying to untie the knot and kiss her at the same time. "I thought my life was over. Thank God you're safe. I thought you were dead until this morning and then I thought I might lose you all over again with all this business."

"Daniel, I can't believe you're here, actually here, out of nowhere. I thought I might never find you when Mary Ibbotson told me she'd seen you go off over the hills. And your eye, what's happened to your eye?"

"Never mind that now," he said, tearing the filthy strip of cloth from round her neck and turning to help Sally. "Don't you recognise who's with me?"

"Hello Lizzie," said David. "Your big brother's home at last."

Elizabeth stared open-mouthed at the near-stranger in front of her."David?"

"That's me," he said.

"But how…?" she said, looking from one man to the other.

"Let's get these ropes off first," said Daniel. "Are you okay Sally? That gag was tied right tight."

"Yes, thank you. I was just so scared. Where's John? Is he alright? Is he on his own with those men? We can't just leave him."

"No-one's leaving him," said Daniel, at last managing to untie all the ropes. He turned back to Elizabeth and drew her close, whispering words of comfort and relief. "I'm afraid all this will have to wait," he said, pulling away. "It's not the homecoming David or me would have planned but we've got to get you two out of here quick and get over to the churchyard. I'm not sure how long John can keep them busy on his own."

"One quick hug, little sister," said David, circling Elizabeth with his one arm.

"Your arm, what's happened to your arm?" she said.

"Like this fine husband you've got yourself said, there's no time for explanations. We'll do all our catching up later, right now we need to make good our escape."

"What about me, mister?" said Porter. "I never done nothing, honest, only deliver a message. That Quinn's a nutter, don't leave me here to him."

"I suggest you scarper," said Daniel. "And if I see you so much as nod in Quinn's direction then I'll deal with you myself. Understand?"

"Yes, mister."

"It's Quinn or him," said David to Porter, "or the police, or you clear off once and for all."

"I've gone, mister. I've had enough. I didn't want anything to do with hurting people."

Porter fled as the rest of them made their way carefully down the stairs and paused in the doorway. They could see John still talking to Quinn in the churchyard, with the two heavies away to either side.

"Elizabeth and Sally, you must hurry off and try to find a policeman. I suggest the direction of the market might offer the best chance," said Daniel. "David, are you ready for this?" he smiled. "I don't see your umbrella."

"Don't you worry about me, my good man, I've got a little surprise of my own."

"Then let's sort this out once and for all."

The two men crossed the road and ambled through the gate.

"WRONG answer Hukin. You see you're not in a position to bargain, in fact you're not in a position to do fuck all. I've got your missus and another pretty girl as a bonus. I've got your snivelling little shit of a nephew here and I've got my old pals Whitey and Bassett to lend a helping hand." With that Quinn whistled. Down at the churchyard gates, John saw Quinn's two thugs get up and walk over. They were big men, both taller and broader than John and although he could have taken either of them in a straight fight – they'd rely on size and intimidation rather than muscle and were soft in the way big men often were – he knew he was on a losing streak with both of them, even without factoring in Quinn, who still had Jimmy and, no doubt, an assortment of lethal weapons about him. Bassett walked past John, shouldering him hard in the process, only to find himself staggering back: the dray man was immovable. Bassett positioned himself behind John on the left. Whitey came up close to John. "Alright Johnny boy," he leered into John's face, "you won't remember me but I remember you giving my young brother a good hiding once. I'm going to enjoy working on you."

Hukin didn't flinch or move at all. Ignoring Whitey's face and remarks, he kept his eyes fixed on Quinn's. In the end Whitey also moved round behind him, he was now surrounded.

"What I believe you don't quite understand, Hukin," Quinn was sounding quite conversational now, "is that I'm in no particular rush to get my money back. Truth be told, it's more a matter of pride than need. You don't have the money? Fine, the money will wait. Fact is I never liked you, you were always too full of yourself. I never liked that worthless excuse of a man you called your father, that's why I stuck a knife in his guts. What I am going to like is to see my two friends behind you try and find out where that money is. Believe me they're hard workers and they enjoy their work. It's amazing how long a man will stay alive before he dies." Quinn sniggered and then absently tossed Jimmy aside. The boy cracked his head on the edge of a gravestone and collapsed in a limp heap.

Hukin remained unmoved, his gaze never straying from Quinn's. Jack's face tightened in annoyance at the lack of reaction. He pulled out his knife and moved closer. "Whether you tell me where that money is or not, you'll die slowly and so will the boy. On the other hand, your lady friends will start working the streets just so they can stay alive. All in all it's a win win situation for me. And for you? Well, quite frankly you're fucked."

"Someone's coming Jack," Whitey rumbled and placed a hand around John's arm, Bassett did the same on the other side.

Quinn looked over his shoulder to see two men: one, one-armed and with a walking cane, and the other, a big man with an eye-patch; they were both smartly dressed and strolling up the path. Turning back to John, Quinn palmed the knife. "Forget it, they're just churchgoers."

"I say, what the devil is going on?" an affectedly posh voice demanded. Daniel stared at David, startled at the transformation in his speech. By now they were alongside. David carried on mincing his words: "I suggest you unhand this man at once. If he is a brigand or a scoundrel then let's call the police and let them deal with the rogue but I cannot countenance you taking the law into your own hands, especially on holy ground."

Quinn turned to David. "Look Sir, this is a private matter and no concern of gentlemen such as yourselves. Now, if you continue on your way, we'll soon be gone."

"Well, if you're sure." David and Daniel made as if to move on but Daniel hesitated and closed in on John. "Wait a moment, aren't you John Hukin?"

"Aye, what's it to you?" John finally spoke, still not moving his eyes off Quinn.

"Bastard, you owe me money." With that Daniel slugged John in the gut. Hukin doubled over with the pain and dragged his captors with him. As the two men lurched forward, Daniel elbowed Whitey in the face knocking him back and punched Bassett in the side of the head knocking him to the side. At the same time Quinn lunged forward only to receive a smart crack on his head from David's stick which sent him reeling backwards.

Daniel helped John upright. "You alright big man?"

Between gasps John managed to splutter: "That was your plan? Walk up and hit me? Jesus, I think it'd have been best if you'd left me with Quinn."

"Don't say you've gone soft on me John?" Daniel said and then saw Whitey and Bassett clamber to their feet. "Please don't say you've gone soft on me John because we've got two huge ugly men behind you and they don't look too happy."

John turned as the two heavies approached. "You take Bassett, I'll take Whitey," he said as he lumbered forward.

"Which one's Bassett?"

"The one I haven't decked."

Whitey lunged for John with both arms, hoping to get him on the ground where his superior weight would be an advantage. At the same time Bassett started to back away from the grim one-eyed man who was stalking him. In one movement, John seized both of Whitey's arms, head-butted him and kneed him in the balls. Bassett turned to run but was plucked back by Daniel's grip on his collar. "Going somewhere?" Daniel asked before spinning the man around and pushing his head into the church wall. The sound of crushed bone, teeth and cartilage made Daniel wince as the man slid down the stonework leaving a smear of blood on the wall.

"You know what?" John was saying over the prone Whitey, "your brother at least put up a fight." He kicked the man in the head. "Can't say the same about you."

Quinn shook his head and tried to get up only to find himself being pressed to the ground by the walking cane held by the one-armed man. "What're you going to do? Stick me to death."

"My dear fellow," David said, although there was no false voice this time, just a deadly serious one. "From what I understand, you've been a bit of a shit. Now, I deal with shits all the time, it's part of the business I'm in. But you've been a bit of a shit to my sister and the last time I saw her was when she was only eleven. I'm afraid I can't forgive that. So what are we to do?"

Quinn saw an opportunity, he also saw a one-armed man with only a cane for protection. "Tell you what, I've nearly five hundred pounds on me right now, what if I gave you that by way of an apology for your sister and then we call it quits. Let me get up and get the money and then I'll be on my way."

David backed off. "Very well, like I said, I haven't seen her for years, she's probably turned into some god-awful harridan. Give me the money and we'll say nothing more about this affair."

"Right you are." Quinn got to his feet and reached into his inside pocket, reaching for a small loaded pistol. David sighed almost regretfully and flicked a switch on the handle of his cane. As Quinn pulled out the pistol the casing fell away from David's stick to reveal a long and lethal rapier. As Quinn aimed the gun, David thrust the blade into Quinn's stomach. The little man fell on to the blade, fell further and further until he met the hilt and began gargling blood.

David let go of the sword and Quinn fell to the ground. David leaned over him. "By the way," he said, "five hundred pounds wouldn't cover my daily wage bill."

THE fire was dying in the hearth back at Bungay Street with only the faintest orange glow radiating out between the greying embers but the room had never seemed so welcoming. The police had arrived in St Peter's churchyard in time to see Quinn pull the pistol and they'd all but thanked David for ridding them of one of the town's most elusive gang bosses: arrangements had been made for the various parties involved to call down to the police station the following morning to make statements but now it was time for everyone to enjoy simply being together.

"Will you bank up the fire, John, while I see to Jimmy?" said Sally.

"Ay, Love," he said. "And then perhaps us men can enjoy those beers we bought."

Jimmy had regained consciousness in the carriage home and loved being the centre of so much concerned attention. He didn't like women fussing over him, even his Mam had sometimes tried his patience trying to get him washed – he could never see the point, he'd only be getting mucky all over again - but this time he gave in willingly as Sally gently cleaned away the dried blood and the dirt covering his legs after his trials at the feet of Whitey and Bassett. She pulled the curtain next to her bed and put him in some fresh clothes.

"And do you know you're one of the top pupils at school?" she asked him.

"Me, Sally? Who said that?"

"Only the headmaster himself, called me in specially to his office to tell me how well you were getting on and that in another couple of years he might put you in for a special scholarship so you could go to a proper big school and learn more. Would you like that? You could learn all about all the different countries all over the world."

"I'd love that. You don't think Mr Quinn would be able to spoil it all do you?"

"That man won't be spoiling anything ever again," she said. "You're safe now, we all are."

"I'm really sorry for what I did, Sally, getting mixed up with Mr Quinn, and for what those men did to you and I couldn't even help."

"Actually I thought you acted like a real hero," she said. "If you hadn't been so brave when those two horrible men were hurting you, they would have gotten fed up with you and turned on Elizabeth and me. So actually, Jimmy, you saved us."

"Do you really think so? I never thought of it like that," he said.

"Well Lizzie and I did, we've got a lot to thank you for and we'll always know who to turn to if we ever need a hero again."

"Just think, Jimmy Urmston a hero."

"Now it's time for Master Urmston to eat. Come on, heroes need to keep up their strength."

Sally pulled the curtain back and everyone applauded the new-look Jimmy. Then he tucked into his scones as if he'd never eaten before in his life. The men held their bottles of beer high while Elizabeth and Sally made do with lemonade and David proposed a toast.

"I'm almost ashamed to say it but the truth is I haven't enjoyed myself quite so much since I was out in India," he said. "It's a long time since this one-armed man has been able to feel quite so useful and for that I thank you all. We've all done some catching up in the cab back here but I know there are so many more stories we all have to tell each other. So I propose that I book you all into my hotel this very afternoon and we can get down to some serious celebrating of all the various reunions that have happened today. I'd like my sister to meet Oonagh, my wife, and I'd like Oonagh to meet as good a bunch of people as she's ever likely to meet, either side of the Atlantic. So, everyone, raise your glasses., or bottles, as the case may be."

"Sally," whispered Jimmy louder than intended, "am I invited to the hotel as well or do I have to stay here?"

"How could we leave you behind, young man, when your actions helped win the day," said David. "You'd make a fine soldier and I'd be proud to have you in my regiment, if I still had one," he laughed.

"Here's to Jimmy," said Daniel.

"I'll second that, it's not every uncle lucky enough a have such a good 'un for a nephew," said John.

"What I can't understand is why I never noticed such an outstanding young man up at Malin Bridge," said Elizabeth. The reference of course led to a moment of sadness, relieved by David as he called for everyone's attention again.

"As from tomorrow," he said, "I intend to sort out the Shaw estate once and for all and to sign over a large portion of the proceeds to Elizabeth and Daniel. I also intend to set some of the proceeds aside for John and Sally here. I've seen and heard enough to realise that their future lies together, even if it has taken them rather a long time to admit it to themselves."

Sally pulled John close to her. "How could you have possibly thought I was interested in Matthew Blagdon," she said.

"Well you kept talking about me and Melanie, as if we were about to get hitched," said John. "And then you kept going out with Blagdon for tea and that. I didn't think I meant anything to you, not in that way anyway. Why do you think I was in such a bad mood for days last week?"

"John Hukin it would have been obvious to any clear-headed man months ago," said Elizabeth. "Didn't you ever wonder why she never missed your deliveries to the pub?"

"Take it from me that the phrase 'clear-headed' has never been applied to John Hukin," said Daniel. "More like pig-headed or bull-headed."

"You all make such a close company of friends that I'd like to play my part in keeping you together," said David. "We can rebuild Willow Tree, perhaps a house this time, rather than a cottage, and how about I use some of the Shaw inheritance to build a pub, I'd never find two people more suited to running the place."

"And Quinn's kindly left us a couple of hundred to help us on our way," said John, at which more cheers were raised.

"Would we go back up the valley?"

It was Daniel who spoke and Jimmy who answered.

"The valley's home," he said, "of course we'll all go back up the valley."

And the bottles and glasses were chinked again.

"By the way, Jimmy, there's a small package on the table for you. Open it, why don't you."

"I was waiting to be asked," he said. "It looks really pretty with the bow, I bet that was Sally did that, Uncle John would never have such a nice idea."

"Don't you be so sure of that," said Sally.

Jimmy ripped off the tie and the paper and uncovered a neat little square box. He took the top off carefully and filled the room with the look of happiness on his face. "Uncle John you remembered," he said, "it's that watch I wanted for my birthday."

***

About the authors

Maggie Lett was born in Liverpool and moved to Sheffield in the late 1970s. A journalist, she worked on Sheffield Morning Telegraph and Sheffield Telegraph before moving to the press office of Sheffield City Council.
Geoff Rowe was born in London and moved to Sheffield in the early 1990s, where he worked at a variety of jobs, from pensions administrator to binman, and played in a number of local bands.
Together they opened Bukowski's Piano Bar and Diner on London Road.
They wrote *Flood Waters* when the bar closed for business.

***

Acknowledgements

The authors wish to thank Sheffield Local Studies Library and Archives Department for their help and support and would like to acknowledge Samuel Harrison (A Complete History of the Great Flood at Sheffield) and Geoffrey Amey (The Collapse of the Dale Dyke Dam 1864) as valuable reference sources.

***